Also by Roberto Costantini

The Root of All Evil

The Deliverance of Evil

THE MEMORY OF EVIL

ROBERTO COSTANTINI

Translated from the Italian by N. S. Thompson

Quercus

First published in the Italian language as *Il male non dimentica*
by Marsilio Editori in Venice in 2014

First published in Great Britain in 2015 by Quercus Editions Ltd
This paperback edition published in 2016 by

Quercus Editions Ltd
Carmelite House
50 Victoria Embankment
London EC4Y 0DZ

An Hachette UK company

A CIP catalogue record for this book is available
from the British Library

ISBN 978 0 85738 940 4
EBOOK ISBN 978 1 78429 988 0

10 9 8 7 6 5 4 3 2 1

Typeset by Jouve (UK), Milton Keynes

Printed and bound in Great Britain by Clays Ltd, St Ives plc

for Milena, Carolina and Fabrizio,
and to the free people of Libya

Tripoli, 31 August 1969

The Killer

Italia was there, standing right in front of me. Her back was turned and she was looking out to sea, her feet only half a metre from the edge of the cliff. Half a metre that separated her life from mine. One step back or forwards that would change everything.

I could feel the way her thoughts were going, but couldn't change them. And I wished with all my heart she could take that step forwards herself, as if the moral responsibility alone could weigh less than being the material cause. But Italia wasn't that kind of person, and I knew that very well. She would never do it on her own.

I don't know if she heard my footsteps or the beating of my heart as I came closer. I don't know if she had any idea whose hands pushed her over, but she never turned round. I don't know if she gave any thought to her favourite son, Mikey, as she plunged towards the rocks below.

No cry came from her as she fell. And that silence changed my life.

Tripoli, 15 August 2011

Michele Balistreri

I've no idea if my mother thought about me as she fell towards those rocks. I hope there's no place from which the dead can watch us and know everything about us. If there isn't, she will never know that while someone was pushing her over that cliff edge, I was far away in bed with her worst enemy, Marlene Hunt.

And that last time I was inside her, I've no idea if Laura Hunt hated me or pitied me. That's the difference between youth and age. Back then I preferred to think it was hate. Today I hope it was pity.

And as the pellet I fired went right through his cheek and tongue, I've no idea if Salim was aware he'd made the biggest mistake of his life when he cut off the ear of his half-brother Karim, because no one lays a finger on any member of the MANK organization and gets away with it.

And I've no idea if Farid remembered the promise the MANK made him all those years before, when he was thrown as live bait to the sharks, minus his penis.

Nor, as we faced each other on that last day of my former life, have I any idea if Ahmed asked himself which of us was the hero and which the villain, which one John Wayne and which Scar, the Comanche chief.

If I look back now, forty years later, on the drifting boat of my life, everything disappears slowly from sight, but among the cloudy memories the one thing I can always see is La Moneta. My body survived the shipwreck and reached a shore of some kind. But my soul stayed there, facing the rocks of that island, facing the coastal lights of Tripoli that became more and more distant as I ran away from who I was.

1 Obedience and Terror

Thursday, 28 July 2011

Zawiya, Libya

In the preceding days, troops had arrived from Tripoli to restore order for the local tribal leader. They passed through Gargaresh, and then Zanzur, with its oasis of palms by the sea, its huge electric power station, which had been hit by NATO bombing, its chaotic clusters of shops and workshops among the trees, and the potholes and dusty squares between, where barefoot boys played with a rag ball among old, abandoned vehicles.

The coast road, which was usually extremely busy with lorries transporting petrol from the large refinery in Zawiya to Tripoli, was pockmarked by craters caused by the bombing and now used only by jeeps armed with machine guns. Two tanks stood at the city entrance, but they were superfluous because now the rebels were either dead, had been taken prisoner or had escaped. But they served to remind the defenceless survivors – the women, children and the elderly – that nothing would be as it had been before and nothing would be forgiven Zawiya's inhabitants. They no longer had any civil rights: not in the present, not in the future. Their houses could be swept away at any moment on the orders of an officer of the forces loyal to Gaddafi.

Leading up to the school was a twin row of twelve poplars, a left-over from the time of the Italian colonists' agricultural estates. The school façade was now riddled with bullet holes, not a window left intact. At the centre of the courtyard in front of the school was a smoking crater, which had blackened and withered the trees when aflame. The smell of petrol and burning flesh hung heavily in the air.

Tied to every poplar with a noose round his neck was a man, a Berber – or Amazigh, as they prefer to be called. They were the first to rise up in rebellion after 17 February, the beginning of the revolution against Colonel Gaddafi. Loyalist guards armed with Kalashnikovs were pointing their weapons at dozens of desperate women, children and elderly, the wives, children and parents of the men about to be hanged.

The single officer in charge was European, possibly Bulgarian or German, and, like many in the Colonel's pay, a mercenary.

Beaten, and now with fractured limbs, the Berber captives stood on chairs taken from the school. The women were screaming abuse at the guards, but no one dared run to their son or husband to offer comfort. Standing round them in a circle was a crowd of silent, terrified city-dwellers, quietly glad they had chosen not to join the Berber rebellion, even though they hated Gaddafi as much as the rebels, possibly even more.

The hot *ghibli* wind was blowing sand in from the desert. Along with the flies, it stuck to the prisoners' bloody wounds and mingled with the relatives' tears. The scene resembled an Old Master painting on a yellowish canvas; the stationary figures were waiting for someone to make a decision.

A black armour-plated SUV – a Mercedes M1 with dark windows – drove up and parked in the middle of the road, blocking it. As the driver switched off the engine, the European officer rushed to open the rear door.

The man who got out was an Arab, about sixty years old, well preserved despite the deep, vertical lines that furrowed his face below his prominent cheekbones. He was wearing civilian dress, a dark suit over a white shirt, but no tie; his hair was still thick, a little crinkled and grey; his eyes were hidden by dark glasses. Part of one ear was missing, as if it had been cleanly sliced off.

'Which one's the leader?' he asked the officer in English, pointing to the rebels strung up on the poplars.

The mercenary had met many cold-blooded murderers in Uganda, Darfur and Kosovo: sadists who took pleasure in killing. But the man with the severed ear was different. There was no emotion when he killed. It was just a job. And it was a job that needed to be done for this man to get what he wanted.

The mercenary pointed to the nearest poplar. The man strung up there was standing on one leg, the other twisted at an angle of thirty degrees; he was covered in blood, his fingers and thumbs broken by hammer blows.

The man with the severed ear went up to him.

'In much pain?' he asked in Arabic.

The Berber made an enormous effort to gather enough saliva to spit in the man's face. But he only managed to produce a thin stream of spit and blood that trickled from his broken teeth down his chin. The man with the severed ear turned to the women.

'Which of you is the wife of this poor man? Come here immediately and wipe his mouth.'

'No!' the Berber rasped.

But the man with the severed ear had already noticed the woman who had started to come forwards. She was swathed in a barracan, only one eye showing.

'I'll give your wife to my soldiers later,' he told the Berber.

He said it in a loud voice so that everyone could hear. He knew that blind obedience could be obtained only by terror.

Suddenly a boy about thirteen emerged from behind his mother, wielding a knife, and flung himself at the man. His eyes were the same as those of the man strung up on the poplar.

With lightning speed, the man with the severed ear took out his pistol and shot the boy in the middle of his stomach, careful not to hit any vital organ and so kill him instantly. It was necessary for everyone to see the boy bleed, to think he could still be saved as they watched him slowly die.

'Bring him here,' he ordered the European, pointing to the boy's body lying in the dust.

The officer hid his look of disgust. He had killed children, but only in the heat of battle. What he was feeling right now was not pleasant. But he was being paid very handsomely, and this was part of what he was being paid handsomely to do.

It took two soldiers to drag the boy's body under the tree where his horrified father was strung up, and four to hold still the mother, who was screaming and gesticulating like someone possessed.

For the man with the severed ear the boy meant nothing. He would bleed to death in a few minutes and die like the thousands who perished in Africa every day through hunger and disease. He felt absolutely nothing: neither pity nor hate. It was just what he had to do to make his audience understand.

Behind his dark glasses he let his eyes run over the silent crowd, the people of Zawiya. These people were the ones he had to convince. These were the imbeciles whom despicable opportunists, extremists and terrorists had persuaded they could fight for freedom. He would make no speeches to counter this, to tell them they were wrong and that if Gaddafi fell they would only find themselves in worse hands. Words mattered only in a democracy, which – thanks to the Colonel – was not how it was in Libya. All he had to do was to persuade these idiots never to try it on again, not even to think about it, no matter who was right or wrong. And he knew people well enough to know that there was only one way.

He turned to the crowd. He pointed to the rebels in the blackened poplars.

'These men are terrorists, friends of Bin Laden. The man Colonel Gaddafi protects you from.'

The crowd hung their heads, many nodding in agreement, in the grip of silent terror. The man with the severed ear took out a knife with a saw blade, ten centimetres long.

'Take a look, rebel swine!' he said to the boy's father, whose eyes were now streaming tears. Tears wasted on the man below. Dribbling blood, he gave a desperate cry as the man with the severed ear cut the boy's throat in one swift movement, then kicked away the chair on which the rebel father was tottering on one foot.

He turned to the European officer, speaking again in a loud voice, levelling a finger at the rebels strung up in the trees.

'Hang the lot of them! Then kill their children, rape and kill the mothers. And as for the fathers of these terrorists, cut off their hands, but leave them alive. I want everyone to know what happens to traitors and those who do not report them.'

He got into his Mercedes and ordered the driver to leave. On the drive towards Tripoli, he didn't give the traitors a second's thought. They were of no interest to him, nothing but dead meat in a war declared when other traitors, like the opportunist Americans, British and French, had joined forces with the cowardly Italians and begun a move against Gaddafi, against a regime that had bankrolled their consumerist populations for years, sometimes their pathetic heads of government too.

He leaned back in his seat and closed his eyes. He was thinking about that day in the *ghibli*'s windblown sand when four boys cut their wrists and mixed their blood. It had been him, his brother, Nico Gerace and, of course, Mikey Balistreri. Almost fifty years had passed. But they were not enough to make him forget.

Tripoli, 1962

Mikey Balistreri

This evening the large forecourt is lit by little lamps along the wall surrounding the two villas. The *ghibli* is blowing sand into the city from the Sahara.

Nico, Ahmed, Karim and me are sheltering behind the Hunt villa in the darkest part of the large garden near the back gate. The car port that William Hunt built to protect the Ferrari and Land Rover from the sun offers only partial shelter from the gusting wind and sand.

I look at my three friends. Sand comes in right under the car-port roof and it gets in our eyes.

'Let's make a pact, the four of us,' I suggest, and ask for Ahmed's knife.

We position ourselves between the Ferrari and the Land Rover. But even there we can't get away from the sand.

Without saying a word, I cut into the back of my left wrist. Drops of blood well up from the cut.

Then it's Nico's turn. He smiles happily, cuts his wrist and looks satisfied when the blood oozes out. To do what I do is an honour for him.

Karim is less keen. He's not happy about mixing his blood with that of two Christians. He makes a small cut. Not much blood flows, and he looks at it, perplexed.

He then passes the knife to Ahmed, who looks into our eyes, as serious as ever. He's not frightened; he likes the idea. He's left-handed, so holds the knife in that hand. In silence, he makes a longer and deeper cut than ours, the blood flowing copiously from his right wrist.

The single light bulb hanging under the Hunts' car-port roof emits a tremulous grainy light, filtered by the yellow sand. There's a smell of oil and petrol. We can hear the *ghibli* whistling, the palm leaves flapping and the shaking of the eucalyptus.

Our four wrists are placed together and our blood mingles, along with the fine sand.

Sand and blood. For ever.

2 The Exterminator of Zawiya

Friday, 29 July 2011

Rome

Rome's like a beautiful woman. Better when she's just woken up than for the rest of the day.

Every morning, just before six thirty, Michele Balistreri walked the same route from his flat down to the office in the city's historic centre. From the silent greenery of the Oppian Hill he went down to the Coliseum and from there passed along the most beautiful three hundred metres in the world, between the Imperial Forums and the remains of the greatest empire history had ever seen. Within half an hour this extraordinary beauty would be invaded, trodden over and exploited.

Things had been better up to a few years ago, but now, with the economic crisis, only a part of Rome could enjoy the summer as it used to. The people who were feeling the squeeze were staying at home and, at weekends, packing on to the free communal beaches of nearby Ostia, while the truly rich were, as usual, already on their yachts at Capri, Elba and Portofino.

If his morning stroll gave rise to a good many grim thoughts, it also helped Michele exercise his knee, which was becoming more and more painful since being fractured five years earlier by the bullets of the Invisible Man's accomplices.

If he could help it, that precious hour between dawn and the incoming tide of vehicles was the only time Balistreri went out and about in the open. These days, he lived his life indoors. The hunt for the Invisible Man and its aftermath had inflicted wounds on his body, which were at least partly healed, but those to his soul couldn't be cured. Now, except for this brief morning constitutional, he tried to stay within the confines of his home and his office. His life had gradually become devoid of all stimulus and opportunity for conversation, socializing or new interests.

Nothing held any appeal for him now. The rare poker games with friends and the few lovers he took had become duties rather than pleasures. In the office he limited his contacts to his closest colleagues and then only to discuss work, which was now based on intercepts and DNA, things of no interest to him.

Although he was at peace, he was bored. He'd slowly emptied himself of everything, but for him this was no Zen exercise or effort of the will. It was the natural consequence of the scorched earth he'd created around his relationships over the course of the years.

At a quarter to seven he went into the tiny bar under his office block, drawn there by his habitual weakness, a well-made espresso. Inside was the usual crowd at that time of the day: the *barista*, the street cleaner, the fruit seller, the high-school teacher. Simple folk he would willingly have spoken to years ago, but now he only gave them a passing nod. But they knew who he was: Head of Rome's Homicide Squad.

Balistreri didn't join in the conversation but listened in silence. These people were normal people: *the people*. They weren't capable of stealing, not even the sweets by the cash desk in a crowded bar. They were the majority, the losers; they were of interest to the powerful only insofar as they had the right to vote.

Now there was the crisis: recession, stagnation, depression. Every day, educated ministers, bureaucrats from banks and treasury departments – all of them overpaid, with too many roles, and sometimes conflicts of interest – explained to these poor souls that they had to understand and accept the sacrifices imposed upon them for the good of the country and for the children. It wasn't clear if this meant the children of the listeners or those of the privileged speakers.

In any case, the people – ordinary folk – could go about complaining, because no one would put them behind bars for what they said. For that, they had democracy to thank.

As he thought these things, there was no anger in Balistreri, or even resignation. The people who complained were likable people, but he no longer felt any solidarity with them. He was fed up of listening to Italians moaning about the politicians they themselves had elected.

The newsreader on the bar radio began to talk about Libya and the war there, which was now entrenched, with no end in sight and costing the earth. Hundreds of millions of euros had been spent, the NATO allies attacking and Gaddafi fighting back to defend his regime. Not to mention the human cost, especially among defenceless civilians. Gazing at the bottom of his cup, Balistreri listened to the reports of a massacre at Zawiya: it had been nothing less than the total extermination of the women, children and elderly there.

He paid a little more quickly than usual, nodded to everyone and went out. If there was one thing he really didn't want to hear about, it was that war between Colonel Gaddafi, the rebels and NATO.

The Colonel's evil, but those who decided to bomb him in order to obtain an extra petroleum contract or two are no better.

At seven, Balistreri went through the grand entrance into the Flying Squad offices situated in the small square. He smiled in response to the obsequious salute from the duty guard. Balistreri had looked daggers at the man until he addressed him as Commissario and not Head of Homicide or, even worse, Deputy Assistant Police Chief.

Gasping a little for breath – he smoked too much, his knee hurt and he didn't do enough exercise – he walked up the three marble flights of stairs to the half-deserted offices of Section III. So far, it was only the switchboard operators in the open-plan office; almost everyone else would arrive between seven and eight o'clock.

When he left the Special Section for Homicide, Balistreri had held on to his old office, even though he was now entitled to a more spacious, modern one with a little reception room attached. But he was used to this ancient, peeling space. It wasn't so much for its view of the Coliseum and the Roman Forum, especially as he almost always kept the shutters closed, but because this room was a reflection of his state of mind; of his increasingly stooped posture; of the white hair on his temples, the grey of the rest. The wood of the door and desk were made of cheap honeycomb core, the springs had gone in the old armchairs, the black leather sofa was worn and wrinkled, the architectural friezes on the little balcony covered in dust and grime.

It was like that myth that dogs end up looking like their owners. If the office had been modern and sparkling clean, it wouldn't have been his. For him, it was something between a den and a tomb. The hunt for the Invisible Man had been the last investigation he'd led out in the field, the last time he'd fired his gun, the last time he'd been overwhelmed by his feelings.

Since then, all that remained for him was the flat and the office – sealed off from the world by double-glazing and shutters, and impregnated with cigarette smoke and the smell of whisky – where, each day, as soon as he'd finished signing all the pointless paperwork, he could stretch out on the old leather sofa to listen to Leonard Cohen, shutting out – at least for a little while – both the infinite beauty and the inescapable sleaze of his city and his country.

On that sofa he could let time pass as if he were on a boat in the sunshine, letting himself be carried by the current to the mouth of a placid river.

I wanted to change the world, but the world changed me. It was all a dream, only a dream.

Tripoli, 1958

Mikey Balistreri

Here in Tripoli, it's mild, even in winter. From the garden in front of the two villas the croaking of frogs breaks the silence of the African night. The two villas are just outside Tripoli: beautiful, comfortable, with air conditioning. Villas for the rich. Behind them lie the olive groves built up over half a century by my grandfather Giuseppe Bruseghin, starting with a stretch of sand, the only thing the Fascist colonial administration would give him after he emigrated to Libya after the First World War had devastated his Veneto region. Grandad had spent years preparing the ground, raising barriers to block the *ghibli* sand blown in from the desert and digging down to the water table to build irrigation channels. Finally, he was able to plant the saplings and wait. Thanks to those years of sacrifice, today Grandad has the largest olive groves in Libya.

My father, on the other hand, can't stand the smell of olives. It reminds him of his childhood in Palermo; for him, it's the smell of poverty. Nor does he like the smell of the manure used to fertilize the olives, the smell that comes from the cesspit where the huts of the sheep- and goat-herders and the shacks of his employees stand.

Tonight, three families are sitting together in our main living room for the grand finale of the Sanremo Song Festival. We're the Italian one, the Balistreri: my grandfather; my father, Salvatore; my mother, Italia; my elder brother, Alberto; and me, Michelino – but I prefer to be called Mikey. The American family, the Hunts, are our neighbours in the next villa: William and Marlene and their daughter, Laura. And the Libyans, the Al Bakri family: Mohammed, the head of the family, and his four sons, who live with their two mothers and their sister, Nadia, in a corrugated iron shack beside the cesspit.

I'm sitting on the sofa between the two most important women in my life. The one who gave birth to me, Italia, and the one with whom I'll spend my life, Laura. On the black-and-white set Domenico Modugno is singing the winning song of the festival.

'*Volare, oh, oh! Cantare, oh, oh, oh, oh!*'

Friday, 29 July 2011

Tripoli

Linda Nardi was lying stretched out fully clothed on the bed in her room in the Hotel Rixos. She had switched off the lights and opened the windows on the blazing red sunset. Everything was warm and peaceful outside; the palms were still and the muezzin's cry was soft and mournful. The war seemed very far away without the noise of the NATO fighter planes that passed over in the night.

She wanted to have a word with Lena, her mother in California, but had called the night before and knew from the terrible cough she had that it was tiring for her mother to stay too long on the phone. She also wanted to talk to her father, but there was no solution to that problem, seeing as she'd never met him, didn't even know who he was. At the very least, she wanted to talk to a man who was pleasant and sensible. But right now there was nobody.

Right now, Linda?

She'd turned forty a few months ago, but there'd been no close connection with men in her life, except for a brief period five years earlier. She thought she'd found that connection – and the one man in the world *right for her* – when she'd gone to the hospital to pick up

Michele Balistreri, there convalescing from the wounds inflicted on him by the killer Manfredi.

They had spent months together, chatting, having dinner and a glass of wine; it had been a closeness based not on words but more on what was not said.

The two of them had never shared even a kiss. That was a door that had remained closed. But after the calm had come the storm. She had emerged from that storm stronger in some areas, but weaker in others, and with a cynicism that made her self-sufficient and incapable of being won over by any ordinary form of courtship.

She pushed the memory of Balistreri aside and tried to concentrate on the job in hand. She was there to report on the civil war. At first it had seemed the rebels were going to win, then it was Gaddafi, and now, with NATO's intervention, the war seemed never-ending and the outcome uncertain. News from the battle fronts was contradictory and, in any case, terrible. On both sides, the war was being fought on the ground by troops who were ever more weary, with ever more insufficient means, and against a background of violence against civilians and bombs raining down in the name of freedom – the freedom of others to have Libya's petroleum. Laura had already filed an article on the mysterious death of General Younis, Gaddafi's former chief lieutenant, who was said to have defected to the rebels but had also been accused of being a double agent. Now she had to write something on this dreadful business at Zawiya.

She couldn't wait to get away from Tripoli and back to the orphanages and hospitals in Central Africa to which she had dedicated herself since Manfredi's death and the split with Michele Balistreri.

There were only a few hours to go. At dawn the following day she had a flight to Nairobi, but this evening she still had to deal with the war.

She rose from the bed, ran her hands over her clothes to iron out the creases, but didn't look in the mirror or even think of putting on lipstick or a bit of make-up. She knew very well that not taking care of her appearance, especially for the benefit of a man, was a hangover from what she had suffered at the hands of Manfredi. But painful memories aren't wiped away by a simple act of will.

She took the lift down to the lobby and went into the hotel bar. It was an obligatory stop each evening to catch up on the latest war news and gather material for her next article. You could always pick up some nugget that slipped out of a fellow journalist's mouth when they'd had too much to drink or wanted to brag.

'Miss Nardi?'

Bashir Yared was a Lebanese entrepreneur whom she'd met in Nairobi. He was around fifty, in construction, somewhat rough and ready, but always friendly and polite, and always chasing after her.

'What are you doing here in Tripoli, Mr Yared?' she asked.

He made a slight bow and kissed her hand. He was dressed in a smart blue blazer and red tie.

'I'm here on business. And to offer you an aperitif, if you would have one.'

As ever on these occasions, she immediately wanted to go back to her room. Solitude was a gift for her, not a burden. But she didn't want to be rude to a man who was fundamentally kind and, as she also had to find a lead for her next article, she took him up on his offer.

They sat down at a table. The bar was noisy, but cheerful, full of men, both Arabs and Westerners, talking more business than war; that is, the business they could do thanks to the war.

No one here in the Rixos will end up dying. As always, the real fighting's left to other poor souls.

Bashir ordered a non-alcoholic beer and Linda a tonic water. He lit a slim menthol, but Linda refused one.

'You don't mind if I smoke, Miss Nardi?'

'No, please do. Only it's a vice I've never . . .'

'I know. It *is* a vice. That's why I promised my wife I'd give it up. I made a . . . how do you say? . . . A . . .'

'A vow?'

'Yes. I made it because, now she's nearly twenty, my only daughter's getting married. They'll be taking her away from me, so I'm thinking of having another . . .'

He was trying to tell her two things. One was his bafflement that a beautiful forty-year-old had no husband. Also that, even at his age, his spermatozoa were strong enough to procreate.

'She's getting married in church,' he continued. 'We're Christians, you see. There'll be three hundred guests.'

Linda wondered if Bashir Yared was more proud about the marriage, the number of guests or his religion. He probably thought the Christians there were more civilized than the Muslims.

'Are you here for work, Mr Yared?'

He looked at her through the spirals of menthol smoke. Everyone was smoking.

'Yes, many contracts, Miss Nardi. Wars are manna from heaven for me.'

He winked at her, as if his witty remark made them somehow complicit.

'And the contract's going ahead for the new hospital in Nairobi?' she asked, as much to pass the time as anything.

He smiled with the air of a man who knows a thing or two.

'Of course the hospital's going ahead, and I have won the subcontract. You double the estimate, win the contract and then give half the money back. In cash and, naturally, under the counter. Italian rules, Kenyan accounting – a perfect combination . . .'

'But isn't it the Swiss Italians from across the border who are building the hospital, not Italian nationals?' Linda objected.

Yared gave a shrug, as if the observation was irrelevant.

'Nothing is ever really Swiss, is it, Miss Nardi? Apart from the chocolate, the watches and the banks. The Ticino consortium is only Swiss on the outside; inside, it's run by Italians for Italian interests.'

Linda had been a journalist for many years. She knew very well how the world worked; it was foolish to be shocked and pointless to be indignant. She had earned her living with stories like this, but every so often she still committed the error of getting emotionally involved and believing that her investigations had the power to change things. In reality, there was nothing new in what Bashir Yared was saying and nothing she could do about it.

Besides, it was common knowledge that this was part of Italy's famous creativity, applied here to balance sheets rather than fashion or the arts. The Italians had become great experts in the art of over-billing, creating slush funds and false accounting.

But people aren't interested in stories like these any more. They're not important, no longer carry a court sentence and are of no interest to journalists. But Bashir Yared knows I'm a journalist and wants to make himself appear interesting.

'You don't surprise me, Mr Yared. Unfortunately, the newspapers don't publish these things any more. The public's heard it all before.'

But he wasn't giving up.

'Finance for the new hospital is also coming from Italian public money. And part of this money will be quietly returned. But not to the public.'

'Nor in Italy?'

The question came out without her really thinking, without any real interest, purely to give him a little satisfaction. Bashir made a face that was even more knowing.

'No, not in Italy, but almost. A state situated in the middle of Rome. And one bank in particular.'

Linda showed slightly more interest.

'Would that be the IOR?'

Bashir nodded.

'Yes, the Institute for Religious Works. God's Bank, isn't that what you call it?'

'Yes, that's what we call it. And how can you be so sure that the kickbacks end up precisely there?'

'Intuition, and a little bit of information. The director of the Swiss consortium building the hospital is an Italian, Gabriele Cascio. He goes to the site each morning, and each evening at seven goes home to his apartment in central Nairobi, then to the Bluebird Club in search of female company.'

Linda smiled.

'Nothing strange there. I don't think . . .'

'Of course, except that on Sundays he leaves two hours earlier and deals with the business of turning his dirty money into clean money. As you know, here in Africa everyone works on a Sunday. Should we have dinner together, Miss Nardi, and talk further?' asked Bashir hopefully.

The invitation was more an act of old-fashioned gallantry than a real move on her. Some men were happier spending money on dinners, jewellery and trips. Others preferred a prostitute.

Linda was tired. What she needed was a lead on the Libyan civil war; she had no real interest in Yared's story. She decided to use the excuse she used with many men, the one that worked best in not upsetting them. In this case, it also happened to be the truth.

'I have to pack. I've got an early flight to Nairobi tomorrow.'

Bashir smiled and tried to make the invitation more appetizing.

'They say that this Gabriele Cascio used to work for the IOR and was the right-hand man of that monsignor who comes to Kenya every so often to set up charitable works, the one with that perfect Italian name – Pizza.'

For a moment, Linda was surprised. Monsignor Eugenio Pizza, who liked to be known more familiarly as Don Eugenio, was the most mysterious and talked-about man in the Catholic Church. His progress through the Vatican's secret chambers was a mystery that time had gradually wrapped in dense fog.

Benefactor or con artist?

'And how come you know this, Mr Yared?'

He smiled again.

'I keep myself well informed. I know everyone in Nairobi, as *you* know . . .'

At that moment a Western woman surrounded by four young men who looked like members of the Libyan Secret Service walked quickly through the bar and the entrance lobby. The woman had blonde hair; beautiful, delicate features; a slim and graceful body. She was well dressed, but not provocatively so. She and the four men were following an Arab man of about sixty, with an olive complexion, hollow cheeks in a deeply lined face and high cheekbones. His thick hair was slightly frizzy and turning grey and part of his ear was missing, as if it had been cut off very cleanly. They quickly entered a lift and disappeared.

Bashir Yared was visibly pale.

'Do you know who that woman is?' Linda asked him.

The Lebanese shook his head.

'No, not her. She'll be an escort for –'

She stopped him short.

'That Libyan? A competitor of yours?'

'He's not a businessman.'

'A friend of Gaddafi?'

Bashir Yared was now feeling the effects of several different things – Linda's breasts pushing against her large-buttoned blouse, his empty stomach and the atmosphere running through Africa because of the revolutions in Tunisia, Egypt and Libya – and wanted to show off even more.

'Have you heard about what happened in Zawiya, Miss Nardi?'

Naturally, she'd heard rumours about the massacre. In fact, they were more than rumours. It was as if the regime wanted to broadcast what had happened, not hide it. As always, Bashir Yared was well informed, even in Tripoli.

'Was that man involved?'

'They say he was the one behind General Younis's death . . .'

Linda tried to get more out of him, but Yared was frightened and suddenly remembered he had some business to attend to. He gave a slight bow, kissed her hand and said goodbye.

Linda went back to her room and jotted down some notes for her article. A massacre in Zawiya: women raped, old people and children murdered, men mutilated. She would be happy to leave.

Here, the world's far worse. There are people here for whom life has no value at all.

Rome

At the end of the day Balistreri was sitting with his painful leg stretched out under the desk, his foot resting on a humiliating footstool, while he smoked away and signed papers he no longer bothered to read.

That was the way Italian bureaucracy functioned. From reports of motorway infractions to the laws of state, the writer drafted a text that was incomprehensible to his superiors, who in turn signed it without reading it. If they had taken the trouble to try to read it, they wouldn't have understood it anyway.

There was a knock on his office door. It was Corvu. He always knocked, had done for years. Balistreri knew he did it for fear of embarrassing him, in case he found his boss on the sofa instead of at his desk. Two taps, a pause, a third tap. He did it in order to be recognized and with the mathematical precision typical of the little Sardinian, who possessed the best analytic mind in the police force.

Balistreri left his paperwork, lit a Gitane and went to lie down on the black leather sofa, trying to look like someone who had been lying there all day without doing a stroke of work. Only then did he call out, 'Come in!'

Corvu entered, well groomed and shaven and even decently dressed, guided by the tastes of his girlfriend, Natalya. The red tie with the grey suit and white shirt evidently owed something to her artistic touch. Embarrassed, Corvu tried not to look at his boss lying on the sofa.

'Nice tie, Corvu, beautiful colour.'

'Thanks, *dottore*. Red's Natalya's favourite colour. She sends you her very best, by the way. And if you'd like to come to lunch on Sunday . . .'

Balistreri was horrified at the thought, even though Corvu was an excellent cook.

The thought of having to make conversation for two hours . . .

'I'd be happy to come. But I promised to take Antonella to the beach . . .'

'Not to worry, that's fine . . .' his deputy mumbled, looking deflated.

Balistreri immediately felt bad. Corvu worshipped him like some old saint, worrying if he lost weight, if he smoked or drank too much, and wasn't happy if he was on his own too much. But Antonella was a kind of reassuring guardian spirit: lover, friend and nurse, when necessary.

Corvu was allowed to think all these things but never to express them openly.

'Could I have a word about Giulia Piccolo, Commissario?'

Balistreri felt a burning in his oesophagus – that blasted reflux. The name was enough to get all the acid in his stomach going.

Giulia Piccolo was a complex case. She had grown up with a submissive mother in an all-male family in a small town on the coast near Palermo. She was 1.87 metres of iron muscle. Needing to escape from her native town in Sicily, she had come to Rome and passed the exams to enter the police force at the same time as Corvu, to whom she was very close.

For Balistreri, she had always been both a gift and a punishment. Piccolo's role had been decisive in the success of many investigations, but her physical strength and complete disregard for danger had led her to make some stupid mistakes.

Five years earlier he'd asked both his deputies to come with him to Homicide. Corvu had accepted without a moment's hesitation, but Giulia Piccolo had declined to be transferred. He'd never asked why. He never asked women for explanations; he considered the words superfluous. From then on, whenever their paths crossed, only a simple 'Good morning' or 'Good evening' was exchanged.

Resigned, Balistreri raised himself from the sofa.

'What do you want to say about Piccolo?'

Corvu coughed and cleared his throat.

'Yesterday there was an enormous row between Giulia and two of her colleagues. They'd stopped two young girls who were kissing each other in a corner of a Metro station and, according to the guys, it was on the mouth and far too passionately. The girls say the officers insulted them. So after one of the girls told them to fuck off, they went to handcuff them.'

Balistreri closed his eyes. He could imagine what was coming next.

'And Giulia Piccolo happened to be passing by at that very moment?' he asked.

Corvu coughed to hide his awkwardness.

'Giulia maintains that she identified herself immediately, but the other two say she didn't show her ID. Result: one colleague with a broken nose, the other with a fractured rib.'

'Witnesses?'

'The two girls say that Giulia was attacked verbally and physically and only acted to defend herself from the two officers.'

Balistreri had no difficulty believing that this was exactly what had happened. But it wouldn't save Piccolo from the sack. The police force wasn't very understanding when it came to hitting colleagues.

'The head of Section II's asked Colombo for Giulia to be dismissed.'

Colombo was head of the Flying Squad, the job Balistreri had declined.

'And so, Corvu?'

He knew he wasn't playing fair. He knew very well what Corvu hoped he would do. But in order to be able to do it, he had to convince his deputy that he wouldn't intervene.

'Commissario, Colombo's about to make a decision. I was hoping that . . .'

Balistreri didn't even bother to reply.

'All right, Corvu, off you go now. And don't ask me again about that woman.'

Corvu bowed his head.

'OK, but you might want to reconsider . . . And, anyway, I wanted to remind you that it's late now. There's nothing urgent here – I'm coming in tomorrow – so if you want to go somewhere with . . .'

The filthy look Balistreri gave him stopped him in his tracks and propelled him on his way.

Balistreri pressed the button for his direct line to Colombo.

'Balistreri! Any good corpses lately?'

The sarcasm irritated him more than the jocular camaraderie. Colombo was a good policeman, but he enjoyed play-acting too much, especially in front of journalists.

'I'm calling about Giulia Piccolo,' said Balistreri, cutting him short.

'Oh, yes, that woman who's always causing trouble.'

'Inspector Piccolo is one of the few real investigators we have, Colombo.'

'Could be,' came the cautious reply, 'But you know there's no excuse for what she did.'

Balistreri wanted to get down to business.

'In the same way, there was no excuse for your son being where he was when I hauled him out of that little party full of underage kids off their heads on cocaine.'

He could hear Colombo swallow on the other end of the line.

'So what do you suggest, Balistreri?'

'Two months' suspension without pay.'

'Three, at the very least,' Colombo replied.

'All right. Not a word to anyone that I've said anything. It'll make you look better then, too, won't it?'

'But when she comes back on duty you can take her on in Homicide, Balistreri. She's burned her bridges in Section II. No one wants her here.'

'We'll see,' growled Balistreri, and replaced the receiver without saying goodbye.

Two hours later, Corvu came in, beaming.

'Giulia's only got three months' suspension. You spoke to Colombo about her, didn't you?'

Balistreri rose from the sofa and took a step towards Corvu, who moved quickly backwards.

'Corvu, if you dare put word around that I did, I'll send you right back to those goats in Sardinia.'

Corvu hid a smile. That's the way Balistreri was. An act of generosity was a sign of weakness. He excused himself and made an even quicker exit.

Alone again, Balistreri cast a casual eye over the daily papers, which he'd still not managed to read. It would be one way to pass the time. In *Il Domani* there was an article from Tripoli by Linda Nardi about the death of General Younis. For some reason, he found the name of Linda Nardi in association with that city deeply disturbing. And it brought to mind all that had happened five years earlier: a love that never got started, perhaps never ended; the crazy hunt for the Invisible Man led by Linda Nardi and Giulia Piccolo, using any means they could, including ignoring the rules and putting their own lives at risk.

They're like those two boys of so long ago, Mikey and Ahmed, who also ignored the rules and scoffed at danger.

Tripoli, 1962

Mikey Balistreri

I'm the son of one of the richest and most influential families in Tripoli, but my real friends are Ahmed and Karim, the younger sons of Mohammed Al Bakri, my father's chief factotum. Then there's Nico Gerace, the class fool, ridiculed by everyone except me, who protects him from the taunts. I prefer to spend my time with them than with the sons of wealthy Italians, English and Americans in the exclusive clubs along the beach. My father's not happy about this.

It's very hot in the garden of the two villas. The sweat's dripping down my neck and the sparrows are making a real racket.

Having come back from prayers in the mosque, Ahmed's waiting for the gunfight, dressed as a cowboy, in the costume they gave me as a present but which I no longer wear.

Laura's standing in the shade of the eucalyptus tree, chatting with Karim. Karim doesn't act in my films; he's very religious and says that films are for unbelievers. Karim and I often talk about things. In contrast to Ahmed and Nico, who follow me in everything, his only guide is the Koran. If he hangs about with us it's for two reasons: one, he has to obey his elder brother; and, two, so he can be with Laura Hunt. She's a beautiful young girl, with light blue eyes that look right into you. Between Laura and me it's a mixture of like and dislike; I like her, and I know she likes me, but we don't say much to each other and, when we do, we communicate in a funny way. In the beginning she used to call me Michelino, just to annoy me. And I called her Bimba. Not any more, though. Our friendship is indirect, like the way we're attracted to each other.

In my version of *The Searchers* it's Scar, the Comanche chief, who kills the Civil War veteran played by John Wayne. I'm not sure if Laura's father, William, would approve of the way I've changed the film's ending.

Today, however, we're playing my version of the gunfight in the last film my grandfather took me to see at the Alhambra, *The Last Sunset* with Kirk Douglas and Rock Hudson.

I go up to Ahmed, hands in my gun belt. I explain the new deal and he shakes his head, at a loss.

'Mikey, I'd rather lose, like I always do.'

'Don't worry, Ahmed, you can lose. But this time I'm going to die, and you stay on your feet.

Karim counted out the steps, then we turned and looked each other in the eye.

Then the two of us shoot. Kirk Douglas falls to his knees: I'm on the ground, a hand on my chest, my eyes half closed. Finally, Laura and Karim take notice. Both are surprised. It's the first time I've lost in a gunfight.

I tell them the new twist to the plot. My pistol wasn't loaded: I'd emptied it before the gunfight so as not to kill my best friend, Rock Hudson.

Ahmed is confused.

'I wanted to be the one who dies.'

Laura darts a glance at him.

'You wouldn't let yourself be killed because your gun wasn't loaded. Not even by Mikey.'

Then Karim steps in.

'I wouldn't let myself be killed for either one of you. But I would for Laura.'

I'm sure he would, and I know that in some ways Karim admires me and in others he hates me. He and Ahmed look similar, but their characters are opposite. Karim lives for ideals and the Koran; Ahmed lives for reality and his knife.

As for me, I live for my dreams.

3 Kickbacks and Bribes

Saturday, 30 July 2011

Nairobi

It was cold when Linda landed at Jomo Kenyatta airport. She immediately felt happy to be there, among the smiling faces in the confusion of Arrivals. The photos of wild animals and incredible landscapes on the walls, the stalls full of Masai handicrafts and the colourful clothing made her feel lighter and full of energy.

She passed through the hellhole of baggage reclaim, where it was only the Westerners who raised their voices and complained about the delays. When she finally got her bag she left the airport and took a taxi, which was immediately caught up in the chaos of the traffic. As they finally drew closer to the city centre, which was clean and modern, the traffic became less congested and more orderly and the lorries, pick-up trucks and carts gave way to cars.

An hour later Linda was in her room in the African Beauty Hotel, but she didn't have the energy to unpack. She was very tired and knew she would fall asleep as soon as she lay down. But the thought didn't cross her mind. She had neither the time nor the money to stay more than two or three days in Kenya and, besides visiting her beloved orphans, she had decided during the flight there that she would investigate what

Bashir Yared had told her in Tripoli. All things considered, it would be worth it. So she took a shower, changed and went out.

She crossed the gardens of Central Park and went straight away to buy a third-hand motorcycle. She had to be able to get about quickly.

She set off and rode easily through the centre: all hyper-modern skyscrapers, shopping centres, elegant shops, flyovers and gleaming hotels. But as soon as she left it she found herself on another planet.

Nobody kept to their lane; everyone sounded their horn and jumped the lights. Progress was no more than walking pace, and you were surrounded by crowds of pedestrians who crossed when and where they pleased, dodging between cars, lorries and scooters, held up by goats that appeared out of nowhere and holes in the road that were more like craters.

Linda crossed the vast city over to the area around the smaller Wilson Airport in Nairobi West and into the shanty towns full of *mitumba* markets. Here, the average income was half a euro a day and the number of HIV sufferers shocking. She pulled up at the orphanage that carried an Italian name, that of Manfredi.

As soon as she entered the building, the nuns came to hug her and all the children ran up to meet her. If she hadn't found the money, hadn't persuaded the authorities and overseen the work, many of those children would be on the street now, perhaps already dead.

She stayed there for hours, playing with the little ones: she had brought Punch and Judy puppets with her and had the children rolling around with laughter; language didn't matter. She ate supper with the nuns and the children, helped to put the kids to bed, and kissed them one by one as she went past saying goodnight.

Then she got back on her motorbike and drove back across the city. Other people might have said she travelled 'from the hellhole of the shanty towns to the paradise of Central Park'. But for Linda it was the exact opposite. Once in her room, she threw off her clothes, jumped into bed and fell into a deep sleep.

Sunday, 31 July 2011

Nairobi

Linda spent the whole morning at the orphanage, dealing with admin and discussing with the nuns how to resolve various problems. She then played with the children, had lunch with them and set off once again on the bike.

She followed the edge of the shanty towns as far as the offices of the Swiss consortium ELCON, on a construction site surrounded by barbed wire and armed security guards. Beyond the wire were mounds of refuse and open drains next to homes made from corrugated iron and cardboard; tangled electric cables dangled from wooden poles, and the inevitable goats, chickens, dogs and skinny cats wandered in and out of the rubbish.

Linda settled into a noxious-smelling bar opposite the site. She ordered a coffee every hour and didn't touch a drop. The cups looked as if they hadn't seen detergent in years, but she had a good supply of bottled water and bananas in her rucksack.

At five o'clock Gabriele Cascio came out for his customary Sunday visit to the bank, just as Bashir Yared had told her in Tripoli. He was carrying an overnight case chained to his wrist and, at his side, two armed guards served to keep away wrongdoers and beggars. They got into a black Toyota pick-up and set off.

Linda put on her helmet and followed at a distance. It was much easier for her to make her way on the bike amidst the melee of men, metal and animals as they headed further west, skirting the shanties around the National Park, then over a reinforced steel bridge covered in mud which spanned a turbid stream full of floating rubbish and excrement. Then they were on to muddy lanes bordered by ditches of stagnant water and banks of stinking rubbish. There were no more goats crossing the roads, but there were huge rats, which Linda tried to avoid. The homes were no longer recognizable as houses, just hovels made out of anything available: corrugated iron, cardboard boxes, carpets, tarpaulin. All the children were barefoot. None of them had even a ball of rags to kick about. But they all smiled at her, just like her orphans.

The pick-up cleared the district and in a few minutes came to a small brick building with a neon sign outside it that read 'International Cooperative Bank'. Half the letters were unlit but, for a bank, neon was thought more suitable than a painted sign.

It was almost six in the evening, and the bank would soon be closing. Linda decided to run the risk of being seen and went in a couple of minutes after the man she was following. This run-down branch of the International Cooperative Bank was on the ground floor. There were two black Africans at the cash desks and several white clients. She could see Cascio through the drooping Venetian blinds of the only office, sitting opposite an African wearing glasses. A peeling sign on the door read: 'Manager'.

Of the two employees, she chose the one who seemed less proficient, a good-looking young Kenyan. She asked for information about opening an account while trying to see what was going on behind the Venetian blinds. She saw Cascio counting out hundred-euro banknotes and the Kenyan manager re-counting them.

This went on for a while, and Linda had no idea what else to ask the cashier, who really was good-looking, probably about thirty years old. He seemed embarrassed, awkward dealing with white women.

'Would you like to have a beer with me?' Linda asked him in English, before she'd even realized what she was saying.

'I'm sorry?'

He was surprised and looked worried. He turned to look at the manager's office. Linda smiled at him and pointed to the time. Five minutes to six.

'Just a beer – five minutes. My name's Linda.'

He gave her a faint smile, not quite believing that she'd asked him, a little anxious but also flattered.

'Okay, I'm John. John Kiptanu. There's an application form to fill out.'

She was amazed at how natural and easy it had been to be so forward. But it wasn't her who was suddenly another person. It was the young man in front of her.

Kiptanu handed her the form, which she pretended to complete so the other cashier wouldn't get suspicious. In the meantime, she saw the manager giving Cascio some deposit slips to sign. The Italian slipped his copies into his trouser pockets and quickly left. Linda positioned herself so he had no way of seeing her face.

When she left the bank with the young cashier the sunset sky was peach coloured. She didn't have any particular plan in mind, nor wanted one. John had never been able to plan anything his whole life, even less anything involving a woman like Linda Nardi.

He looked at the motorbike with a mixture of attraction and fear.

'Is this yours?'

Linda handed him a helmet and helped him fasten it. Then she had him get on behind her and off they set to the centre, the only two motorcyclists wearing helmets in the whole of Nairobi. John clung on to her. Linda could feel him trembling as he pressed close to her, out of fear, not desire. So she dropped her speed to that of the cyclists, and he began to relax. But, that way, it would have taken three hours to get back to the centre. She pulled over, switched off the engine and turned to face him.

'Have you never been on a motorbike before?' she asked.

John looked back at her, his irises an intense black in the white of the corneas.

'No. Only on a bicycle. But I do trust you, miss.'

He looked ashamed, embarrassed to find himself on the back of a motorbike behind a beautiful, independent-minded white woman.

But I do trust you, miss.

It was the loveliest, most honest thing a man had ever said to her.

And what Michele Balistreri denied me.

Linda got back on the bike and told him to put his arms right round her, even if it did make him feel awkward and uncomfortable, and they set off again.

'Sorry, miss,' he kept saying at every pothole that thrust him against her.

Once back in the centre, she parked near the hotel.

'Just a beer and something to eat, okay?'

She pointed to a restaurant where she had often been on her previous trips to Nairobi. John stopped her outside the entrance. He pointed to his sandals and faded jeans.

I can't go in here. I haven't got any money.'

He must have seen lots of Western television films in which successful men offered a girl dinner. But, with a salary of seventy dollars a month, John Kiptanu couldn't even afford an aperitif. Not here, or anywhere else.

Linda took him inside. The elderly black waiter looked disapproving, but after a glance from Linda he led them to a table for two with wooden chairs in the shape of giraffes. She ordered beer and roast crocodile meat for both of them.

Between mouthfuls, John stole furtive glances at her.

'How old are you?' Linda asked him.

'I'm not sure. My passport says thirty, but it could be more.'

Given the local habit of registering babies only when they had their first serious illness, it was likely that John was thirty-two or thirty-three, even though he had the body of a twenty-five-year-old and the careworn face of a man of forty. He seemed tired, sleepy.

'Are you tired?'

'Yes, I'm sorry. After the bank, I usually have a sleep, because I have another job at night.'

She looked at him in surprise.

'What type of job?'

He studied his hands. She wasn't used to a grown man being so shy; it was so different from the men she knew, always so ready to boast about themselves and their success. It was almost as if she were committing an offence just being with him.

'From ten to one I sing and play guitar in a night club,' he said, avoiding her eyes, as if he were admitting being a drug dealer.

Linda was suddenly aware of an emotion she hadn't felt for many years. Everything was beating faster: her heart, her breath, her life.

'Do you have a girlfriend, John?'

If a man with dark skin could blush, John Kiptanu would have.

'No, no girlfriend.'

'But you sleep with girls, right?'

He looked at her, amazed. No one had ever spoken to him like this. He was embarrassed, curious, but not flattered, as a Western man would have been. And he replied with an honesty that would be alien to any Western man.

'Well, for the sex, yes; not for love.'

'And you'd like to have love, a wife and children?' Linda asked.

He stared at her with those black irises in their stark white corneas.

'I don't have enough money to marry. And I don't want children.'

'Why not?'

The question hung in the air over the abyss that separated their two worlds: their desires, their expectations, even the value they put on existence.

'Maybe five or ten years from now I'll be dead from AIDS, you know that? Everyone gets it here, sooner or later.'

Linda tried to stop herself, but those words of his, that smile, that unconditional trust offered in exchange for nothing, was pressing on the defences she had built up over the years.

She looked at the man in front of her. He was wearing the white, short-sleeved shirt of a bank employee, its collar worn but clean. This was the half of him the customers saw above the desk. Below were the torn, faded jeans and sandals that were the real John Kiptanu.

He lives in a shanty town and has no future. He works in a bank, plays the guitar and sings to get by until the moment comes. He couldn't wish for anything which, for him, was simply impossible.

John had to leave to get the bus to the nightclub where he played.

'I have to go now, miss,' he said.

'My name's Linda, not Miss.'

'Yes, Miss Linda.'

'Where do you sing?'

From his wallet he took out a creased business card. He held out his hand, shook hers, made a small bow and smiled.

'Goodnight, Miss Linda.'

Kiptanu left, and Linda walked over to African Heights. Inside, it was full of locals and Westerners, tourist couples, businessmen, girls in miniskirts and vertiginous high heels, all flocking into the

Bluebird Club. Linda sat in an armchair in the lobby, where she could see people entering and leaving the club. She knew that Cascio was inside.

The Italian came out at about ten thirty with an East European blonde. She was tall and slim, elegant, wearing little make-up, black leather trousers and a pair of cowboy boots; her long, straight hair hung down below her waist and her fingernails were painted black.

Linda was satisfied. It was important to understand what sort of woman he liked. With her body and features, it wouldn't be difficult to become the right type for Signor Gabriele Cascio.

Having checked out Cascio, she took a taxi across the centre of town to the hotel where John was performing. The nightclub inside was overflowing with Westerners, all of them tourists. Onstage were not only local girls but also good-looking local men, there to attract the eye of female tourists.

Linda remained standing at the bar, half hidden by a column, sipping a mineral water. John's act came on at midnight. He walked on barefoot in his stage clothes: skintight black trousers and bare torso, a pirate bandana around his head.

Linda felt angry and put out as the women nudged each other at the sight of his athletic, muscular body and the perfect features of his face.

It was John's job to sing requests for the women, the songs chosen by a horrendous bidding process, the winner throwing banknotes on to the stage as a tip. An attendant collected the money, which without a doubt went largely to the establishment, with only a small percentage to John.

His jaw dropped when he found her waiting outside the club. They walked off together in silence and, when they arrived at her hotel, he stopped.

'I can't go in here, can I?'

Linda took him by the hand and they went up in the lift. John looked around the tidy and well-furnished little room as if he were lost. Naturally, he had had sex with local girls in the shanty towns, on beaten-up old mattresses among the other huts and the rubbish. But he had never seen such an elegant bed as the one in this room.

Linda looked out of the window at Central Park. Neither of them knew what to do or say. Then John plucked up his courage. From the back pocket of his jeans he pulled out a tattered wallet and handed her a piece of paper and a condom.

'I had a test last week. Here's the certificate.'

So this was John Kiptanu's proposal for sex: a condom and a certificate. Well, it was more honest than a thousand dinners.

They kissed and undressed quickly. Linda was relieved to find that she didn't feel embarrassed. She was even more relieved to realize that John was looking into her eyes far more than at her body.

The awkwardness of first-time lovers soon dissolved into passion in the arms of this man who kissed her and looked in her eyes, then caressed her, still looking into her eyes.

Sex with John was different from anything else she had experienced. At a certain point with previous lovers her body became a separate thing, her mind detached as she watched the man trying to please her; she went along with it for his pleasure. During sex, her soul seemed to leave her body and only returned when it was all over. But now her soul was fully present, and perhaps more excited than her body; it was the total absence of assumptions and expectations. She felt liberated.

As for John Kiptanu, he had nothing to offer and nothing to ask. One day he would die from AIDS, reduced to skin and bone in his shanty on the Nairobi outskirts.

Perhaps that day I'll be sipping a cocktail in Piazza di Spagna with another man.

But it was this man without a future that she guided inside her. He lifted himself up above her and looked at her with such adoration it was as if a boiling liquid were coursing through her arteries and veins, as if she were giving herself for the very first time that day. Her body and her soul were reunited, were melding together in his embrace.

Linda felt connected to this young man by something quite ordinary, but it was something she had never felt before: the feeling that *this was something very beautiful.*

Before he left, John pointed to Linda's still-unpacked suitcase.

'Are you leaving?'

'Tuesday morning. Tomorrow's my last day here.'

There was a sad smile on his face, but it disappeared instantly, probably because he didn't want to upset her.

'If you want, I can come back tomorrow. I think I love you.'

No Western man would have said such a thing so suddenly and so openly.

Without thinking about it too much, Linda made a decision. She knew that, in some way, she had to be honest with John. So she explained that she'd gone into the bank as part of her work, following the man who had come in to see the manager. Kiptanu listened to her story almost as if she were the heroine of an adventure story.

They agreed to meet at midnight in the hotel the following night.

Monday, 1 August 2011

Nairobi

Linda spent the whole day at the orphanage, eating an early supper with the nuns and children, then returned to her hotel and made herself up to play an exotic woman of the night.

At the Bluebird Club, Cascio noticed her as soon as she came in and sat down at a small table in a booth behind a screen. Tall in six-inch heels, with platinum blonde hair (extensions), black leather trousers and shoes and black enamelled fingernails, she had dressed for the part.

Just the kind you like . . .

Cascio made his appearance a few minutes later. There was some subdued chatter from the other booths and music from the bar, but it felt as if it was just the two of them. And he was dressed to kill – or rather to pull: a blue Armani jacket, white shirt, grey slacks and suede moccasins.

'Mind if I sit here?' he asked in English.

She replied in Italian, with a slight French accent.

'If you must,' she said, sounding bored, almost not looking at him.

This was not the reply of a prostitute in search of a customer. Cascio was surprised.

'You're Italian?'

He used the familiar *tu* form, ignoring the fact that she seemed not to care whether he was there or not.

'Half Italian, half French.'

'I haven't seen you here before.'

She carried on ignoring him, staring instead at the dance floor, where a flabby American was dancing with two local girls.

'I arrived yesterday. My name's Catherine.'

'And what are you doing in the Bluebird, Catherine?'

'I'm here on a whim. I'm married to a man who's too rich to take any notice of me.'

For a moment he was speechless. Linda went on, almost surprised at how easily she was playing her role.

'Every so often I take a trip around the world and find places like this one. And then I choose what I want there.'

The message was clear. Just as it was clear he wasn't the type Catherine would be looking for.

But he was hooked by the challenge. Cascio usually bought his women, but money wasn't enough with her.

'And your husband isn't here, I take it?'

He's an accountant. A cautious man.

'He's in Paris. I'm here just for tonight. Tomorrow I'm off to the Seychelles.'

A dream scenario for the Cascios of this world.

He ordered champagne and lit a cigar. Linda looked around her as if checking the place out for someone more interesting, then deciding it was time to give him a helping hand.

'And what are you doing in Kenya?' she asked, as if she couldn't care less what he did.

Cascio had his own vision of the world of women. If you wanted to win them over, you had show how important you were.

'Business, finance, property. I'm here to see if purchasing the Bluebird would be a good business move.'

She showed a first sign of interest.

'You're a banker?'

Cascio felt that he'd found the right way to impress her.

'I worked in a bank in Rome for many years.'

She pretended to be disappointed.

'Oh, what a shame! Bank employees are ever so boring usually. It's different with bankers . . .'

Cascio hesitated, then decided what he might tell her wasn't too confidential. And there was no other way of winning her over.

'I was a manager in a very special bank, Catherine. Perhaps, as you're half Italian, you'll have heard of it: the IOR. The Institute for Religious Works.'

Linda stopped looking at the dance floor and turned towards him for the first time.

'Ah, God's bank, isn't it?'

Cascio gave a satisfied smile.

He's blessing Marcinkus, Sindona and all the others who contributed to making the name so famous . . . or notorious . . .

His foot brushed against Linda's ankle. Just a slight contact, but enough. She didn't move, but neither did she return the gesture.

'I see you know what that means, Catherine.'

She smiled at him.

'What did you say your name was?'

He moved his foot a little closer.

'Gabriele Cascio.'

He was getting cocky now. Linda gently moved her ankle away.

'So, you were one of God's bankers, Signor Cascio. Doing business in Kenya must be very dull for you . . .'

He wasn't sure how to go on. True, he could make something up, but he wanted to impress her.

'I'm here for a very important project — hospitals for the poor. With Islamic and Italian funds. I'm the director of a Swiss consortium, ELCON.'

She looked disappointed again.

'Oh, the poor, they're such a pain. And the IOR is so interesting!'

By now it was clear to Cascio that it was only the IOR that excited her — while what excited him was the idea of having a woman without having to pay her. Linda studied him: a grown man, uncertain as a little boy, wondering whether he could steal some sweets and get away with it.

She got up and went to the bar for a cigarette, which she didn't inhale, and came back to Cascio at the table, giving him plenty of time to appraise what lay underneath those black leather trousers.

'Well, the building site I'm looking after is linked in part to the IOR. But this is confidential information.'

What a lack of imagination: you're almost telling me the truth . . .

She stretched out one leg under the table and placed her stiletto heel delicately on the fly of his trousers. He was so surprised that he spilled champagne down his front.

'You know, Gabriele,' said Linda, looking him in the eye as she started to massage him, 'confidential things excite me. They're a kind of challenge for me. I'll do anything to find out what they are. Anything.'

Five minutes were enough to bring him almost to orgasm. When Linda realized from his breathing that he was ready to come, she took her foot away.

'I don't want you to stain your clothes, Gabriele. Not here, at least.'

He looked at her, his eyes inflamed with desire.

'We could go to my place?' he suggested.

She pulled a face.

'I've told you I'm not a prostitute. But I want to be paid in some way; otherwise, there's no fun in it.'

'How much do you want?'

'Have you no imagination? I don't want money. My husband's filthy rich.'

'So what do you want?'

'I want to feel something. I want to play. I want to go somewhere exciting.'

'All right, I'll get the best suite in the hotel.'

I have to get him to take me to where he keeps his papers.

She pulled an even sulkier face, looking bored.

'Luxury is part of my everyday life, Gabriele. Can't you give me anything a little different? Somewhere I'd never go without an adventurous man like you?'

She saw the idea slowly making its way into Cascio's mind.

'What about the building site I run in West Nairobi? That's a dangerous place. It's in the outskirts.'

She stared at him with her glorious green eyes.

'And do you have an office there, with a desk?'

Cascio had a momentary vision of what they could do on that desk. But he didn't like the idea of venturing out into the shanty towns. Linda could see it in his eyes, so she had to push him into it.

'You're not afraid, are you?'

Cascio had begun to sweat, despite the air conditioning. He shook his head and forced a laugh.

'There's a loaded gun in the car.'

'Good. Then buy some champagne, and let's go.'

Cascio came back with a bottle and two glasses, and five minutes later they were in his Toyota SUV, heading for the construction site. He drove for half an hour, the pistol beside him. Anxiety about being held up kept him from putting his hand between her thighs. He only relaxed when they reached the site gate, where there were armed guards on duty. They drove through and then another half a kilometre, and parked outside the motor home that served as his office.

They went in and he switched on the light.

'Do sit down, *signora mia*.'

Linda's eyes took in the desk covered with papers, the filing cabinets and, lastly, a small safe built into the wall. There would have to have been one, seeing that Cascio kept a lot of cash there.

'Is that the safe where you keep all your secrets, Gabriele?'

She took off the jacket she was wearing, over a white blouse buttoned right up to her neck. Then she pushed all the papers off the desk, him watching her all the time, fascinated and excited.

'We'll need some space on here in a while. Now give me the bottle.'

He passed it to her and she opened it, poured champagne into the two glasses and offered one to him.

'Let's drink to our secrets!' she said.

He emptied his glass and started to move in close, but she stopped him.

'Oh, Gabriele, don't be so obvious, or I won't feel like it any more. Let's play a little game. Just use your imagination. Come on, it'll be fun!'

'What do I have to do?'

'We trade secrets. I'll give you one, if you give me one. If you've no secret for me, then I won't have one for you.'

Linda put her fingers to her blouse and undid a button. Cascio finally cottoned on. Linda watched him as he made up his mind.

Of course you'll try to befuddle me, telling me anything you like, all useless information. But what I need is for you to open that safe.

'Gabriele, you mentioned that the site here's linked to the IOR.

But outside there's the nameplate of a Swiss consortium, this ELCON . . .'

Cascio gave a sly smile and poured himself more champagne.

'The ELCON consortium's only a cover.'

'For what, Gabriele?'

Cascio was wavering, hovering between fear and desire.

'An Islamic trust. I don't know who's behind it. It's someone in Luxembourg linked to some Italians.'

Linda knew that the Valium she had slipped into his champagne would soon take effect. She had to get Cascio to open the safe before he fell asleep.

She undid the belt of his trousers and the second of her six buttons.

'Italians? So what's the IOR got to do with it?' she asked, in the most vacant way she could manage.

He was breathing hard, his voice hoarse.

'The Luxembourg trust has an account with the IOR. Now, will you please take off your clothes?'

She smiled at him. Cascio had downed half a bottle of champagne, his eyes were on stalks and he was staggering. She took a step back and gave him a serious look.

'I don't believe you. Only priests are allowed accounts with the IOR. And you're nothing but some weedy little accountant who's not worth my trouble. Show me some proof or take me straight back to the Bluebird.'

She saw Cascio's eyes shoot to the safe, then back again. He grabbed the champagne bottle and finished it off. Linda had taken only a few sips from her glass.

'My head's spinning,' Cascio mumbled as he made for the safe. While he punched in the code Linda took a heavy metal binder from a shelf and, as soon as the safe was open, let it come down heavily on his head. Cascio fell to the floor like a ripe fruit from a tree.

It took her only a few minutes to find the memorandum of

association, signed by a notary for the Swiss consortium ELCON. Headquarters: Lugano. The investment companies forming 50 per cent of the consortium were GB Investments (head office: Luxembourg) and Charity Investments (central office: Dubai). Two pieces of information of which it was difficult to make sense.

Unfortunately, there was no trace of the bank accounts relating to the transfer of monies from the International Cooperative Bank of Nairobi. They were probably in another safe in Cascio's home. But there was his secret weapon, the one with which he had probably hoped to seduce her: a visiting card with a single name printed on it: Monsignor Eugenio Pizza.

Below the name was a handwritten mobile-phone number with the Switzerland prefix. Linda jotted it down.

She made a copy of the memorandum, put the original back in the safe and closed it. Cascio wouldn't even remember he'd opened it.

She dragged his body towards the desk. That way, he'd think he'd banged his head, falling down drunk. She emptied his glass into the sink and rinsed it, together with the bottle and the other glass. She then put on her jacket and went out to get help from the guards, who called for a taxi to take her back to her hotel.

On the way, it began to rain. She thought about that name. Monsignor Eugenio Pizza.

Just as Bashir Yared had led her to understand. The éminence grise *behind the Vatican's finances, or a true benefactor of the world's poor?*

Back in her hotel, Linda had just enough time to take a shower. At midnight, John arrived. He had to call from the lobby because they wouldn't let him come up. She had to explain that he was a guest.

When he came in he was soaking wet from the rain, but he had brought two presents. The first was three roses, which were also soaking wet and must have cost him half a month's salary. Linda tried to find a vase to put them in but, obviously, there wasn't one. They had to make do with the tooth glass from the bathroom.

By morning they'll be dead, just like our love affair.

John had taken a great risk in obtaining the second gift. He had used his own keys to enter the bank when it was closed and had unlocked the manager's desk.

He handed her photocopies of the deposit and transfer slips filled in by Cascio at the bank. There was a number for an IOR account in Rome, but no name for the account holder.

Perhaps Monsignor Eugenio Pizza's visiting card was the answer to that.

That night, which was both very long and very short, Linda asked herself several times what was stopping her giving it all up and not going back to a world where she had no life and staying here instead with John and the orphans.

But going away and running away aren't the same thing.

Rome

Several thoughts kept Linda awake during the return flight from Kenya to Rome.

There was the IOR account and Monsignor Eugenio Pizza's visiting card in Gabriele Cascio's safe. It could all be true, and then she would make the headlines. But there were plenty of things in the way. There were few Italian newspapers that went in for real investigative journalism. It was nothing but a fairy tale circulated to an innocent public that an interesting investigation would always be published.

It depended on who was being investigated, the political climate and how dangerous the reaction might be.

Mentioning the IOR was like entering a minefield, and Monsignor Eugenio Pizza was untouchable – if he could even be found. She had thought about this a long time and, unfortunately, the only way of moving on was through Senator Emilio Busi.

The senator was as exceptional as he was untrustworthy. Exceptional as a politician and a director on various management boards, but untrustworthy as a man. From the moment his star had begun to rise in the 1970s, he had built up his power base day by day, buying the public's soul, distributing floods of growing good fortune to everyone: electorate, collaborators, friends and adversaries – especially the adversaries, so that they never became enemies. The result? People were glad to have dealings with him. They trusted him.

From 1970 onwards, his rise in politics and business had been as unstoppable as it was exceptional, aided by an initial personal fortune of no very clear provenance, and created by means of a brokerage firm that dealt with petroleum securities in the Arab states, which Busi had sold for huge profits when he was first elected to Parliament.

By the beginning of the 1980s, Busi had been in Parliament for some time and it was said in the Italian Communist Party that he was the true intermediary with the Christian Democrat Party, thanks to his excellent friendships in the Vatican.

With the fall of the Berlin Wall, Communism – even in its Italian version – had an identity crisis. And in 1992 the so-called 'Clean Hands' investigation into the 'Tangentopoli' culture of bribery and corruption in Italy almost swept away the Christian Democrat Party and the Socialist Party and destroyed the careers of a lot of entrepreneurs and directors. But there was nothing on Busi.

With the death of the Christian Democrats, the Left seemed finally destined for power in the 1994 elections and Busi on the brink of great things: a ministry, at the very least, if not Speaker of the House.

But just before the election he had put on a tie that matched his shirt and jacket – something he had never done in his life – and had gone on to the most popular Italian talk show, on which he had never before wanted to appear. There he had confirmed two things: that the destruction of the political parties by the judiciary in the 'Clean Hands' investigations would only bring trouble to Italy; and that Communism had clearly shown itself to be a mistake: it went against reality – the claim that everyone could be equal in poverty was made possible only through the use of tanks and the Gulag.

And to be consistent with this, he said, he was withdrawing from political life and would not be standing for Parliament again.

This gesture proved to be a real stroke of genius. Against all predictions, the Left lost the 1994 elections and, in a very short time, it was the Centre Right who came looking for him.

From then on, as the Centre Rights and Centre Lefts came to power and went, Emilio Busi was the shadow minister for infrastructure in governments of whatever stripe.

Then, for his great merit and innumerable services to the state, he was nominated a senator for life, re-entering Parliament in triumph, and now, at the age of sixty-six, his word was law, even for prime ministers, and particularly in the field of energy and industry.

Linda had known him personally for less than six months, since a foreign journalist friend of hers had passed on rumours about a business deal regarding contracts for military aircraft commissioned from Busi's Gruppo Italia by several foreign countries. It was hinted that the contracts had been obtained by bribes and other unorthodox means.

When Linda had contacted Busi's personal assistant for an interview about these contracts, she had expected to be refused.

Instead, Busi had received her in his private chamber in the Senate. After that interview, as polite as it was inconclusive, a discreet courtship had followed, subtle but insistent, which had enabled her to understand the man much better.

Busi had never forced himself upon her. As a truly powerful man, he expected that she would take the first decisive step and offer herself to him.

But although she found Busi's intelligence fascinating, Linda was aware he had a vision of the world with which she could never agree. Not even for one night.

It would have been the slow crumbling of the conscience that goes on to corrupt the soul.

Wednesday, 3 August 2011

Rome

Linda woke up, made a strong espresso, had a shower, then sat down on the terrace and called the number of the secretary of Gruppo Italia's chairman.

A young male voice passed her on to Beatrice Armellini, Busi's personal assistant.

'Linda, dear, what an unexpected pleasure!'

Linda bore no ill will towards women like Beatrice, who prettied themselves up to please the men on whom they depended to make them happy. She understood them well enough and felt no superiority, just a genetic difference.

'I've just come back from abroad and need some professional advice from the chairman,' she confided politely.

'He's in the Senate for the vote on the new budget,' Beatrice replied.

'OK, then I'll call back later, perhaps when he has a free moment.'

Beatrice gave a little laugh.

'Actually, this really is the time when he's most free. And then he'd be angry with me if he knew I hadn't passed you on to him. Hang on.'

Linda had no time to say that this didn't seem to be the right time, but after a moment Busi was there on the line.

'It's always a pleasure to hear from the country's most beautiful journalist,' he said.

In the background she could hear a senator speaking about the Italian fiscal system.

'I'm sorry to bother you, Senator. This doesn't seem to be a good moment . . .'

'It's the best moment there is, Linda. I have some real business to attend to after the sitting in this chamber, where it's nothing but pointless talk. And even if this mobile phone is being tapped, which it most certainly is, you can call me Emilio. Just don't mention those nights of passion we . . .'

He laughed. Linda did not. Obviously, there had been no nights of passion. And she was certainly not happy about using his first name. But this was the way this highly influential man reminded her that she was special – although not that special: he could have plenty of women who were younger and more attractive. It was up to her to make a move.

'I need to speak to you in private, Emilio. Do you have a moment?'

She had used his first name, despite not wanting to. He was obviously pleased by this first small concession.

'Are you looking for contributions to your charity work?'

'No, this isn't about orphanages, Emilio. I'd like to interview Monsignor Eugenio Pizza.'

Busi was quiet for a moment as he weighed up the pros and cons. Asking a favour of Monsignor Pizza was not a problem for him, but it was well known that questions asked by Linda Nardi could be very irritating.

'I've been invited to the Italy–Middle East Economic Forum tomorrow. A meeting of delegates that's a complete waste of time – no one ever does any business – but as Gruppo Italia's chairman I have to be there. There's dinner and a night on board a cruise ship sailing from the island of Elba to Civitavecchia.'

He let it hang in the air. She hesitated, and he realized she needed more.

'Monsignor Pizza will certainly be there, so I can introduce you. There will be separate cabins, of course.'

Emilio Busi chuckled at the last detail and left the choice up to her: refuse and have no help, or be his prey in return for a little favour.

Linda knew very well how to keep even Emilio Busi at bay and needed his help, so she accepted. Immediately afterwards, however, she felt the need to take another shower.

Tripoli, 1962

Mikey Balistreri

According to my father, Don Eugenio — who takes us for catechism —
is a generous man of the cloth, very able at managing the alms he gets
to promote charitable works. But he doesn't know that Don Eugenio
also has the habit of letting his hands wander where they shouldn't.
Not on me, of course, the son of Salvatore Balistreri, but those boys
like Nico: the weak, the kids of nobodies, the ones no one can protect. Under the car-port roof, which gives us no shelter from the
ghibli, I'm furious. I look at Ahmed. I can see him as he cuts the eye
out of that dog and then slits its throat in revenge for poor Jet, my
dog, who caught rabies.

'We have to get him to stop it, the pig. I've got an idea.'

The sand getting everywhere, into our clothes, they all listen
closely to me. Karim stares in admiration, Ahmed nods silently, but
Nico has a problem.

'I can't do it, Mikey. I'm too scared.'

I try to persuade him. I have to, or he'll be a victim for ever and
become a coward. 'Nico, if you don't do this, you'll always be scared
of him and he'll be able to carry on doing those things to you. If you

go along with me, you won't be frightened of him any more, nor of anyone else.'

'Can't you do it instead of me, Mikey?'

He's so scared, he's lisping.

No, Nico. I'm Ingenere Salvatore Balistreri's son. Don Eugenio wouldn't dare. You're the outcast.

'And we're Libyans, Mikey,' Karim cuts in. 'What if Don Eugenio has us arrested?'

'I'll protect you. If he reports you, he'll have to report me as well, and he'll never do that.'

Ahmed takes out the Swiss knife he used to kill the dog that infected Jet. I gave it to him as a present on his last birthday.

'If it doesn't work, I'll take care of that priest.'

As usual, Karim doesn't agree. But we were then united by a pact of blood, a brotherhood; no one could touch a single one of us. He knows that, too. And so, although he's unwilling, Karim accepts the plan: four young teens against an important adult.

Next day in the confessional, Nico begins his confession as planned.

'We touched ourselves. Myself, Mikey, Ahmed and Karim. All four of us pulled down our underpants. Then we measured our peckers.'

Don Eugenio comes out of the confessional. His light blue eyes fix on Nico.

'How far down did you pull your underpants? Get up, let me see.'

Closing his eyes, Nico does as he's told. His shorts and underpants drop down to his knees. He's trembling. We should wait a little longer, but Karim can't hold still.

He pops out from under the desk and takes snaps with the old Kodak. Click, click, click. Don Eugenio is about to react, but out jump Ahmed and me. We're double trouble for him, Ahmed, because he goes to get him away from Nico, but above all me, because I'm the son of Salvatore Balistreri, the most important Italian in Tripoli. Ahmed has a knife in his hand, the one from the blood brotherhood, the one with which he kills scorpions and cuts the throats of rabid dogs. He presses the knifepoint at the priest's Adam's apple. 'If you touch my friend again, I'll slit your throat, you queer. Understand?'

A few droplets of blood form. A thought enters my head.

The first drops of so much blood.

The trap we laid for Don Eugenio turned out well, but tonight I can't get to sleep. I want to talk to someone, but my brother's in London, studying English and making useful friendships. *And learning how to steal legally,* as Italia maintains. When she tells him this, he gets very annoyed. Mamma says nothing to him and smiles at me instead. As if, for her, it's enough that I understand.

I get up to have a drink of water in the kitchen. My mother's not asleep. She's on her own. As usual, she's got a cigarette in one hand and in the other a glass of that dark-golden liquid Papa calls her poison.

The hot air of the African night enters through the two open French windows, along with the croaking of the frogs. And swarms of mosquitoes, attracted by the light.

'Don't the mosquitoes bite you, Mamma?'

'No, Michelino, only Alberto and Papa. They have sweeter blood.'

'And the two of us?'

She smiles. 'Ours is sour; it's like poison to them.'

'Like what you drink?'

She looks at me with a frown.

'You don't have to parrot everything you hear adults say, not even if it comes from your father.'

'But is it bad for you or not?'

'It's called whisky. And it can damage your health if you drink too much of it.'

'I did something very serious today, Mamma. A mortal sin.'

'Michelino, I just told you not to parrot things you haven't properly understood.'

'But there are the Commandments, Mamma. They were written by God.'

She looks at me indulgently. She knows I haven't believed in Father Christmas for some time.

'And how do you know who really wrote them, Michelino?'

I'm left speechless. If they'd heard her in Tripoli, they would have reported her to the Pope in Rome. They would have excommunicated her. If Papa had heard her, it would have been worse still.

I tell her about Don Eugenio. She listens to me in silence. When I give her the photographs that Laura developed, the shallow lines in her face become deeper.

'Listen to me now, Michelino. We're not going to tell your father about this business. I'll take care of Don Eugenio.'

4 Ghosts From the Past

Thursday, 4 August 2011

At sea, off the Island of Elba

Everything on board the cruise ship spoke of wealth, power and the future, from the business stands to the napkins on the tables laid for dinner.

Linda immediately went off to her cabin on one of the lower decks, the less luxurious ones. But it was still clean and spacious. She didn't want to go on to the bridge deck and mingle with the other journalists. In fact, she didn't want to talk to anyone until dinnertime, when Emilio Busi was due to arrive and would introduce her to Monsignor Eugenio Pizza. She didn't want any of her colleagues to wonder why she was there. Nor did she wish to be hit on by some powerful man who hadn't brought his wife, lover or an escort along.

She lay on the bed and thumbed distractedly through *Il Domani*. On the first page she noticed the interview with Gruppo Italia's chairman, Senator Emilio Busi. The headline was both interesting and surprising. *OLYMPIC PARKS AND A BRIDGE ACROSS THE STRAITS OF MESSINA: WILL THEY REALLY HELP ITALY?*

These were two vast projects that had been talked about for years. And Gruppo Italia's chairman had been a strenuous advocate of them.

But doubts and objections about both had been raised on all sides, both about financing and the risk of infiltration by the criminal underworld, which in Italy was always ready to make money out of public works like these.

Linda read the interview closely. In effect, Busi wasn't denying the need to go ahead. But *Il Domani*'s staff writer had highlighted the real news in the section about the world economic crisis, which, Busi said, would give 'the opportunity for a serious check into the financial backing'. Others had voiced the same opinion but, coming from the mouth of Gruppo Italia's chairman, it indicated that there was a remarkable rift in the group that was pushing for the projects.

She put the paper down, took a long shower and started to get ready for cocktails and dinner. She had hired the evening dress that morning in Rome before leaving. She had never had occasion to wear such a thing before, and she couldn't see it happening again. The one she had chosen was high necked, long and loose fitting. Over it, she was wearing a grey jacket. On account of the air conditioning, she would say.

The lounge bar where drinks were being served was an enormous panoramic room but still overflowing with more than five hundred guests. Almost all the Italians knew one another: politicians, entrepreneurs, managing directors and journalists. All were faces known to the newspapers. They saw each other, embraced and exchanged nods and winks. Only the few who had half-decent English were speaking with the guests from the Arab states.

Linda found Beatrice Armellini at a table with several journalists. She was perfectly at ease acting out her role in designer evening wear, her hair up in a chignon and wearing horn-rimmed glasses.

Linda sat opposite her and watched as she drank a non-alcoholic sparkling wine with evident distaste. Then she smiled at the new arrival.

'Dear Linda, we're so happy to have you here.'

Linda wasn't there to spend the night with Busi, as Beatrice Armellini thought, but she couldn't bring herself to explain.

'Has Senator Busi arrived?' she asked.

Beatrice gave her a complicit smile.

'His helicopter's just landed on the ship. Several of his friends were on it with him also. He's in his suite now. I'm sure he'll be down in a moment. He doesn't want to mingle too long with these people.'

'Aren't they his guests?' Linda asked.

Beatrice looked around.

'Italian entrepreneurs complaining about the state of Italian politics to foreign ministers? Italian politicians complaining to Arab backers about Italian entrepreneurs' lack of competitive spirit? No, Senator Busi prefers the company of a few long-standing friends.'

The man himself then entered the bar, impeccably turned out in black tie and accompanied by three people. The one with the dog collar, the rosy complexion of a baby and thin white hair which once must have been blond, had to be Monsignor Pizza.

Then there was an elderly Arab gentleman with a heavily lined face and, lastly, another elderly gentleman in a white dinner jacket, still very handsome despite his years, almost the double of the older Clark Gable with his white locks, still-gleaming smile and deep, dark eyes.

'Who's the Arab gentleman with him?'

'A Libyan VIP, an old friend of the senator who's very close to Colonel Gaddafi. His name is Mohammed Al Bakri.'

'And the older man in the white dinner jacket?'

Again Beatrice gave her a complicit smile.

'Yes, he must have been gorgeous when he was younger. I think you were close to his son a few years ago.'

For a moment Linda was speechless.

So that's where I've seen those eyes before.

She remembered that Michele had always steered clear of mentioning him. He had introduced her to his brother, Alberto, and had talked to her with sparkling eyes about his mother, Italia. But when she had asked about his father, the reply had always been: 'He doesn't live in Italy any more. I haven't heard from him in twenty years.'

Busi introduced her to his friends and then Linda was seated between Monsignor Pizza and Salvatore Balistreri.

Don Eugenio struck up a conversation with her, perhaps because he had been asked to by Busi, or perhaps so she wouldn't hear what the other three were saying, even though she would have had no idea in any case, because they were speaking in Arabic.

'Senator Busi tells me that you travel a lot.'

'I'm a journalist. I was in Libya covering the war there. And I was in Kenya a few days ago.'

'And what were you doing in Kenya?'

There was something in the man's politeness that Linda found annoying, like chocolate sticking to her fingers.

'I go there a lot. I have a charity there. We've opened a children's hospital.' Monsignor Pizza nodded and only then pretended to recognize her.

'Of course, now I remember who you are. Excellent! God will reward you for all you do. I also have an interest in helping out the poor in that part of the world, whenever I can.'

Monsignor Pizza touched the arm of the older man in the white dinner jacket.

'Salvo, Signorina Nardi isn't only a distinguished journalist. She does wonderful work in Kenya!'

Salvatore Balistreri slowly turned to look at her. Linda had the impression that he was not at all happy to see her at the table.

'And whatever brings you on to this ship, Signorina Nardi?'

His manner was polite and his voice low, warm and gravelly from smoking; his Italian tinged with an American accent. Linda decided to tell him at least part of the truth.

'I have to talk to Senator Busi about an investigation I'm working on, so he invited me here. He didn't have any time in Rome.'

As she gave it, the explanation seemed suspicious, even to her. Monsignor Pizza was deep in conversation in Arabic with Busi and Mohammed Al Bakri. Salvatore Balistreri looked at her with those eyes, as deep and dark as Michele's.

Similar, and yet so different.

'The senator is most obliging. But I don't think he likes journalists very much.'

Linda realized that his words contained a warning. She wondered why. Knowing Emilio Busi's weakness for young women, was Salvatore Balistreri putting her on her guard?

But why? What does he care?

Then the other three men ended their conversation in Arabic and the dinner continued with the usual comments about the world financial crisis. And yet Linda felt a hidden tension round the table, as if her presence there was preventing the men from getting to the heart of the matter. At the end of the meal, Salvatore Balistreri went behind Linda's chair and stood to pull it out from the table.

'Shall we have coffee together?' he asked her.

Linda was taken aback for a moment. Then she followed him to the bar. They picked up two coffees and went out on the balcony. The sun had set some time ago, but the air was still warm and the lights on Elba were glittering in the distance.

'Would you mind if I smoked a cigar, Signorina?'

She indicated that she didn't. She was confused, but not uncomfortable and she was curious to know more about Michele Balistreri's father.

'You live in America, don't you, Signor Balistreri?'

It was difficult to know how to address him.

'Between America and Dubai,' he replied.

It was clear he wanted no more questions on that particular subject.

He exhaled a little cigar smoke, taking care that none of it blew her way. He seemed pensive, as if her presence had triggered something inside him, partly annoying, partly happy.

Annoyed that I was at the table with them, happy that I'm now out here with him.

'Several years ago I read your articles on the Invisible Man. You really are *overly* courageous, Signorina Nardi.'

It was the second sentence that struck her.

A compliment and a warning.

That was the difference between father and son. Michele was incapable of ambiguity, of living with conflicting emotions. She found herself saying something that was apparently unconnected to his comment.

'Your son's an excellent policeman, Signor Balistreri.'

He looked surprised, as if he had put a foot wrong, but only for a second. Something passed across his face, perhaps thoughts about a son he hadn't seen for more than twenty years. Again, the capacity for ambiguity.

Regret or resentment?

'I know,' he said after a moment. 'My wife predicted as much when he was still a child. And Italia was always right.'

Then this handsome elderly gentleman, who looked so like Clark Gable despite his white hair and moustache, handed her his business card and took his leave of her with a simple '*Arrivederci*'.

Emilio Busi was standing at the bar with Beatrice Armellini, Monsignor Pizza and Mohammed Al Bakri. He took her aside for a moment, his hand touching her bare arm.

She was expecting an invitation to his suite and some questions about what she wanted with Monsignor Pizza, but Busi seemed upset by something, as if some complication had arisen.

'I have some business to see to, Linda. I'll give you a call as soon as I'm free. Keep your mobile on . . .'

She felt relieved. Perhaps Emilio Busi had found other company for the night and was no longer interested in her. That was fine with her, as she had now made a first contact with Monsignor Pizza.

She watched the Gruppo Italia chairman return to the bar and rejoin Pizza and Mohammed Al Bakri. Together they went over to a lift, in front of which stood an attendant. He motioned them in and the lift acsended.

After a while Linda went up to the attendant.

'Can I use the lift, please?' she asked.

'I'm sorry, madam, this lift is private,' he replied.

Linda hung around the lounge for a while but, seeing her alone there, too many men came up to talk to her. She took the stairs down to her cabin. On each level she saw an attendant by the private lift. Out of curiosity, she went down to the very lowest deck with cabins, which was just above the engine room.

This deck was deserted, except for another attendant outside the private lift in a half-lit corner of the passageway. Just as Linda was about to go up again, the lift doors opened.

Out walked a refined and beautifully dressed young woman. It was the one Linda had seen a few days earlier in the Hotel Rixos lobby in Tripoli. Now she had a pretty little girl in her arms. The young woman noticed Linda and came towards her. The little girl gave Linda a beaming smile, but her mother looked nervous, strained. Nevertheless, she forced a smile.

'You're Linda Nardi, the journalist, aren't you?'

Linda was surprised. Up until a few years ago she had often taken part in debates on television talk shows, but now she did so only rarely, and only in order to talk about the orphanages in Kenya and to appeal for funds.

'Why, yes, I had no idea I was so well known . . .' She smiled, trying to make light of it.

The young woman tried to smile back. She wanted to be friendly, but it was obvious she was distraught. She had a foreign accent, but her Italian was excellent.

'I always read your articles, and I admire what you do in Kenya. Forgive me if I seem intrusive, but do you think we could have a few words?'

'Of course, whenever you like, Signorina . . .?'

'My name's Melania, and this is Tanja. We could do it straight away, but little Tanja has to go to sleep.'

'Of course. Do you have a number I can call?'

'We're getting off early tomorrow morning, at Civitavecchia. I'm taking Tanja to stay with a friend of mine, Domnica, in Ostia. She works in a bar, the Stella Polare. You could reach me there . . . any time during the day . . . I can offer you a coffee, or whatever you like and . . .'

Linda was puzzled, but the little girl was yawning and the young woman seemed to be in a big hurry and not very keen to give out her number.

'All right . . .'

'Thank you,' said Melania, interrupting her. 'Now, I have to run. Tanja must get to bed.'

For a moment, her face relaxed and she looked like the beautiful young woman Linda had noticed in the Rixos lobby.

'Good night,' said Melania, and off she went before Linda could ask her anything more, dashing off towards the last cabin at the end of the passageway.

Linda went back to her own cabin, but the ship was full of noise and her mind full of thoughts. She was afraid that Emilio Busi might call at any moment.

Come up to my suite.

But the phone didn't ring and Linda fell into a fitful sleep.

Rome

Balistreri was in a bad mood. The image of the girl's body surrounded by people taking photos with their mobile phones had given him no peace all night and all day.

But why should you care? What's it to do with you?

He was indignant, and understandably so, but still too much relative to the level of indifference he hoped he had reached towards what happened in the world.

On top of that, his knee was swollen from the strain, and extremely painful. So much so he'd had to give up on his daily walk and be taken to the office and home again in a police car.

A little before midnight Balistreri glanced at the newspapers, more to distract himself and settle his mind so that he could sleep rather than out of any desire for news. He opened *Il Domani* and saw the lead article. It was an interview with the man who was perhaps the most powerful in the country, Senator Emilio Busi.

One of Papa's old friends. One of my old enemies, forgotten like all the rest.

He was struck by the headline.

OLYMPIC PARKS AND A BRIDGE ACROSS THE STRAITS OF MESSINA:
WILL THEY REALLY HELP ITALY?

A bridge to link Sicily to the Italian mainland had been an obsession of his father's for a long time, but Mikey had scuppered the plan in 1983, thanks to the lethal weapon given him in the form of a letter from Tripoli. Now, surprisingly, having always been so supportive of the bridge, Emilio Busi was, in this moment of deep economic crisis, expressing doubts about the funding for the projects.

The man has no conscience. I know him too well. It must be in his interest somehow.

Tripoli, 1967

Mikey Balistreri

The Underwater Club's terrace is crowded, as usual at the weekend. The band is playing 'Ruby Tuesday' and sitting around the restaurant table are the Balistreri–Bruseghin family and my father's guest from Italy.

Emilio Busi is a lean young man, with thick hair that is always dishevelled and horrendous square black glasses. He chain smokes nauseous plain-tipped cigarettes and wears short-sleeved check shirts, high-waisted trousers too short in the leg and white socks and sandals.

After abandoning a career in the Carabinieri paramilitary police and having joined the Italian Communist Party, Busi first worked for the Italian petrochemical firm ENI in Sicily and then moved permanently to Tripoli. He says he is a business consultant to various Italian companies that want to do business in Libya, but he never mentions any names.

Towards the end of the meal Papa turns to Grandad Giuseppe.

'It may be that our family and some of Signor Busi's clients will become future business partners.'

'And what business would that be?' my mother asks in her usual manner, cool but polite.

Papa turns to Grandad again, speaking to him in the hope of convincing her.

'The future of any business links between Italy and Libya will be based on two things: petroleum and cars. Enrico Mattei always said so. If a country wants to produce cars, it also has to have petrol. And it was thanks to Italian exploration that petroleum deposits were found in the Libyan Desert in 1939. Then, unfortunately, the war broke out and Anglo-American interests took over.'

My mother gives Grandad no time to reply.

'Signor Busi, the Anglo-Americans were able to win thanks to an Italy teeming with traitors and turncoats. Like the Mafiosi who helped the Americans enter Sicily.'

My father is visibly embarrassed and upset. Things are not going at all as he had hoped. He tries to find a way of soothing Italia's antipathy towards the Anglo-Americans.

'Italia, Libya's oil now runs the risk of ending up totally in the hands of Esso and Mobil. And the car market in those of Ford and General Motors. Isn't it about time we Italians started to claw something back?'

'And what does our family have to do with all this?' Italia asks Busi.

He looks at her coldly from behind his thick glasses.

'Olives are excellent, but the future lies under the sand, not above it. Italy's only now coming out of the ruin and poverty that Fascism caused. The people of Italy need cheap petrol, and they need work.'

'And where do we come in?' asks my mother.

Busi puffs out a cloud of nauseous smoke.

'If you're agreeable, your family can become the minority partner in your country and you'll become truly wealthy. You can help to speed up what in any case is inevitable. Italy will go ahead, no matter what.'

That last whispered sentence has the effect of an earthquake or a declaration of war. The Balistreri family are the most important Italians in Tripoli; they are not nobodies. And, by choosing them, Italy is conferring an honour on them.

Alberto intervenes.

'Signor Busi, in order to become partners in big business, you need to have a great deal of money, which we don't have.'

My father laughs that habitual good-natured laugh of his.

'As always, my son Alberto's right. He's going to university in Rome to study engineering. One day, he'll lead an industrial empire.'

About little Mikey, the son he didn't want, Papa says nothing.

Friday, 5 August 2011

At sea off Civitavecchia

Linda was woken at first light by the announcement that in one hour they would be docking in Civitavecchia. She dressed, then went up to the saloon deck, from which the passengers would disembark. There was no sign of Emilio Busi and his friends. They were not the sort of people to disembark with ordinary mortals. Probably, they had already left by helicopter. She looked for Melania and Tanja but couldn't see them. The Gruppo Italia car was waiting for her to take her back to Rome.

Rome

Balistreri was woken by the telephone. He had only just fallen asleep. It was Corvu, sounding slightly hesitant. A delicate situation had come up.

'*Dottore*, sorry about the time, but they've found two bodies on a cruise ship just off Civitavecchia.'

'It's in our jurisdiction, but don't they need Homicide?' asked Balistreri, hoping to be able to go back to sleep.

'It seems a young woman shot her two-year-old daughter then killed herself. The cabin was locked from the inside.'

'Well then, the Civitavecchia police can shift themselves and get down there.'

Corvu coughed.

Here goes: now for the bad news.

'There were some VIPs aboard. One of them was no less than Senator Emilio Busi.'

'Then Civitavecchia can certainly handle it!' Balistreri exploded, and put the receiver down.

But there was no question now of his going back to sleep. In the end he got up and drank a cup of extra-strong coffee on an empty stomach, against all the advice of his gastroenterologist. Then he lit a cigarette and put a Leonard Cohen CD on the player. But, whatever he did, nothing worked.

As soon as she arrived home, Linda learned of the death of Melania and Tanja Druc from the eight o'clock news on the radio. The information was very basic. According to the police, the young woman from Moldova had first killed her little girl and then put the pistol to her temple. For the moment there was no doubt that her death was suicide, given that the cabin had been locked from the inside and the key had been found on the bedside table.

The news item had come at the tail end of the broadcast, amidst the local news, after the latest on the economic crisis, the index of public debt and the all-round necessity for Italy to tighten its belt.

To try to get over the shock, she undressed and took an ice-cold shower, hoping to fight off the sense of guilt she felt.

I should have understood how distraught she was.

She hated that side of herself: she was forever thinking she hadn't done everything she could. She couldn't get the faces of that little girl and the frightened woman out of her mind.

I have to talk to someone. Get some advice. Even help.

Giulia Piccolo was the right person. Despite their different characters, with Giulia she had formed the most precious friendship she had ever had.

She called her on her mobile and Giulia arrived a few minutes later on her Ducati Monster 900 Dark. She was wearing black jeans and a purple sweatshirt that matched the colour of the streaks in her hair. She hadn't always looked like this, only in the past five years, since deciding not to follow Michele Balistreri into Homicide.

They sat down in the kitchen and had a cup of tea. The sun was streaming in from the French windows on the small terrace overlooking St Peter's cupola, and the atmosphere was one of domesticity and calm, but Giulia had noticed Linda's strained face and the dark shadows under her eyes.

'What's happened?' she asked.

Linda told her about Melania, from the day she first saw her in the Hotel Rixos in Tripoli to the previous evening on the ship, when she'd asked Linda if she could speak to her. But she mentioned nothing about Busi, Monsignor Pizza and Salvatore Balistreri, not even indirectly.

'Are you sure it was the same person you saw in Libya?'

Linda had seen her only from a distance in Tripoli, and in a poorly lit passageway on board the ship but, as always, she trusted her instinct.

'It was the same person. She didn't have the little girl with her in Tripoli, but it was her, I'm certain. I should have stayed with her, tried to understand what she wanted . . .'

Giulia shook her head, passing a hand through her purple highlights.

'It's not your fault, Linda. You were ready to listen to her straight away.'

She thought for a moment.

'What were you doing on the ship anyway?'

It was the question a policewoman would ask. Linda told her about the kickbacks, the slush funds, the IOR and Monsignor Pizza's business card. She passed over how she had managed to extract the information from Gabriele Cascio, and also over her relationship with John Kiptanu.

You wouldn't believe it anyway, Giulia.

'During the cruise Senator Busi introduced me to Monsignor Pizza,' she concluded.

Giulia looked concerned.

'Linda, Monsignor Pizza's one of the untouchables. As for the IOR . . .'

'I know, I know. But, as a policewoman, perhaps you can help me in this.'

Giulia looked outside across the small terrace.

'Yeah, a policewoman who's been suspended. I had an argument with two colleagues. Things got a bit heated. They were hassling two girls they found kissing. I tried to reason with them, but when they told me to get lost I kind of lost it . . .'

Linda made no comment. She could have said that violence isn't fought with more violence. But she knew very well this was only true up to a certain point.

'Have you been expelled from the force?'

'No. Only suspended. Three months' enforced leave. Surprising, really.'

'Surprising?'

Giulia bit her tongue and opted for a partial truth.

'You usually get fired for those kinds of things.'

She didn't tell Linda what she'd learned from Corvu, who'd got it from a cousin who was personal assistant to Colombo, head of the Flying Squad, that Michele Balistreri had intervened and saved her from getting the sack. She knew that it was forbidden to mention her ex-boss in front of Linda. Although it was an implicit rule between them, Giulia Piccolo was always in two minds about it. On one hand, after the split between Linda and Balistreri, she'd taken her friend's side; on the other hand, deep inside her, she hoped the two would get back together.

'So, how can I help?'

Linda handed her the payment details John Kiptanu had given her. Piccolo looked at the sheets of paper. Then at Linda.

'Is this what you were telling me about? The account that pig in Nairobi was paying the kickbacks into?'

'Yes. We need to get into the IOR.'

Giulia smiled and shook her head.

'Really? Is that all? Well, we could go together one night, like the good old days at Casilino 900. Look, it's much more difficult getting into the Vatican, believe me.'

Linda smiled, too, remembering the mad time that had bonded their friendship. It had been nothing to do with courage, just that stupid, insatiable desire for justice of hers.

'No, I'll go there by myself. You're already in trouble. I don't want you to risk your job.'

Giulia sat in silence for a moment.

'Hang on, Linda. I think there is a way of getting in . . . without actually getting in.'

'Getting in without getting in?'

Giulia burst out laughing.

'You're behind the times, Linda. These days you can get in anywhere thanks to the internet.'

'The internet?'

'Yes, but I need to speak to someone.'

'And do you think it will work?'

'I'll call a friend of mine. But you'll have to be patient. I haven't heard from her for a while.'

'And she'll do you a favour? It seems a bit risky.'

There was a smirk now on Giulia's face.

'I think I can persuade her.'

Corvu saw Balistreri lying sprawled on his office sofa wrapped in a cloud of smoke and distractedly signing documents. Five years ago he had seen his boss's attitude at work as an obvious manifestation of alienation and indifference and had thought of it as an illness. He had even resented it, sometimes angrily; then, with the passing of time, he had come to realize that the situation wasn't how he'd imagined it; it was perhaps worse: Balistreri no longer seemed interested in life. His perspective on time, that vision of the future that keeps us alive, had shut down at the end of his involvement with three people in that year of 2006: the Invisible Man, Angelo Dioguardi and Linda Nardi.

It had become almost impossible to shake him out of it and Corvu only rarely attempted it, but now he decided to try again.

'Commissario, what do you make of taking on board a stewardess who has to bring a little girl with her?'

Balistreri nodded; it was certainly odd. Except there could have been a thousand explanations and he had no intention of thinking about any of them.

'The Civitavecchia police have started an investigation. Let's leave it to them, Corvu.'

'Well, I've never heard of anyone working as a stewardess and having to take a two-year-old girl with her,' Corvu went on, regardless.

'What were the names of the victims?' Balistreri asked, with a sigh of resignation.

'Melania Druc, thirty years old, from Moldova. And her daughter, Tanja, aged two.'

Corvu watched his boss for a reaction. Once, such a young victim would have at least stirred up a little emotion in him. But now he went on smoking and signing papers without even reading them. Corvu tried again.

'A forensic report's being done, but it'll take a few days. If it turns out there are doubts this was suicide and it becomes a homicide, then the case will come back to us.'

'In that case, we'll see. But let's hope not. For the moment, it's not our problem.'

Corvu scratched his head and remained standing in the room, not saying a word.

'Is there anything else, Corvu?'

'There were some important passengers on board.'

'I don't see why that should concern us.'

'Among them was a certain Senator Busi, Commissario. I'm certain I mentioned it.'

Balistreri buried himself in his papers again.

'Another reason for not getting involved.'

But Corvu caught a glimmer of interest. And he was a very stubborn young man.

'We've got the passenger list of all the official guests, but it's incomplete. I spoke to the Civitavecchia police . . .'

Balistreri looked up.

'You did what?'

Corvu turned slightly pale but kept his composure.

'Nothing formal. I've got a friend there.'

'Yes, you have friends everywhere – we know. And so?'

'They say that Senator Busi came and went in a helicopter with several friends who weren't listed among the guests.'

Balistreri went back to signing documents and switched on Leonard Cohen. It was the signal for Corvu, who made a swift departure.

Balistreri lit a cigarette. The shutters were drawn but they let in some daylight, as well as the sounds of people and traffic on the street below.

Several friends not listed among the guests. Ghosts, Michele. Ghosts you ran away from. By going off to a war.

Cairo, June 1967

Mikey Balistreri

Ahmed and Karim came running up to me.

'Mikey, a war's broken out!'

We raced into Tripoli on our bicycles and stopped at the Esso petrol station before entering the city itself. Nico was standing in his overalls in the middle of the empty forecourt by his two pumps, looking in amazement at the crowds travelling past.

'What's happening, guys?'

Karim looked at him in exasperation.

'Don't you know there's a war on? We've invaded Israel!'

Nico laughed out loud.

'Look, this isn't *Lawrence of Arabia*, and you aren't Omar Sharif. The Israelis'll kick the shit out of you.'

Karim was about to get off his bicycle, but I stopped him.

'Leave it, Karim. Nico, shut up shop and let's go.'

We entered Tripoli through the Garden City and came into the Cathedral Square and Corso Vittorio, where all the Jewish shops already had their shutters down.

Piazza Italia, or Maydan as-Suhada, was overflowing with crowds that stretched as far as the castle and the Adrian Pelt promenade. Loudspeakers were broadcasting Radio Cairo. People were shouting with joy and swarming in from the twin columns on the promenade, Corso Vittorio, Via Roma, Via Lazio, Via Piemonte and Corso Sicilia.

Masses of kids had climbed up over the archway of the Souk el Mushir. Ahmed, Karim, Nico and I were jostled by the thousands of people there. The square was full of police and military, many of them very young and carrying pistols in their hands. Some were shooting up in the air in celebration.

The speech of the Egyptian president, Gamal Abdel Nasser, was broadcast live from all the Arab stations, working up the crowds:

'O most merciful Lord and my brothers, we have been attacked by the Zionist empire. All the Arab armies are marching to the front, where the Zionists will be destroyed. Israel will be wiped off the map and Palestine restored to our Arab brothers.'

'We have to go, right now,' said Karim. The crowd was pushing us in all directions.

Nico burst out laughing. 'You're only fifteen, Karim. Where do you think they'll let you go?'

But Karim ignored him and turned to his elder brother.

'Didn't you hear the president, Ahmed? Even boys can fight against the Zionists. We really must go and fight. Allah wishes it, not only Nasser.'

The two brothers were so alike in appearance, but so different in character: one an idealist; the other a pragmatist. And Ahmed was older.

'Our father won't let us go, Karim.'

'Our father can't stand against the wishes of Allah. Didn't you hear? The Libyan army's setting off tomorrow for the front. They're asking for volunteers from the age of fifteen up. I'm going, brother, with or without you. I'll be smoking a *shisha* in Jerusalem by the end of the week.'

Ahmed looked at the poorly armed young soldiers around us. They weren't trained for war. He shot a glance at me.

Nico's right. The Israelis will massacre us.

Ahmed was my greatest friend and the one who was most like me. He was my companion in games, martial arts, fishing and hunting. We had everything in common, nothing between us.

'Libya's our homeland, Ahmed,' Karim insisted. 'I'm going.'

I looked at the faint white scar on my left wrist. Our blood brotherhood of five years ago.

I turned to Ahmed and Nico.

'Five years ago, we made a pact. And Libya's my homeland, too.'

Ahmed had too much respect for – or fear of – me to reply.

Don't be stupid, Mikey – this isn't your homeland. Your home is way across the sea.

I heard Nico mouthing curses under his breath.

Another one who's afraid to tell me I'm mad.

In the end, Ahmed gave in.

'All right, Karim. Let's go and talk to Father.'

So we followed Karim to Cairo to fight in the holy war against Israel, bound together by our pact of blood. And I wanted to escape from a father who wouldn't accept me because I refused to grow up in his likeness and be like him. I won't study, won't mix with the right people and I despise his dealings with Busi, Don Eugenio and Mohammed.

When we arrive in Cairo three days later in a dilapidated truck, the war has already been lost. It becomes clear the further we go into the city. There are thousands of refugees with neither destination nor hope fleeing from the Israeli air-force bombs in Sinai. The radios in the bars and on balconies continue broadcasting scarcely credible hymns of glory, while old people crowd at the windows and on the balconies, looking in fear towards the horizon: the fear of seeing the Star of David on the oncoming tanks.

Evil-smelling rubbish litters the streets: rotting fruit and vegetables picked over by beggars and ravaged by huge rats; children run barefoot among the dung of horses and asses.

It's almost dark when we get to the square behind the Al Azhar Mosque, and there's a stream of refugees and young Egyptian soldiers, many without shoes after leaving their boots behind in the Sinai Desert so they could run more quickly over the sand as they fled.

While Ahmed and Karim go to ask if we can stay at a relative's house and Nico wanders about the square looking at the cinema posters, three Egyptian soldiers surround me. One of them, armed with an old Russian pistol, sticks the barrel in my ribs. They are two or three years older than me; the only one with boots is the one with the pistol. The second is wearing flip-flops and the third leather babouches of two different colours.

They push me to the back of an alley that ends in a two-metre-high wall. '*Filuss, dollars!*' they bark. Then they'll kill me. And no one will go looking for my killer here.

Then Ahmed comes up from the square. One of the two guys holding my arms turns towards him.

'Get lost, kid!'

Ahmed pretends to be nothing but a harmless seventeen-year-old and grins idiotically. He steps forwards and says to me in Italian, 'Take the one with the gun!' Then he unleashes a *tae* kick to the soldier's chin while I launch one at the guy with the gun.

There's a sound of breaking teeth, jaws and ribs, and cries of pain. The third terrified Egyptian tries to run away towards the square, but Nico lands him among the refuse with a *kwon* to the temple.

Karim looks on, appalled. He came to help Egypt's troops and is now seeing them laid out by the other members of the blood brotherhood. I know he'll never forget this; it will be another rift between us.

Ahmed goes up to the soldier on the ground, pulls out of his pocket his new knife with a saw blade and grabs him by the hair.

'No, brother!' Karim blurts out desperately.

'Quiet,' Ahmed orders. He is the elder brother and Muslim custom binds Karim to obey him. Then Ahmed looks me in the eye. He needs my say-so.

'If we let them go, they'll only report us, Mikey. They'll shoot us straight away.'

I try to say no, but nothing comes out of my mouth as Ahmed slits the man's carotid artery.

One of the other two tries to recover the gun, but Nico gives him another painful *kwon* to the chin.

Ahmed calmly goes up to the other two, who are now on the ground, and cuts their throats. First one, then the other, without a moment's hesitation.

Now I know where our brotherhood of blood and sand is leading us. Perhaps it was always written in our destinies, in our genes, in those endless afternoons we spent skewering scorpions and shooting turtledoves, harpooning groper and learning martial arts.

Laura's right: we'll turn into gangsters like Ahmed.

Friday, 5 August 2011

Rome

Corvu came back into Balistreri's office looking worried but decisive.

'We spoke to the shipping line,' he announced.

Balistreri didn't even look up from the papers he was reading.

'On what grounds?'

'Not everyone who works on that ship is up to date with their tax returns.'

'And what has the Homicide Squad got to do with tax returns?'

His deputy gave a sly grin.

'I had a colleague in the Guardia di Finanza call.'

Balistreri couldn't keep back a smile. Corvu's network of friends and relatives was an intricate web composed of a thousand threads. His deputy went on, satisfied.

'The Finanza asked to see the contracts of all the employees on board. And, obviously, the shipping line were worried.'

'All right, Corvu. If you really must tell me, go right ahead. Why did the shipping line give Melania Druc a job as stewardess even though she had to bring a little girl on board?'

'Because someone told them to. It came up on the database under her name. She had a special recommendation.'

'Who recommended her?' asked Balistreri, trying to show as little interest as possible, just enough to placate this young policeman, who was so diligent and yet so stubborn.

'A well-known Catholic humanitarian organization. It's called Porte Aperte. 'Open Doors' in English. It's been going for more than fifteen years; it helps poor kids from all over the world get legal entry into Italy. It offers them somewhere to stay to start off with and a place to work. Melania went through them to come to Italy when she was twenty-three.'

Balistreri gave a shrug.

'There you are, Corvu. All quite normal, everything in order. It's perfectly logical for Porte Aperte to recommend Melania Druc to the shipping line. It was thanks to them she came to Italy.'

Corvu shook his head doubtfully.

'Commissario, she came in 2004. And seven years later Porte Aperte recommends her for a job when she has a two-year-old baby girl . . .'

'Perhaps they did it precisely because she was a young mother?'

Balistreri lit another cigarette. He had no intention of dealing with Corvu's doubts or a case that might involve Senator Emilio Busi.

He sent his deputy away and went to lie down, but the old sofa was unusually uncomfortable and the office, full of smoke and in the shade, seemed suffocating. And it was all Corvu's fault, him and his bloody questions.

Why had Porte Aperte recommended Melania Druc for that work so many years after she'd first come to Italy? It was a very good and reasonable question.

'Oh, all right, then,' he muttered, getting up and limping over to the computer. He typed 'Porte Aperte' into Google and looked around the humanitarian organization's site, with its mission statement, values and projects. They even had a chart of who worked for the organization. His eyes came to rest on a particular name.

President: Monsignor Eugenio Pizza.

He stared incredulously at the computer. Emilio Busi had been on the ship where Melania and the little girl had died. His old acquaintance and associate Monsignor Eugenio Pizza was president of the organization that had brought Melania Druc to Italy seven years earlier and had recommended her to the shipping line as a stewardess, despite her having to bring a two-year-old girl with her.

There are no such things as coincidences. Only the results of mistakes, rashness and arrogance on the part of the guilty.

What came into his mind were the guests not on the official list, the ones who came and went in Emilio Busi's helicopter. He felt a burning sensation in his oesophagus and a subtle disquiet that seemed to come from very far away.

He cursed Corvu and then called him. He tried to cover up his sudden interest by being surly and offhand.

'Graziano, so that we're not caught out unprepared, see what we have on this case. Get some info on Melania Druc, Porte Aperte and its president, Monsignor Pizza. Nothing official, mind. All right?'

The diminutive Sardinian hid a smile and hurried off. Balistreri lowered the shutters even more on the outside world, lit a cigarette, poured himself a whisky and lay down on the sofa.

There was something that didn't add up.

A young woman with a little girl gets taken on as a stewardess on a cruise ship. Already something odd there. Then what does she do? Goes on the ship in order to kill herself and her daughter?

His instinct told him that this wasn't what had happened. Melania Druc had gone on that ship for a different reason. Almost certainly to meet someone. Except it went wrong.

Unregistered guests in the helicopter. Friends of Busi. Powerful friends. With the power of fear.

Tripoli, Friday, 1 August 1969

Mikey Balistreri

All four members of the MANK organization were back from Cairo. In our two years there we'd been hugely successful. The money was pouring in from the restaurant we had on the Nile, and from other, more clandestine and more profitable activities we had. We had come back at my father's request, but I certainly hadn't done it as a favour to him, but rather to be with the two most important women in my life, Italia and Laura. Laura's eighteen now, and her body's developing and becoming more and more like her mother's, although her personality is completely different. Apart from my mother, Laura's the only person who can see inside me. She sees what pleases me and what upsets me, but she never tries to change me. Our love doesn't need words. It isn't made of declarations; it's a secret between the two of us and still hasn't led to a single kiss. But she's the reason I've come back.

It's sunset, and Laura and I decide to celebrate my and the others' return by going into the city centre for an ice cream. We call to invite Nico and go off to pick up Karim and Ahmed.

When we get to the Al Bakri shack next to the cesspit, Mohammed is there with his two elder sons, sitting on the ground outside, smoking a *shisha*. They're drinking tea from chipped enamel cups which must have been handed down from our kitchen at home. Their tea is excellent, made by his two wives, who take it in turns each day in a kind of competition. Mohammed has the right to the first infusion, which is strong and bitter; once cooled and heated again, it goes to his sons; heated a third time and diluted, it goes to the wives and his daughter, Nadia.

Nadia's being pushed on the swing made out of a lorry tyre suspended on a rope between two trees. Ahmed is practising his knife throwing.

'Signor Michele, this is an unexpected visit,' Mohammed says.

I have to ask permission to take his sons with me, which wouldn't be necessary in the Balistreri family. But Islamic etiquette doesn't include an evening stroll into the city centre to get an ice cream, and Mohammed doesn't want any friction between his sons and any Italian boys. That would mean trouble for him and my illustrious father. But I'm his boss's son and, although he's not happy about it, he agrees to let them go.

There's a large walkway under the colonnades of Corso Vittorio, and the ice-cream parlour's crowded. Laura stays outside with Karim.

When Nico, Ahmed and I come out with everyone's cones, four rough young Italians are standing in a circle round Laura and Karim. The biggest puts a hand on her arm.

'You're the daughter of that tasty American piece, right? Fact, you look just like her, you know that?'

Without a second thought, although he's on his own against four older guys, Karim steps forwards to protect Laura.

'Don't you have any manners, you big slob?'

While the big slob makes a fist, I feel a surge of adrenalin shoot along my spine. I give him a *tae* kick in the stomach and the lout bends double and begins to retch. The other three come closer. I look over to Ahmed, who's ready and waiting. We could make mincemeat out of them, but Mohammed would be angry with him and Karim.

'Not you, Ahmed. Nico and I will take care of this.'

It's an order. And, as always, he has to obey it. But then Girus's owner comes rushing out, called by passers-by. The owner of the ice-cream parlour recognizes the situation and knows what to do. He has the magic formula. He turns to the four louts, a harsh frown on his face.

'You should thank the son of Ingegner Balistreri that he hasn't called the police. Now get on home, you little shits!'

The four look at each other, confused, now they know who I am. They don't want to be the cause of their fathers losing their jobs. They apologize and go off, cursing under their breath.

I've seen the huge power that fear has. And Laura's seen into that side of me.

Friday, 5 August 2011

Rome

Linda had fallen asleep on the sofa, exhausted. The ringing of her
landline woke her. She'd slept the whole day and the sun was now
setting. She ran to answer. It was Giulia.

'Linda, aren't you answering your mobile?'

'Sorry, Giulia, I fell asleep . . .'

'Asleep? Is that what you do when you're home alone?'

'I'm tired, Giulia. Libya, Kenya, then Melania and Tanja . . .'

'Well, get yourself together. I've got great news. My hacker's
done it!'

'Fantastic. What have you found out?'

'The account's in the name of Monsignor Eugenio Pizza.'

Linda looked outside. She could see the wonderful cupola all lit up.
And over there in a corner off St Peter's Square was Torrione Niccolò V,
the great round tower that was the Vatican Bank's headquarters.

She said goodbye to Giulia and made a herbal tea. She didn't want
to go through Emilio Busi a second time. She had Pizza's Swiss
mobile number, the one on the business card she'd found in Gabriele
Cascio's safe in Nairobi.

Perhaps I should give all this up and go back to my orphans in Kenya. And John . . .

Her thoughts weren't that confused. There was a common denominator.

It's much easier to divide the world into the privileged and the destitute than divide them into representatives of good and evil.

She picked up her mobile and called the number she'd copied from the card.

When he'd stubbed out his tenth Gitane, the daily limit fixed by his GP, Balistreri usually considered that his day was practically over. But Corvu had given him the additional information for which he'd asked, so he decided to read it before going home.

As usual, Corvu had been lightning fast. He'd done a good job, the result of a few hours at the computer and a chat with a friend of his in the Secret Service.

Balistreri started to read what Corvu had discovered about Don Eugenio.

Apart from occasional hiccups, the name of Monsignor Eugenio Pizza was linked solely to charitable works. But those hiccups were very interesting.

In 1982, Roberto Calvi, chairman of Banco Ambrosiano, which was heavily in debt from its loans to the Vatican, was found hanged under Blackfriars Bridge in London. Some said it was suicide; some that it was the hand of the Mafia. Among the many things never mentioned in public, according to the Secret Service contact, was the fact that one of the clergy officiating in the church that Calvi attended in Milan was a certain Don Eugenio.

Then, in 1986, Michele Sindona, chairman of Banca Privata Italiana and, earlier, Franklin National Bank, died in prison from a poisoned coffee. The same source in the Secret Service revealed that Don Eugenio had been his confessor in prison and that Sindona had made what turned out to be his last confession with him on the very morning of his death.

And, in 1990, Archbishop Paul Marcinkus, founder of the IOR, the Institute for Religious Works, had left his job as head of the Vatican's finances. At the same time, Monsignor Pizza disappeared, and no one heard any more of him for fifteen years. Every so often a little article based on someone's indiscretions appeared in an international newspaper, from which it could be gleaned that Pizza had climbed up the clerical hierarchies to the level of archbishop, a role he executed in parts of the world that had significant financial importance. He had been papal nuncio in Colombia and Washington DC; that is, one country where the greater part of money laundering originated, and the other the most concerned about fighting it.

Then he was back in the Vatican with a seat in the Roman Curia. But still, little was said about him. Friends praised his highly active support for the dispossessed in the world's poorest regions. His enemies whispered about a certain casual assurance in financial circles, about a very powerful gay lobby in the Vatican and even told stories about a secret location for thought and prayer, but also for sex and covert plots.

In February 2006, Monsignor Eugenio Pizza was conspicuously present at the funeral of Paul Marcinkus in Sun City, Arizona. But, from 2005, there was a German pope who was very keen to shed some light on the obscure finances of the IOR and other internal questions about the Roman Curia. And the Monsignor's presence at the funeral had not been appreciated.

And so Monsignor Pizza came to be transferred from Rome to the much more modest diocese of Lugano, his choice from the alternatives offered. It leaked out from the Vatican that, as with Marcinkus, Monsignor Eugenio Pizza was not to be made a cardinal. And that he was by now over the age of seventy-five, which meant that, according to canon law, he was obliged to relinquish all clerical offices.

But Monsignor Pizza was still active as chairman of the humanitarian organization Porte Aperte, which gathered funds from all over the world, from Gruppo Italia to Arab sources from Dubai and Libya. For years, rumours had circulated about certain Sicilian friends the Monsignor had who were not exactly squeaky clean and about various accounts in the IOR, used perhaps for laundering money of dubious provenance. But these were merely gossip; nothing concrete had been proven.

Balistreri absorbed all the information quickly, without a great deal of interest.

I know all this. I've known Don Eugenio for nearly half a century.

Corvu had inserted in the dossier what little personal information was held on Melania Druc by Porte Aperte, the organization that had brought her to Italy in 2004, together with her friend Domnica Panu. Melania had been born in Tighina on 1 February 1981, the last of seven children in a very poor family, the father an unemployed, alcoholic ex-miner, her mother a cleaner in a school. In that difficult environment Melania had nevertheless shown herself to be so academically gifted that she obtained several grants, which had enabled her to graduate with a degree in political science and communication with the highest grades and the publication of her thesis.

Then, because of the lack of opportunity in her country, she had come to Italy with her friend and lived in the Porte Aperte hostel.

Melania didn't stay long at the hostel and disappeared for seven years. There was no trace of her: not a credit card, a social security number, mobile-phone or any contracts of employment or for renting property.

Balistreri read that passage twice. Corvu was always like that, analysing what was there, proofs and clues, but using his instinct to work out what was not said and fill in the gaps.

It was as if Melania had melted into thin air. Impossible, even for a clandestine worker. Someone had hidden her, given her protection.

He sat on the sofa and studied the photocopies of her passport passed on by Porte Aperte. Melania Druc was a woman with delicate features, a beauty that was elegant without being provocative, and intelligent eyes.

Too refined to be on the game and too beautiful to work behind a bar.

There was something in Melania Druc's story that worried him. Something about the first idea that came into his mind, that she was an escort, didn't ring true.

He made a decision, trying to convince himself that he was only doing it to help out Corvu. He called Colombo.

'There's something not right about this case on the cruise ship in Civitavecchia. Have you read the report?'

As usual, Colombo hadn't read anything, but he wasn't going to admit it.

'Yes, yes, of course. I had some –'

'Right, well, starting now, we're taking on the case, OK?'

'OK. You'd better inform the public prosecutor and the Civitavecchia police, then.'

Half an hour later Corvu knocked on the door. He was beaming.

'So we're taking it on?'

Balistreri made a gesture of resignation. It was better not to ask how his deputy had found out.

'Look, Corvu, this is just routine, enough to get us up to speed if the ballistics report and the autopsy . . .'

'Of course, Commissario. We'll have them tomorrow. Is there anything else I can do?'

'Nothing official. Use your many relatives and friends. I want to know why there's no trace of Melania Druc in Italy for seven years. I also want to know who it was who arrived on the ship by helicopter with Senator Busi. And get me the official passenger list.'

If Corvu noticed the difference between a routine check and the amount of orders he'd just been given he was very careful not to let it show. He was used to working through the night.

Balistreri shut himself in his office with its worn furniture, smoke and the music of Leonard Cohen. He couldn't care less about this investigation; it wasn't even, strictly, an investigation. He'd seen lots of poor women and children murdered in his career. But there was something in Melania Druc's case that worried him, like the first signs of a tooth that's about to go bad. And it was because of those two names.

Emilio Busi. Don Eugenio Pizza.

He'd wiped both names from his memory since they'd surfaced again in 1983, in the course of the investigations into the death of Anita Messi. Every so often he'd read about Emilio Busi or Monsignor Pizza in a newspaper, some political matter or the inauguration of a hospital in Africa or Asia. At first he'd been angry, then just irritated; now, he felt nothing.

I've got used to a world in which the front pages of the newspapers are split between people who have been sent to jail and those who should be.

But there was something else that worried him.

A young woman and a child. What sort of twisted killer was that?

Tripoli, 1962

Mikey Balistreri

A few days after our little confrontation with Don Eugenio, two bodies were fished out of the cesspit next to the Al Bakri shack: a young woman and a baby girl.

During my father's weekly Saturday evening get-together, I overheard a conversation between him, Don Eugenio and General Jalloun, Tripoli's chief of police, a brown-noser who does everything the influential Westerners in the city tell him to do. There was only a little skin left on the two corpses, but what there was was dark.

'They were from the Sahara,' says Don Eugenio, the priest with the wandering hands, as if he were talking about camels.

'Poor things, coming in from the desert at night. They must have fallen in,' says my father.

Jalloun listens to them, agreeing.

'They've been there some time, although it's impossible to say how long. No one's been asking after them and the police don't have time to carry out an investigation on people like that,' he says.

I relate this to the others in our pact of blood: Karim's the youngest, but he's the one who prays five times a day and knows the Koran by heart. He's beside himself.

'If they were two Westerners, Italian or American, then the whole police force would be working on it.'

This time Karim's right. I'm only ten, but I'm beginning to understand how the world is around me. In this sick world the law isn't the same for everyone. Some people's lives are worth no more than monkeys'.

5 God's Bank

Saturday, 6 August 2011

Rome

When Linda Nardi called Monsignor Eugenio Pizza the night before, he was moderately surprised and extremely courteous. He hadn't asked her how she had got his mobile number, and arranged to meet her after seven o'clock mass in San Pietro, in Vincoli, near the Coliseum.

The morning promised a clear, warm day when Linda walked up from the Coliseum towards the Oppian Hill. She passed by the Engineering Faculty and came to the church. The little square in front of it was completely deserted; there was no other sound than the sparrows singing in the leafy trees. It was as if the beauty of the place had bewitched and stilled everything.

Inside the church was Michelangelo's *Moses*, one of the most extra-ordinary sculptures ever created, and also Monsignor Eugenio Pizza: for many, a great benefactor; for others, a man who had been able to manipulate Vatican finances behind the scenes for decades.

Linda went in once Mass was over and stopped at the end of the central nave. Monsignor Pizza was surrounded by several elderly female parishioners. That good-natured face, the blue eyes and his soft, smooth, white hair gave him the appearance of an ages-old child as he dispensed his wisdom: a humble priest in a simple cassock at the service of the souls of the faithful and *one of them himself*. A priest known for the charitable organizations with which he was involved, and for the funds he raised to help the world's poor.

When he's dead and gone, some pope will make a saint of him.

When the last old lady had disappeared, Monsignor Pizza came up to Linda, smiling and holding out his hand.

'Signorina Nardi, how nice to see you again, after such a short time – although I imagine it's work that brings you here. Some gossip about plots against our German pope?'

Linda rose to the bait.

'Investigative journalism isn't gossip – it's looking for the truth.'

Monsignor Pizza studied her and shook his head.

'And you think there's an indissoluble link between goodness and the truth?'

Linda pointed at the crucifix over the altar.

'I seem to think there's a commandment that says that very thing.'

Monsignor Pizza nodded, but avoided looking at the crucifix.

'An early version, if you'll allow me, written somewhere between the Stone Age and the Middle Ages.'

'Then why not abolish the commandments and sacraments, Monsignor?'

'Because they give many people comfort, Signorina, just like wine and cigarettes. However, the rules are a little rigid and shouldn't become an obstacle to the performance of good deeds.'

'The commandments are obstacles?'

The smile was that of an experienced religious instructor to a naive student.

A new version of the catechism for the modern era.

'Beneath the altar of this church lie some chains. Legend has it they're the chains with which St Peter was bound, first in the Holy

Land, then here in Rome. But if we're in chains, how can we perform good deeds?'

'So it's permissible to break the commandments if you're convinced you're doing it for good? Such as stealing, for example?'

Monsignor Pizza winced slightly, as if he had detected a bad odour.

'I don't agree with the verb you use, Signorina. It's too harsh and crude.'

'But Jesus Christ would be more in agreement with me than with you, Monsignor . . .'

Monsignor Pizza sighed, as if his student were failing to grasp what he was saying.

'Jesus Christ . . . If we who represent him on this earth presented ourselves to the common people as he did – immaculate, completely cleansed of every sin, perfect – well . . . everyone would feel excluded. Religion would be so rigid it would make them feel constantly guilty. Christianity would just disappear.'

'So creating an understanding with evil is a marketing tool for modern Christianity?'

'I have just celebrated Mass, Signorina Nardi. I have preached about tending towards the good, not the perfection, of sinlessness. People listen to me because I'm a human being. If I were Jesus Christ, they wouldn't come back each Sunday. No one likes to have to face their own guilty conscience.'

He looked at his watch.

'Unfortunately, I don't have time for theological discussions this morning, Signorina. What can I do for you?'

Linda decided that the only way forward was the less prudent one. She took out the photocopies of the bank statements which John Kiptanu had given her only a few days – although it seemed like a century – ago, and handed them to him. Monsignor Pizza stared at them in silence through his bifocals.

'Do you know whose IOR account this is, Monsignor?'

Slowly, very slowly, he gave her back the photocopies. His face was impassive. He didn't seem to be at all worried. The Institute for Religius Works was his domain and it was certainly not open to any inspection by the Guardia di Finanza.

'I don't know how you came by these statements. I hope it was legally.'

'Within the limits of legality that you've specified yourself, Monsignor. Ignoring one or two rules perhaps, but all in a good cause.'

He smiled good-naturedly.

'I see. *Touché*. Will that be all?'

He was an intelligent man, cautious; he'd won his expereince in a thousand battles fought between St Peter's Square and Piazza del Gesù, where the old Christian Democrats headquarters used to be. As his guru, he had the prime minister, the Christian Democrats' most cryptic and powerful member. So Pizza knew how to handle certain problems. And Linda knew that the only way to deal with men like this was to catch them off guard, but she couldn't think how. This man was untouchable, as were his friends. But then she thought about the cruise and something came to mind.

'There were two deaths aboard that cruise we were on, Monsignore. Did you know the woman and her daughter?'

He nodded slowly, as if considering for the first time that she might constitute a slight risk. Then he shrugged, as if he'd decided the matter were irrelevant. Standing below that crucifix, he looked at her with his pale blue eyes and smiled.

Ferocity with a sugar coating.

'I must now take my leave, Signorina Nardi.'

Linda felt words coming to her lips which the most basic common sense would have told her to hold back. But she was so angry she couldn't.

'Melania wanted to speak to me, did you know that? She was

extremely upset and made an appointment to meet me at her friend Domnica's.'

A network of little lines appeared on the priest's soft features. Then he turned his back on her and walked away.

Balistreri arrived in the office on foot at seven. Corvu was already there, in the next office, probably having spent the night. This sudden activity was upsetting. This cruise-ship business had caused Balistreri to sleep badly and he was irritated when he found that his office windows had been left wide open, on to the Roman Forum's early-morning silence, by the cleaning lady, in an effort to air the smoky room. As he did every day, he closed the windows, pulled in the shutters and switched on the lamp by the sofa.

On his desk he saw the Civitavecchia police report and the first autopsy report on the deaths of Melania and Tanja Druc. He put them to one side, picked up the bundle of newspapers and started to leaf through them. A report of the double homicide/suicide in Civitavecchia was given two small columns in the local news. He also found a short article on Libya. The war there was in stalemate, the battlefronts unchanged for three months. Gaddafi's son Khamis was dead and it seemed the tight circle round the Colonel was crumbling because of the enormous cost of the war. There was also the question of the strange death of General Younis – Gaddafi's old friend who had betrayed him. Had it been the rebels or someone at the top of the Secret Services?

Amidst all the drama, there was also the ridiculous. Articles about the so-called *gheddafine*, three models who were part of the group of hostesses hired by Gaddafi during his triumphant visit to Italy a few months earlier and who had now gone to Tripoli to offer their support. Support to whom was not made clear.

But it was the *gheddafine* that led him back to a woman in another league altogether.

Tripoli, 2 August 1969

Mikey Balistreri

I saw how Laura looked at me after last night's fight in the ice-cream parlour. She's beginning to have doubts now about whether I'm Kirk Douglas against Rock Hudson or just a hood like Ahmed, as she'd said.

At nine o'clock on the second day, the *ghibli*'s blowing strongly. I head for the Hunts' house, drawn by the smell of French toast and bacon. I'm hoping to see Laura to say sorry about last night, but it's just William Hunt sitting in the large kitchen.

He's only been back from the United States with Laura and Marlene for two days, but I haven't seen him since I left for Cairo.

'Hi, Mikey, come on in. Marlene's out for a run, despite the *ghibli*. Laura has an upset tummy. One of those girl things. So it's just me here, all on my own.'

'OK, I'll go back home, Mr Hunt. Sorry to bother you.'

'Won't you have breakfast with me? I'm having it in here because there's too much bloody sand outside, but there's cornflakes, French toast, bacon, pancakes.'

The invitation takes me by surprise. I've never been alone with

Mr Hunt, and he's never shown any particular interest in me. He prefers Alberto. But it's difficult to refuse.

'Oh, well, thank you, Mr Hunt. I'd like that.'

We start eating in silence. It seems impossible to think of a subject we have in common that we could chat about, as he and Alberto do about international politics and the Vietnam War. But William Hunt has something on his mind.

'You like Laura, don't you?' he asks me out of the blue.

Now I knew where Laura's habit of asking direct questions comes from. But it's difficult to know how to reply.

'Laura takes beautiful pictures. She'll be a professional one day.'

'Isn't there anything else you like about her?'

Again, I'm lost for words. I stare at the bowl of cornflakes.

Here's a man who never stands for any 'bullshit', as the Americans say.

'She's very beautiful, Mr Hunt.'

He laughs.

'Of course, she takes after Marlene, who's also a beautiful woman. Don't you think?'

This is too much. I'm caught off balance.

'Laura's very serious, as well.'

William Hunt abandons the subject of Marlene and whatever he wanted to imply and takes up the compliment about Laura.

'She's taken that from me, Mikey. She has the qualities of both her parents.'

'And the defects?'

I'd only thought it, I believed. But the question slipped out.

He doesn't bat an eyelid. Rather, for the first time since I've known him, William Hunt looks at me with real interest. He thinks about it for some time, as if the question needs a considered response. Then he says something surprising.

'Marlene hasn't any defects at all. As for mine, I really do hope Laura hasn't inherited those.'

Not to see any defect in Marlene means he is either blind or deluded. But William Hunt seems to be neither. As to his defects, I've no idea what he means.

'Your Uncle Toni died in the war, didn't he, Mikey?'

Now I can follow him.

His defects. The pointless sacrifice of heroes like Toni, like those in the Folgore Division, like his friends who died in Korea and Vietnam.

'Yes, sir. And you fought against the Communists in Korea, didn't you?'

I know a little from my mother telling me, a little from Laura. A desperate battle against 300,000 Chinese, a human avalanche that swept down upon the South Koreans and the Americans, including the X Corps of Marines. The Yalu River was frozen, there was a single wretched bridge, dead bodies everywhere and countless prisoners and civilians. At Ch'osan Reservoir, the Marines were surrounded. A few men parachuted in to help, William Hunt among them.

Heroes. Men ready to die for their principles.

William Hunt nods.

'War's ugly, Mikey. It leads you to do things you'd never, ever want to do. It changes you, for ever.'

At that moment Marlene comes back from jogging, dripping with sweat. She pops her head into the kitchen, waves a hand at us and goes upstairs, while I avoid following that exceptional body with my eyes.

William Hunt gets up. His orderly's arrived in a jeep to take him to Wheelus.

'I know you read Nietzsche, Mikey. So you'll know that there are no essentially *moral* things, only moral *interpretations* of things.'

He goes out and climbs into the jeep, leaving me alone in the kitchen, speechless, with my French toast, eggs and bacon.

★ ★ ★

Ten minutes later, I'm still there, eating, when Marlene comes in. She's changed out of her shorts and running vest and is now in a bikini, ready to go and sunbathe on the veranda. I try not to look at her. I've already had enough dealing with her husband.

'Thank goodness you're here, Mikey. Laura's asleep. I could do with a hand.'

She hands me the sunblock and I stare at it in the middle of a bite of French toast. She turns away and stops in front of a mirror. With one hand, she lifts her hair off the nape of her neck and holds it. With the other she lights a cigarette, her dark eyes watching me in the mirror.

'Come on, Mikey, let's be quick.'

I try to protest.

'But the *ghibli*. You'll be covered in sand.'

She laughs back.

I feel my forehead redden and my legs turn to jelly. I spread a little cream around her neck, then stop. She looks at me in the mirror, the cigarette hanging from the corner of those generous lips.

'And the rest? Do you want me to get sunburn all down my back?'

I spread cream on her shoulders, avoiding her gaze in the mirror. When I reach the strap of the bikini top I stop again.

'You'll have to undo it; otherwise it'll leave a stripe.'

She says it just like that, totally casual. Of course, I'm so nervous my fingers can't undo the two hooks. She stares at me in the mirror.

'You're almost nineteen, Mikey. You must have undone a bra or two. Am I making you uncomfortable?'

She puts out the cigarette, throws her long hair forwards over her shoulders, brings her arms behind her back and her hands guide mine to the fastenings. I feel my hands trembling as I undo them. She takes her hands away so she can hold the top of the bikini over her magnificent breasts.

I close my eyes, praying she won't turn round and see the large bulge in my jeans. I begin spreading the cream with both hands, up and then down, getting ever closer to the elastic of her bikini bottoms.

An uncrossable border, the entrance to a forbidden paradise.

'It should be my husband doing this, but he's always at work or travelling. And here am I alone, in the middle of all this sand.'

Her voice wavers between joking and bitterness.

'I'm sorry,' I say stupidly.

'What are you sorry about, Michelino?' Now there's a scornful tone to her voice.

I've come to the edge of her bikini bottoms now and can feel the elastic under my fingertips. I try to lower it in my mind, but fail.

'I'm sorry, but I have to go now.'

Horrified, I hear my adolescent voice turn raucous and guttural, wavering.

She fastens her top and turns round, facing me. I'm one metre eighty and taller than she is by several centimetres, and yet I feel like a child caught *in flagrante*, red-faced and dumbstruck. I'm terrified she'll see the erection pressing against my jeans.

Marlene stares straight into me for a moment with those eyes that make you feel like you are the only man in the world. And the most stupid.

'You have beautiful hands, Mikey. You use them well. Perhaps we can do this again.'

She gives me a little pat on the chest with two fingers and, electric shock waves running through my body, she turns away and goes off upstairs.

I stopped at the edge of that bikini bottom as if on the edge of an abyss.

I go outside into the baking sun. In the garden my father's chatting with Don Eugenio, Emilio Busi and Mohammed. Four pairs of eyes follow me.

I run off, not looking at them, but I know I'm not invisible.

Saturday, 6 August 2011

Rome

After her meeting with Monsignor Pizza, Linda walked down Via Cavour to Via dei Fori Imperiali, and from there along the Roman Forums to the Coliseum. Mock-centurions were charging five euros to be photographed with the tourists. It was a job, though, and more dignified than stealing money from the public purse.

To be given to the poor, Signorina. You don't understand.

She looked up the number of the Stella Polare in Ostia and called it. A woman answered in a foreign accent.

'Domnica?' asked Linda.

There was a moment's silence.

'Sorry, who is it?'

'I'm a journalist. My name's Linda Nardi and I'm writing a piece about your friend Melania Druc. Can I come over to Ostia and ask you a few questions?'

A longer silence.

'You pay for interview?' said Domnica at last.

Linda smiled. It was only fair.

Sure, like the Roman centurions, we all need to make a living.

'A hundred euros for half an hour of your time, Domnica.'

'All right. But come now. Bar empty. Later, many people coming.'

Balistreri was lying on the sofa resting his knee when he opened the report on the homicide/suicide of Melania and Tanja Druc. The cabin had been locked from the inside. The key was found on the bedside table next to the one single bed, on which the little girl was lying, a bullet hole in her right temple. Melania was sitting in the chair facing the desk, also with a bullet hole in her right temple, her body slightly inclined to the left, her right arm hanging loosely down and the pistol on the floor, forty centimetres away from her hand. There were technical terms that were difficult for the layman to understand. But Balistreri had read dozens of these reports in his thirty years with the police. Yes, the gun was there beside her right hand and the woman hadn't been left-handed, so this could confirm the suicide theory. Also, the gunshot-residue analysis had revealed traces of gunpowder on Melania's right hand. But there were also things that didn't add up. From the photo and the measurements, and Balistreri's experience and intuition, the weapon seemed slightly too far away from her hand. The cabin floor was covered with fitted carpet and the gun hadn't fallen from a height that would have made it bounce further away, assuming, that is, that Melania had fired – if she had fired – while sitting on the chair in front of the desk.

And perhaps it would have been more likely that a mother would shoot herself straight away, standing. Or else lying beside her daughter.

There was something wrong. Leading towards the theory of homicide/suicide was the fact that the cabin door had been locked from the inside and the key found on the bedside table. The door had been opened by a crew member with a pass key when Melania and Tanja hadn't come up to disembark.

But the gun's serial number had been filed away.

What the hell was a young Moldovan woman doing with a gun whose serial number had been filed away? That was something you found with gangsters' guns.

The first autopsy report said that Melania's stomach was empty. She hadn't eaten, although dinner time had long passed. On the other hand, Tanja's stomach was full: she had eaten some sole two hours earlier.

She gives her something to eat, then kills her two hours later?

Then Balistreri read the next sentence and the acid reflux rose up his throat. He read it, once, twice, and yet again.

The tip of the middle finger of the child's right hand is missing. The knife was found in the cabin. On it were traces of the sole and Tanja's blood.

The Civitavecchia police report said that the tip of Tanja's finger had been found in the toilet. On this detail, the police had no working hypothesis.

Could an accident on Melania's part while cutting the fish have frightened her so much that she shot the child and killed herself?

Impossible.

And the autopsy was quite clear on this point.

Very little bleeding. The fingertip had been cut off after death.

Balistreri left his office and rushed to the bathroom. He was just in time to vomit into the toilet bowl, just as he'd done that day.

Tripoli, 3 August 1969

Mikey Balistreri

Nadia's been missing since the morning. We all search for her for hours, between the villas and the Al Bakri's shack, even by the cesspit where, seven years earlier, those two poor creatures were found, the woman and child from the Sahara. But it's all in vain. My father and William Hunt call the police.

General Jalloun arrives in record time with no fewer than ten policemen. This is not efficiency but the influence of the powerful Balistreri–Bruseghin family.

'Does Nadia have any friends in the city, Ingegnere?' the general asks, addressing my father obsequiously and studiously ignoring Mohammed. My mother cuts in immediately.

'Shouldn't you be asking her father or brothers, General Jalloun?'

Jalloun is offended. Giuseppe Bruseghin is his friend, but his daughter's an arrogant fascist. She's also married to Salvatore Balistreri, the most important Italian in Tripoli.

'Very well, let's hear what Mohammed has to say.'

At that moment, Laura comes in from the neighbouring villa. I can feel her eyes on me, but I avoid them. Now that I've put sunblock on her mother's back and shoulders, stopping at the edge of those bikini bottoms, I can't look her in the eye. My mind's only on that body. Even in this moment, all I can think of is that Marlene Hunt's alone in the villa next door.

Trying not to be noticed, I slip out into the garden, drawn by an irresistible force and go over to the Hunts' house. I peer in through the half-open door, then quietly cross the threshold and begin to climb the stairs.

Marlene appears at the top of the staircase, completely naked. She stops to look at me, and it's like a *tae* blow in my chest. I stagger and fall back, rolling to the bottom of the stairs.

As I get up, bruised in body and pride, I hear her laugh and the terrace door close.

I'm on fire as I run towards the back gate and then on towards Grandad's olive grove.

The *ghibli*'s last howls hit me in the face as I run, my mouth and eyes caked with sand and the sweat pouring down my spine. I get to the Al Bakris' shack in less than twenty minutes. I go quickly past the cesspit and on into the olives. The sun's starting to set, looking like a ball of fire on the horizon now that it's able to penetrate the *ghibli*. Every so often along the path I can see the goatherds' tin sheds. I can hear the goats bleating, tended only by the dog that keeps an eye on them.

But the dog's barking too much. It's agitated, sniffing at the door of the old olive press. A parallelepiped shape, this shed was where the olives were pressed for years, thanks to a mule that trotted round, turning the two enormous millstones that crushed the fruit. One day, the shed caught fire, but the charred ruin had been left standing, although it had been shut up for years.

The dog's barking outside it and there are flies buzzing around; too many, given that the wind is still blowing hard. There's a small lock on the door but no sign of rust. I glance in through the window, its glass opaque with years of dirt. The sunlight barely gets through and all I can see is the sinister outline of the two huge millstones.

The goatherd's dog is still barking furiously at the door. In front of it, the ground's been disturbed and, caught in a bush, there's a paper handkerchief stained red.

I pick it up and put it in my pocket. My mind and body are paralysed. I refuse even to think about it. I could break the glass and look in. But I can't. I have to go back to the villas to sound the alarm, but first I have to stop and heave up everything I can.

Rome

Linda took the Metro from Trastevere to Ostia and immediately found the bar. It was just on nine o'clock and the seafront was almost deserted, except for joggers, cyclists and dogwalkers. In two hours, when Rome's sunbathers arrived, it would turn into one of the crowded circles of hell.

She found Domnica Panu in the spacious bar of the Stella Polare beach resort. She was blonde, her features too mousey to be attractive. She certainly had none of Melania Druc's charm, but she had a good body with curves in all the right places, although she was carrying a bit too much weight. She'd let herself go a bit, despite still being young.

Linda had come at a good moment. There was only one other person serving at the bar and very few customers. She and Domnica went and sat outside, looking directly on to the sea. Linda put her recorder on the table and switched it on.

'Now, Domnica, I'm going to ask you a few questions. I'm recording your answers so I don't have to take notes. Then, if the paper approves, I'll publish an article on Melania and how the two of you came to Italy via Porte Aperte.'

She didn't like lying, but Domnica was only interested in one thing, the money.

'You pay even if they don't publish?'

Linda put a fifty-euro banknote on the table.

'And another fifty after this interview, if you can give me some useful information for the article,' she said. But she was ill at ease: getting information like this went completely against the grain.

'All right. You can start, I have only half-hour. People come after nine thirty. I work here five years and always all in order.'

The two Moldovan girls were so different. Melania Druc was exceptionally beautiful, intelligent and elegant. And certainly not the type for that bar and the work there. Domnica Panu had a bland face and a body that was a little too provocative. And, she was certain, once they'd arrived in Italy, Melania had mixed in circles that would have been closed to Domnica.

'Did you know Melania since you were little?'

'We went school together. Always together, and Italy together.'

'You came to Italy together, is that right?'

'Yes. In Tighina, cold and hunger. No hope there.'

'How did you get to Italy?'

'We go to Chisinau. Office there of Porte Aperte. They ask if we cook and serve tables, so to work in Italian bars and restaurants. We say yes. They put us on coach for Rome.'

'And when you got to Italy?'

'They put us in hostel near Rome. After two weeks come first job.'

'Where was that?'

'In poker club.'

'You went to work in a poker club?'

Linda had done various investigations in this area. Over time, many activities had been legalized, but poker clubs at that time were still illegal.

'Outside, it say Billiards Hall, near Ciampino airport. After certain hour it shut and if you are friend you can stay and play poker.'

'And what did you and Melania have to do?'

She shook her head with a sour look.

'I only waitress. Melania croupier. In Moldova she has degree in political science and communication. She is very good, very intelligent.'

Linda nodded. The difference in appearance and education explained a good deal. But there was no jealousy in Domnica. Rather, she spoke about Melania with evident care and feeling. She had probably idolized her. Capable, intelligent, beautiful.

'But you also left the club, Domnica. You said you'd worked here in Ostia for five years.'

The young woman let a tear fall and turned away to the sea.

'Yes. Work in poker club disgusting. After one year I have enough. No more.'

'Disgusting work?'

Domnica stopped. She stared at the recorder.

'You write my name and I lose work here.'

'I won't give your name. Only the initials.'

This imaginary article was almost becoming real.

'I am waitress. They say always be nice to customers, but not prostitute, only company, drinks. No sex. Then they introduce another person. Italian lady, very beautiful. She promises much more money if I do sex with rich people, important customers. Not in poker club. Other places, much more beautiful.'

'What was her name?'

'I never know. Others call her *Fratello*.'

'*Fratello*? Brother? But isn't she a woman?'

'Yes, but in poker club they call her that.'

'And then?'

'This lady she organize parties. Men rich, famous. I see them on television. Much, much money they have. Parties in lovely houses — very, very lovely. And much cocaine . . .'

'Did they force you to have sex?'

'The woman dried a tear.

'Not force me with violence. But everyone there easy like that, clothes off, lap dance, cocaine. Men dress up like politicians, actors, ancient Romans, cardinals. The girls like nurses, nuns, sheep. At end, if you go away, then no money. Much money only for sex.'

Linda remained silent. Domnica stared at the ground, avoiding looking at her.

'Is cold in Tighina, Signora. Hunger there. They give money, much, much money. Difficult say no, all say yes to sex. First only one man. Then two. They give money, cocaine. I fine, then frightened, very frightened.'

'Why?'

'Cocaine too much. They play games, first only handcuffs, blindfold, vibrators. Then very dangerous. One night I naked with five, ten, I not know. They want whip me, no stop, I am crying, I say stop now. Then they put rope round my neck and have thing, a pulley. I pee myself so frightened, and they all laugh. Day after I stop.'

Linda looked at the sea, as smooth as a mirror. And the blue sky that was rapidly clouding over. Melania and Tanja were up there, somewhere.

This is the world we live in. Nothing new about it.

Domnica was in tears and Linda put a hand on her shoulder.

'OK, no more, I have enough. Can you tell me about Melania? Was she involved in these parties?'

'No, she different level. She bring in customers, but no sex. Three year ago she meet important man and then work no more in poker club. He look after her.'

'And he's Tanja's father?'

'Yes.'

'Do you know his name?'

'Melania she never tell me this, ever. Secret. I don't know where she live even.'

'When was the last time you saw Melania?'

'One morning she leave with Tanja for Elba, on cruise ship. She came here with Tanja to say hello, after so many months.'

'Was she happy?'

Domnica thought for a moment.

'At first Melania always happy. But last times no. That morning she very worried. I thought because little girl too young for cruise, I not know.'

'But why did she come that morning? Just to say hello?'

Domnica looked at the sea, then shook her head.

'No, she say when she get back Rome I take Tanja with me for some days, because Melania not happy at home.'

Linda remembered Melania Druc's agitation on the ship as she was coming out of the private lift with little Tanja in her arms. Her friend was right: that was a frightened woman.

Tears were streaming down Domnica's face, mingling with some drops of rain that were beginning to fall. Perhaps she was regretting not having stayed in her native country with Tighina's poor but honest people. To die from cold, perhaps, but not from men wanting to string her up, laughing as she wet herself.

'You really don't know who Melania took up with? Tanja's father?'

They heard thunder and it started to pour. Domnica shivered.

'Before she leave on cruise to Elba, she say he on ship.'

Linda felt a shiver down her spine. She thought about the men on board, sitting round that table: the Libyan Mohammed Al Bakri, Monsignor Eugenio Pizza, Senator Emilio Busi, Salvatore Balistreri.

'But you have no idea of his name?'

Domnica avoided her eyes.

'Melania never say.'

Linda stared directly at Domnica and switched off the recorder.

'And the real name of the woman they called *Fratello*?'

A gust of wind chilled the air about them. Linda studied the horizon. A small, dark line, then bolts of lightning. Domnica had come to a stop, as if in front of a doorway too dark to enter. She began to tremble.

'You not here for interview,' she muttered.

Linda got up, holding out her card and two hundred-euro notes. She had the feeling that Domnica was wondering whether to tell her something else. Domnica took the card, but not the money.

'No, thank you, Signora. I know you come here for you care about Melania and Tanja. You here for justice, not interview. I don't want money for justice.'

Linda embraced her, Domnica Panu's tears wetting her cheeks. But it was useless taking this any further right now. Linda said goodbye and quickly crossed the road along the front.

'Signora!'

Linda heard the cry when she was already across the road.

Domnica was on the pavement opposite, outside the bar, under the downpour of the summer storm.

She's followed me out to tell me the names of Melania's lover and that of the woman.

Linda started to move towards her, but Domnica had already stepped off the pavement and was crossing the small square towards her. The van came up at over ninety kilometres an hour and hit her full on, hurling her another twenty metres forwards. The driver made no attempt to stop.

When Balistreri had finished vomiting into the toilet bowl, he put his head under the cold-water tap, then went down to the bar and had two double-strength espressos. Then he went back to his office.

Tanja Druc's middle finger in 2011. Anita Messi's middle finger in 1982. Nadia Al Bakri's middle finger in 1969.

He remembered perfectly well the letter that came from Tripoli in 1982, typewritten in English on cheap paper:

Signor Commissario Balistreri,

We receive the Italian newspapers in Tripoli and have come to know of Anita Messi and the amputation of the middle finger of her right hand. We should like to inform you of a similar mutilation found on the body of a young girl murdered in Tripoli on 3 August 1969. A photograph of the victim's hand is enclosed.

Yours faithfully,
PO Box 150870

The fifteenth of August 1970 had been his day of reckoning. That night he had left Libya for good.

That letter had triggered the manhunt.

But the killers of Anita Messi and Nadia Al Bakri had been found and both died in 1983.

He'd already smoked three cigarettes one after the other and now he wanted to know everything about the Druc case, right away. He called Corvu into his office, which was now swathed in a wreath of cigarette smoke.

'So, Corvu, found out anything else?'

Corvu stared at him in surprise. In the face of his boss, a man tired and unmotivated, he could see a light he couldn't remember seeing since the days of the search for the Invisible Man.

'A few things. First of all, we've gathered a bit more information about Porte Aperte.'

He held out a leaflet and Balistreri read the list of sponsors: Gruppo Italia, Libyan Charity Fund, Dubai Charity Fund.

Again, he felt the acid in his stomach. But he had already vomited everything, except the two coffees. He looked at Corvu, who had still more papers in his hands.

'There's more?'

Corvu was tense.

Bad news. As if the missing middle fingertip wasn't enough.

'Yes, thanks to my contact in the Secret Service. Monsignor Pizza uses a Swiss SIM card with which he speaks only to other foreign-SIM-card users: another Swiss, a Libyan and someone in Dubai.'

While the burning in Balistreri's stomach was spreading, his thoughts were stirring with ghosts from the past.

Was it possible or impossible?

'Have you got the ship's passenger list, official guests and unofficial?'

Corvu looked even more tense.

'Only those officially registered.'

He handed him a list. It was in alphabetical order and under 'B' was Senator Emilio Busi. Under 'N', Linda Nardi.

Balistreri had always considered four-letter words a sign of weakness. His mother Italia had drummed it into him when he was a child.

'Shit,' he mouthed.

Then he shot an irritated look at Corvu.

'Nothing else? What about the passengers in the helicopter with Busi?'

Corvu shook his head. Even with all his contacts, he'd come to a dead end on that one.

'Couldn't manage it, Commissario. The helicopter took off from the roof of Gruppo Italia's tower block and returned there. I haven't been able to find out anything else.'

Balistreri was getting more and more impatient. He felt an anger rising up in him he'd thought he'd overcome.

'And you've found no other traces of Melania Druc? How could she have vanished for seven years?'

Corvu was disconcerted by his boss's sudden proactive mood, and upset by his reproaches, but he was happy that his boss seemed to be his old self.

'I haven't uncovered anything yet, but I'm working on it.'

Balistreri banged the autopsy report on the table.

'There's not enough here, Corvu. Have you read about this bloody middle finger or not?'

Corvu had read everything, of course. He was careful not to remind Balistreri that it was he who had first asked him to take a look at the case. He felt suddenly angry, but tried to put it aside.

'I do have one thing. Civitavecchia's sent over everything they found in the cabin. This is Melania's BA thesis.'

Balistreri glared at him.

'And what do I do with that, Corvu? You want me to read a Moldovan escort's BA thesis in the original?'

'Melania Druc was fluent in three languages. This is the Italian version.'

Balistreri stared at the bound copy and sighed.

'And how the devil is Melania Druc's thesis going to help?'

'To know her better, *dottore*,' Corvu replied.

But Balistreri wasn't interested. He had other things on his mind. *Ghosts from the past. A severed middle finger.*

'Come on, Corvu, try to get things moving. We need to find this friend of hers she came to Italy with. She must know something about her.'

Corvu nodded.

'Domnica Panu. I'll see if she still works at that bar in Ostia.'

The answer came that moment on the computer screen. It was tuned to the channel that gave updates of ongoing police investigations, and Balistreri kept it on out of habit. There was a newsflash.

A hit-and-run driver has killed a woman outside the Stella Polare beach resort in Ostia. The victim's name is Domnica Panu.

Balistreri was speechless, and stared at the screen. Another film was running backwards before his eyes, going from Melania and Tanja Druc to Anita Messi and Nadia Al Bakri.

And then to Italia Balistreri.

Tripoli, Sunday, 10 August, 1969

Mikey Balistreri

It's been a week since Nadia's death. That worthless crook General Jalloun's arrested an old, half-blind goatherd who couldn't harm a fly.

It's late afternoon and in the garden in front of the villas the air is finally a little more breathable. Italia's sitting on her own on the swing seat out on the veranda. She's drinking whisky, smoking and reading Nietzsche's *Beyond Good and Evil*. I sit down next to her.

'How are you feeling, Mamma?'

She raises her eyes from the book and smiles. There are lots more lines around her eyes these days.

'I'm tired, Mikey. I can't get used to the idea that Nadia's dead.'

I pull the crumpled sheet of squared paper from my jeans on which Ahmed and I have written down in pencil the alibis of all those we consider suspects. She scans it in silence, reading the names, including that of her husband, my father. Practically everyone except for the three Hunts, who had been watching a baseball game at Wheelus Field.

'I need your help, Mamma. Where it says "check".'

She could tell me, as my father would, that I'm only a kid and these are things for grown-ups and the police.

Instead she smiles at me, folds up the piece of paper and places it in the Nietzsche book.

'Very well, Mikey, I'll check. But you're not to do a thing.'

Perhaps she's seen something on the paper that I can't see.

The next day, the old, half-blind goatherd become scapegoat kills himself in prison. The investigation is closed.

Saturday, 6 August 2011

Rome

Giulia Piccolo arrived on her Ducati half an hour after Linda Nardi's phone call. She found Linda sitting at a table outside the Stella Polare, her eyes staring wide at the pathetic sheet with which the traffic police had respectfully tried to cover Domnica's body.

The sun had come out again after the storm, and all around them life was going on as usual: sunbathers under umbrellas, children with ice creams, the strident horns of drivers irritated by that sheet blocking half the carriageway.

Linda gave her statement as an eyewitness. The van was white, possibly a Fiat Ducato; she hadn't seen the number plate. There was only one person inside, and they'd made no attempt to brake.

Then Giulia took her home, gave her a sedative and forced her to go to bed. She lay down beside her quietly until she saw that Linda was asleep.

'Come on, Corvu, let's get going.'

Although he hated leaving his office, Balistreri was in a hurry to get to the accident scene in Ostia, and Corvu was driving. During the journey they didn't exchange a single word. Balistreri seemed suddenly animated. Corvu couldn't quite believe it.

Once at Ostia police station, they quickly read the traffic police report. The van hadn't braked but rather accelerated and immediately driven off. Then, among the eyewitnesses, they found that name again: Linda Nardi.

Balistreri swallowed a swear word. He was a man who didn't believe in coincidences when they cropped up in an investigation. Or in life. *We're the authors of our own destinies.* Corvu had heard him say it many times over the years.

'OK, back to Rome,' said Balistreri.

In the tense silence during the trip, his thoughts were giving rise to contrasting feelings: anger, regret and his fear of having to deal with them again. Only by discipline and force of will had he been able to suppress his imaginary conversations with that woman over the last five years. It had taken a long time before they had worn themselves out, along with any desire to see her again.

So as not to think of that night any more.

Friday, 21 July 2006

Rome

She turned her face away so as not to look him in the eyes as he tore off her panties. He had to stand up to unfasten his trousers. He was ready. But in that moment when their bodies separated in the dim light and the total silence was broken only by his own heavy breathing, Balistreri saw the slim figure of a semi-naked woman with her clothes torn, her breasts shielded by her arms, her pubis exposed. It could have been Elisa, Samantha, Nadia, Ornella, Alina or Saint Agnes. It could have been another woman, one he hadn't forgotten since that last night in August 1970.

And, as Linda had predicted, he saw the first glimmer of truth. It was only a sensation, not a real and proper idea. Incredulous, horrified, he took a step back, staggering. He crashed into the table lamp, which fell and broke, and left the flat in utter darkness. He took advantage of it to escape into the night.

Saturday, 6 August 2011

Rome

Linda woke up towards the end of the afternoon and joined Giulia on the little terrace. She was still suffering from shock, had no energy to speak and handed her tape recorder to her friend, who listened in silence to the conversation Linda had recorded that morning with Domnica. Her face hardened as she heard what Domnica had to say.

'More than Melania's lover, it's that woman who took those poor girls to those filthy-rich pigs who makes me sick. We know what men are like, but a woman doing that . . .'

'Do you know anything about this Porte Aperte organization Domnica was talking about?'

'Never heard of it, but there are so many of them. Let's take a look online.'

They found the Porte Aperte website easily and, like Balistreri, found themselves looking at a name. *President: Monsignor Eugenio Pizza.*

They stared at each other in amazement.

'A ridiculous coincidence,' Linda whispered.

Giulia Piccolo thought about what her ex-boss Michele Balistreri used to say about coincidences. But she was careful not to mention his name.

Then Linda's mobile rang and she recognized the number on the display.

'Graziano . . .'

The little Sardinian's voice was gabbling in agitation, his consonants doubling as he spoke.

'Linda, that accident in Ostia, you were there, weren't you?'

'Yes, Graziano. I was on the other side of the street when . . .'

'He wants to see you, right away.'

Linda was silent. She could always refuse, but then Balistreri would be forced to bring her in officially with a warrant for questioning.

It would be worse. I'd have to answer too many questions.

'Tell him I'm on my way.'

Giulia Piccolo took her on the bike and prudently left her at a block some distance from the Flying Squad offices. Linda was tired and tense at the end of a long day that had begun with her visit to Monsignor Pizza and then gone on to the death of Domnica Panu. And she had no desire to see Michele Balistreri again.

Corvu came out to meet her and accompanied her to the room at the end of the corridor. Nobody was in it. It was the first time she had seen the armchairs with the broken springs, the worn leather sofa, the ancient, peeling desk full of papers, the closed shutters, the bluish smoke filling the air.

But she knew whose office it was. In some way, what lay before her was what she'd understood that day she had expelled Michele Balistreri from her life.

A man who's no longer living. Dead before he gives up the ghost.

Seeing the empty room, Linda gave a sigh of relief. Perhaps Graziano would be interviewing her and she could avoid Michele Balistreri altogether.

Corvu looked upset.

'Linda, what are you thinking . . .'

Balistreri came in at that moment.

'You can leave us, Corvu. And you can take a seat, Dottoressa Nardi.'

The return to formality reminded her of their first meeting, in the church of Sant'Agnese in Agone in Piazza Navona, when she had told him about the terrible violence that men had inflicted on Agnes and he had almost laughed in her face.

Corvu left the room without a word. Linda moved to a lighter side of the room.

'I'll stand. I'm only staying for a minute.'

Balistreri lit a cigarette and sat down, leaving Linda alone in the middle of the room.

'OK, as you wish. But this is a murder inquiry and we will take all the time that is necessary.'

He looked at the computer, at the papers on his desk, at the glowing point of his cigarette. Linda felt the anger rising up from her heart to her brain.

'Aren't you able to say my first name, Michele?'

An interminable moment passed in which he neither looked at her nor said anything. Linda almost feared he might attack her again, as he had on that night five years ago.

Then he stubbed out the cigarette, got up and went to open the windows. He turned round and finally looked her in the eyes.

Five years ago I didn't want to believe you. I desired you without even knowing how to kiss you. I attacked you and didn't protect you, leaving you alone with a killer.

Like Linda, he was angry with himself for thinking about the past, but he pushed his memories to one side when he spoke.

'You can't leave whenever you feel like it. So, please take a seat, Linda.'

The words were harsh, but the use of her first name was a concession, if not a capitulation. For a moment she was caught between
rebellion and giving in. Then she chose a middle path. Her body
refused to move. She didn't try to leave, but neither did she sit.

'What do you want to talk to me about?'

'A great deal, starting with the death of Domnica Panu this morning in Ostia.'

'Is Homicide now dealing with hit-and-run drivers?'

'Is that what it was?'

'Can you tell me why it might not be?'

'No. It's you who has to tell me what you were doing there this
morning.'

This quick going back and forth, brute force against scorn, was all
that was left between them after five years. They both felt it; they
both thought it.

Neither of us wants to be here right now.

Balistreri stared at those light, transparent eyes, where he had one
day thought he'd found everything he'd never had: fidelity, sharing,
even love. He stared at Linda as a shipwrecked sailor might look at an
enchanting sea the moment he'd escaped his death there. It was only
once he had been exiled from it did Balistreri realize what he had lost.

Linda was also studying Balistreri. His hair was too long and turning grey, his clothes were rumpled, his cheeks sunken and there were
dark rings under his eyes. This was the man who'd declared his love
for her with the words *You're mad.*

You must have been a different person at one time, Michele.

She sat down in the armchair in front of the desk, looking Balistreri in the eye, as he had done to her, forcing herself to concentrate
on the events of the day and to answer his questions.

'I was on the other side of the road along the front when she was
hit. I gave my statement to the traffic police . . .'

'I know – I've read the report. But the woman on the cash register says that you and Domnica had spoken at length, right up to a minute before the accident.'

'It was an interview, for an investigation I'm undertaking.'

'What investigation?'

'Michele, there are laws protecting privacy . . .'

'Linda, I am the law and this is an inquiry into a possible murder. Or, rather, three murders.'

Linda looked at him. 'What are you talking about? What murders are these?' How could he know?

He looked directly into her eyes.

'Those of Melania and Tanja Druc.'

She stared at him, waiting for more. But Balistreri had no intention of explaining what he knew. All at once she felt vulnerable and exhausted. The man in front of her was the one she had thrown out of her life. But perhaps he was the only one who could get to the truth, no matter who tried to stop him, even a man like Monsignor Pizza.

She pulled the tape recorder out of her bag and pressed play. Balistreri listened right up to the end of the interview without making any comment. He called an officer in and told him to make a copy straight away. He gave the tape recorder back to her, knowing very well she'd already have made a copy for herself.

'And don't even dream of using the contents of this pseudo interview for an article,' he warned her.

She picked the tape recorder up. She wasn't taking any orders from him. On the contrary.

'Someone has to find Melania's lover boy. Domnica says he was also on the ship. Together with that woman, *Fratello*.'

Balistreri stared at her for a moment in silence.

'You don't have to find anyone, Linda. We, the police, will see to that. Now tell me why you were on that ship from Elba.'

Linda tried to collect her thoughts.

He's the worst kind of man, but an excellent cop. This is the right question to ask. One that opens up a very different front.

'I was there for work.'

He pressed her for an answer.

'What work?'

'My work. I had to speak to someone.'

'Who was that?'

'I'm a journalist, Michele. I have the right –'

'You have no rights here. I've already told you that this is an inquiry into three homicides. Who did you have to speak to?'

Linda breathed a long sigh and told half the truth and half a lie.

'Senator Emilio Busi.'

Balistreri lifted his gaze, and his eyes held a different light above those dark rings.

'Busi's a friend of yours?'

Linda picked up on something behind the question.

Bitterness, anger, fear.

She felt a wave of tenderness that she immediately swept aside with her answer.

'It's none of your business if he's a friend or not, is it?'

'What did you have to speak to him about?'

'He was going to introduce me to Monsignor Pizza.'

Balistreri gave a slight start, then his mood darkened further. He lit a cigarette.

'Why did you want to meet Monsignor Pizza?'

'I'm making investigations into the IOR.'

Balistreri kept silent, waiting.

Linda observed him. After she'd mentioned the names of Emilio Busi and Eugenio Pizza, something in the hardness of his face had slipped away. He now seemed more concerned than angry, and a mental picture came back to her, the distraught Michele Balistreri who ran to save her from Manfredi.

A last reflection of the man he had once been. Loyal, courageous, good.

She told him everything then. The conversation with Bashir Yared in Tripoli, the building site in Nairobi, the slush funds used for bribes, the Swiss group's memorandum of association, the IOR bank statements, the account held by Monsignor Eugenio Pizza. She left out her affair with John Kiptanu and the way she'd dealt with Gabriele Cascio.

You wouldn't understand. Only judge and nothing more.

'And you came to know all this via legal methods?' Balistreri asked her when she'd finished.

The same question Monsignor Pizza had asked. Put by the priest it had been a provocation; with Michele it expressed concern.

'A journalist can do things the police aren't allowed to do. Those two investment companies that run the Swiss consortium, for example. You would have had to send an international letter rogatory to find out who's behind them, they would oppose it and a whole year would go by. I can use other means.'

'The same methods you used to obtain the memorandum of association and the bank statements?'

Linda looked him straight in the eye.

'I got them by adopting the manner you men want women to have: by behaving like a whore. And this morning I went to see Monsignor Pizza and threw them in his face.'

Balistreri stubbed out his half-finished cigarette.

'You did what? Linda, are you completely mad?'

She observed him, eyes gleaming.

'Do you know how Melania and Domnica entered Italy? Thanks to Porte Aperte, whose chairman happens to be Monsignor Pizza.'

Balistreri knew this very well, but he didn't want the conversation to go in that direction. He was hesitant for a moment, hovering between anger about what Linda had done and fear about what might happen to her.

Because I know them very well. I know what they're capable of.

'Did you tell him that you were going to see Domnica Panu?' he asked her.

He could see Linda thinking; she was trying to remember. Then a vertical line creased her forehead, her features shrinking in anger and pain.

'Not exactly,' she whispered, 'but I said something that could have made him suspect it. I wanted to scare him.'

And you succeeded, Linda. You have no idea who you're dealing with.

'Let me get this straight. Busi introduced you to Monsignor Pizza on that cruise, right?'

Linda nodded and sighed.

'I had dinner with them and two other men.'

Balistreri felt an uncomfortable feeling stirring within him, the burning sensation rising up his oesophagus along with the thoughts spreading from his heart to his brain.

Busi, Don Eugenio, the helicopter, the other guests, the missing fingertip. OK, Michele. That's enough. Stop right here, right now.

But he couldn't.

'And who were the other two?' he asked.

He could feel the uncertainty in his own voice; it was almost a plea. *Tell me it isn't true.*

She looked up into his face, and their eyes met. She was worried and apologetic.

She's sorry for me, not for herself.

'With Senator Busi, there was Monsignor Eugenio Pizza, a Libyan named Mohammed Al Bakri and . . . your father.'

Balistreri was dumbstruck. It was impossible this was all coincidence.

He had to think fast, get his mind around it all as quickly as he could.

'How did you come to know Domnica Panu?'

'By speaking to Melania on the cruise. She approached me. She wanted to tell me something, but was clearly frightened. She told me to get in touch through this friend of hers, Domnica.'

'You spoke to her on the ship?'

'There was a private lift between decks that Busi and his guests used. I went down to the bottom deck to have a look around and Melania came out of it with her little girl . . . I recognized her straight away.'

Balistreri made a frown.

'You recognized her? You knew her?'

'I'd seen her a few days before.'

'Where?'

Linda sighed.

'In the Hotel Rixos, Tripoli. She didn't have the little girl with her then. She had an escort of Libyan special agents and she was with a man. The one they were saying was responsible for the Zawiya massacre and the death of General Younis.'

Balistreri again felt the twinge of anxiety he'd felt when he'd read Linda's article about it.

It was a presentiment.

'Young man or old?'

Linda tried to cast her mind back.

'He was thin, slender, olive complexion, curly grey hair, about sixty. A piece of his ear was missing.'

Balistreri was stunned. It was too much. All his old enemies. Tanja's missing fingertip and that missing part of an ear were dragging him back to that old promise he'd buried in his conscience.

In a month, a year, a hundred years, I'll find out the truth about my mother's death.

He accompanied Linda to the door.

'Leave this business to the police.'

He said it in a tone that didn't allow for any objections. She left without saying a word.

6 One Half of the Truth

Tripoli, La Moneta, Saturday, 30 August 1969

Marlene Hunt

This summer's been hell. First, the vacation in America, a real drag, with Laura thinking only of Mikey, and William of the Libyan situation and Gaddafi. Then coming back to this red-hot sandpit, Nadia's tragic death and then the two worst bits of news: Laura and Mikey falling in love and William announcing that in a few months we'd be moving to Vietnam.

Fortunately, after Nadia's death, there was the extra vacation with Laura. London, Paris, Rome. And there, finally, was Salvatore Balistreri. Every day after our dinners in Rome, I wondered how to speak to him and convince him to leave Italia. I thought about it while he was in Italy with Mohammed a few days ago. Then he came back, but now he's always busy with those two, Busi and Don Eugenio, always up to his eyes discussing who knows what.

Then at last the moment comes: the invitation to the party for Salvo's forty-fourth birthday, which is going ahead despite the Al Bakri family being in mourning for Nadia's death. But then, the killer has been found, that goatherd Jamaal, and he committed suicide in prison. So, case closed.

The party's being held on the small island of La Moneta which Salvo bought and developed, a few miles offshore. Because of the mourning period, Italia's halved the festivities: there'll be just one dinner tonight with a dance afterwards, and only a few close friends will stay over on the island. Among them, us, obviously. Italia's taking good care of us because of Laura and Mikey. But she has no idea what she's in for . . . This invitation's the first step to breaking three ties: between Laura and Mikey, Salvo and Italia, William and me.

The first one will be easy. It's my speciality.

I start off on the motorboat, because we and the Balistreri family are going to La Moneta together. Italia's wearing one of her long dresses, down to her ankles to protect her milky-white skin from the burning sun. She looks like an Egyptian mummy. She's also wearing a light scarf over her short hair and huge sunglasses. She's standing in the bows looking at the coast, her back to us, smoking.

I take off my pareo. Underneath I'm wearing one of the skimpy bikinis I bought in London. It gleams white against my suntan. And I always have a suntan.

Look at her, Salvo, your wife will soon be an old woman. And now look at me!

Mikey's at the helm, Salvo behind him, keeping an eye on where we're going. They need to keep looking ahead.

'The sea's like glass. Can I stretch out on the prow?' I ask Mikey.

He looks at me, perplexed. We're almost there; another ten minutes and I could sunbathe comfortably on the beach. I know what he's thinking: I'm a spoilt narcissist. But Salvo's the perfect host.

'Of course, Marlene,' he says. 'Mikey, watch the sea, and careful with the waves.'

I lie face down on a mat, my head towards the prow, my feet towards them, and unhook my bikini top. I know what Salvo and Mikey can see. Dark hair pushed sideways, my naked back suntanned down to my bikini bottoms, the elastic hem that follows the curve of my hips and bottom and goes down between my thighs, which are close together, but not that close. Just enough for men to fantasize . . .

'Watch out, Michele, there's the skin divers' buoy!' Salvo shouts.

Mikey makes a sharp turn, the boat swerves and a wave splashes my back. I yell out.

'Mikey! *Mi hai schizzata!*'

Salvo's calm but irritated. He orders Mikey to leave the helm and has a word with him in Sicilian dialect.

'How about having a bit of a break, eh?'

Perfect.

It's two thirty when we get to La Moneta's little jetty, and it's boiling hot. Everything's already been prepared by the Al Bakri family, with the help of Nico. The gazebos are in place to give us some shade, deckchairs are laid out on the beach, the large white villa is perfectly set up.

It's everything Salvo wants for his important guests. And he's the perfect host. His hair, combed back, is still all black; his moustache is trimmed and neat. He's suntanned, relaxed, obviously well satisfied with himself. He's wearing a spotless white linen suit, a blue shirt and a light blue tie. Beauty and power are an excellent combination. And yet I'm neither in love nor even particularly sexually attracted by Salvatore Balistreri.

But he would give me the life that's been taken away from me.

William goes into the guesthouse to take a shower and get out of the heat and Laura goes off with Mikey and his friends to the cliff on the other side of the island. I lie down on the beach by the sea. I don't have to worry about the sun with my dark skin.

I want everyone to see my body; I want everyone to want it so that it'll infect both Salvo and Mikey with feverish desire.

Groups of other guests arrive, brought over in two motorboats, one piloted by Farid, the other by Salim. Ambassadors, dignitaries from King Idris's court, two ministers, the heads of Italian, English and American companies in Libya. And, naturally, Busi and Don Eugenio.

While Salvo welcomes everyone, the guests can't help but look at me. The men with desire, the women with envy.

I know that Salvo's noticed this, taking in their reactions, feeling how it would be if I were at his side instead of that fake pale queen of his who keeps to herself, smoking away, wrapped up in her kaftan and scarf to protect her delicate skin.

After they've all seen the possible, and dreamed the impossible, I go to the guest house to change. After a shower, I change into a light-coloured, low-cut dress I bought on Via Condotti in Rome. I look at myself in the mirror to adjust my cleavage and the curve of the dress over my hips.

Just right: all that's needed to set the imagination and the desire going.

As soon as I'm out among the crowd, the men start coming over to greet me. William watches, as always, neither worried nor upset. He's proud, more than anything else, that I'm his and his alone. But, like most men, my husband hasn't picked up on the signals.

William smiles at me and sets off round the back of the villa towards the path that leads to the cliff, leaving me alone with all those eyes on me, happy that I'm admired. Perhaps in his primitive male mind he believes that the admiration makes up for my unhappiness.

Italia receives the guests with a cold and formal cordiality. She disapproves of the party, it being less than a month since Nadia was killed. But there's something more than that.

Perhaps Salvo said something about the two of us when he came back from Rome. Or perhaps she simply suspects.

Then she, too, sets off behind the villa. For a moment I wonder if she has a meeting arranged with William, then I shake my head, amused.

Wouldn't that be the limit? Nothing happening between Salvo and me, while those two cold fish are doing it under our very noses!

But it's more amusing than a probability.

She would never leave Salvo for the love of another man, although she might if he betrayed her . . .

I have to make this happen.

Then I see Mikey setting off behind his mother, trying not to be seen.

An hour later William comes back along the same path that Italia, and then Mikey, took. He's got an envelope in his hand; his face is tense. There's a worried look in his eyes. I don't think I've ever seen him like this before. He signals to me, comes over and we go off to our room in the guest house. He tells me to sit down on the bed.

'Marlene, we only have a few minutes to decide about something very important. Or, rather, two very important things that are connected.'

He's never spoken to me in this tone before. It must be the one he uses to his men in battle: calm, efficient, decisive. He passes me the envelope.

'Italia gave me this envelope a few minutes ago on the cliff.'

I stare at him, not understanding.

'What's in it?'

He doesn't hesitate but replies immediately.

'The copy of a letter Italia intends to send to General Jalloun within forty-eight hours. It's time for me to make a safe exit from Libya. She's offering me this chance because I'm Laura's father.'

I feel my pulse quicken. I'm seeing the other side of my husband, the one I've never seen in action but over the years have slowly come to realize was there. A soldier, a war hero, a CIA agent, and – now, I'm sure of it – a man capable of anything.

'What's in the letter?' I ask him, feeling all the energy draining out of me.

He shakes his head, as if it doesn't matter right now.

'It's something I could be shot for. You can read it later, if you want. But, right now, we have to deal with the situation.'

I realize that, for the first time, he's asking for help. For my help.

'You want me to help you escape? Surely you don't need . . .'

He shakes his head.

'I can't leave this country in under forty-eight hours. There's a work matter I have to sort out.'

'A work matter?'

'Italia has her suspicions, but she doesn't know for sure. Langley told me that, tomorrow night, Mohammed's going to Benghazi . . .'

'Will, I've no idea what you're talking about . . .'

My husband stares at me for what could be a second, a minute, an hour. Then he decides he can't do anything but tell me the truth, and I know I should shut my ears, throw away the envelope and run away. But I stay put and hear him out, in shock.

'Salvo Balistreri and his friends Busi and Don Eugenio are involved with Mohammed in plot to overthrow the monarchy and have all Westerners expelled from the country. Which of course will leave them to grow very rich.'

For a moment my mind can't make the connection; I can't understand what he's saying to me.

'Will, are you crazy? What the hell are you talking about? What's Salvo . . .'

He leans over to his briefcase, the one he's never separated from, puts in the combination, opens it and takes out a photograph, which he hands to me.

It's a sharp image in black and white, taken in front of the Grand

Hotel in Abano Terme in the north of Italy. Two men smile as they shake hands. One has *Corriere della Sera* from two days ago, 28 August, folded in his pocket. That man is Salvatore Balistreri. The other man is much younger, his features clearly those of a Libyan from the desert.

'Who's the second man?'

William again hesitates a moment, then shakes his head.

'Muammar Gaddafi, a young lieutenant who's head of the rebels. The man who'll govern Libya in a few days' time, thanks to Salvo, Busi, Don Eugenio and their friends in Italy. If we don't stop them, that is.'

We being the CIA.

I look at the photograph in my hand. An idea's starting to take shape in my head.

Italia would never leave Salvo for the love of another man. She would leave him if he betrayed her, but he's meticulously careful. There's another kind of betrayal, though, an even more serious one, perhaps, in Italia's eyes. And it's this that William's offering me on a silver platter.

I get up from the bed. My legs are trembling, but my brain's now clear.

'What do you want me to do, Will?'

'I have to leave staight away for Benghazi, get in touch with Langley and see what Washington wants to do. You stay here on the island.'

'And then?'

'Call me tomorrow morning at Benghazi and I'll tell you if you can show this photograph to Italia.'

'But Salvo'll be shot . . .'

William nods.

'Of course, if I hand the photo over to General Jalloun before the *coup d'état*, then Salvo would be executed. You have to explain to Italia that if she sends that letter exposing me to General Jalloun, then the general will receive the negative of this photo. Italia won't let the father of her sons be shot. She'll agree. Then she can tell our fancy man Salvo Balistreri to go to hell.'

I'm both petrified and over the moon.

Fate is handing me the opportunity I've been looking for.

'OK, understood. I'll do everything you want, William.'

William smiles at me, satisfied.

'I'm counting on you, Marlene. Now, hide the envelope and the photo under the mattress and let's go back outside.'

I feel like I did after that first snort years ago on that Hollywood producer's couch. I no longer have any fear.

That photograph will destroy the bond between Italia and Salvo. She'll save his life because he's the father of Alberto and Mikey, but she'll never forgive him for what, for her, is the greater betrayal of all. I'll also save William's skin and pay off my debt to him. Then Salvo and I'll be free, free to be together.

We go outside, and William asks Salvo if he can use the villa's phone and leaves me with him. Behind us the sea is smooth as olive oil. In front of us, people are all happily dancing away. Everything seems perfect. I smile at Salvo and caress his hand in a barely perceptible gesture, but it's too brazen for him and he immediately takes his hand away.

He's so frightened of being suspected of marital infidelity! He, who's always impeccable, untouchable. But now, a little less so.

I know I shouldn't, not here and not right now, but euphoria has made me brazen.

'So you went to Italy for the thermal baths?' I say.

For the first time I see this man who's so sure of himself, imperturbable, turn pale and flinch.

You have to understand, Salvo. I'm neither like Italia nor a little tramp you can pick up for a quick one-night stand.

Slowly, very slowly, Salvo regains his composure and attempts to smile.

'I've been having some back pain. I had three days of mud-bath therapy.'

But I have to go further. I'm feeling strong, unbeatable.

'Great. The spas at Abano Terme are good for that.'

He staggers like a boxer caught by a deadly right hook. He's about to ask me *How do you know?* But at that moment William comes back.

'You'll have to excuse me, Salvatore. Wheelus Field's been on. Something urgent's come up. I'll have to go.'

Salvo looks concerned. I've never seen him so agitated. It makes him a little less fascinating, but more human.

'But it's late now, William. Can't you go tomorrow?'

'Sorry, Salvo. Marlene'll sing "Happy Birthday" to you for both of us.'

Salvo has to give in. Or perhaps he's thinking that, without William, it'll be easier to ask me how I know he's been to Abano Terme.

'All right. I'll tell Farid to take you back to the Underwater Club.'

William thanks him and then turns to me.

'I need to have a word, darling. Would you excuse us, Salvo?'

'Of course, of course. I'll go and see to the motorboat for you.'

We slip away to a place where no one can hear us. William has the calm air of someone who knows what he's doing.

'Everything's fine – I'm off to Benghazi. I'll have instructions from Langley by tomorrow morning. Call me to get confirmation, then go to Italia with the photo and explain the alternatives.'

'OK. Will do. Till tomorrow. You can count on me.'

Sure, Will. You can count on me to save your life. But then I'm going to ask you a favour. I want you to let me go.

I can feel Salvo's eyes on me and I know that at this moment he's not thinking about my body. He's thinking about Abano Terme. I have to give him the right message, keep him hanging until I've had a chance to speak to Italia.

The band's playing 'A Whiter Shade of Pale', the perfect slow tune. Salvo's in a corner talking with Emilio Busi, Don Eugenio and Mohammed. As I approach them, four pairs of worried eyes study me.

'Salvo, I'd like to dance.'

It's an order, not an invitation. He hesitates a moment, then remembers the thermal-spa business, smiles and takes my hand, leading me to the centre of the dance floor, which is full of couples. We observe the formalities and dance well apart. But we know we're the best-looking couple and that everyone is looking at us.

Salvo smiles at me.

'This business of the mud-bath treatment at the spa. How do you know about it?'

From my husband, who works for the CIA and is having you followed everywhere. But this isn't the moment to tell you. Maybe after we're married.

'I've a friend who works at the Grand Hotel in Abano and she told me there was a guest from Tripoli. I asked her who it was and she gave me your name. Now hold me a little closer.'

He does so, as little as he can get away with, but at least he does what he's told.

A rational, prudent man.

Laura and Mikey are dancing a few metres away from us. My daughter's eyes are asking a silent question: *Is everything OK with Dad?* Mikey's eyes are two live coals.

Are you furious, Mikey? Because you saw me naked and you rolled down the staircase and I laughed at you? Because you know I'm about to break your beloved mother's heart? Oh, please be angry, Mikey. That's how I want you, wild, losing your senses, so I can take you to a place from which there's no going back. So everything can be settled, tomorrow.

The party's over. The guests have gone off in the motorboats. There are a few of us still left on La Moneta. Myself and Laura, Busi and

Don Eugenio, Mohammed and his four boys, Nico Gerace and, obviously, the Balistreri–Bruseghin family members. Fifteen people in all, going off in little groups to sleep, the Balistreri family in the villa, the guests in the various guest houses.

I'm alone in my room, and Laura's sleeping in the one next to me.

You have to do it, Marlene. You have to read it so that you'll have both William and Salvo in the palm of your hand.

I take it out from under the mattress, open the envelope my husband gave me a few hours ago and slowly read what Italia's written to General Jalloun.

General,

The black African girl found in the cesspit with her daughter in 1962 was killed on the orders of William Hunt. She was a housemaid at Wheelus Field who had stolen a top-secret document from his desk and demanded money for its return. Nadia Al Bakri saw William Hunt with the girl and the baby, but only recently, by pure chance, did she make a connection. Unfortunately, besides telling me, she also told someone else she trusted, who then told William Hunt. He had Nadia killed by his hired hands.

I'm terrified that Laura has heard these words through the wall, even though I've only read them to myself. I go and vomit up everything in my stomach and more.

The well-mannered soldier I've been living with is nothing but a monster.

I need to be cool and clear-headed. That man saved me from prostitution and, most importantly, he is Laura's father. If she knew of this, she'd die. As could William and Salvo.

Very slowly, my brain calms down and starts functioning again.

The plan doesn't have to change. I'll blackmail Italia with the photo, so she won't accuse William of being responsible for those deaths. She'll leave Salvo. I'll leave William. And he'll be eternally grateful to me, as he should be.

I need some air, and go outside. The night's very dark. I see four men underneath one of the beach gazebos: Salvatore, Don Eugenio, Busi and Mohammed. They don't notice me, hidden in the darkness behind another gazebo.

'Is everything ready?' Salvo asks, turning to Mohammed.

'Yes. The Al-Aqsa Mosque in Jerusalem was set fire to recently by a Christian extremist, and the Libyan police have been mobilized round the clock to stop any protest demonstrations by Islamic extremists here. The alert will end tomorrow in the early afternoon and, after three sleepless nights, General Jalloun will send them all home to rest. Tomorrow night, Tripoli will be without a police force.'

'Is General Jalloun on our side?' Emilio Busi asks, puffing out a cloud of his revolting smoke.

'No,' Mohammed replies, 'he's loyal to the Senussi royals. But he's scared. He won't do a thing, He wants to ingratiate himself with the new regime.'

Don Eugenio interrupts in his usual mellifluous tone.

'This sudden trip of attaché Hunt worries me. Are we agreed nevertheless for tomorrow night?'

Busi replies straight away.

'I've already checked with Rome. Our man in SISDE assures me that all the information about us is absolutely secure. Unless something leaks out here in Tripoli . . .'

Mohammed interrupts him. His manner is brusque. He no longer seems to be just Salvo's dogsbody.

'It won't. These junior officers risk being hanged for high treason. And we still haven't given the go-ahead, so, officially, no one knows a thing. William Hunt will have been called away because of the worsening situation in Vietnam.'

'Are we sure about the new leader X?' Busi asks, still uncertain.

Salvo waits a moment, then makes up his mind to speak.

'We met him a few days ago at Abano in Italy. Everything's OK, isn't it, Mohammed?'

So William wasn't kidding. It's all true.

'He's a young man with backbone and grew up in my own tribe. I know his family and we're very good friends.'

'We're not concerned with your family's friendships here, Mohammed, but with this X's future relationship with Italy,' Busi protests.

Salvo replies in that calm tone of his, before Mohammed can get angry.

'Did you know that X is a Juventus fan? He's said that, one day, when he's in power, he'll buy some stock in it. Doesn't that set your mind at rest?'

But Busi's in no mood for jokes.

'Great, we can all go together and watch matches with him. But, for the moment, I think we should stick very close to him.'

'Of course,' Mohammed replies curtly, 'I'm leaving for Benghazi tomorrow, and tomorrow night I'll be right at his side.'

Don Eugenio breaks in again.

'It's essential to avoid any bloodshed.'

'Yes, that way the West will confine itself to working out who the leader is and what he's thinking,' Busi adds. 'I know my fellow Party members. They'll be sceptical to begin with, but they'll support the change if there's no violence.'

Don Eugenio sighs. He's playing the part of the clergyman, which I suspect is difficult for him.

'We seem to be forgetting about God, gentlemen. I was talking about that, not about what the politicians want.'

Mohammed's tone is icy. He can't disguise his scorn.

'There'll be no deaths, gentlemen. Perhaps several old men might die of fright and a few of the powerful of a broken heart, but no

Libyan would give his life for this pro-Israeli and pro-American king.'

The four men get up and disappear. If I had any doubts about William's story, they have vanished.

I go back to my room and take out the photo of Salvo at Abano Terme with this Gaddafi they call X and think of the face he'll make when he sees it. But William said to show it to Italia. And that's what I'll do, not only for William's sake, but for mine.

Tomorrow I'll explain to Italia what Salvo's got himself into. Although now I've heard the conspirators myself, I feel doubt creeping up on me.

Italia's a dyed-in-the-wool fascist and a stupid idealist. In other words, she's mad. I don't want to take even the minimum risk that she's so mad she'd turn Salvo in and have him shot. But my head's clear, and I can see how I can deal with this eventuality. I take the pair of nail scissors from my vanity case and cut the photograph in half. Now Salvo's in front of the sign for the Grand Hotel in Abano Terme, the *Corriere della sera* for 28 August in his pocket, his right hand shaking another hand. But the owner of that hand is in the other half of the photograph.

I'll show her both halves, but give her only the half with Gaddafi, and the half with Salvo I'll hold on to. That way, whatever happens will be up to me. And whatever happens to everyone else.

7 Past Becomes Present

Sunday, 7 August 2011

Rome

Balistreri hadn't slept a wink. The man with the severed ear who Linda saw with Melania Druc a few days earlier in Tripoli, and Tanja Druc's missing fingertip, have brought together two events separated by almost half a century.

He couldn't stay shut in his office smoking and waiting for life to end any more. That option had been taken away from him.

Taken away deliberately. Otherwise, why cut off the tip of a little girl's finger after shooting her?

Corvu had found the name of the religious house where Monsignor Pizza stayed when he was in Rome, and early in the morning Balistreri set off there, limping on his painful knee.

He crossed the Sant'Angelo bridge over the Tiber to the famous castle and again saw an image of his life as a boat running smoothly over calm waters towards the sea. But now there was an unnatural current opposing him, putting a stop to that peaceful end. And it was unnatural, because instead of carrying him towards the river mouth and the sea it was dragging him back against the current towards its distant source in a harsh, wild and violent country from which he'd escaped and which he had then buried away in his memory.

He stepped into the narrow alleyways south of Borgo Pio behind the castle, which were full of locals and tourists, then came to the hostel in the vast square dominated by the sunlit cupola of St Peter's. Nearby was the headquarters of the IOR, the Vatican Bank, and in the surrounding few square kilometres stood the world's greatest and most enduring power.

The power of fear that replaced the power of reason. A power that's tolerated everything over the centuries in the name of faith. Even men like Monsignor Eugenio Pizza.

The man at the hostel desk was a polite young priest.

'Monsignor Pizza's in his room. He's had breakfast and I think he's now in prayer before going out.'

'I'm an old friend. Do you think you could tell him I'm here?'

While the man delivered his message over the phone – *There's a Signor Michele Balistreri here to see you, Monsignor* – he wondered how Don Eugenio would react.

He's a very intelligent man. He knows it's the head of Homicide that wants to see him and he'll ask me to come up.

The young priest smiled at Balistreri.

'The Monsignor's waiting for you in his room.'

The religious hostel was clean and silent. Balistreri went up in the lift to the second floor and Don Eugenio opened the door before he could even knock.

'Come in, Michele. Please sit down. I'm sorry, there's not much space. It's a very small room.'

The man facing him had the same smooth skin and rosy complexion he'd had all those years ago. The same intelligent light blue eyes. The same excessive friendliness. But the untroubled façade was betrayed by a look Balistreri had come to know well during his thirty years as a cop.

Perhaps it's my visit. Perhaps Linda's.

The little room was simply furnished: wardrobe, desk, bed. A prie-dieu underneath a crucifix. Pizza's clerical dress was almost threadbare.

A humble servant of God, espouser of charitable causes.

But Balistreri was well acquainted with this man and knew how deceptive appearances could be. Here was an old man, his hair now white, with the face of a child and that same benevolent look. But he was also the man who had attempted to molest Nico and who had been there on La Moneta that terrible day Italia had died.

All that stands between him and evil is a wall of thin air.

'There's only one chair,' he said, pointing to it as he went towards the bed.

Balistreri sat down. Those light blue eyes were following him, and Balistreri again felt himself back with Nico at their school desks in front of the teacher.

'Out with it, Michele. Is this an official visit? Should I call my lawyer, perhaps?'

Balistreri caught the hint of anxiety in the typical sarcasm of his old religious teacher. Monsignor Pizza wasn't at ease; he was just keeping himself under control.

'Not yet, Monsignor. I've nothing to accuse you with. Today, that is. Only some questions.'

'I'm all ears, Michele.'

The same words Don Eugenio had used in Tripoli when his father Salvatore had made him confess so he could take communion.

I'm all ears, Michele.

'Yesterday Linda Nardi came to see you. She asked you two questions. One about Melania Druc and one about an IOR account. But you didn't answer them.'

Don Eugenio seemed not the least concerned.

'Are you going to ask me them again, Michele? Is there an investigation underway?'

His tone was as calm as ever.

'There's no investigation. Even though Domnica Panu died just after Linda Nardi had spoken with you.'

An expert fighter, Don Eugenio took the blow, but a slight shadow, like a very faint breath of air, passed across his face.

A tiny ripple across a calm sea. The cold wind of fear.

Then Don Eugenio nodded, as if following his own thoughts.

'I don't remember Signorina Nardi mentioning that name. But what is it you want to ask me, Michele?'

'Who was at your table on that cruise the night Melania Druc and her daughter died?'

'Linda Nardi hasn't told you? She was there, as I'm sure you know.'

Balistreri let that go.

I'm no longer Michelino, and you're no longer my religion teacher.

'Perhaps she did, but I'd prefer to hear it directly from you, Monsignore.'

Don Eugenio sighed and nodded, as if he were still dealing with Michelino, his most unruly pupil. But it was also the sigh of someone having to reveal something he'd prefer not to.

'There was myself, Senator Busi, Mohammed Al Bakri . . . and your father, of course.'

Don Eugenio studied him with his kindly eyes. Linda had already told him that his father was there, almost apologetically. But coming from Don Eugenio, the same words were pure poison. And this time the taunt found its target. Balistreri's voice was angry.

'My father's not even supposed to set foot in Italy!'

Keep calm, Michele, this man's known you since you were a boy. He knows how to stop you thinking about things; he only has to touch your wounds.

'Really, Michele? I didn't know that he'd ever been expelled.'

The unruffled response, soft voice and provocative tone, as well as his memories, were making him lose focus.

I kicked him out, with that photograph that came from PO Box 150870 in Tripoli in 1983. The photograph of him with Gaddafi at Abano Terme just before the coup d'état.

Balistreri tried to control himself. But what was rising up in him was too strong to control.

'And why were you all together there?' he asked.

Don Eugenio smiled softly.

'We're all old friends, Michele, as you know. It was business, pleasure – the usual things.'

Balistreri couldn't contain himself any longer and made one of those mistakes he always taught less experienced investigators to avoid.

'Which required the use of foreign SIM cards to communicate, of course.'

The Monsignor remained silent, lost in his thoughts. But now there was something that really did look like fear at the back of those light blue eyes. His gaze turned back to Balistreri. He was no longer smiling.

'But that's no business of yours, Michele. And there's nothing illegal about it.'

'Except that a young woman and her daughter were killed on that cruise.'

For a moment Don Eugenio's jaw dropped, but he was soon in control of himself.

'That's not what I've heard, Michele. Rather, it was a murder and a suicide. Perhaps the poor young woman was depressed . . .'

Balistreri remembered the two-year-old's missing finger, and then Nico with his shorts pulled down in front of this priest. He got up, took the paper knife off the desk and went up to Don Eugenio, who sat back further on the bed.

'There was no suicide, Monsignore. Melania Druc wasn't depressed, she was frightened. Linda Nardi told me so, because she'd spoken to her shortly before she died. Both she and Domnica Panu had come to Italy via Porte Aperte. And Melania was on that ship thanks to a reference from Porte Aperte!'

Now Balistreri could clearly see the fear in those eyes. Monsignor Eugenio Pizza realized who he was dealing with. And it wasn't Deputy Assistant Police Chief Michele Balistreri, respected head of Homicide, but the young boy from all those years ago.

Young Mikey and his friends in the MANK.

'Domnica told Linda Nardi that Melania Druc's lover was on board that ship, and Linda had also seen Melania in Tripoli a few days before. She was with a sixty-year-old Libyan man who people were saying was behind the Zawiya massacre and the death of General Younis. Now listen, priest, you tell me the truth or I'll do to you today what Ahmed wanted to do to you all those years ago.'

You remember that knife?

Don Eugenio was petrified. But he wasn't looking at Balistreri, nor at the paper knife.

He's struggling between two different fears. And the other is far stronger than the paper knife.

'I can't,' he whispered feebly.

That 'I can't', spoken by such a powerful man with a paper knife at his throat was both a confession and an undeniable concealment of the truth.

The priest looked at Balistreri, his blue eyes full of fear.

'You managed to save yourself that time, Michele. Now you either forget this, or this time you will die.'

But what he said didn't seem like a threat, and it was this that really made Balistreri fearful.

It's a fear that comes from a long way back in time.

He went out, leaving the paper knife on the table.

Tripoli, La Moneta, Sunday, 31 August 1969

Mikey Balistreri

There are certain things no one would do. But I'm the son of that no one. These festivities for my father's birthday, less than one month after Nadia Al Bakri's death, are absurd, as is Marlene Hunt's presence on the island. All she wants is to destroy my parents' marriage, and she does nothing to hide it. I saw them dancing together last night, my father and that *gahba* talking softly to each other as if my mother weren't there.

I thought about it all night, a night without sleep, a night without dreams. At first light I can't stand being in bed any more. While Alberto's still asleep, I get up and go out into the warm mist, which promises another blistering day.

My mother's alone on the veranda, sitting on the swing seat with an almost empty bottle of whisky and an ashtray full of cigarette ends. She must have spent the whole night out here. I sit close by her and, for a while, we're silent. The only sound is that of the tide in the early dawn. Lying next to her is Nietzsche's *Beyond Good and Evil*. A sheet of squared paper is sticking out of the last pages.

'Are those my notes on Nadia's death?'

Italia nods. I'm sure she remembers her promise to look at them. Her silence confirms it. It's strange she hasn't kept her promise.

'Did you manage to check the alibis of the grown-ups for that morning?'

A shadow crosses her face.

'The matter was closed after Jamaal's suicide, Mikey.'

'So you think Jamaal was guilty as well? Just because he committed suicide?'

'No, not because of that. If someone takes their own life, then people think they're either mad or guilty.'

'Jamaal didn't kill Nadia, Mamma.'

She gazes out to sea. It looks as if she is following a train of thought, or a seagull.

'Of course he didn't. He was just mad.'

'Or else, he was neither mad nor guilty.'

Italia turns to look at me, dark rings in her pale face. Her eyes have a worried look.

'Michele, you must promise me something.'

I already know what she's going to ask.

'Do I have to make you a promise to show you I love you, Mamma?'

She gives me a sweet smile, her hand tracing out the movement of a caress in the air, but she stops halfway, as if something's blocking her, something in the air that separated her from me.

'No, I know you love me. But you must show more love for yourself, Michele. You're not the loser your father says you are, nor are you the crazy hero your Uncle Toni was. And now you have Laura, and I know you're perfect together.'

But this isn't enough for me. There's no peace without the truth.

'Mamma, Nadia will never get any justice . . .'

She smiles at me again. The same sweet smile as when she sang me that mournful song to get me to sleep when I was tiny. Now I want to go back to sleep on the swing seat with my head resting on Italia's shoulders, as I did when I was a child. But I'm nineteen and that time's long past.

Sunday, 7 August 2011

Rome

It had seem'd to Linda Nardi that the night would never end. The meeting with Michele Balistreri in police headquarters had brought only ugly memories and negative feelings. One was that he wouldn't be able to open an investigation and confront such powerful men.

Besides, there was no concrete proof. Monsignor Pizza and Senator Busi were part of an untouchable circle, and neither ELCON nor the IOR could be so much as touched by the Italian justice system, it was so concerned with protecting civil liberties.

But I'm not Italian justice.

At seven in the morning she woke Giulia Piccolo, who was sleeping on the sofa.

'We have to find out who's really behind that Swiss consortium and GB Investments in Luxembourg and behind Charity Investments in Dubai.'

Giulia lifted her head.

'No, Linda, give it a rest. We've had three deaths, and Balistreri's right. Leave it to the police now.'

'The police won't be able to discover who it is that controls

ELCON's shareholders – they'd need a warrant signed by a judge, an international letter rogatory to Dubai and also one to Luxembourg. The two of us can do it much quicker.'

Giulia was now wide awake and totally against the idea.

'Listen to me, Linda. First let's find the woman that Domnica Panu told you about, the one they call *Fratello*.'

'What use would that be, Giulia? Even if we did find her, we'd only be where we were before. Going nowhere fast.'

Giulia sighed.

'So what do you want to do? I don't think my hacker friend's going to be much help this time.'

'Come with me to Lugano. There's a flight at nine. Let's get going.'

Arriving at headquarters, Balistreri found Corvu in his office. He had the red eyes of someone who had worked all night, and his crumpled clothes were those he had been wearing the day before. Balistreri told him about the conversation he'd just had with Monsignor Eugenio Pizza. But only insofar as it had to do with the present investigation. He avoided mentioning Libya, his father, Nadia's missing fingertip and the man with the severed ear. If he'd done so, he'd have been forced to move on to other investigations and he had no intention of doing that right now.

Corvu heard him out. At the end, he drew the obvious conclusion.

'After Linda's visit, perhaps the Monsignor told someone she was going to see Domnica Panu. It was probably Melania Druc's lover.'

'I worked that out by myself, Corvu,' Balistreri shot back rudely. 'Only we don't know who he is.'

Corvu smiled and handed him a photograph.

'Perhaps we do. My Secret Service friends sent me this.'

The shot showed Melania Druc getting out of a luxury saloon with dark windows outside a small main door in a square in Rome's historic centre.

'That car's part of the escort of Gruppo Italia's chairman, Senator Emilio Busi, which is why they were following it. As you know, the Secret Service keeps tabs on everyone, even itself.'

Balistreri nodded. But it wasn't enough.

'Have you identified which apartment she was going into?'

Corvu shook his head.

'There are ten of them, and not a single name on the entry phone.'

'Check the deeds in the land registry to find out who owns them. Something's bound to come up.'

But Corvu had been working through the night.

'Already done that. The whole block's owned by Gruppo Italia and all the apartments are rented out at ridiculous figures. But not one of them to Melania Druc.'

Balistreri knew that Corvu was doing exceptional work, and he should have congratulated him. But his mood was dark and his thoughts were still upsetting him.

'The trouble is, Corvu, that none of this proves that Melania was Busi's lover, nor that he had anything to do with the deaths of her and her little girl.'

Corvu replied patiently.

'But, Commissario, perhaps this photograph explains why there's no trace of Melania Druc anywhere in Italy in seven years.'

Balistreri lit a cigarette to give himself time to think.

Corvu's right. If Melania was Emilio Busi's lover, he had every reason to keep her well hidden. Yes, I have to move on this, right now.

'Get me Senator Busi's number, Corvu.'

The young Sardinian wanted to tell him *Wait, it's too soon*, but the look on Balistreri's face told him not to.

Alone, Balistreri recalled Domnica Panu's words on Linda's recording.

Melania was educated, a degree in political science and communication. But in my mind she's nothing more than an escort.

He started to look for the bachelor's thesis that Corvu had unsuccessfully tried to get him to read. He found it at the bottom of a drawer where he'd tucked it, thinking it was pointless to look at it.

But the title of the thesis immediately caught his attention: *Large-scale Public Works and the Criminal Underworld in Italy.*

He began to read. It was a serious study, the result of dedicated research. Public tenders falsified with expertise and skill, repeated contact between public officials and entrepreneurs, connections between entrepreneurs and the Mafia, the 'Ndrangheta and the Camorra. Things that everyone talked about, but of which Melania Druc had gone to great lengths to collect official data over the last twenty years, and not only in Italy. Nothing original perhaps, but the thesis left no doubt.

This wasn't an escort who'd entrapped a wealthy man. Perhaps she was just a deluded idealist who thought she could cure evil with love.

Hidden in the fold of the last page was a photograph of Melania in front of St Peter's with little Tanja in her arms. On the back of the photograph, which was perhaps never given because it was too compromising, was a handwritten dedication.

To Emilio, with all our love from Melania and Tanja.

Melania Druc had told Domnica Panu that Tanja's father was also on the ship. And Senator Emilio Busi had been on that ship. And it was him in the dedication.

Balistreri remembered the article in which, for the first time, Busi had voiced doubts over the possibility of constructing a bridge across the Straits of Messina.

Had Melania been trying to convince him? Perhaps yes, perhaps no.

His acid reflux was rising and burning his gut.

Four men who'll stop at nothing have a project. An idealistic and inflexible young woman tries to stop them. The young woman dies.

Those four men were on the cruise ship between Elba and Civitavecchia.

Those four men were on La Moneta the day Italia died. With them, too, was a boy who later had part of his ear severed. And Nadia Al Bakri's killers were also there. They were all there.

Tripoli, La Moneta, Sunday, 31 August 1969

Mikey Balistreri

Around eight, Marlene joins us on the veranda. She's in running vest, shorts and trainers, ready for her jog. Her tanned complexion and black hair, swept back in a long ponytail, contrast with my mother's paleness. Italia greets her unusually politely.

'May I give William a call?' Marlene asks.

'Of course. Mikey, show Marlene to Papa's study, where she won't be disturbed.'

I show her the way. As we enter the study, I feel her breast brush against my arm. Did she do it on purpose, I wonder. The *gahba* smiles at me.

'Thanks, Mikey. Now, a moment of privacy, please. You know, things between a man and his wife . . .'

I leave her in the study and go back to the veranda. I can still feel the tip of her nipple on my arm. I want to strike her with my fists. Or strike myself.

You're just an oversexed little boy. She can do whatever she wants with you.

Italia's smoking in silence, her eyes hidden behind her large sunglasses, her body covered by a long kaftan. Her exposed arms are very thin and white, her veins showing through.

'What are you going to do today, Mamma?'

'I'll go up to the cliff to read in a while.'

'Aren't you coming with us to lunch at the Underwater Club?'

'No, Mikey. I'd rather stay here.'

This self-imposed solitude is the protective shell around her sadness. I want to say something to her, but I don't know what. While I'm trying to think of something, Laura comes out. Her tired eyes show she's slept badly. Too many thoughts, the same as me.

Our parents' marriages are falling apart.

She kisses Italia first, then me. I'm about to say something to her, to ask her help, when Marlene comes back from the study. Her face is tense, as if she's made an important decision.

'Italia, I need to talk to you.'

I hold my breath. It's the most surprising request I can imagine. And yet my mother seems unsurprised. She replies in the friendliest manner I've ever seen her use with Marlene.

'You can come with me to the cliff top, if you like.'

Marlene looks at Laura, who's evidently concerned. As am I.

'I'm going to do my hour of jogging and then I promised I'd spend the morning with Laura on the beach.'

'Well, then we can speak when you've come back from lunch at the Underwater Club,' my mother offers.

I could see that Marlene wanted to talk to my mother before she talked to William again.

'William's expecting me at Wheelus at two thirty, when he's back in Tripoli.'

My mother doesn't seem put out at all. Perhaps she, too, wants to clear up something she can no longer put off.

'Then let's do this, Marlene. I'm going up to the cliff top now, but I'll be back by half past twelve. I've already asked Farid to stay here and grill some fish for me. If you like, we could eat together while the others are at the club and then, when they come back, you can go and meet your husband.'

Marlene smiles back at her. She, too, is being unusually accommodating.

'Thank you, Italia. I really appreciate it.'

They're sharpening swords for the duel. But this isn't a film, young Mikey.

Marlene goes off for her jog and Laura goes to the beach. I go to my father's study and see the notepad by the phone. There's nothing written on the top sheet, but I check the wastepaper basket. There's a single ball of paper inside. I open it out and find a line of numbers scribbled on it.

Do you want to be a policeman when you grow up, Mikey?

I dial the number. A voice in English answers; it's the switchboard of Benghazi's military airport. I put the receiver down and questions start to crowd my mind.

William Hunt's in Benghazi. Marlene's just called him there. But what has he gone there to do?

I go back to the veranda, having made up my mind to speak to my mother. But it's too late. I can see her walking to the rear of the villa where the path dividing the island starts. Her pale skin's protected by a hat, sunglasses and the long kaftan.

The image of the sad queen.

Sunday, 7 August 2011

Rome

Corvu came back a few minutes later with the number of Gruppo
Italia's switchboard, but getting through to its chairman, Senator
Emilio Busi, was much more difficult than reaching Monsignor
Pizza.

On the phone, his personal assistant, Beatrice Armellini, sounded
like a cross between a television announcer and a rigid military chief.
Only by mentioning what had happened on the cruise ship and by
resorting to a veiled threat to bring the senator to the Flying Squad
offices was Balistreri able to arrange a brief interview. But he had to
be there within half an hour at the most.

Balistreri had a driver take him. Gruppo Italia's front offices were
located in an eighteenth-century building behind Piazza Navona. Its
façade was dominated by a grandiose main door below an architrave.
In that mass of friezes, marble columns and capitals, Emilio Busi ran
an economic empire with the light but sure hand that enabled him to
look nonchalantly and from on high at the comings and goings of
prime ministers, governments and parliaments.

Emilio Busi wasn't one of the many politicians who waste time winning a handful of votes, or who exploit their momentary power for personal gain and sooner or later end up on the scrapheap or in prison. Busi was at the centre of political, economic and media power, he knew the system inside out and he dominated it with the astute and cynical ease of a puppetmaster who plays at making it seem as if the puppets are playing their part. He hadn't appeared on television for years and only occasionally granted an interview to a newspaper, as he had done a few days earlier with *Il Domani*.

A security guard opened the inside gate, which led on to a huge rectangular courtyard bordered on three sides by arcades. In the middle were the remains of ancient statues and a fountain. A doorman in a dark blue uniform took Balistreri to reception, where ancient and modern were blended with great taste, then to the panelled lift, which had a red seat. He turned the key to the top floor and pressed the button.

Another doorman met him at the other end and pointed to a long corridor with walls and ceilings decorated by sixteenth- and seventeenth-century artists. At every turn there was another desk with a doorman to show him the way.

The last man took him across the council chamber, a room as large as a tennis court with a marble floor, a frescoed ceiling and walls covered in a series of paintings, tapestries and mirrors that would not have disgraced the Louvre.

Finally, the man showed him into a small waiting room, all wood panelled, with sofas upholstered in alcantara, and beautiful photographs of Rome on the walls.

The person with whom he had spoken on the telephone greeted him with a cold professional smile.

'Beatrice Armellini. I'm the chairman's assistant.'

She was a splendid woman of about thirty-five, as smart as the furnishings: her black hair was rolled into a chignon, her spotless iron-grey suit a discreet but slightly teasing cover for an impressive figure that not even a nun's habit could have totally deadened. Glasses in a grey frame completed the impression of refinement.

Balistreri thought he'd seen her somewhere before, but couldn't remember where.

'The senator's very busy, Commissario. He can only see you for a few minutes.'

Balistreri followed Beatrice into the large, beautifully furnished office. The window that took up almost an entire wall framed a spectacular view of Piazza Navona's rooftops with St Peter's cupola on one side and the Roman Forums on the other.

When they entered, Gruppo Italia's chairman was on his feet with his back to them, watching a newsflash about Libya on a large plasma screen. He didn't turn round. NATO was dropping bombs on Tripoli.

Balistreri saw a transformation in Emilio Busi that wasn't there in Don Eugenio. He'd already seen a first change in 1983, but now the makeover was complete.

He'd first known Emilio Busi as a young man, when he dressed in the most appalling mismatch of clothing and smoked hideous plain-tipped Nazionali cigarettes. His once unruly and uncombed hair was now very short and grey. His dress was in keeping with the place and his role in it. No more horrendous short-sleeved check shirts over a white vest, no high-waisted, shapeless trousers, no more short socks and worn-out moccasins. Busi now sported a Marinella tie, Church's shoes and a Rolex on his wrist. His cigarettes were no longer Nazionali but long, slim Dunhills. Over the years he had become a very powerful man, with longstanding links to the Left, new links on the Right and, via Monsignor Pizza, with the Vatican. There was not a large-scale work financed from public coffers that didn't cross his desk.

A man for whom olives were of no use at all.

Only at the end of the news item did Busi turn off the sound and face Balistreri. Neither man smiled. Nor did they shake hands.

'Commissario Balistreri. I didn't think we'd meet again. I imagine you're happy they're dropping bombs on Gaddafi.'

It was a cruel, sarcastic remark from a man who knew very well that the other man's mother had died a few hours before Gaddafi came to power.

And perhaps because of it.

Balistreri replied in the same vein.

'Everything has to end, sooner or later, Senator. Even the Communism that you admired so much . . .'

Busi made a brief gesture with his hand, as if to brush away an insect as annoying as the memory.

'Communism was a stupid idea, even if it was necessary at a certain time to get rid of that fascist. It's a world where the best rule and others accept it or disappear. After 1989 it no longer served its purpose. Anyway, none of this has any importance. What did you want to see me about so urgently?'

'Melania and Tanja Druc,' replied Balistreri curtly.

Busi gestured for him to sit in one of the luxurious armchairs. His face was inscrutable, a mixture of cynicism and toughness, but the mention of those two names had created a tension that deepened the furrows in his brow.

Fear, remorse, pain?

'Fire away, Balistreri. I can only reply to things I judge to be relevant.'

Busi wasn't even bothering to put up a front. He didn't need to. He was in the circle of the untouchables. A circle inside which everyone knew everyone else and everyone helped each other out. The same schools, the same gyms and clubs, the same parties and, in some cases, the same churches.

'Did you know Melania Druc?'

Busi shut up like a clam. But, unexpectedly, faced with a question to which he could have replied *And who is she?*, what Balistreri read in the senator's features wasn't reticence or fear. It was anger.

He handed him Melania Druc's bachelor's thesis.

'The title page is enough, Senator. Although I think you already know what it says.'

Busi studied it for a few seconds, then handed it back. His wrinkled hand was that of an old man, and was shaking slightly. Balistreri produced the photograph of Melania and Tanja in front of St Peter's. He handed it over and Busi studied it carefully.

'Do please turn it over, Senator. It's addressed to you.'

To Emilio, with all our love from Melania and Tanja.

The senator's lips trembled. But he immediately checked himself and gave the photograph back. Again, he said nothing. But that silence didn't deny a thing; it was only the silence of a man who for the first time in his life finds himself without anything to say.

'Senator, I'm opening an investigation into a homicide. And the first thing I'm going to do is ask for a comparison of the little girl's DNA and yours.'

Busi shrugged, as if this were completely irrelevant.

'Commissario, if I oppose this, you won't even get an investigation started.'

Balistreri ignored the threat. He knew that the photograph and its dedication had shaken Busi, and he wanted to push home his advantage.

'Melania Druc died because she opposed the plans of someone who doesn't like to be stopped. Does that remind you of anyone, Senator?'

Busi remained silent for some time. When he eventually spoke, his voice was less certain than usual.

'The past usually helps us to understand the present. But not in this case. You'd do well to accept that fact.'

Balistreri tried to contain his anger.

'Senator, my mother died in 1969. It's out of time and out of my jurisdiction. But not the deaths of Melania and Tanja Druc. If you had nothing to do with it, then tell me who is responsible. One of those men you speak to when you use those foreign SIM cards, I imagine.'

Busi lit a long, slim cigarette with his Dunhill lighter.

'Balistreri, you should have grown up by now. Please stop chasing these ghosts from the past.'

Balistreri looked him right in the eyes.

'A few days ago Linda Nardi saw Melania at the Hotel Rixos in Tripoli. She was with a man who had a severed ear. Was he a ghost, Senator?'

Emilio Busi turned pale, now showing all of his sixty-six years. A spider's web of lines scored his face, and his ice-cold eyes closed in the effort to suppress something.

Regret, anger, fear, pain.

Finally, his lips moved in a whisper that would never have left his mouth in the past and would never again.

'Balistreri, you don't understand. You haven't understood for forty years. There are businessmen, and then there are killers. Have you still not got over the desire to get yourself killed?'

The chairman of Gruppo Italia had recovered his icy calm. He pressed a button on his desk and his assistant immediately came into the room.

'Commissario Balistreri is leaving, Beatrice. Would you see him out?'

Balistreri got up. After what Busi had said, he was now certain. *Everything started on that day.*

Tripoli, La Moneta, 31 August 1969

Mikey Balistreri

I hang around on the swing seat on the veranda and, over the next hour, everyone comes out in little groups. First Alberto, Nico, Ahmed and Karim. Then Grandad, Papa, Mohammed, Don Eugenio and Emilio Busi. Farid and Salim appear last, with tired, red eyes that indicate they've only just got up after a few hours' sleep. The day before, they had ferried the guests back in the two motorboats until late.

Breakfast takes place in an unreal silence, as if each of us were there alone for a celebration that wasn't a celebration and should never have taken place.

As soon as breakfast is finished, the grown-ups set off for Tripoli in one of the two motorboats. Grandad, Papa and Don Eugenio have to go to Mass, Mohammed to the office and Busi to the Italian embassy.

'Please make sure you're at the Underwater Club on time,' my father says.

He says this to Alberto, naturally.

The son he can trust.

We boys start to take the gazebos down. We want to finish before the sun becomes too strong.

Marlene comes back from her jog straight after they leave, almost as if she wanted to avoid my father. She joins Laura and they talk as they walk along the water's edge. It doesn't look like an easy conversation.

A storm also seems to be brewing in the Hunt household.

You have to tell her, Laura. Tell her to leave my father alone.

We all pull together and, by eleven, the gazebos are dismantled and stored aboard Farid and Salim's large Zodiac rubber dinghy. Now there's nothing more to do until lunchtime.

'Why don't we all go fishing?' Salim suggests. 'We'll show you a new place that me and Farid found.'

'I have to stay and cook for Signora Italia and Signora Marlene,' says Farid.

'I want to stay here on the beach. I have to study,' Alberto says.

The four of us in the MANK organization look at one another. By now, I can't bear the atmosphere on La Moneta any longer.

'OK, Salim, we're up for it.'

I'm still the head of the organization. Nico, Ahmed and Karim make no objection. They never do.

Sunday, 7 August 2011

Lugano

The flight from Fiumicino took an hour. From Lugano's tiny airport, Linda and Giulia quickly arrived in Collina d'Oro by taxi. Everything there was perfect, clean and calm. Low houses nestled in the greenery and below them lay the lake.

They had the taxi stop outside the address shown on ELCON's memorandum of association, which Linda had photocopied in Gabriele, Cascio's office.

'OK, Giulia, you stay here. If I don't come out in half an hour, you come in and get me out the Piccolo way.'

'So we can end up eating chocolate in a Swiss prison?'

Linda touched her arm.

'It's a civilized country. They won't treat us badly.'

The office was in a small, single-storey villa, very simple. There was no ELCON sign, only a plaque below the bell, which read 'Certified Accounting Associates'.

Linda rang the bell and the door was opened by a middle-aged lady who must have been the secretary.

'Good morning. How may I help?' she asked.

Linda showed her the photocopy of the consortium's memorandum of association.

'I'm from GB Investments in Luxembourg. I need to speak with whoever deals with ELCON's accounts in Nairobi.'

The lady looked puzzled and Linda added the magic words.

'It's a highly confidential matter.'

The lady thought for a moment. She wasn't prepared to make the decision herself.

'We only see people by appointment.'

Linda adopted a serious tone.

'Something important is happening in Italy.'

'Very well, take a seat. I'll call Signor Milani right away.'

She showed Linda into a little lounge with a table and four chairs. Signor Milani arrived a few minutes later, a pleasant man of about forty and very self-confident.

All the better. It'll make it easier.

'What can I do for you, Signorina . . .'

'Nardi, Linda Nardi.'

She showed him her passport before he could ask for it. Signor Milani examined it, comparing the photograph with her face.

He handed the document back and smiled at her. She returned the smile; he could interpret it as he wished.

'And so, Signorina Nardi, what is this about?'

Linda spoke in a low voice.

'The judiciary in Luxembourg have asked us for the names of the real owners of the company. It seems there's been a request by the Italian Guardia di Finanza.'

Milani looked at her, at a loss.

'I don't understand . . .'

'We have our sources, Signor Milani,' said Linda conspiratorially. 'The Guardia di Finanza have been investigating the IOR for some time. And what's come out is that there have been several payments by ELCON to a certain Monsignore.'

Milani turned pale. As he kept the accounts, he couldn't be unaware of the payments.

'An international letter rogatory's been sent . . .' Linda added casually.

Milani was now sufficiently alarmed and confused.

'Signorina Nardi, I can't possibly discuss these matters with you without the authorization of GB Investments. You understand, we have to observe confidentiality. I don't know who you represent.'

Linda gave him an encouraging smile, no longer so difficult to interpret. Then she tried her bluff, as Angelo Dioguardi had taught her in poker all those years ago.

The more impossible it sounds, the more credible it is.

'You can call Giacomo Busi directly. He's the one who sent me.'

Milani was speechless. Linda knew she had hit the bull's-eye. 'Give me five minutes to make a call.'

Milani got up and left the room. Linda sneaked out immediately after him.

'I'm going out to have a cigarette,' she told the secretary.

As soon as she was out, she got into the taxi, where Giulia Piccolo was waiting for her.

'Airport, please!' she ordered the driver.

Giulia looked at her.

Linda smiled.

'Bang on target.'

Rome

Beatrice Armellini accompanied Balistreri to the main entrance.

'Commissario Balistreri, I have to speak with you. But not here, if you follow . . .'

'Would you like to come to my office later on?'

She shook her head.

'That's not the right place, Commissario. For the very same reasons.'

'Then you say where.'

Beatrice Armellini took off her glasses and smiled. Once again, Balistreri had the impression he'd seen that smile before.

'This needs privacy, Commissario. If you don't find it too awkward a proposition, I'd suggest a drink at the Sky Suite. I have a dinner engagement earlier, but we could meet there later on.'

Balistreri had heard of the reputation of the new establishment on top of the Janiculum. It was the most fashionable and pricey in Rome; you could drink and dance on its panoramic terrace or stay the night in its magnificent suites, all of which had views over the city.

Definitely a place for confidences.

Balistreri knew that it was rash to accept, but past and present were coalescing and he couldn't resist.

He nodded to Beatrice Armellini.

'I'll see you there.'

Off he went, on foot among the tourists. It was hot, very hot.

Tripoli, La Moneta, Sunday, 31 August 1969

Mikey Balistreri

We're a little late getting back to La Moneta: it's just after twelve thirty. Laura and Alberto are already waiting on the jetty, Farid beside them. Salim brings the motorboat up next to the dinghy and Laura and Alberto step quickly on board.

'Has Mamma come back?' I ask Alberto.

'Yes, I saw her a few minutes ago, coming down the path to the villa.'

'And she's going to stay here?'

'I haven't spoken to her, Mikey. We were already out here waiting for you on the beach when she came back.'

I catch Laura's eye. She's definitely upset, but she gives me a silent warning to keep quiet.

Let them talk between themselves. We can't do anything.

Alberto loosens the moorings and chivvies me along.

'Come on, Mikey, we're late. It's better if we don't make Papa angry.'

He's been telling me this my whole lifetime: *We mustn't make Papa angry.*

Instead, I get out of the boat and take hold of Laura's hand.

'Can you make do with a bit of fruit?'

She nods and gets out of the boat. Alberto looks at me, resigned, while Salim gets the motor running. They leave to meet the adults at the Underwater Club.

Now Laura and I can talk about our mothers.

We go into the kitchen. At the end of the hall is the lounge. Marlene will be telling my mother how everything's about to change.

Your husband doesn't love you any more, Italia. He wants to live with me. You'd better get used to the idea.

'Do you want to go and eat with Signora Italia and Signora Marlene?' Farid asks, looking anxious.

He's seen the anger in my face. Even Laura's worried, I look so furious. Her answer's also directed at me.

'No, thanks, Farid. Mikey and I'll eat some fruit on the beach.'

We should leave them in peace. We can't interfere.

I know she's right, as she nearly always is. I know we can't do a thing. We go back down to the beach in silence and lie down in the sun, while Farid goes to sit on the veranda in the shade.

It's one o'clock. Laura and I are still on the beach when the phone rings in the kitchen. Farid gets up and goes into the house. He comes out after a few seconds.

'That was Salim on the phone. They're coming back.'

'Already?' I ask.

Farid shrugs and sits down again on the veranda to smoke. Laura's in a deckchair beneath a sun umbrella, while I'm a few metres away on the burning sand under the sun, each of us caught up in our own thoughts, waiting for what fate has in store for us. In silence I watch the coming and going of the two coastguard launches. I know very well what's happened.

Papa's frightened that Marlene will tell Italia the truth. That's why he's rushing back.

Sunday, 7 August 2011

Lugano

'So would you mind telling me how you did it?' Giulia asked as they were waiting for the return flight to Rome.

Linda was thoughtful rather than cheerful. She'd managed it partly due to an intuition, and one that wasn't too difficult to fathom. And it made her think about the arrogance of the men in power in Italy.

'The children of powerful men are often so stupid. They think they're above the law and become reckless. Using their own initials for the name of a company, for example . . .'

'You mean "GB" stands for Giacomo Busi? How on earth did you think of that?'

'It was Domnica Panu who told me that Busi was involved.'

'But that's not true, Linda. You played me the recording of your interview with her and she never mentioned Busi at all.'

'She said that Tanja's father was on the ship. And that Melania had kept his name a secret. It had to be someone really very important who liked young women. That fits Emilio Busi . . .'

'Busi was Tanja's father? At his age?'

Linda smiled.

'Grand old powerful men can always find novel ways of doing things, Giulia. From Viagra to those little suction pumps . . . Also, Domnica mentioned a few other things that made me think of Busi.'

'Such as?'

'That woman *Fratello* – wasn't she a procuress who found clients for Domnica in return for a certain percentage? And she took Domnica to them.'

'What's that got to do with Busi?'

'Do you know how I got to meet him? It was during an inquiry into the very informal methods used by Gruppo Italia to influence its potential clients.'

Giulia looked at Linda as if she had wings and a wand. Then she smiled.

'You make me feel so stupid sometimes, Linda. So now what do we do now?' she asked.

Linda's face clouded over. She was remembering that Clark Gable face with white hair and moustache, the soft but firm manner with which he had both praised and warned her.

You really are overly courageous.

'We now know that Emilio Busi's behind GB Investments in Luxembourg, and that the IOR account's in the name of Monsignor Pizza. That leaves Charity Investments in Dubai. And there was also a man who lives in Dubai at the table on the ship with Busi and Pizza.'

'You never said anything about that. Why not?' Giulia asked, slightly resentful.

'Because his name is Salvatore Balistreri.'

Giulia Piccolo turned pale. She brushed a hand through her highlights, which were now green, and shook her head.

'Linda, there are newspaper articles about Salvatore Balistreri going back years, from before he left Italy in 1983 . . .'

'What articles?'

'He already had the idea back then of constructing that bloody bridge between Calabria and Sicily, a bridge over the Straits of Messina. Perhaps it was idle speculation or malicious gossip, though he was never accused of anything. But there's also objective proof against his four elder brothers in Palermo. They had a leading business in Sicily's earth-moving sector and owned land, betting offices and bars. One of them, the eldest, was put on trial, accused of having links with the Mafia . . . You follow?'

Linda Nardi nodded slowly. She well remembered the grim face Michele Balistreri made whenever she mentioned his father.

The very Michele she had sent packing because he didn't want to shoot anyone any more.

Perhaps this is the last thing I can do before going back to John Kiptanu and my orphans in Kenya. So I can leave without feeling I'm running away.

Out of her purse she took the business card Salvatore Balistreri had given her out on deck between Elba and Civitavecchia. There was a mobile number that began with the prefix 00971: Dubai.

'Don't do it,' Giulia begged her.

Linda smiled at her.

'Giulia, I want to leave Italy for good. But if I leave this business halfway through it would be like running away. I couldn't ever forget that.'

She dialled the number and after a few rings heard a warm voice, a little throaty and a little gravelly.

'Hello . . .' he said in English.

'It's Linda Nardi,' she said simply.

There was a moment's silence.

You can hang up and keep me out of all this. But if I've understood correctly, you won't.

'So I did well to leave you my card, Signorina.'

There was no irony in his voice. And no surprise or irritation either. Perhaps a touch of concern, that was all.

You really are overly courageous.

'I need to talk to you, Signor Balistreri, if you're still in Rome.'

'I am in Rome, but I'm about to go to the airport, I have a flight to Geneva.'

'I'm also about to get on a flight. I'll be in Rome in an hour. Could we meet at Fiumicino?'

'Of course. Where are you coming from?'

Linda had a moment's hesitation, then decided it was better to be cautious.

'From Turin. Where shall I meet you?'

'At Alitalia's Freccia Alata lounge in International Departures. I will see you then.'

Rome

All four of them were on that ship together. Exactly the same as that day on La Moneta.

Balistreri called his brother's mobile. As ever, whether he was in a meeting with a minister or having lunch with his wife and children, Alberto answered on the first ring.

'Michele!'

He hated asking him the question, but there was no avoiding it.

'Is Papa in Italy, Alberto?'

He didn't speak for a moment.

'He's been here for a few days, Michele. He had some urgent business to sort out, but he's leaving today.'

'I think I need to talk to him.'

Alberto again hesitated, but only for a second.

'He's got a flight to Geneva at three o'clock. If you hurry you'll find him in Alitalia's Freccia Alata lounge in International Departures.'

Balistreri went on foot to the Metro to get to Fiumicino, his mind troubled by old ghosts as he walked under the burning sun.

Today's dead are the offspring of yesterday's dead. The explanation lies there.

Tripoli, La Moneta, Sunday, 31 August 1969

Mikey Balistreri

It's just after half past one when I see the motorboat coming from the Underwater Club. The heat's unbearable even over the water, turning the view into a kind of gleaming mirage. Salim's at the helm and from the beach I can see Ahmed going to the bows to help with the mooring. About a hundred metres from the jetty, the motorboat slows down further. A breeze is stirring.

'Should I go?' Farid asks us from the veranda, about fifty metres from the jetty.

Laura and I are much closer.

'We'll deal with it.'

We get up on the jetty and get ready to receive the mooring ropes. While the motorboat is coming to, travelling at less than two knots, I see my father deep in conversation in the bows with Busi and Don Eugenio. He looks drawn, and at a certain point I see his worried eyes looking towards the villa.

I turn to look as well, shading my face with an arm. The villa door's open, and Farid is next to it, talking to my mother, a cigarette between his lips.

She looks at us briefly from behind her dark glasses, her hair in the usual scarf, her body enveloped by the long linen kaftan that leaves her thin white arms bare. A book is sticking out of her pocket, probably Nietzsche.

Without smiling, she raises an arm halfway up in a kind of unfinished greeting. Then she stops, as if she's done all she can. Then she turns and heads off quickly.

Italia doesn't want to see Papa. Not now.

She leaves us all wondering. In those two or three seconds, on that jetty struck by the sea, wind and sun, I can distinctly feel the fear around me. Not just of one person, but of everyone.

They begin to disembark, unloading the food and water. I help for a couple of minutes, but in that silent half-hour waiting on the burning sand I've made up my mind. And that melancholy gesture from my mother has removed any lingering doubts.

I'll take care of the American gahba.

I set off towards the villa. Laura sees me, but says nothing.

Don't do it, Mikey.

But I can't trust her blindly like that. I know she loves me and also that anything I say to Marlene will be useless. But what's driving me is stronger than either reason or love. Farid is still on the veranda next to the door.

'Where's Marlene?' I ask him brusquely.

His coarse features twist in concern. He blocks my path.

He, too, can see I'm crazy.

'I think she's in the bathroom taking a shower before she leaves.'

'I have to speak to her. You stay here.'

I push him rudely aside and enter the villa. I've got no more than two minutes before the others arrive. The door to the guest bathroom is closed. From outside, I can hear the noise of the shower. I knock three times, loudly.

'Yes?' comes Marlene's voice.

'It's me.'

The son of your lover and the woman whose heart you're breaking.

The key turns in the lock and the door opens a hand's breadth. Marlene's wet face stares at me; her body's hidden by the door jamb. The scents of shampoo and body lotion hit me.

Immediately, desire mingles with my anger. It's an unbearable animal desire, made even more unacceptable by the hate I feel for her at this moment.

Her naked body is only twenty centimetres away. Again, I catch the scent of her body lotion.

'I have to speak to you, right now.'

My voice sounds wavering and weak, and this makes me even more angry.

She looks at me with that mocking half-smile of hers.

'I'll be home at three. Now go and take a cold shower. You're far too hot.'

She shuts the door in my face and I make it down just in time to be back on the veranda before the others arrive to eat the now-cold hamburgers. Everyone, that is, except my grandfather. But perhaps he's the one that can tell me what to do.

'Where's Grandad?' I ask Alberto.

My brother's uncharacteristically subdued.

'He preferred to stay at the club. He's waiting for Farid and Salim to come with the gazebos to put in the warehouse.'

I then go up to my father.

'I have to talk to you.'

He doesn't even glance at me.

'Not today, Mikey. Tomorrow.'

But tomorrow will be too late, Papa.

I look for Laura, but she isn't there. I'm alone with myself.

Alone with my anger.

★   ★   ★

Five minutes later, suntanned in a short white skirt and pink T-shirt, looking as beautiful as a goddess, her black hair loose, Marlene Hunt comes out on to the veranda, followed by Farid, who's carrying her luggage, a large, black leather bag with Marilyn Monroe's face on it.

She gestures to my father.

Here, Salvo. As if to a little puppy.

For a moment I have the impression that Papa's about to resist, but he looks afraid and goes over, while I follow behind. I'm prepared for anything, but not the exchange I hear.

I told her everything, Salvo.

You're crazy, Marlene.

Have I heard them right? Or did I imagine it? I'm not sure.

Marlene then goes off to the jetty, where Farid's stowing her bag on the boat. Salim's ready in the rubber dinghy with the gazebos.

Farid helps Marlene get on board.

There's no more time. I have to decide. I can go to my mother on the other side of the island and try to comfort her, or I can go and face my father and threaten to cause a scandal. Or I can follow Marlene Hunt, the real guilty party.

I get into the dinghy. Lots of pairs of eyes are following me, but my mind's made up. I'm going to have it out with the American *gahba*.

Sunday, 7 August 2011

Fiumicino

Linda and Giulia talked the whole flight back. Giulia was worried and thought the meeting was a bad idea. As a good policewoman, she knew that what they were doing was not only illegal but very likely to be dangerous too. But her friendship with Linda outweighed these considerations and when they landed at two in the afternoon she went with her to International Departures.

Linda tried to allay Giulia's fears.

'No one's going to kill me here at the airport, especially not in Alitalia's VIP departure lounge. Go to my place, Giulia, and I'll meet up with you there,' she told her, and went in.

The lounge was quite crowded, but she spotted Salvatore Balistreri immediately, sitting in an armchair reading the *Financial Times*. He was beautifully dressed, as usual, in a blue sports jacket with grey trousers, a white shirt and a midnight-blue tie.

As soon as he saw her, he got up to meet her and shook her hand with a smile. But this handsome elderly gentleman was not interested in her in the way that men like Emilio Busi or Bashir Yared were.

'I'm happy to see you again, Signorina Nardi.'

He seems genuine . . .

Linda forced herself not to lose sight of the facts: this man was a friend of Monsignor Eugenio Pizza and Senator Emilio Busi, both of whom were involved in this business, as was Salvatore Balistreri himself perhaps, according to ELCON's memorandum of association. And all three were on that cruise where Melania and Tanja Druc died.

Linda accepted his offer of an iced tea from the bar and they went to sit down in front of a window where you could see the aeroplanes lined up by the runways. He could see that she was tense.

'You were different on the cruise. Has something happened, Signorina?'

Indeed, Signor Balistreri. Melania and Tanja Druc and Domnica Panu are dead. And I've found that your friends are behind the slush funds and the IOR account. Which just leaves your role in it all.

Linda thought for a moment. Then she decided that there was no other way to approach it than to tell him everything, or *almost* everything.

'Yesterday morning I went to Ostia to meet a certain person.'

He just stared at her, waiting. Despite his cheerful, smiling manner and his courteousness, this old man struck a fear in her that she'd never felt before.

He knows I'm an investigative journalist. Why is he so polite?

'She was a friend of the young woman found dead with her daughter on the cruise,' Linda went on.

Salvatore Balistreri didn't move a muscle, or even frown. Only after a little while did he nod and lean over towards her.

'And why did you go to Ostia to see this woman?'

Linda looked out of the window. An aeroplane was taking off. She imagined herself getting on it, escaping all the horror. But that was precisely what she didn't want to do: run away.

'To find out the truth . . .'

Her voice was faint.

This time he did frown, but not because he didn't understand; rather, the opposite.

He's understood who I am, how I am.

'You suffer a great deal, Signorina Nardi. I feel very sorry for you.'

It was absurd but, despite coming from Salvatore Balistreri, who was probably a very shady businessman, perhaps a Mafioso, even worse, the words managed to sound sincere.

He really is sorry. Perhaps he's sorry he's going to have to kill me.

He bent forwards and smiled at her.

'Come on, tell me why you came on that cruise. Was it to meet Monsignor Pizza?'

Looking into his impenetrable yet understanding eyes in that moment, Linda was convinced that there was no other way of fighting and winning against this man, to see if he really was sincere, than to tell him the truth. Lying to him would only be pointless and perhaps even more dangerous. She decided to tackle him head on, regardless of the consequences.

'It's an ugly business, Signor Balistreri. Would you like to hear about it?'

He poured her out another iced tea.

'Of course, Signorina Nardi. I will listen very closely to what you have to say.'

Linda told him the whole story, starting with the information she had got from Bashir Yared. Then she went on to Nairobi and Gabriele Cascio, the bank statements and the account in Monsignor Eugenio Pizza's name. She also told him of the meeting she'd had with Monsignor Pizza in San Pietro in Vincoli just over twenty-four hours earlier, the conversation with Domnica Panu and her death, the trip to Lugano and the discovery that Emilio Busi's son was behind

GB Investments. The only thing she didn't mention was Michele Balistreri.

As she told him these things she gradually felt lighter and less worried about what might happen to her.

Salvatore Balistreri heard her out in silence, his eyes closed, as if he were searching in his memory for the answers to her questions.

Tripoli, La Moneta, Sunday, 31 August 1969

Salvatore Balistreri

After an hour of exhausting discussion, Busi and Don Eugenio went to their rooms to rest.

'What should we do, Ingegnere?' Mohammed asks me.

I look at my right-hand man. How much he's changed over the years. He used to be a dogsbody, and now he's playing a key role in a *coup d'état* that's on the verge of collapsing because of a spat between two women.

I have to know if Marlene's spoken to Italia . . . Because, in that case . . .

'Could we put it off for a day or two, Mohammed?'

'No, Ingegnere, we have to move tonight. This is the last possible day before Omar Al Shalhi gets back into Libya. He and his brother Mansur Aziz run the police and the generals loyal to the king. They'd make dangerous enemies.

'And the king?'

'King Idris is also abroad. We won't get another moment like this.'

He's right there's no alternative. There's only one thing to be done. *It's today. Now or never.*

'All right, Mohammed, you go and rest as well. It's going to be a long night.'

Sunday, 7 August 2011

Fiumicino

At the end of her story, Linda stopped, and Salvatore Balistreri opened his eyes.

'Why did you call me, Signorina Nardi?'

The tone of his voice was warm and polite. Linda plucked up her courage.

'To find out if you're the man behind Charity Investments, Dubai, the other partner in the Swiss Consortium.'

He nodded and continued staring at her. She thought there was a great deal behind those staring eyes. They were the same as Michele's, but also very different.

Such huge contrasts. Hard and soft. Determination and regret.

Salvatore Balistreri bent forwards and looked her in the eyes. There wasn't a trace of resentment or threat in his look, nor in his voice.

'I'm no longer an Italian citizen, Signorina Nardi. It wouldn't be considered a crime, and no one could accuse me of a thing. The information is no consequence to me, nor of any use to you.'

Linda nodded slowly. The man was right. Even if he had admitted, *Yes, I'm behind Charity Investments, Dubai*, he would have risked nothing in terms of criminal prosecution.

'And why did you go to see Dominica Panu?' he asked her.

'Because Melania Druc mentioned her. I spoke with her briefly on the cruise. She was worried, scared. Very different from the other time I saw her.'

Salvatore Balistreri frowned.

'The other time?'

'A few days ago I saw her in the Hotel Rixos in Tripoli. She was with an important Libyan, a member of the Secret Service. A man of about sixty with a severed ear.'

For a moment Linda saw a shadow cross the old man's face. Then he sighed.

'I've already had occasion to tell you, Signorina Nardi. You are overly courageous.'

'And so what should I do now, according to you, Signor Balistreri? Go to the police or forget all about it?'

He reflected on this for some time, his eyes closed so he could concentrate better, as if the question really were of considerable importance. Finally, he looked her again in the eye.

'Neither the one, nor the other, I think. As to forgetting all about it, I fear that's not in your character.'

He said this with a smile. But Linda knew that smile could mean anything.

'So what should I do?'

'You're a journalist, Signorina. Leave those poor victims to the police, and don't bother yourself with them any more. You have solid proof enough for the other story, which is your real field. You can write a good article about that.'

Linda shook her head.

'I don't think you spend enough time in Italy, Signor Balistreri.

Not even *Il Domani* would publish any article that involved Senator Busi and Monsignor Pizza.'

He nodded.

'I understand, but you undervalue certain men and think too highly of others. Write a piece based solely on the established facts and call *Il Domani*'s editor personally. He'll publish it. Otherwise, the *Financial Times* or *Le Monde* will. You'll see.'

In that *You'll see* was the absolute certainty of a man who can accomplish anything. It was pointless asking how, or why, or who. Utterly pointless.

'I thought Monsignor Pizza and Senator Busi were your friends . . .' Linda said.

He shook his head and continued to smile.

'Friends are another matter, Signorina. My brothers, my cousins, are the only people I call my friends. Anyone else is just an acquaintance. Or perhaps I should say ex-acquaintances.'

Linda was lost for words. The last sentence, spoken completely calmly, had something final and terrible in it.

Salvatore Balistreri rose to his feet.

'I have a flight to catch. I have a meeting at Geneva airport. Try to do as I say. I'll be back from Geneva this evening. By all means call me again, if it would help.'

They stopped just outside the door to the lounge. He took her hands between his. They were the hands of an old man, well manicured but covered in liver spots and with thick veins under the wrinkled skin.

He looked at her directly and spelled out his words very clearly.

'I would hate anything untoward to happen to you, Signorina. You will promise me you will be careful?'

Linda stood stock-still as she watched him disappear, those two contradictory phrases ringing in her head.

A threat posing as concern. Or concern posing as a threat?

*   *   *

Having arrived at Fiumicino, Michele Balistreri hid behind a notice board. From there he kept an eye on the Freccia Alata lounge, waiting for his father to exit towards the departure gates.

He had no idea what to say to him, or what to ask.

Are you behind that investment company in Dubai? Did you push my mother off that cliff?

He was well aware of the inappropriateness of both these unconnected questions.

Or perhaps they were linked, by an extremely long, invisible thread.

He wanted to leave, shut himself in his office full of smoke and continue his calm voyage towards the mouth of that river and the sea. It was Mikey, not him, who wanted to confront this man and who had those thoughts that Michele couldn't manage to dispel.

The VIP lounge door opened and his father came out with Linda Nardi. Balistreri couldn't believe his eyes; he was frozen in shock. Those were two people he had never wanted to see together.

He watched his father clasp Linda's hands and whisper something to her. On his lips he could read: *'I would hate anything untoward to happen to you, Signorina. You will promise me you will be careful?'*

For Balistreri, who had known this man for so long, those words were very clear. In the end, it was his father who had made him run after Marlene Hunt that day.

Tripoli, Sunday, 31 August 1969

Mikey Balistreri

We get to the Underwater Club at ten past two. While Farid takes her bag to the Ferrari California in the car park, Marlene and I walk along the jetty in silence.

I can't see her eyes, but I hear her whispered words.

'Today's the day, Mikey. It's now or never.'

The words destroy any sense of calm I still had. Grandad comes up to us. Marlene says hello to him and goes off to her Ferrari.

'Are you coming with us to the olive grove, Mikey?' Grandad asks me.

I shake my head.

'I've got a headache, Grandad. I'm going home.'

A moment later, I'm in the jeep. I follow the Ferrari at a distance of a hundred metres. Perhaps Marlene can see me in the rear-view mirror, but it makes no difference.

The red Ferrari travels slowly along the Adrian Pelt coast road, crossing the empty city. The palm trees are motionless and everyone is hidden away in the cool and shade of their houses.

All this peace around about, and all this fury inside me.

Marlene's at the Wheelus Field entrance a little before two thirty. I park the jeep at a suitable distance from the air base. While Marlene shows her ID, a military aircraft lands on the runway.

There's a pair of binoculars in the jeep that we use when we're out hunting. I get them out and through the perimeter fence see William Hunt exiting the plane. Marlene is waiting for him with the Ferrari directly below the air stairs. There's no hug, not even a kiss. They're immediately in deep conversation in the aeroplane's shade. In fact, it's Marlene who speaks, while William listens.

As I watch them through the binoculars, I try to read her lips and imagine what she's saying.

It's over, William. Salvo told his wife yesterday and I said the same to her today.

William Hunt is a dangerous man, an ex-Marine with ice-cold eyes who, I'd heard, works for the CIA. A man who's always been in command and has never been betrayed or humiliated. He listens intently, impassively, like a soldier getting ready for action.

William says something to his wife. I can only imagine what.

I'd rather kill you, Marlene, than let you go off with that Italian fancy man.

Then he gets into the Ferrari with her and they drive to the office blocks on the other side of the base. After less than five minutes, the car appears at the entrance bar, Marlene alone at the wheel.

She waves to the guards and takes off towards Tripoli at high speed, the Ferrari's tyres squealing. I follow in the jeep, but the distance between us grows. Marlene's driving along the coast at nearly a hundred and twenty miles an hour. I know she's seen me in the rear-view mirror. It's a challenge.

Frightened, little Mikey?

At the crossroads before entering Tripoli, the Ferrari turns off towards Garden City and Sidi El Masri at sixty miles an hour, and I have to let her go; otherwise, the jeep would overturn. She's only going home. And, there, we'll settle things.

Rome

Arriving back home in the middle of the afternoon, Linda told Giulia about Salvatore Balistreri.

'You shouldn't have told him everything, Linda. He's a very dangerous man. He threatened you.'

'He didn't threaten me, Giulia.'

'He said, "I would hate anything untoward to happen to you," didn't he? Will you listen to me? He also said that his only real friends happen to be his family in Palermo, and those are people who . . .'

'I don't think Salvatore Balistreri would have me killed, Giulia. Not now, at least.'

'Exactly. He had you promise that you wouldn't do anything more, otherwise . . .'

'That wasn't what he meant, I'm sure.'

'All right, so how do you want to go on from here?'

'I'll do what Salvatore Balistreri said. I'll write the article and then call *Il Domani*.'

Giulia Piccolo ran her long, strong fingers through her highlights. As a policewoman, she knew exactly what she should do.

Notify Michele Balistreri and the Homicide Squad.

Linda went to the computer and started to write. In half an hour she had finished the article. She mentioned Kenya, Gabriele Cascio, the slush funds used for kickbacks deposited in Monsignor Pizza's IOR account and the fact that GB Investments was run by Giacomo Busi, son of Gruppo Italia's chairman, Senator Emilio Busi. Nothing about Melania, Tanja or Domnica.

I'm doing what you suggested I do, Signor Balistreri.

Then she called the office of *Il Domani*'s editor. Linda had known Salvatore Albano since she'd started on the paper as a trainee. He was an excellent journalist, but also a well-balanced and prudent man who would never put his newspaper at risk for the sake of an article. He might not even answer the call, given that — among other things — it was almost eleven o'clock at night, the busiest time, just before the paper was put to bed. However, his secretary put him on the line straight away.

'I was expecting your call, Linda. I'd have preferred you to get in touch directly, though, without someone else giving me advance notice.'

So no pressure there . . .

'I'm sorry,' Linda said. 'This isn't exactly my idea. But would you like to read the article?'

'We're nearly out of time. And we'd have to show it to our legal office, Linda. Can you send it to me right away, and I'll call you back?'

She sent him the piece and he called back in fifteen minutes, his voice deadly serious.

'We'll put it on the front page, Linda. But you know what you'll be facing, don't you?'

You'll hang me out to dry, no doubt about that. But what you don't know is that this isn't the whole story: there are three murder victims as well.

'OK, Salvo, thanks. And please don't worry about me.'

Albano sighed, and his voice became animated.

'It's an excellent piece of work. I'd publish it no matter what. Try to trust other people a little bit more, will you? And well done – I know how important this is.'

Linda ended the call. Another interminable day was coming to a close. She and Giulia settled down on the sofa to watch a black-and-white 1950s movie.

It was a love story.

Tripoli, La Moneta, Sunday, 31 August 1969

Don Eugenio Pizza

At a quarter to three I decide to make the telephone call. Very reluctantly. It could cost me a lot. But not making it could be lethal.

The secretary doesn't want to put me through. It's after lunch on a Sunday, the prime minister's having coffee with some of his supporters. *My faithful mendicants*, as he calls them, in a mixture of irony, affection and scorn. But I have to insist.

'My dear Don Eugenio,' he says, greeting me with friendly formality. But his tone is cold. I try to tell him what I have to.

'I have to confess . . .'

'My dear Don Eugenio, you are the confessor.'

'There are problems between the Ingegnere's wife and one of his friends, an American woman. As you can understand, Prime Minister, a fight between two women at this point could be dangerous.'

The brief silence is followed by the prime minister's icy, nasal voice.

'Don Eugenio, the Vatican Bank oversees business operations far more complicated than problems between a man and his wife.'

The conversation is over. For a moment I imagine the prime minister examining the photos of me with Nico Gerace. The ones Mikey

Balistreri gave to Italia, a woman who would stop at nothing. I can see Italia Balistreri handing the envelope containing the photographs to the prime minister and feel gooseflesh all down my spine.

Forget the Vatican Bank. This could be the end of me. I have to act immediately.

Today's the day. It's now or never.

Emilio Busi

I've thought about it again and again. With the risk I'm facing in the form of Italia Bruseghin, I can't make a move without consulting them. After all, they're my past, present and future. Without them, I'll never be what I want to be.

At three I make the call. My contact in SISDE listens in silence while I explain the problem.

'Very well, Busi. Call me back in five minutes.'

He needs to consult with his people.

I can picture the scene: two flights of stairs, a corridor, the last door on the left. I call back exactly five minutes later.

'You've sorted out far greater problems than this. A lot of people are counting on you here, and they wouldn't be pleased if anything went wrong.'

Call over. I sit down in an armchair and think things over. A fight between that American whore and Balistreri's fascist wife can't be allowed to upset things. The *coup d'état*, my career, my life. There's no alternative.

Today's the day. It's now or never.

Mohammed Al Bakri

It's three thirty, and in two hours I'll be at the airport to take the six-thirty flight to Benghazi. I'll be at the side of Signor X during the hours that will change Libya's destiny, and also that of my family. I must try to control my feelings. I have to.

Nothing can stop history. Not even this.

I cross the beach in the suffocating heat on my way to the servants' quarters. My thoughts are troubled and as painful as the burning sand in the afternoon sun. Thanks to their work, Farid and Salim are starting to earn a little cash. But I have to think of Ahmed and Karim's future, about my two intelligent sons, the ones who should have an education. They're clever, as Nadia would have been had I sent her school instead of her working for the Balistreri family.

I brush away the thought of my dead daughter. I can't allow myself to feel guilt or regret. Especially not today, when the whims of two women risk upsetting everything. But it won't happen.

No, I won't have Ahmed and Karim grow up in poverty as I did, and fearful of the Italians. No one can stop the plan. We can't put it off, whatever the cost. What will be will be.

Today's the day. It's now or never.

Sunday, 7 August 2011

Rome

The Sky Suite Hotel's roof garden was crowded. Most of the men were over fifty and most of the women under thirty-five. In the majority of cases, the couples were clandestine. The whole set-up spoke of money, power and sex and the flaunting of all three.

Balistreri didn't see Beatrice Armellini when she first came in and initially became aware of her only by the reaction she caused among those already seated at the tables – lasciviousness in the men, jealousy in the women. The transformation in the woman he had met only hours before in Gruppo Italia's offices was extraordinary.

But this is the real one.

Gone were the thick grey glasses, the chignon, the pale make-up, the severe clothes. The person entering the room was a woman close to forty who looked less than thirty, beautifully made up, her black hair loose on her tanned shoulders, wearing contact lenses and a mid-thigh red, sleeveless dress that both clothed and exposed her terrific figure. Again, Balistreri wondered where he had seen her before.

She came over, smiling, as he rose to greet her. She was conscious of the reaction she created and did nothing to minimize it.

'Good evening, Commissario Balistreri. Oh, I feel so important. Fancy the Head of Homicide taking the trouble to meet me, especially in a place like this!'

'I imagine you're used to feeling important. Should we take a seat at the bar?'

'I'd prefer somewhere away from people's stares, Commissario. If you feel comfortable with the idea, let's take a suite.'

She laughed, and Balistreri called the maître d' over.

'Have you already booked, sir?' he asked.

'No.'

'Then I'm sorry, everything's already taken.'

'Oh no,' Beatrice muttered.

Balistreri took out his wallet, but the man looked apologetic.

'It's not a question of tipping me, sir.'

Balistreri smiled. This was a typical Italian reaction. But over the years he'd learned how to deal with Italians. His took out his police ID, which stated that he was in charge of Section III, Flying Squad, and showed it to the man.

'Section III is Homicide,' Balistreri explained. 'Now please have a suite made ready.'

The maître d' blanched.

'Of course, sir. I beg your pardon. Please come this way.'

Balistreri smiled at Beatrice.

The maître d' accompanied them to a suite on the eleventh floor: living room thirty metres square, dining table already laid out on the terrace facing the city, flat-screen television, CD and DVD player, adjustable halogen spotlights in the ceiling and floor, a master bedroom with an enormous four-poster bed, strategically placed mirrors and a bathroom with a jacuzzi.

'The floor waiter will be with you straight away,' he said.

Then he bowed and left them alone.

Tripoli, Sunday, 31 August 1969

Mikey Balistreri

It's half past three when I draw up to the iron gates bearing my parents' linked initials. The Ferrari is parked in front of the Hunt home, and the pair of villas are wrapped in complete silence, as if the torrid heat of this last day of August has rendered even the sparrows, the cicadas and the frogs mute.

I try to think about things, about my mother alone on that cliff edge with her sad eyes, ruminating on the end of her marriage, the humiliation and the loneliness. I picture that half-raised hand again, just as the motorboat was docking, and suddenly have a feeling something terrible is going to happen.

She wasn't waving at us, or at anyone else. She was saying goodbye. Goodbye to life.

Anger and anguish churn uncontrollably in my blood. I get out of the jeep and stride in the direction of that she-devil's villa.

As usual, the door to the Hunt villa isn't locked. I know that when I open that door I will close lots of others. I stand there motionless, like a compass needle caught between two opposing forces.

Good and evil.

I swear to myself that I won't touch her, just speak to her. I'll persuade her to leave my father alone.

When I enter the villa, it's enveloped in shadow, a thin strip of light coming from under a door at the end of the hall where the bedrooms are. William and Marlene's bedroom.

I walk slowly in silence. On the living-room carpet are scattered the few clothes Marlene had been wearing. I pick up the pink T-shirt and little white skirt and smell her scent on them: her body lotion, her sweat.

That's why I'm here. Not for my father or my mother, not out of fear or resentment.

But for her temptress flesh.

Sunday, 7 August 2011

Rome

Linda and Giulia were exhausted. The trip to Lugano, the meeting with Salvatore Balistreri, the article for *Il Domani* . . . At least the old black-and-white love story had a happy ending.

'If only love was really like that . . .' Giulia muttered. 'But it's not women's fault. It's men who make us give the worst of ourselves . . . The trouble is, we're capable of lowering ourselves to their level, like that woman who took Domnica to Gruppo Italia's clients. They called her *Fratello*, exactly as if she were a man . . .'

Suddenly a face popped into Linda's memory.

'Beatrice . . .' she whispered to herself.

'Who the hell is Beatrice?'

Linda went to the computer and Googled Beatrice Armellini. Wikipedia came up with the biography of the winner of *Grande Fratello*, Italy's *Big Brother*.

Michele Balistreri and Beatrice Armellini were sitting on the terrace with an excellent bottle of white wine. Beatrice wanted to take her time, so Balistreri let her talk: the economic crisis, inept and corrupt politicians, the euro and all the poor people who were losing their jobs.

He'd decided to wait, given it was Beatrice Armellini who had asked to speak to him. And indeed, after a couple of glasses of wine and a little chitchat, she loosened up a little.

'You're looking into the deaths of Melania and Tanja Druc, aren't you?' she asked.

'Is that why you wanted to meet me here?'

Beatrice smiled.

'For that, and a little more. Assuming you're interested, of course.'

'I'm interested in what you have to tell me, Signorina. Assuming you're not going to tell me any lies.'

She licked a drop of wine off her lips with the tip of her tongue.

'And how would you deal with those lies, Commissario? Corporal punishment?' Balistreri lit a cigarette. He had to put a stop to this. Beatrice was steering the conversation in a direction where she felt more at ease. But he had neither the time nor the desire for it.

'Why has Senator Busi sent you to me, Signorina?'

She smiled again.

'Because of the questions he couldn't answer. But also to propose a deal.'

'I don't do deals.'

Beatrice wasn't put off in the least.

'Let me tell you something, Commissario, then you can decide if you want to go forwards.'

Balistreri said nothing. He was trying to ignore the low-cut dress, the thighs, the eyes, all the provocative ways in which Beatrice Armellini was trying to make him more malleable. It was a game at which she was an expert, and men had taught her that it worked and paid off.

'I've been Senator Busi's PA for years, Commissario. And since he became chairman of Gruppo Italia I've been in charge of the special entertainments programme.'

'And what does "special" mean?'

Beatrice leaned gently towards him. It was obvious she wasn't wearing a bra.

'The word speaks for itself. Each time Gruppo Italia invites important guests to Rome, whether Italian or from abroad, I look after their stay here, right down to the last detail.'

She stopped for a moment and smiled at him. That word 'detail' was said just for him.

'What kind of detail?'

'Our important clients are almost always men, and you know what you men want, don't you, Commissario?'

'Why don't you tell me in your own words, Signorina?'

Beatrice leaned even closer. She looked directly into his eyes, and now Balistreri couldn't help but let his gaze be drawn to her nipples.

'At the age of fifty and over, it's no longer enough for a girl to give you oral stimulation. You need to feel that you really turn her on. And that you become erect by yourself, not because she's done her best to arouse you for half an hour.'

She laughed, putting the glass to her lips, well satisfied with her crystal-clear explanation. She looked at him, putting a hand on his arm.

'I hope I haven't shocked you, Michele?'

Balistreri made no reply and stared at the city many metres below the terrace, the penthouses and church domes all lit up, the stream of cars along the Tiber.

This is a game, Michele. Watch out: she can play it even better than you can.

Beatrice got to her feet, swaying gently on her heels, a cigarette in one hand, glass of wine in the other. Balistreri stared at her: he remembered now. It was that pose – perhaps even that dress – on the front pages of the newspapers. The year that Bea won *Grande Fratello*. He recalled the conversation Linda had recorded with Domnica Panu.

Others call her Fratello.

'All right,' said Balistreri. 'I'll offer *you* a deal. If you can convince me that you and Senator Busi had nothing to do with the deaths of Melania, Tanja and Domnica, I'll leave you in peace. Now tell me who did kill them.'

'The person under interrogation would like to ask for a break, Commissario, and a little gift. A dance. If you won't, I won't be able to talk any more.'

She switched on some background music, then took his hand, made him get up and led him to the space between the table and the terrace balustrade. With the palm of his hand on her spine, Balistreri could feel her soft, naked skin as they slowly danced. She lifted her head, and their lips were only centimetres away.

'Is there anything else you want from me, Michele?'

Tripoli, Sunday, 31 August 1969

Mikey Balistreri

When I open the door, Marlene's sitting on a chair, busily brushing her shiny, wet, black hair. She's wrapped in a towelling dressing gown, tied at the waist.

What's she wearing underneath?

She looks at me in the mirror.

'What are you doing in my bedroom?'

'You said I could find you here.'

'And you come in without knocking, while I'm half naked?'

I'm livid. More at myself than with her.

'The front door was open,' I say weakly, trying to justify myself.

She gives me that sarcastic smile again.

'Perhaps I should call the police. But then you're not a dangerous thief, are you, Michelino? Just a thief who comes in and looks, no more than that, taking nothing away. A thief who only wants to talk and talk and talk.'

She's on the dividing line between provocation and derision. I should get out of there right away.

She's a she-devil, Mikey. You'll lose everything. Laura, your mother, yourself.

Marlene looks at me. Then she says it again, and this time I'm sure what I'm hearing.

'Today's the day. It's now or never, Michelino. Either rise to the challenge or go and get lost.'

I grab her by the collar of her dressing gown. Her eyes open wide with surprise. Then the green of her irises becomes dark as the winter sea.

'Are you upset, Michelino? Do you want to hit me? Is that what you want to do?'

'You'll be used to that with your Marine of a husband.'

My anger and desire give me away. I feel like a boat in a storm at sea and she's the storm. She's in charge here. She makes the decisions.

'Michelino, you don't think for a minute that William is the kind of man who would hit me, do you? It's only you Italians who do such things to women. Ask your father.'

I rip the dressing gown off her and throw her on the bed. She's wearing a bra and briefs underneath. I throw my eighty-five kilos on top of her, while she kicks and screams and hits me furiously in the face. She scratches my shoulders and I feel the blood trickling down my back.

But I'm heavier and stronger than her. I give her a slap and take hold of both her wrists in my left hand as she fights to free herself. Then, with my right hand, I rip off her bra. The sound of the material tearing only augments my strength and my anger.

Marlene spits in my face. I grab the elastic of her briefs with my free hand and pull hard, but they won't tear.

'You're not strong enough, Michelino. Too much jerking off, thinking about me.'

I can't see anything any more. I let go of her arms and tear off her briefs with both my hands while she tries to claw at my face. But she's a prisoner under my weight. I get up on my knees, straddling her naked body so I can look at her.

She's underneath me, naked, sweating, her hair all over her face. She wrestles against me, screaming insults, her eyes as green as a stormy sea. And I'm there, tossing about on those waves, raging with hate and desire.

I pause for a moment on the edge of the abyss, trying to calm myself down. Then she stretches a hand out to my jeans and has them undone in three seconds. I hear her speak, her voice hoarse with emotion.

'Tie my wrists to the bed, Michelino. Then I won't feel it's my fault.'

I tie her to the bedhead with the belt of the dressing gown and pull off my jeans and briefs.

I want to devour her, destroy her, do to her body the most ugly, vulgar and insulting things.

As I penetrate her she bites my lips and draws blood, then she spits my own blood mingled with her saliva into my eyes. Now she wrestles even more, but in a different way, so that I can penetrate her more deeply, with the fury of desperation.

This is the devil; this is hell: blood, flesh and flames.

Sunday, 7 August 1969

Rome

Beatrice steered him to the metre-high balustrade. It was about thirty metres above ground level and Balistreri felt a little dizzy, while Beatrice sat easily on it, her back to empty space. As she crossed her legs, it was evident that she wasn't wearing any underwear.

'The senator told me several things about what you were like when you were young. You were crazy, but women were also crazy about you. Can you still drive them crazy, Mikey?'

That name echoed in Balistreri's brain.

Mikey.

His gaze travelled from Beatrice Armellini to the space below the balustrade.

Just like that damned cliff.

Beatrice lifted her dress and straddled the balustrade, one leg dangling outside, one leg inside to balance herself on the terrace floor, her naked buttocks on the concrete ridge.

'Sit up here with me, Mikey, and I'll tell you the truth you so much want to hear.'

Balistreri took a look down and stepped back. He had twice

jumped from that height on La Moneta, but below had been the sea, not asphalt and parked cars. And too many years had passed.

She smiled at him; she was prepared for this. She knew how to capture him.

'You're not interested in today's truth, are you? Come up here with me and I'll tell you the truth you really want to know . . .'

The truth. Yesterday's truth. The only truth.

As if in a trance, Balistreri went up to the balustrade and cautiously lifted one leg over it, his knee crying out in pain, then sat himself down, one leg dangling in the void, one firmly inside on the terrace. He tried desperately not to look down.

Beatrice lifted her dress up to her waist and slowly unbuttoned his trousers. Then she put her mouth close to his ear, kissed it, licked it and whispered something barely audible.

Do you remember that afternoon, Mikey? You were in bed with Marlene, while your mother was breathing her last.

Balistreri wasn't sure if she'd really said this or if he'd only imagined it. But he had no time to consider. Beatrice lifted herself up, sat on his lap and guided him into her.

The legs inside the terrace brushed the tiled floor, those outside swayed in empty space. She was close to him, and they moved gently backwards and forwards, life on one side of them, an abyss on the other. She again put her lips to his ear.

'Your friend with the severed ear's been waiting many years for you, Michele. He wants to tell you the truth.'

At that moment, Balistreri heard the hiss of the bullet. Beatrice Armellini's face exploded, and her blood, brains and fragments of her skull spattered over him and all over the terrace.

Tripoli, La Moneta, Sunday, 31 August 1969

Ahmed Al Bakri

On the beach here with Karim, Nico and Alberto, time passes very slowly and the day seems endless. We swim, kick a ball about a bit, have another swim. But all I can feel is anger at that little *gahba*'s words echoing in my head.

Mikey's mother also thinks he should steer clear of you.

I grew up with Mikey Balistreri. If there's one person in the world whose judgement Mikey trusts more than his own, it's his mother's. I have to do something.

It's getting close to four and even the sea breeze has died down; you can't breathe on the beach.

'I've had enough,' says Alberto. 'It's too hot. I'm going to my room to study with the air conditioning on.'

'I'm going to look for Laura,' Karim says.

'I'm going to flop down on my bed,' says Nico.

I look at them, happy they're going to leave me in peace.

'I'm staying on the beach.'

There's no more time for hanging around. It's time to act.

Today's the day. It's now or never.

Salvatore Balistreri

At a quarter to five Mohammed Al Bakri drops into my study to say goodbye. His face is hollow, much more so than usual. There are dark rings under his worried eyes, but he has a determined look about him.

'I'm off to the airport, Ingegnere. Farid and Salim are coming to pick me up in a little while.'

He doesn't ask my permission, or my opinion. He's frightened of a last moment of weakness.

'What time do you leave?'

'The flight's at six thirty. I'll be dining with him and his men this evening. Everything's settled for tonight.'

'You look tired, Mohammed.'

'As do you, Ingegnere. It's been a long day.'

Mohammed goes off, and I mix myself a third Martini. I've done a great deal, a very great deal.

Today's the day. It's now or never.

Rome

Linda and Giulia were still debating how to deal with Beatrice Armellini when Sky 24 broadcasted the news just in. A young woman had been killed by a rifle shot at the Sky Suite Hotel. Nothing was known about her identity, but it said that also present at the scene of the crime was the Head of Rome's Homicide Squad, Michele Balistreri.

The two women stared at each other a moment. It could have nothing to do with anything, but both felt shaken. Giulia grabbed her mobile and pressed the button for Graziano Corvu's number. He replied, struggling for breath.

'This isn't a good moment, Giulia. I'm rushing to a crime scene.'

'Can you tell me the woman's name?'

'What woman?'

'The one killed at the Sky Suite.'

'Are you crazy? I can't . . .'

'Was it Beatrice Armellini, by any chance. Busi's PA?'

'How the hell did you know that?' yelled Corvu, not thinking.

Giulia ended the call.

'Well?' she asked Linda.

Physically, Linda was exhausted, but her mind was wide awake.

'Call your hacker friend and tell her to get into Porte Aperte's database. We want the names of all the girls. And their mobile numbers, if they have them. Then we'll get in touch with them, straight away.'

'Linda, it's almost two in the morning.'

'Don't pretty much all of them work at night? We have to find at least one girl, Giulia, and right now. Just one, with the courage to speak out. My piece is publishing in *Il Domani*, and all hell's going to break loose. We have to be ready.'

Giulia Piccolo ran a hand through her green highlights. She remembered the day she and Linda had gone into the Casilino 900 camp to face the gang there.

'All right. I'll do it, but it's going to end in trouble. Big trouble . . .'

Balistreri called Corvu. In a few minutes, everyone was there. Forensics, Colombo, the duty public prosecutor and Police Chief Floris. The hotel was both surrounded and invaded by police.

Sitting in the suite, Balistreri gave them all the details up to the meeting with Beatrice Armellini and the balancing act on the balustrade. He kept Linda Nardi out of it, and Armellini's last words to him. Neither was relevant.

They had to do with another crime, another time, another justice.

Naturally, there was an outcry. Balistreri's violations of investigative procedure couldn't be tolerated. An investigation in which leading members of the country's governing class were involved had been seriously compromised by the direct involvement of the commissario's father – as Balistreri himself had admitted – and by illegal questioning.

But Police Chief Floris had a lot of respect for him. He was also one of the few politicians who were honest and had balls.

'All right,' he said. 'I'll call the interior minister right now. If he's agreeable, we'll request an official interview with the senator tomorrow. But you, Balistreri, will not say a word to anyone. Is that clear?'

The public prosecutor pointed to the outside-broadcast vans already parked around the hotel.

'The media mustn't know the identity of the deceased until we can see Senator Busi.'

Balistreri's boss, Colombo, took him by the arm.

'Now keep out of this, Balistreri. You've already caused enough trouble.'

But Balistreri was no longer even listening. He couldn't care less about rules and regulations, about his pension or the police. The only thing occupying his mind was that island, La Moneta. And Beatrice Armellini's last words.

Your friend with the severed ear's been waiting many years for you, Michele. He wants to tell you the truth.

The truth of past and present were one and the same. One single truth.

Tripoli, La Moneta, Sunday, 31 August 1969

Mikey Balistreri

Marlene Hunt gets up and puts her dressing gown back on.

'Get dressed and go, Mikey. Now. It's already five fifteen.'

She shuts herself in the bathroom and I dress in a hurry. I want to be out of the villa before she comes out. All hell's raging inside me. In one stroke I've betrayed the two women who mean anything to me, Italia and Laura. I dash out of this she-devil's lair just as the telephone starts to ring.

My head's about to burst; I must have a temperature. I arrive at the Underwater Club at a quarter to six, just as Farid and Salim are getting out of one of the motorboats. They'd gone to pick up Mohammed on La Moneta and were taking him to the airport.

'Can I take the boat?' I ask.

Mohammed stares at me, his lean features forming a silent query.

Where have you been, Mikey?

'Yes,' Farid replies. 'We have the dinghy.'

It's a little less hot on the water; the wind from the land has died down and a sea breeze is blowing. But I feel red hot. In the thirty minutes it takes to reach La Moneta I can't put a single sensible thought together. I have a premonition of disaster. Something awful lying ahead.

The sun is setting over the island when I moor the motorboat to the La Moneta jetty. There's a certain excitement on the little beach: everyone's down there, the adults and the teens.

Papa looks at me, rubbing a hand over his suntanned face. His dark eyes look unusually worried.

'Where've you been, Mikey?'

Fucking your woman, Papa. Instead of going to look after my mother.

I make no effort to reply.

'Where's my mother?' I ask instead.

Everyone looks at everyone else; it's as if I'm talking about an extraterrestrial.

'She'll be in her room, won't she?' my father replies.

I turn my back on everyone, go into the villa and knock on Italia's door. No reply. The door's unlocked, the room tidy and unoccupied, the windows are closed and there's no smell of cigarettes. My mother's still not back.

I go outside and shoot off up the path to the other side of the island, knowing very well there's no reason to run. A few minutes won't change a thing. But I run just the same, Ahmed at my side and Alberto struggling behind

It's almost totally dark by the time we reach the cliff, but the always foresighted Alberto's brought an electric torch and switches it on. The area underneath the large olive bent by the wind is deserted. There's only a folding chair and my mother's copy of Nietzsche's *Ecce Homo*. That book left open on the chair is the silent witness that something out of the ordinary has happened.

I look down over the steep crag into the impenetrable dark that ends on the rocks a good many metres below. I know it's a steep and slippery descent, dangerous even by day. To go down in the dark is almost insane. But it's the least I can do.

'I'm going down.'

'No, Mikey,' Alberto says. 'Let's go back to the villa and call someone from the police or the coastguard.'

'Leave me the torch, Alberto. You run back and call the others.'

It's the first time I've given an order to my elder brother. But the exceptional circumstances had reversed our roles, and Alberto went running off to the villa.

'I'll come with you, Mikey,' Ahmed says.

Telling Ahmed that it's dangerous would be both offensive and useless. I make no reply and Ahmed follows as I start to climb down, the torch in my hand.

You can't see more than a metre ahead. We move slowly, one step at a time, first testing the ground cautiously. When we come to the steepest part, I stop.

'Watch out. There's loose gravel in this stretch,' Ahmed warns me.

Too late. My standing foot loses its grip.

If I try to resist, I'll tumble off into mid-air.

I let myself slump on my bottom and slide straight down until I manage to grasp at a twisted root with my right hand, and my legs trace an arc in mid-air and bang against the rock face.

The pain rises piercingly from my ankle. Perhaps I've cracked something, but that's the least of my worries. I'm grasping the root and my arm muscles tense; I can only hold on a few seconds.

Lying flat on the ground, Ahmed comes worming his way towards me, using both hands to stop himself from slipping down and falling on top of me.

'Ahmed, stop, or you'll fall as well.'

He doesn't even listen to me, he's so focused on what he's doing. He slips his right ankle under another root that's sticking out.

'It won't bear our weight, Ahmed.'

'It doesn't have to take it all.'

He's lying horizontally against the descent and stretches his right arm out to me. Like this, only half his weight's pulling on the root.

His right hand comes slowly towards mine. His foot's held by the root, but it's slowly rising. His hand locks around my wrist like a vice.

'Leave me, Ahmed, it's impossible.'

'The left one, Mikey.'

With a huge effort, I lift my left arm up and stretch out my hand. I still need two or three centimetres to reach his arm. My ankle feels as if it's being wrenched off my leg.

'One last effort, Mikey. First, a big breath out. Empty your lungs.'

I gather my strength, breathe out and lunge upwards as my left hand grasps his right arm. The pain in my leg is now so strong I feel sick.

'Keep holding on to the root with your right hand and pull yourself up with the left.'

I should thank my father for having paid for years of training in the gym, and paying for Ahmed as well. Our honed muscles are as taut as violin strings. Now we can't fall, but we're stuck.

We stay like that, in total silence. I see the scar on Ahmed's right wrist, where we mingled our blood as kids.

If the root gives way, we'll fall together. And the pact of sand and blood goes with it.

I don't know how much time goes by. Alberto comes back with the adults, bringing a rope with him. They lift us up, one at a time. I try to stand up, but my ankle gives. I try to scream. I try to breathe. As I'm bent double being sick, I feel a cool hand holding my forehead. It's Laura's. My vision begins to cloud. Before I faint, I have one last thought.

Marlene.

Monday, 8 August 2011

Rome

Senator Busi had just gone to bed, but he couldn't sleep. He had received a phone call from a contact in the Secret Services who told him that *Il Domani* was going to press with a piece by Linda Nardi about him, Monsignor Pizza, Gruppo Italia and the IOR. He didn't know what was in the article but advised him to stop it being published, if he could.

Before calling *Il Domani*'s editor, Busi opened his safe and found the photograph, now almost six years old: it showed him and Melania together in a Bahamas hotel room, where he had taken her to be away from prying eyes. She looked radiant, and was gazing at him contentedly. And he was smiling.

Yes, I was happy that day. I was happy with her, with her and with Tanja.

But that was when the trouble had started. Melania had become even more combative, having found out more about the kind of contracts he dealt with, and had no wish for the father of her child to finance public works in which people and businesses with dubious backgrounds were involved. He had resisted as he had agreements with associates that went back forty years and which couldn't easily be dissolved.

Then had come the Arab Spring, and in Libya as well. Initially, Busi had exerted all the pressure he could in Gaddafi's favour. He had done all in his power to avoid NATO becoming involved – or at least Italy – but not even he, with all his political clout, had been able to convince the government. On the other hand, the Americans, British and French were all too ready to let the bombs drop in the name of liberty and petroleum.

With NATO's intervention, the risk of finding himself on the losing side – something Busi hated – had become very real. It had been then that he had decided to use Melania as an excuse, and the means to distance himself from his associates.

He had sent her into the lion's den in Tripoli to tell Gaddafi's men that she had nothing against them, the problem was the links with Dubai and the Sicilians: she didn't want the father of her child to have anything to do with people like that. They had told her that if Busi stopped supporting them, he would be considered a traitor.

Busi became more and more certain that NATO would win and that continuing to support Gaddafi and the projects that helped finance him would mean that he would end up on the wrong side. So he had engineered that interview in *Il Domani* about the bridge over the Straits of Messina where he'd expressed doubts about the financial backing. To his associates, he had said that he'd been forced to do it, otherwise Melania Druc would have revealed their relationship and the fact that he was the father of her child.

So Mohammed Al Bakri had brought them together on that cruise and asked Busi to bring Melania along as well. He wanted to persuade her to wait until the end of the war. Busi had asked Don Eugenio to have Porte Aperte recommend her so she could be on board without being linked to him in any way. Melania had wanted to bring Tanja with her because there was no longer anyone she trusted in Rome.

During dinner Busi had explained to his associates in Arabic that Melania's blackmail could destroy him. In reality, he was depending on Melania's determination in order to be able to jump ship so as not to end up on the losing side.

After dinner there was a heated argument in his suite between Melania and Mohammed Al Bakri. Salvatore Balistreri hadn't been invited because Melania hadn't wanted to discuss any matters with *that man*.

And, as Busi had anticipated, Melania would not give in. What he hadn't anticipated were the consequences. Melania and Tanja had died that night. It was an unambiguous message for him, the would-be traitor. He should have understood that. They were people who would stop at nothing. As he had known for more than forty years.

And yet he wasn't frightened, neither of them nor of Linda Nardi's article. There was only one thought running through his head.

Melania would have wanted to see Linda Nardi's article in a newspaper. And now I do, too.

He felt better. He decided to let the article decide his fate and perhaps that of the war in Libya. He decided not to call *Il Domani*'s editor to try to stop it being published.

Instead he called Monsignor Pizza on his mobile. A few coded words were enough to get the message across. Soon afterwards they were in Busi's car, heading towards the nearest motorway.

Benghazi, Monday, 1 September 1969

The radio station in the centre of Benghazi is a bare two-storey whitewashed building.

The twenty-six-year-old junior officer whom the Qadhadhfa tribe had placed at the head of the Libyan revolution arrives in a dusty jeep just before two in the morning with an armed escort and Mohammed Al Bakri by his side. The few armoured cars have been more than enough to convince any rebels to stay at home.

In front of the microphone, Mohammed hands him a sheet with the speech he has prepared with Busi and Salvatore Balistreri. It is a very short speech, which Muammar Al Gaddafi reads out, a little unsure of himself. There will be no violence; the cities and frontiers are secured; everyone is to stay at home; a curfew is in place. Gaddafi doesn't give his name. It's all part of the agreement.

At that time of night, there are few Libyans awake and listening to the radio. The message is really for the leader's supporters, who have already occupied ministries, radio stations and airports all over Libya, without meeting any resistance, And it is they who, during the night, spread the news to the rest of the population, firing celebratory shots into the air from rifles and pistols.

Salvatore Balistreri and his friends are in the lounge of his villa on the island. They are in contact by phone with General Jalloun, who is desperately sorry; he's been trying to gather his forces to start looking for Italia, but the police are confined to their barracks by the military, there are roadblocks everywhere and even the general himself isn't free to go out.

That night Ingegnere Balistreri and his associates are among the few people listening live to the short broadcast in which Gaddafi announces the end of the Senussi reign and the birth of the Libyan Jamahiriya. They have waited so long for this moment, but not one of them dares to smile.

In a silver frame by the radio, it's as if Italia's watching them from her photograph.

Monday, 8 August 2011

The Autostrada del Sole

They turned on to the motorway, heading north. For a while neither of them said a word.

'Were Melania and the little girl murdered?' Don Eugenio asked.

At the wheel, Busi nodded.

'Michele Balistreri's convinced it wasn't a case of homicide followed by suicide. And I think he's right.'

Don Eugenio leaned back in his seat.

'I didn't think it would end like this. And I have Domnica on my conscience. I should never have told them about Linda Nardi's intentions. The Lord will never forgive us.'

The memories began to turn into regrets.

Tripoli, Monday, 1 September 1969

Mikey Balistreri

I wake up where my mother gave birth to me, a hospital bed in the Villa Igea clinic. I have no recollection of the motorboat taking me ashore, nor of the ambulance to the clinic. It seems they've pumped me full of tranquillizers and put my ankle in plaster.

Half awake during the night, in the dim light of the hospital's bedside lamp, I glimpsed Laura sitting beside me, holding my hand in hers. Ahmed, Karim and Nico were in the furthest corner, listening to a transistor radio with the volume turned low.

I try to fight against the sleeping tablets and painkillers they've given me. When I wake up, the room is empty, and so, it seems, is Villa Igea. Total silence. There are a few sounds coming through the window, like the noise of lorries. Then I hear isolated shots. I ring the bell and, after a while, a nursing sister comes running in, panting and out of breath.

'Have they found my mother?'

She looks at me, surprised.

'Your mother? I've no idea. There was a *coup d'état* last night.'

I have no idea what she's talking about and begin to shout.

'My mother, you fool, my mother! Have they found her?'

The sister runs away. After a few minutes Ahmed appears, his bony features even more sunken and morose than usual.

'Sorry, Mikey, we were on the floor below. The military's outside. No one can leave the building. There's a curfew in place.'

Perhaps this is a nightmare. Perhaps I've gone insane.

I start to shout again. A doctor comes running in with a syringe. It takes four of them to hold me down to give me an injection to make me sleep.

I wake up again in the late afternoon. There are no more sounds outside the clinic's windows. It's as if the whole of Tripoli's been abandoned. Then I hear distant shots and shouting. But the shots must be shots fired into the air in celebration, because the shouting seems to be full of joy.

The members of the MANK organization are in the room.

'Have they found my mother?'

Silence. Then Ahmed speaks.

'They've given us permission to leave the clinic for an hour, but only to go home. Mr Hunt came a little while ago to pick up Laura.'

I couldn't care less.

'Have they found my mother?'

Ahmed replies in a sullen voice.

'Mikey, there's been a *coup d'état*. The monarchy's fallen; armed troops have taken over the city.'

I look at him. Ahmed's never lied to me. He'll never lie to me.

'Have they found my mother?'

'I don't know, Mikey. Your grandad called. They've been stuck on La Moneta all last night and this morning. They only managed to get back to Sidi El Masri a little while ago.'

Anyway, we're allowed to leave. I sign my hospital discharge and soldiers escort us home, given there's a curfew. We drive through the deserted city in the MANK van, followed by the escort jeep. There are more soldiers than passers-by, and more military jeeps than cars.

The young soldiers, all of whom are carrying weapons, look at us hostilely. Various military vehicles are parked outside the royal palace with its two golden domes, including two armoured cars. But no one fires a shot. My head's throbbing, as if there's a sponge inside it that's swelling and swelling. We draw up to the villas and stop outside the gates. I don't want anyone with me, not now.

'You go on home, guys. We'll be in touch later.'

As I hobble off on my crutches, Ahmed gets out and catches up with me.

'I'll take Karim home and then come back, Mikey. I'll sleep outside this gate. I'll be here if anything happens.'

I know he'll always be at my side.

'You can sleep at home, Ahmed, it's already happened.'

He shakes his head.

'It won't happen again. I'll be here. Now go.'

Alberto comes out to meet me. His eyes are red and sunken, underscored by dark rings of grief. I stop, breathless on my crutches.

'Where's Papa?'

'He's in his study with Grandad and the others.'

'I'm going in to see him. I want to know what's happened to Mamma.'

Alberto tries to stop me.

'Mikey, let me make things clear. Leave him alone right now – he's in pieces. He really is.'

I make no reply, but limp on to the study. Resigned, Alberto opens the door for me.

My father's at his desk, as usual. Sitting opposite him in the armchairs are Grandad, Emilio Busi and Don Eugenio. They all look terrible. But Grandad's the worst; he's deathly pale.

My father hasn't even shaved. I think this must be the first time since I was born. The knot in his tie's twisted and one of his cuffs is slightly stained. This is unimaginable in my father. He doesn't wait for my question. His voice is sorrowful but calm, like an announcer on Italian state television when they broadcast a funeral.

'The Libyan coastguard found your mother's body out at sea this afternoon.'

Italia's body?

'What kind of bullshit is this, Papa?'

He carries on as if I'd said nothing.

'The police couldn't look for her before. General Jalloun and his men were confined to their barracks during the curfew.'

'So?'

'Italia's body was swept out to sea by the current and the tide after sunset. She fell from the cliff near the old olive tree in the afternoon, when the water was at its lowest. There are traces of her on the rocks.'

Those were his exact words. *Traces of her.* Something was ablaze in me. In my stomach, my heart, my brain. But only one question comes to my lips.

'And who pushed her?'

My grandfather shoots me a look of alarm. Busi and Don Eugenio look out of the window at the garden. Behind me, Alberto takes a deep breath. Only my father remains unmoved.

'No one pushed her, Michele. Your mother, sadly, decided she no longer wanted to live and threw herself off.'

'Do you think Mamma was mad, Papa? Or that she had something to hide?'

Those are the words of your wife, Papa, a few hours before she died. Do you think they're the words of a woman who's about to commit suicide?

'I don't know what you're talking about, Mikey. Your mother committed suicide. It's unfortunate, but that's how it is.'

'And why would she have done that?'

But I know very well why.

Because of you and that whore Marlene Hunt.

'We'll talk about that another time, Mikey. Now, go and rest — you have a broken ankle.'

I put my weight on my left crutch and try to hit my father with the other. Alberto throws himself between us. The crutch catches him on his head and blood starts to ooze out, but he doesn't make a sound, holding on to me tightly so I can't do any harm to myself or anyone else. The tears coursing down his face, mingling with the blood, take away my last reserves of strength.

Perhaps they're right. Perhaps she wasn't saying hello but goodbye.

From that day on, both my life and that of Libya changes.

8 An Old Friend is Waiting for You

Monday, 8 August 2011

Rome

Thanks to some tranquillizers, Balistreri was asleep when the telephone rang. It was a breathless Corvu.

'Read *Il Domani, dottore*. Right now.'

Still drowsy, Balistreri thought he meant that something about Beatrice Armellini's murder had leaked out, despite the precautions taken by the public prosecutor and Police Chief Floris. Taking his time, he dressed and went down to the news stand on the street below.

When he saw the article, which took up nine columns, it was as if an electric shock ran through him.

Goodbye, Italy. Goodbye, Gruppo Italia. An epitaph and an answer.

Seeing the name of Linda Nardi instantly produced the usual burning feeling of acid in his stomach.

Balistreri took the paper back to his apartment, lit his first cigarette of the day and began to read. The article began with a detailed reconstruction of the granting of a contract for a hospital in Nairobi to the Swiss consortium ELCON: false invoicing, GB Investments in Luxembourg and Charity Investments in Dubai. It had come out that the owner and administrator of GB Investments, an unknown company, was Giacomo Busi, the son of Senator Emilio Busi, chairman of the committee that had awarded the contract in the first place. Then the article followed the trail of ELCON funds from a small bank in Nairobi to an account in the Institute for Religious Works, otherwise known as the Vatican Bank in Rome. Sources which could not be named confirmed that this account was held in the name of a Monsignor Eugenio Pizza.

Next to Linda's article was a brief editorial from Salvatore Albano.

We want a country in which the young of the working class can win a public works contract and in which the young of politicians and the wealthy are also among the workers. We want a country in which the ruling class is composed of the most able young people and not the offspring of that same ruling class. We do not want monies from the Italian people to end up in unknown foreign companies. We want a Catholic Church that has no need of a bank.

Balistreri switched on the computer and the television, flopped on to the sofa, stretched out his painful leg and waited for things to unfold.

Linda, they're going to tear you to pieces.

Lugano

In the little villa in Collina d'Oro facing the lake, lost in an unreal tranquillity, Senator Busi and Monsignor Pizza calmly read Linda Nardi's article on the webpages of *Domani.it*. It was a problem, but one that could be solved. All they had to do was give the system and public opinion enough time to let the dust settle in the time-honoured Italian way. The real problem was Gaddafi and their former associates. They had heard the Pope's appeal, launched during his

Angelus from Castel Gandolfo, on the war in Libya. *The force of arms cannot resolve . . . Peace needs to be found by means of negotiation . . .*

But they knew Gaddafi and his friends much better than did the Pope. Five months of war were nothing to the Colonel; nor was NATO bombing his people, who now couldn't sleep for fear of it; nor was the lack of electricity that caused food to rot in the August heat; nor having to fight on an empty stomach during the day because it was Ramadan. Gaddafi was a leader who had come to power without violence, thanks to the help of a good many interests and the weakness of those who had preceded him. In his tribal mentality, honour was a value that sanctioned any amount of atrocity.

'They'll be looking for us, Emilio. But we have friends and money everywhere. We can disappear,' Don Eugenio suggested.

'But first I want Melania and Tanja's killer put in jail,' Busi told him.

Don Eugenio nodded slowly. He was tired; worn out by that senseless race towards nothing that had consumed him for more than half a century.

'I'm with you, Emilio. And I have an idea of how we can bring that about before we leave.'

More than regret, it was exhaustion that struck them then, like it hits a marathon runner when he crosses the finishing line, because they both knew this was the end of a journey that had begun *on that day.*

Rome

Reaction to the article on both sides of the Tiber, initially via the online press, television and social networks, was what Balistreri expected from those in power. They showed no concern for what the public might think: it was simply a unanimous chorus of outrage against the mudslinging press, bringing together politicians of various stripes, Vatican spokespersons, senior judges and journalists:

some defending Busi, others defending Monsignor Pizza. In reality, everyone was defending everyone else, because they knew the story could drag not only those two into the mire but also expose and put at risk Italy's largest and most flourishing business, that of corruption and privilege.

By means of a series of finely drawn distinctions, Linda Nardi would be slowly alienated, isolated and then left exposed to reprisals from her enemies. It was a well-known method, tried and tested, particularly by certain parts of the political and business class. It had worked well against the lawyer Giorgio Ambrosoli, against Carabinieri General Carlo Alberto Dalla Chiesa and the anti-Mafia judges Giovanni Falcone and Paolo Borsellino, all of whom had been assassinated for having tackled the Mafia head on after first being marginalized by those whose eyes and ears were shut to the evidence.

Balistreri felt more and more uneasy and called Colombo.

'So when is Senator Busi in for questioning?'

A morose grumble came from the other end of the line.

'The interior minister's at a conference in Palermo. When he returns, Floris will see him to get the necessary authorization. Come on, Balistreri, your friend Nardi may be right, but she's crazy. You need to do these things calmly, not like this!'

Balistreri put the phone down on him.

People like that made him sick. First, so as not to appear reactionary, they made comments supporting the obvious criticisms, but then came the appeals for caution and, finally, the thousand cavils and subtle excuses offered so that nothing would ever really change. He was sick of a country where the political leaders were old men who talked with heartfelt concern about the future for young people, when it was they who had taken that future away. He was sick of a country where funds allocated for public education were swallowed up by illicit activities, where lots of jobs were given as the result of political patronage, and a country where a terrifying bureaucracy armed with countless purposefully complex and hair-splitting laws produced a caste of unproductive workers who had slowly squashed the life out of the healthy and productive part of the world. In short, he was sick of a country where the people of good will who wanted change were either rendered impotent or killed off.

And how did you come to accept this change, Michele?

Immediately after lunch Linda Nardi went into Sky's television studios for the talk show that followed the news.

Facing the cameras were several representatives of the political parties and the press. None of them attempted to greet her and many ostentatiously turned the other way as she came in. Only the presenter offered her a courteous handshake, but even he did not smile. He had been forced to accept her on the show by London central office, which Linda had contacted to let them know of her willingness to appear.

She sat down in the armchair indicated and the presenter introduced the first round of comment. It started with the usual dance around the need for defending civil liberties, defending the state and the need for sober judgement. Without stating so openly, the senior voices appeared supportive, speaking with good-natured condescension about this article by a young freelance journalist, emphasizing especially the 'young' and 'freelance'. In Italy, being young and without a permanent position meant being less credible than someone who had held such a position for half a century, completely undeservedly, with perhaps the addition of extra earnings and rewards on the side offered by trade unions and boards of directors.

And in subtly different ways, the young, fresh-faced MPs hinted in a grave manner about the risks of crowd pleasing, political nihilism, defeatism and also the serious damage caused to Italy's image by investigations of the type carried out by Linda Nardi.

They all spoke about the necessity for clarification and for change, but surrounded what they said with countless banalities and quibbles — the need to be tough while preserving civil liberties, the importance of protecting the offices of state from the errors their representatives made, the respect that was owed to the millions of good Catholic citizens and the ever more questionable methods used by investigative journalism — all rounded off with the usual hackneyed warnings not to make a mountain out of a molehill or throw the baby out with the bath water.

Linda watched them all in silence, calm and composed, her mind wandering between her orphans in Africa and the faces of the invited guests.

Some of them were indeed more reform minded, advocating change. They edged towards some criticism of the system and ventured to say that, for all their parliamentary privilege and Vatican immunity, perhaps — but only perhaps — Senator Busi and Monsignor Pizza did deserve some blame and censure. But nothing more than that. What was not said and could not be said was obvious. A simple and powerful weapon was pointing at every one of them. Busi and Pizza had something on all of them: a contract awarded here, a job offered there, a daughter taken on by a ministry, an apartment owned by a public body given at a peppercorn rent.

During this orchestrated dance, Linda Nardi sat silently in her seat, making no interruptions or contradictions, nor responding to any of the provocations. Initially, the presenter, the other guests and the audience thought she was having some kind of difficulty or was too embarrassed, then concluded she was simply an arrogant snob. But gradually that prolonged silence became more deafening than any reply.

When everyone had had their say, the presenter was forced to let Linda have hers. Taking out a sheet of paper, she began to read from it and did so without even looking at the camera. She wanted her message to be devoid of anything that could be interpreted as manipulation of the unfortunate general public by such means as body language, eye contact and the rest, methods taught by PR consultants and communications science for telling lies and wriggling out of corners.

'Since last night there have been new developments to the story that I wasn't able to include in the article. Decisive new developments.'

She paused and took a look around the suddenly astonished faces. The disgust on some deepened, the fixed and mocking smiles on others became clownish caricatures.

Linda then continued reading.

'Last night we collected the testimonies of several foreign girls who came to Italy thanks to the non-profit organization Porte Aperte headed by Monsignor Pizza, and who were housed in properties owned by Senator Busi's Gruppo Italia.'

The tightly controlled body language of the other guests began to crumble. Hands gripped arms, arms were folded across chests, feet tapped nervously on the floor. The manifest disintegration of the establishment on live television was a spectacle somewhere between burlesque and horror show.

Linda had asked for and received a hand-held mic. She held it in one hand and the sheet of paper in the other, which was trembling slightly. But it was clear to the millions watching that her trembling was bottled-up anger, whereas the other guests were shaking with fear.

'The job of these girls included *speciality* dinners with influential people involved with Gruppo Italia's affairs. The specialities weren't the dishes served up but the costumes the girls were forced to wear — of animals, nuns or nurses, and Angela Merkel or Condoleezza Rice face masks. The guests were a speciality, too: influential men and, unfortunately, also women of the privileged classes. Two of those girls are here in the studio right now.'

The presenter and the guests exploded in protest.

'You'd better be able to prove what you're saying!'

'You should be ashamed!'

'You'll answer for this in court!'

'You'll never write for another newspaper!'

Linda did not respond. She rose and handed the microphone to a young girl who looked less than eighteen and was sitting in the audience next to a tall, muscular woman with green highlights in her hair. The young girl had been well briefed by Linda and began speaking straight away before anyone could stop her.

'My name is Annika. I came to Italy through Porte Aperte and was then chosen for the parties held for Gruppo Italia's clients. I took part in many parties in private houses, hotels, beach resorts and even offices. Basically, it was a question of lap dancing or games where the men put on wolf masks and we girls put on those of sheep, or they dressed up as hunters and we dressed up as pigs. Sometimes we were tied up, hung up and whipped. I had sex with several participants each time I was ordered to and snorted coke with them. In return I received money, drugs and a free apartment. Many of these men are well known. I've seen them in the papers and on television. I've given their names to Signorina Nardi.'

All hell broke loose. Several guests got up and left the studio. The director cut the sound but left the vision on. In the confusion, a politician already well known for having insulted various journalists advanced towards Linda in a threatening manner, but he didn't reach her. Giulia Piccolo cut him off, placed a hand on his shoulder and stopped him in his tracks.

'Beat it, you conniving piece of shit. You and all the others like you.'

The man met her gaze, saw her muscles and did a silent about-turn. Giulia's words were lip read by an expert and posted on Facebook. Once her words had been translated into twenty languages, the 'likes' soon totalled six million.

Sky's switchboard was overwhelmed by viewers protesting about the break in transmission. The presenter received a call from London. He was told to resume broadcasting and let Linda have her say. All the foreign stations were frenetically trying to link up with Sky. Nothing like this had ever happened in the history of television.

In a glacial silence, Linda Nardi picked up where she had left off. She still had the single sheet of paper in her hand.

'Here are the names of the people we already know are involved. I've sent them to the public prosecutor's office, which will look into the rest.'

At this point Linda met the eyes of Giulia Piccolo, who was desperately signalling 'No!'

No, sister. They'll kill you.

Then she read the last words in a voice that was the most violent whisper ever heard on television.

'The person who recruited these girls was Beatrice Armellini, Senator Busi's personal assistant. She was killed by a sniper's bullet last night here in the centre of Rome. Two of her girls, Melania Druc and Domnica Panu, have also been killed in suspicious circumstances in the last few days. Melania's little daughter, Tanja, also died, on the cruise ship she was on between the island of Elba and Civitavecchia. Also on board were Senator Emilio Busi, Monsignor Eugenio Pizza and other very important individuals whom the police will seek to identify.'

Linda put down the microphone and left the television studio, followed by Giulia Piccolo and the young girl who had testified. The show was over.

Lugano

In the little villa in Collina d'Oro, Senator Emilio Busi and Monsignor Eugenio Pizza were watching Linda's appearance live on Sky.

When it was over, they exchanged looks. They had just witnessed their own downfall, and they knew it. And yet they felt lighter, almost relieved. What Linda had said had made their future irrelevant and removed any lasting doubt. They had spoken at length earlier, but the chat show had made everything simpler and more inevitable.

By phone and online they could give all the necessary banking instructions, country by country. Transfer of funds, blocks of funds. The accounts were almost all in their personal names, including those in the Vatican Bank. Mohammed Al Bakri was the only other person who could observe these operations, but he could not intervene. This had been the agreement for more than forty years. And it had worked perfectly well until the start of that damned war in Libya.

Monsignor Pizza switched on the computer.

'We only need a hundredth part of that money to live on happily for the rest of our lives, Emilio. The rest we can transfer to Catholic organizations who deal with the world's poor.'

Busi nodded.

'That's what Melania would have wanted. Let's do it, then let's book the first flight out to the Caribbean. We'll be safe there. They'll never be able to extradite us.'

They sat down side by side at the computer and connected to the internet. As they shifted enormous sums of money from one part of the world to another, from secret accounts in tax havens to those of humanitarian organizations, slowly, they began to feel younger.

They directed the fruits of evil to works of charity with a lightness of spirit they had entirely forgotten: that of the young boy who wanted to become a priest to serve God, and that of the young boy who wanted to become a *carabiniere* to serve justice.

In between the two spirits, young and old, a lifetime had passed. This ending could not change what they had been, but for once it was not the result of convenience, but of genuine emotions of remorse and vindication that they themselves had always found to be irrational and a sign of weakness.

Rome

After the Sky chat show Linda and Giulia took refuge in Linda's flat. They re-examined Porte Aperte's entire database, in particular the lists of girls who had come to Italy in recent years. There were dozens of names. Many of them had gone to work for Gruppo Italia as cleaners or working in bars, the more educated as secretaries.

'That bitch Beatrice, she deserved what she got . . .' said Giulia, scanning through the list.

'I heard that you spoke to Corvu again, Giulia. What was Balistreri doing with that woman in the Sky Suite Hotel?'

Giulia looked at her in surprise. She had finally mentioned him, saying 'Sky Suite Hotel' and 'that woman' with evident disapproval.

'Corvu told me they'd taken him off the case . . .'

'Why?'

Giulia shook her head.

'I'd prefer not to say, Linda.'

'Why is that?'

Giulia decided that, in the end, it would be better tell her the truth so she could wipe that unpleasant and arrogant old misogynist from her mind for ever. He was incapable of really loving a woman in any case.

'When whoever it was shot at Armellini, she and Balistreri were sitting astride the terrace balcony, thirty metres above ground level, screwing.'

Linda looked out of the window towards St Peter's Square. It was full of noise and people. Then she shut herself in her room and threw herself on to the bed fully dressed.

She felt empty, worn out, without even the energy to move her little finger, but her mind continued to thrash about like the tail of a lizard detached from its body. She couldn't stop the thoughts coming. *Balistreri and Beatrice on that balustrade.*

In the end she fell into a fitful sleep.

Half asleep and half awake, in her mind the images tumbled together.

Balistreri and Beatrice clutching each other on the terrace. Her and John Kiptanu in Nairobi. Melania at the Rixos in Tripoli. Melania and Tanja coming out of the private lift on that cruise ship.

All of a sudden, she was awake. She hadn't slept more than an hour. It was still only five in the afternoon. But something in her sleep had disturbed her. She forced herself to remember.

Melania.

She tried to focus on the thought. In the Rixos, Melania had been surrounded by Libyan security men following one of Gaddafi's men, the one responsible for the Zawiya massacre, as the terrified Bashir Yared had told her. A man with a piece of his ear cut off. Her mind had preserved these images, like certain photographs seen once then put away.

Melania in Tripoli at the Hotel Rixos in the company of that man with the severed ear. Melania on the ship with her little girl, coming out of the lift on the deck where her cabin was, a security guard standing by. She'd been asked if the woman she'd seen in Tripoli and the one on the ship had been the same, and she'd said yes. And they were. But no one had asked her the other question.

Was it the same man? My memory's only very indistinct, but yes, it was the same man. He had the same severed ear. I just caught a glimpse of it in the dim light. I have to trust my memory.

At that moment her mobile rang. It was early morning in San Francisco, and Lena must have just got up.

'Linda, dear, I switched on the computer and found the whole world's talking about you!'

Her cough was worse. Linda sensed two feelings behind what her mother had said: one was pride and the other was concern. Both understandable.

But Lena knew only part of the story. Senator Busi and Monsignor Eugenio Pizza were certainly not as dangerous as the man with the severed ear.

'Would you like me to tell you the whole story, Mamma? It's very long.'

She told her everything, from that first meeting with Melania and the man with the severed ear in the Rixos to the one on the cruise with Senator Busi, Monsignor Pizza, Mohammed Al Bakri, Salvatore Balistreri and – once again, as she now remembered – the man with the severed ear. And then all the rest, right up to that very moment.

Lena listened to her without interrupting, except for fits of coughing. In the end, she did speak.

'I'm coming to Rome, dear.'

Linda was floored. There was something decisive and urgent in that sudden decision. And yet Lena, who was always so generous and open-handed with her explanations, was giving nothing away. Linda heard her mother coughing as she checked the flight timetable.

'There's a night flight to London that leaves this evening, then from there I can get one to Rome. I'll be with you tomorrow afternoon. In the meantime, don't do anything that might be dangerous.'

Words similar to what Salvatore Balistreri had said.

I would hate anything untoward to happen to you.

She found it difficult to make any objection. Lena said goodbye and ended the call. Linda remained flat out on the bed, happy and exhausted. It didn't occur to her to tell Michele Balistreri. She didn't tell him either that the man beside Melania Druc in the Hotel Rixos was the one by the lift on that ship.

The man with the severed ear.

Tripoli, Saturday, 11 October 1969

Mikey Balistreri

Everything changed in the space of forty days. My father sold the villas in Sidi El Masri. He and Alberto are now living in Rome, and for Grandad and me he's rented a maisonette in Garden City. Then Grandad died, after agreeing to the sale of his olive groves. The Hunts moved to a house along the coast road, and Laura is far away in Cairo. The Al Bakri family has left the corrugated metal shack next to the cesspit among the olives and moved to an apartment near Piazza Castello, which Gaddafi now calls Piazza Verde.

To keep myself busy, I have my three friends and the MANK organization. It was Ahmed who told us that Farid and Salim make money out of selling contraband goods. The idea that we should take a piece of their business came from Nico and Karim, as did starting the MANK's business up here in Tripoli. I'm not at all interested in Farid and Salim's business and agree to Ahmed's plan just to satisfy the group and to keep myself from thinking gloomy thoughts.

The colourful market of Souk Al Mushir is crowded all day. When evening comes, the Italians go home or to the places that sell alcohol, like the Gazzella and Waddan hotels. The Libyans divide into two groups: the women and children go home, the men to smoke *shisha* in the bars around Piazza Castello.

Farid and Salim are drinking *chai*. Karim, Nico and I are hiding behind a car, crouching well down so as not to be seen. Ahmed's already at the port, to note down the mileage of the motorboats before they go out for the night. A bicycle stops in front of Farid and Salim's table. It's one of their fishermen, who gets off and says something to them. He seems agitated. The two brothers immediately jump up, get on their bicycles and head off along the coast road in the direction of the port.

'They've seen him,' Karim says, already getting on his bicycle.

'Stay here, Karim. Nico and I'll go to the Underwater Club and take Papa's motorboat so we can follow them.'

But Karim doesn't reply; he's already pedalling off to the port.

'Damn. Nico, can you follow him and keep an eye on him? I'll go and get the motorboat.'

On the Triumph, I get to the club in less than ten minutes, and I'm within sight of the port just as Farid and Salim set out to sea. Karim and Ahmed are nowhere to be seen, only Nico on the quayside, but I haven't got time to go into port and bring him on board.

The only lights on the water are those of their boat in front of me and the coastguard patrol boats in the distance. I follow them at a distance to La Moneta, where they moor at the jetty in front of the villa. A hundred metres away, I put the engine in neutral. Using my infrared binoculars, I watch them get down on to the beach below in the dim light of the lamps on the little quay.

Salim has a knife in his hand and is pushing Karim, who has his hands tied behind his back. Then comes Ahmed, also with his hands tied. Lastly, there's Farid, with another knife. They bind Karim and Ahmed each to a lamp post with ropes they have on board.

I don't need to think. I don't hesitate; I have no doubts.

I suggested the blood brotherhood, not them.

Using the oars, I bring the motorboat to seventy metres off the beach and take my old Diana 50 from the locker in the bows, a lead pellet already loaded in it. I put a handful more in my pocket and station myself in the bows with the binoculars and the rifle.

Laughing, Farid grips Karim's head, while Salim holds the point of the knife to his throat. This is a justifiable vendetta against their younger brothers. Both are better looking, harder working, more intelligent. As a boy, Karim dared to throw Salim in the cesspit, and now Ahmed's spying on their business.

'Let them go! Now!'

My voice shatters the tranquil night. There's a moment's silence on the beach, then an oily laugh from Farid.

'Well, well, Signorino Michele, as well, eh? Instead of hiding in the dark out at sea, why don't you come on out and enjoy the show from here?'

'Because he doesn't have the balls, that's why!' Salim shouts.

With his sharp knife he cuts off the end of Karim's right ear. Karim's cries of pain drown the coarse guffaws of his two torturers. Salim then turns triumphantly towards me, holding the bloody trophy between his two fingers.

'And now,' Salim screams, 'I'm going to cut off something more important from that nosy best friend of yours.'

For the first time since my mother's death I feel alive. I don't give Salim time to get anywhere near Ahmed. The Diana 50's pellet passes cleanly through the hand holding the knife and he begins to screech like an eagle.

After a moment's indecision, Farid runs towards Ahmed. I reload and slip the fisherman's knife in my belt. I put the engine in gear and set off for the jetty, ready for action.

'If you shoot again, Mikey, I'll cut his throat.'

Farid's voice is less confident as he points the knife at Ahmed. The motorboat touches the jetty. Without bothering to moor it, I put the engine in neutral and jump out, pointing the rifle at Farid.

'If you touch him, Farid, you won't leave here alive.'

He stares at me, stunned: the middle-class Italian kid, his boss's son. He wonders if I'll really shoot. Not sure what to do, he lowers the knife. Ahmed's kick catches him in the testicles, making him bend at the knees and drop the knife.

Although he's wounded, Salim grabs the knife and tries to throw himself on Ahmed, who's still tied up.

You don't know who you're dealing with, guys.

I shoot and the Diana 50 pellet pierces Salim's cheek and tongue, coming out on the other side.

I feel neither fear nor remorse. I know I've come to the point I was heading to sooner or later, anyway. I throw the empty rifle down and take out the fisherman's knife with the saw-tooth blade. I cut Ahmed loose, while Farid backs away down the jetty.

Ahmed takes the knife from my hands and goes up to Salim, who's now lying on the ground, moaning about his wounds. Farid watches him, terrified. He can't believe what he's seeing: the savage beasts that have been beside him all these years. Ahmed calls out to him in Arabic.

'Watch closely, Farid, so you'll remember this as long as you live.'

I know what he's about to do. I think about stopping him, but only for a moment.

Ahmed grabs Salim's head by the hair and pulls it back. Farid and Karim cry out as the knife slices cleanly through Salim's carotid artery. Ahmed lets him fall to the sand. Then he goes up to Farid, his knife dripping with blood.

'Ahmed, for the love of Allah,' Farid mumbles, terrified, dropping down on to his knees.

'Do not blaspheme, my brother. Allah doesn't listen to worms.'

No, that's enough. There's no point.

'Ahmed, no. Not him.'

It's an order, and Ahmed knows it. I've given him hundreds, since we were little boys. He's always obeyed without a word.

But things are changing between us.

'If we don't kill him tonight, Mikey, we'll come to regret it one day.'

I'm not discussing it with him; I'm still the boss. I turn to Farid.

'We won't kill you, because you can be useful to us. Tonight, you'll take us with you to whoever supplies you with the cigarettes, and you'll tell them we're to be trusted. From today, we're taking over your business. Got it?'

Farid nods repeatedly, his mouth gaping open and his eyes staring wide.

'Tomorrow, you will tell Mohammed that you had an accident at sea and Salim drowned.'

Farid signals his assent like an automaton. But Ahmed sticks the knife to his throat. Promises like that aren't enough for him.

'Lastly, brother, I don't want to see you in Libya ever again. Tomorrow, you pack your bags, tell Mohammed you want to try your luck somewhere else and leave. If I ever see you again, I'll cut your dick off and make you eat it. Have you got that, Farid?'

Farid's already nearly dead with fear. While we tie him up, he's still begging Ahmed to spare his life. We free Karim and tend to his ear as best we can with alcohol and gauze from the villa. The upper quarter's been sliced right off. It'll always be a reminder of this night. But what can we say about it?

I know there's only one solution, although even that's shaky, and suggest it.

'Karim and I can say we had a dare with the knives. And that, without meaning to, I wounded him in the ear. Whether he believes it or not, Mohammed's not going to report me, is he? And Karim will back the story up.'

'All right. Papa will have his doubts, but he'll never report Mikey,' Karim says.

He's right. Gaddafi or no Gaddafi, I'm still an Italian and the son of his boss.

Ahmed also agrees.

'You go off with Karim while I clean up and put the body in their boat. Then I'll tie two stones to his ankles. When you get back, we'll dump him in the open sea. Then we'll go with Farid to meet the smugglers. When we get back, we'll take the motorboat to the rocks and crash it into them. Farid will escape. Salim won't.'

Autumn 1969

Mikey Balistreri

In the end, Mohammed had to accept the story, because I was still the son of his boss, Salvatore Balistreri. Farid went off to Tunisia, leaving the field clear for us and, within a month, the four of us had transformed a little cottage industry of smuggling into one of industrial proportions. The MANK organization didn't exist on any business register, yet its profits were real and substantial. And, from cigarettes, we went on to currency, seeing that Gaddafi had drastically limited its export and the Italian and Jewish communities were desperate.

Currency smuggling is certainly dangerous, but much more profitable than smuggling cigarettes. Cash takes up less space and is worth a thousand times more. All we had to do was get the money out of territorial waters, deposit it in the Banco di Sicilia on Lampedusa, then transfer it from our account to whoever had entrusted us with it, minus our 30 per cent. We had my father's motorboat, contacts within the Italian community, impunity because of my father's name and the balls for the job.

Karim was against it initially. It's against Islamic religious principles to take a percentage. What's more, we were violating the laws of his beloved Gaddafi and robbing the Libyan people. In the end, we came up with a compromise. Karim went back to Cairo, where he wanted to be, to look after the MANK's business there, and where he could help finance his beloved Muslim Brotherhood. Only with his share of the proceeds, naturally.

The money is no compensation for the absence of the two women most important to me, one dead and one far away. But there's so much cash we can't keep it in my cellar any more. Ahmed has an idea. He has a blacksmith friend of his build four metal strongboxes, similar to the safety-deposit boxes they have in banks. Sturdy, spacious and absolutely watertight, and each with a ring welded on to it so that a steel cable fitted with a lock can be threaded through it and they can be tied together securely.

One initial is engraved on each box: 'M-A-N-K'.

Ten kilometres out from La Moneta, a large rock surfaces from the water. No one goes fishing there, because, by a quirk of the wind, the current's very strong. Several metres down, almost at the base of the rock, there's a cave that goes upwards to a point where it emerges out of the water.

Once a week we take the money there, already divided into four waterproof plastic sacks. After we place them in the boxes, we thread the cable through the rings, linking them together, wind it round a large rock and lock them all together. It's a complex operation, but our treasure's worth protecting.

We all have the key to our own strongbox, but in order to take the boxes away you need the key to the lock that secures the steel cable around the rock. And I alone have that key.

I am the boss, as always, and I always will be. And not even Colonel Gaddafi can change that, even though I know that the MANK's fourth member, Karim, hasn't thought so from the very start, and now thinks it even less.

Sooner or later the boy with the severed ear will break up our brotherhood of blood.

Monday, 8 August 2011

Rome

Balistreri's stomach was suffering a major acid burn after Linda Nardi's appearance on Sky. And he was furious. She had not stuck to his order to keep away from this story and in a very short time had found out who was behind GB Investments in Luxembourg. And with that last sentence of hers she'd openly challenged the police – namely, him – and also some very dangerous people.

Also on board were Senator Emilio Busi, Monsignor Eugenio Pizza and other very important individuals whom the police will seek to identify.

But those other very important people weren't like the senator and the Monsignore. Busi had told him straight after he'd mentioned the man with the severed ear.

There's a great deal of difference between businessmen and killers.

Balistreri was getting more and more worked up. He got up and hobbled over to the telephone and dialled Colombo's mobile.

'Have you found the senator and the Monsignore yet?'

'Not yet, Balistreri.'

'Well, if you don't find them alive now, later they'll be dead. This is about Libya. They haven't helped the people they should have and those people don't joke around with people who betray them.'

He heard a sigh, then the barely contained anger in Colombo's voice.

'We've warned you already. Forget this whole business. Including Libya.'

Balistreri put the phone down and went back to lie on the sofa. He couldn't forget Libya, not now. He had left the two women he'd loved there. One was dead, and he hadn't ever wanted to know anything more about the other one.

Tripoli, Sunday, 21 December 1969

Mikey Balistreri

We haven't seen each other for four months when I find her waiting for me in front of the Garden City maisonette. At eighteen, Laura Hunt has her mother's body and the clear, intelligent eyes of her father.

'Aren't you going to invite me into your new house, Mikey?'

There are a thousand things I want to tell her, but she hasn't come to talk. As ever, she's thought about it and come to a decision.

'Have you got any protection, Mikey?'

I shake my head, puzzled. She smiles.

'I've got one. I got it two months ago, thinking of you at New York airport. I hope these things don't go out of date, like medicine.'

I've always loved you, but the woman I've fucked is your mother.

'There have been other girls, Laura.'

She starts to laugh.

'I never had any doubts, Casanova. An ugly moron like you, all muscle and no brain . . . I'm not surprised some poor girl might have found you interesting.'

Laura gets on top of me. And everything is there. Love united with passion, inexperience with desire, trust with the wish to grow together. But as I enter her I can't block out the image of Marlene tied up under me, spitting my own blood back in my face.

This is love, but it will end.

'Did your mother and my father have an affair?'

She shifts over in the bed, props herself up on one elbow, her eyes focused on a memory.

'That awful day on La Moneta, I thought my parents' marriage was over. I was ready to do anything to stop that. But Marlene assured me that she and William would stay together. Then your mother died and things between them calmed down. It was almost as if nothing had ever happened. I never heard them argue again.'

'But you haven't answered my question. Did they have an affair?'

'Why go on about it, Mikey? You'll only hurt yourself, and others. Your mother . . .'

She doesn't say *is dead*, or *killed herself*, or *was killed*. She says nothing more.

I hold her close, the most wonderful creature in the world, the only person apart from my mother who doesn't want me to change. In this embrace there's love, warmth, peace. But no future. That's already behind us.

Monday, 8 August 2011

Rome

Balistreri was totally overwhelmed by all these things coming one on top of the other. He couldn't put any order into the facts he knew. Tanja Druc's missing finger dissolved into that of Nadia Al Bakri, Melania Druc's face into that of his mother; the image of the Zawiya exterminator became that of Karim Al Bakri, the kid with the severed ear who now must be a man. And then there was his father and his three long-time buddies.

He knew the key to everything lay there in that tangle of past, present and future. But there were too many threads; he couldn't find a place to start.

Of course Beatrice Armellini had told him who he should contact: he wants *to tell you the truth.*

Your old friend is waiting for you . . .

Balistreri thought about that absurd moment of intimacy, suspended between life and death. She certainly hadn't done it out of passion. It was almost as if she were an actress. After all, hadn't she won *Grande Fratello*? But then, why do it without an audience . . .

But there had been one . . .

She had been acting for whomever was watching, except she thought she was being observed through a pair of binoculars, not the telescopic sight of a gun.

Beatrice Armellini was acting the part that her real boss – not Senator Busi – had ordered her to play. But why?

The answer came floating up, like a piece of cork from the depths of the sea.

To take you back where you don't want to go. It was the killer who sent her to you. He didn't shoot too late. He waited until she'd passed on the message.

All his experience as a policeman and his rationality as an adult, all the efforts he'd made over the years to forget, to let the roots of evil dry up and wither inside him: everything was telling him the same thing.

Call Colombo and Corvu. Wait till they find Busi and Don Eugenio and question them.

But that was Michele Balistreri, the adult who was rational, wise; an experienced policeman near retirement. But through Beatrice Armellini, the man with the severed ear had sent his message to Mikey Balistreri.

He's waiting for you after all these years and he'll tell you the truth.

9 Appointment with a Killer

Tuesday, 9 August 2011

Lugano

It was almost dawn. Don Eugenio Pizza and Senator Emilio Busi were sleeping in the living room. They had collapsed after having emptied all the accounts and made the last phone call.

At a certain point Don Eugenio opened his eyes. A faint light was coming from the kitchen. It was the light above the extractor hood. And yet he was certain he had switched it off. Unsteadily, he got to his feet. He was overcome with tension and tiredness.

He woke Busi and pointed to the light. Together, they went cautiously towards the kitchen.

The light above the extractor hood was switched on and the door that opened on to the lawn that gave on to the lake was open. They could see the dark waters and the street lamps that illuminated the Riva Paradiso. The sky was showing the first light of dawn and the moon was slipping gently away.

The man sitting at the kitchen table was staring at them. He had a Walther PPK in his hand. Neither man needed to ask him what he was doing there. They had known him for many years. They knew very well why he was there and what he was capable of doing.

He could put an end to their lives, as he had done with so many others.

Rome

Giulia was sleeping on the sofa, but Linda hadn't slept a wink. She had lain on the bed with the television on and the sound off. But the images running through her mind were completely different to those on the screen.

Melania and Tanja, Domnica, the man with the severed ear, my mother coming to Rome. What should I do?

At nine o'clock the faces of Busi and Pizza came on the screen. Linda immediately switched on the sound and heard about the discovery of the two bodies in Lugano.

Giulia was still asleep in the living room. She ran to wake her. Together they listened to the latest news from Switzerland.

Giulia Piccolo's face went pale.

'This is it, Linda, no more. We have to tell the police. And you need to be somewhere safe.'

'Why?'

'Because you know too much. Remember which one of us happens to be a policewoman?'

'Where should I go?'

'As far away from here as you can. What about your mother's in California?'

Linda smiled.

'My mother's already on a plane for Rome. She'll be here this afternoon.'

'No, Linda. You're not safe here. You should go to California. Please listen to me. As soon as your mother gets here, both of you go back to San Francisco. I'll come with you. I already have a US visa, and you have an American passport. We'll go this evening.'

Linda shook her head. After the deaths of Senator Busi and Monsignor Pizza she no longer had any doubts.

I can go away, but I can't run away.

'We'll go and pick my mother up, Giulia. We'll speak to her and then decide.'

At nine in the morning, Balistreri's mobile began to ring. Slowly, the ring tone penetrated his artificial sleep, brought on only by the sleeping tablets he'd taken the night before. At every ring his conscience became clearer, but his mind resisted. Eventually, he answered it.

Corvu gave him the news, but made no comment.

Two hours earlier, the bodies of Senator Emilio Busi and Monsignor Eugenio Pizza had been found at Busi's son's house in Lugano by the young woman who went to clean every morning. This was as much as was being made known to the public.

Then there was the confidential information supplied by the Swiss police. The two bodies were face down on the kitchen floor, each shot by a single bullet to the back of the head. Among their personal belongings were two mobile phones with Swiss SIM cards.

'The numbers correspond to the ones we know about,' said Corvu, in conclusion.

Balistreri remained silent. Then, while his deputy was asking him what he wanted to do, Balistreri ended the call, switched off his mobile and unplugged the land line.

He lit a cigarette and lay down on the sofa. He could picture those two old cronies kneeling next to each other with the barrel of the pistol a few centimetres from the back of the head, conscious that their lives were about to end right there. He felt no pity for them.

More than forty years ago four men had come together to bring about a certain end. My mother was against it, and died. Today we have the same four men again. Except the pact they had has come apart, like the MANK back then.

Almost all the news on the radio was taken up with the mysterious deaths of Senator Emilio Busi and Monsignor Eugenio Pizza. With extreme caution, it was suggested there might be a *possible* link with Linda Nardi's investigation.

Balistreri got up off the sofa to go out and get some more whisky and cigarettes. On the floor near the front door, was an envelope. It looked as if it had been there for nearly thirty years, from that winter in 1983. It was unmistakable, brown and with no stamp. Inside a sheet of white paper with an address typed on it:

Via dei Pini 1952

Signed: *PO Box 150870*

Balistreri could see the city outside through the windows. It was Rome right now, in present-day Italy. This invitation to an address came not from the living city out there but from somewhere else, and was written on an old typewriter in another time, dictated by a different code of honour.

A duel. One you cannot refuse.

Almost without being aware of what he was doing, Balistreri went over to his bookcase. *Beyond Good and Evil* lay buried under a mountain of books, but he had never forgotten where it was.

As with all his dreadful memories.

Inside that old book was all the correspondence from 1983: copies of the letters sent and received, together with photographs. He hadn't looked at them in almost thirty years. But neither had he destroyed them.

There was the photograph of his father, Salvatore Balistreri, with the young Lieutenant Muammar Al Gaddafi at Abano Terme a few days before the *coup d'état*. The photograph with which he, Michele Balistreri, had forced his father to abandon the project of the bridge over the Straits of Messina and go into voluntary exile.

A gift from Karim for having given him Nadia's killer.

The last envelope was dated 5 February 1983 and contained a short typewritten page and two smaller envelopes.

In one was Laura Hunt's letter. He had never reread it and had no wish to now. That letter had drawn a line between forgetting and avenging that had lasted a lifetime. A barrier which Laura had offered him as the only means of living with remorse without destroying himself in a fruitless search.

Your mother killed herself right after you went off with my mother. There was nothing you could have done.

He had also thought of that letter as another gift from Karim Al Bakri for having shed light on the death of his sister, Nadia. And perhaps it was, in part. But there was something missing. Balistreri had known it back then, because Karim had never tried to hide it from him. And he had even told him, in that brief typewritten note.

Our correspondence ends here.

But now something had changed. After more than forty years, the regime that had been born out of injustice was now in collapse, traitorous Italians were to blame and time was running out.

And Karim wants justice for Ahmed. In exchange, he's offering me the truth about my mother.

Balistreri looked again at the colour photograph, taken with a powerful telephoto lens from the stern of a boat in the open sea. Farid Al Bakri's face was contorted with pain and terror, he was tied to the game chair of a fishing boat, his own severed penis stuck in his mouth, a stream of blood and two shark fins circling him.

He was conscious of never really having looked at it.

Only now did he fully comprehend the deeper meaning. Nadia Al Bakri had been raped, killed, and one of her fingers had been cut off. Now he could see clearly not only the terror in the eyes of Nadia's killer but the photographer's pleasure in that horrific scene.

Beware that, when fighting monsters, you yourself do not become a monster . . . for when you gaze long into an abyss, the abyss will start looking into you.

He had been the one to read these fragments of Nietzsche to Karim, Ahmed and Nico. He had been the one to persuade them there was a world *beyond good and evil*, that everything was permissible *in love* and therefore also *in hate*.

That was why he'd thought of it.

The Koran. An eye for an eye, a great grief for a great grief.

He was now certain. Linda was to be the vehicle of his grief. He grabbed his mobile and dialled. The ring tone went on for some time, then he heard Linda's voice.

'What do you want, Michele?'

'Where are you?'

Silence. *None of your business, Balistreri.*

'Linda, that man's here in Rome. You're in danger.'

My father told you so, as well.

Silence. *And what will you do about it, Balistreri? Leave me to fend for myself, like with Manfredi?*

'I'm with Giulia. She'll protect me.'

Then Balistreri heard a sigh. It was like a last feeble remnant of whatever it was there had been between them.

'That man in the Rixos, the one with the severed ear . . . I've thought about it, he's the same man as the security guard near the lift on the cruise ship, when I saw Melania and Tanja . . .'

The call ended. Balistreri tried calling back, but there was no reply. There was no longer any doubt in his mind.

Either I accept his invitation, or Linda Nardi dies.

He called Corvu, who answered on the first ring.

'Graziano, put Linda Nardi under police protection. Have someone follow her immediately, twenty-four seven. Giulia was with her a little while ago. And not a word to anyone. I'm putting you in charge of this.'

At any other time, Corvu would have objected, having no liking for anything that resembled American police methods. But he caught the same desperation in Balistreri's voice he had heard there five years earlier, when they were coming back by helicopter from a false trail, leaving Linda to face Manfredi alone.

Corvu called back after five minutes.

'I've put two plainclothes men outside Linda's block. I also called Giulia Piccolo. She didn't want to tell me exactly what was going on, but she said they were getting their bags ready.'

'They're leaving?' Balistreri asked in alarm.

'They're going to America. They've got two seats for Los Angeles at nine o'clock tonight. Then, from Los Angeles, there's a connection to San Francisco.'

'Oh, they'll be going to her mother's,' Balistreri said, slightly relieved.

'Yes, but we can't follow them all the way to America. Fortunately, Giulia's going with her.'

Balistreri hesitated a moment. He could do nothing to stop them. And then, perhaps Linda would be safer in America, at least until he had gone to the address he'd been directed to.

'Speak to Piccolo. Tell her to be on the look-out. Have them followed right up to boarding, and make sure they take off safe and sound.'

Balistreri ended the call. He wondered if these precautions would be enough.

If I refuse this duel, I can't protect Linda Nardi for ever.

He wondered if he was over-dramatizing things. But on the rational rather than the emotional plane, it was clear that Melania had been killed, along with Tanja, as revenge, Domnica killed like a dog and Beatrice first used and then also eliminated.

There's nothing else I can do, other than go where Karim's asking me to go. I can only hope that Linda gets safely on that plane.

* * *

It was just before eight in the evening when Corvu called.

'Linda and Giulia are at the airport now. They've checked in and they're going through Security. I made it clear to the men that they should follow them right up to boarding and make sure they take off safely. Don't worry.'

'All right. Call me on my mobile when they're boarding.'

He ended the call, went to the desk and looked in the last drawer. There was the Beretta. It hadn't fired another shot since that night five years earlier when he'd been shot in the side and his knee had been fractured. He looked at it for a little while and left it there.

It wouldn't be any use.

He had to take his old Fiat Ritmo, and punched the address into the satvav: Via dei Pini 1952.

Obviously, he knew what he should have done as a policeman: notify his colleagues and go with back-up to Via dei Pini. But he knew the killer who had slipped the address under his door.

That invitation is for me alone. Otherwise, Linda will die.

Ciampino

He drove to the ring road and from there to the Via Appia. After the turn-off for Ciampino airport, he turned into a dark road: Via dei Pini. He travelled several kilometres through countryside lit only by the moon. He had no fear for himself: he never had had, and even less so now. His only fear was for Linda Nardi.

The narrow road ended in an unmetalled path which led to a large green gate bearing the number 1952. It was very secluded; the ideal place for a killer on the run. A hundred metres from the gate he glimpsed a huge, dimly lit farmhouse with a powerful Kawasaki parked in front of it.

Balistreri looked at his watch. It was 9.05. He called Corvu, who answered on the first ring.

'Have they left?'

'The plane for Los Angeles took off a few minutes ago, with Linda and Giulia on board.'

'You're sure? You had them followed right on to the plane?'

'Of course. The officer followed them right up to the last moment of boarding.'

'No one came back down the jet bridge?'

'No one. The officer had confirmation from the hostess via the intercom that Linda and Giulia were on board. And his colleagues didn't move until the plane doors were closed. For the next fifteen hours Linda and Giulia will be on a flight to California. There's no need to worry.'

But Balistreri wasn't satisfied. Something was telling him that it wasn't that simple.

'Corvu, are you sure someone wasn't following them? Someone who got on the plane?'

There was a brief silence.

'Well, actually, I can't be sure. I'm just telling you what the officers who were following her have told me.'

'I want you to do two things. Check the passenger list. And get copies of all the footage from the airport's CCTV cameras where Linda and Giulia can be seen.'

'All right, will do. But where are you? Are you at home?'

Balistreri ended the call and took the battery out of the phone. It was ten past nine.

He looked at the gate and felt a warning twinge in his knee. But he ignored the pain and climbed over it.

He had almost reached the farmhouse when he felt a gun pressed against his neck.

'Welcome, Commissario Balistreri. Place yourself against the wall with your arms and legs spread out.'

The man spoke in English with an African accent. He checked to see that Balistreri was unarmed and took his mobile and the battery. Then he led him into the farmhouse and into a large, simply furnished room.

'Turn around, very slowly.'

Balistreri turned around. The man with the gun was a black African, probably a member of the Libyan Special Forces. He was ten centimetres taller and twenty kilos heavier than Balistreri, and many more years younger. And he was holding a gun which he showed every sign of knowing how to use.

'You've come here alone, unarmed, and taken the battery out of your mobile so that your colleagues can't trace you. Aren't you afraid of dying?'

Balistreri ignored the question.

'I'm just here to see your boss. After all this time, I think he wants to see me before killing me.'

'Well, I'll ask him that. Meanwhile, get walking.'

At gunpoint, Balistreri walked down a long, almost dark hallway, up to an open iron door with three steps leading down from it.

'In you go,' ordered the man with the gun.

Balistreri walked down the steps and found himself in a cellar lit by a single bulb, with two chairs in the centre.

'You see those handcuffs, Balistreri? Put them on your wrists and lock them. That's it, excellent. Now hand me the key and sit down there. You won't have long to wait – he'll soon be here, but you'll have some time to say your prayers.'

Balistreri heard the heavy door close. Then the key turning in the lock. He thought about the person who was about to arrive, but he wasn't afraid. That person would never shoot him in cold blood, handcuffed.

That would be too much, even for Karim Al Bakri. Or too little.

*   *   *

After ten minutes he heard the sound of the Kawasaki setting off.

Then he heard the cellar door open and hesitant feet come down the three steps.

The footsteps of an old man.

Although he was the same age as Balistreri's father, Mohammed Al Bakri looked a lot older. His face was deeply lined, and he had only a few white hairs on his head and a good many dark blotches. He was very bent and wore very thick dark glasses.

'Sit down, Signor Michele. And keep still. Otherwise I won't hesitate to shoot.'

He spoke in Italian, using the same respectful title he used with Balistreri senior when he was his gofer. He was struggling for breath a little and his bony hands were shaking a great deal, but in the right one he held a Smith and Wesson.

He's shaking, half blind, but from three metres away he can easily kill me with a gun like that.

It was now that Balistreri began to feel afraid. Mohammed Al Bakri was very different from Karim. He could shoot him in cold blood, no problem. And, in the meantime, Karim could kill Linda.

The perfect revenge. You killed Ahmed; we'll kill Linda.

The words that came from his mouth sounded pointless, stupid.

'I'll do whatever you like, Mohammed. Just don't harm any innocent women.'

Mohammed Al Bakri took off his dark glasses. His eyes were red and misted with cataracts. But his scorn was clear. It was the same scorn Mikey had read in his eyes the day he'd reproached Mohammed for not wanting to find his daughter's real killer.

'We're not here for your *gahba*, Signor Michele. We're here for my son.'

'Karim? He's killed all those women, and Busi and Don Eugenio as well.'

Mohammed Al Bakri nodded.

'Collateral damage of no consequence, or else traitors to Colonel Gaddafi. But I'm not talking about the son who's alive, Signor Michele. I'm talking about the other one.'

The other one. Ahmed.

Mohammed stared at him.

'Karim doesn't want me to avenge that wrong here tonight. He's a poor, deluded man who talks about an old brotherhood of blood and the stupid things you did as boys together. He wants you to go to Tripoli to settle matters. He doesn't understand that you're a coward, like all Italians, and would never go there.'

'I'll go, Mohammed. If you can promise me that no harm will come to Linda Nardi.'

Mohammed Al Bakri spat on the ground and looked at him with such deep hatred that Balistreri no longer had any doubts.

I'm going to die here, tonight. And then they'll kill Linda.

'In exchange he'll offer you that truth you care so much about.'

That truth. That wretched day Italia flew off the cliff.

Mohammed went on, sneering.

'When your mother set off for that cliff, a real son would have gone after her and tried to comfort her. But no, you went off to Tripoli with that American *gahba* . . .'

Balistreri couldn't utter a word. He felt an intense pain in his stomach and his chest.

So this is how he wants to kill me: not with the gun but with a memory.

'While the boys were on the beach, myself, Busi, the priest and your father talked in the living room for an hour, then Busi and the priest went off. Your father was very agitated, so I went up to the cliff to persuade your mother not to do anything stupid. I got there at three.'

The truth you no longer wanted to hear, Michele. The truth you'd sworn to seek for ever.

Mohammed paused, either to remember better or to catch his breath.

'Your mother wasn't there. And yet we'd all seen her go off just before you went off with Marlene Hunt. It was strange.'

'Did you look down to the rocks?' Balistreri couldn't stop himself asking.

Mohammed Al Bakri nodded thoughtfully.

'I went partway down the slope, until I saw her body on the rocks.'

Balistreri couldn't contain himself. He made to get up and Mohammed pointed the gun at him.

'Do you want to die right now, Signor Michele?'

Balistreri tried to keep himself in check, but competing with his terrible rage was the desire to kill Mohammed Al Bakri.

'And you kept quiet about this, Mohammed? My mother could have still been alive . . .'

Mohammed shook his head, the lines in his face looking even deeper.

'She'd fallen from a height of twenty metres. Her body was covered in blood . . .'

'You couldn't have seen any blood . . .'

'I saw it. It was on her bathing costume, everywhere . . .'

'You're lying, Mohammed. When they picked her up out of the sea, she was wearing her kaftan over her costume.'

His father's old retainer snorted. He was tired, and fed up with this old story. He had only told Balistreri these things because Karim had told him to, but that didn't mean he agreed with his son.

He knows I'd never go back to Tripoli, not even for the truth about this.

'You haven't changed, Signor Michele. A fanatical loudmouth who's never understood anything.'

'There's only one thing to understand, Mohammed. One of the four of you killed my mother.'

Mohammed Al Bakri revealed his yellowed teeth in a mocking, scornful grin.

'There are two sides to every truth, Michele. You only want to believe the one that suits you. But that's enough for now. I'm going to speak to Karim. I'll remind him that, in Muslim families, the father rules, and then I can shoot you.'

The old man walked up the three steps with difficulty, then Balistreri heard the click of the lock and the turning of the key.

Three minutes of absolute silence went by. Balistreri thought hard. The possibilities were limited. He was bound in handcuffs and, no matter how poor his health, Mohammed had a Smith and Wesson and had certainly used it many times.

He stood up and went up the steps. But the door opened inwards. He would have to be at least a metre away.

Too great a distance, and too much time.

In that moment there was a gunshot. For a minute he was unsure what to do, then in the distance he again heard the sound of a motorbike departing.

Then he made a move. There were various tools in the cellar, including a pickaxe. He grasped it, went up the three steps and began to hit the door with it. It wasn't particularly strong and it took only a few minutes to break it down.

He dashed out into the hallway, but there was no one there. Mohammed Al Bakri's body lay in the middle of the entrance hall, face up on the parquet, next to a small table on which were Balistreri's mobile and battery. Mohammed had been killed with a single shot to the chest. There was no sign of a gun. The killer must have taken it with him.

Balistreri knew what was waiting for him. Expulsion from the police force; perhaps the accusation of obstructing an enquiry. But he couldn't have cared less. A single thought was tormenting him.

Karim's going to kill Linda as well.

He put the battery back in the mobile, switched it on, called Corvu and sounded the alarm.

*   *   *

They were all there within half an hour, just as before at the Sky Suite Hotel. Police Chief Floris, Colombo and Public Prosecutor Madonna. And they were all furious.

'We told you to keep out of this business, Balistreri, and what do you do? You go to meet the chief suspect and confront him alone. This is Italy, not the Wild West,' said the public prosecutor.

'And it's not Libya either,' Colombo observed.

Madonna stared right at him.

'You didn't happen to shoot him, did you, Balistreri?'

Balistreri didn't care what they thought. All he wanted to do was to check that Linda Nardi and Giulia Piccolo had arrived safely in the United States.

'If I'd come here with the intention of killing him, I think I'd have been a little more careful . . . after all, I am – or was – Head of Homicide!'

'It's not that you got here all nice and calm and then changed your mind?' Colombo asked.

'There's no gun, Colombo . . .'

'You could have got rid of it.'

'Then swipe me. You'll find no traces of gunpowder on my hands.'

Madonna shook his head.

'You could have used gloves.'

Balistreri shrugged.

'So find them, then, these gloves. They must be somewhere around.'

Madonna turned to the police chief.

'I spoke to the chief public prosecutor. Until we have proof positive of Balistreri's innocence, we can't rule him out as a suspect.'

Floris was clearly unhappy.

'All right, then. Test him for gunpowder and look for a weapon and those damned gloves. Until then, you're suspended, Balistreri. And keep away from this investigation, for your own good.'

Balistreri turned his back on them and went off to his car, accompanied by Corvu, who spoke to him in a low voice.

'Tell me where you hid the gun and gloves. I'll make sure they disappear.'

Balistreri put an arm round his shoulders.

'I didn't kill him, Graziano. And I don't want you to get into any trouble. Now, tell me instead about Linda and Giulia. Are you sure no one could have followed them on the plane to San Francisco?'

Corvu hated not being able to reassure him.

'Our men were following Linda and Giulia and so were obviously focusing on them, not on anyone who could have been following them. They are certain they were on board at the moment of take-off. Absolutely certain. And I've checked the passenger list, and there are no names on it that give cause for suspicion.'

'Send it to me at home, will you? Have you checked the CCTV footage?'

'The technical staff are preparing a DVD with all the footage from when Linda and Giulia appear at the airport entrance to boarding.'

'Good. Study it carefully. Check everything: anybody who looks somehow strange, people who crop up in two different places; any meetings, no matter how brief. See if anyone was following them. And let me know at home. I won't move from there.'

Wednesday, 10 August 2011

Rome

Balistreri spent a sleepless night, his memories giving him no rest and that one fixed idea in his head. Linda and Giulia would be on board their flight for hours and he could do nothing for them.

Linda was sitting by the window, Piccolo by her side to protect her. But it wouldn't be enough.

He was still thinking about it when his mobile rang. It was 7 a.m. Corvu sounded tired but cheerful.

'Forensics haven't found either a weapon or gloves. They have nothing on you. They found the rifle that killed Beatrice in the Ciampino farmhouse and, in the garage, the van that ran down Domnica Panu. The murder weapon has disappeared, but Ballistics says it's the same gun that killed Emilio Busi, Eugenio Pizza and Mohammed Al Bakri.

'I don't really care, Corvu. Have you checked the CCTV footage from the airport?'

Of course, Corvu had worked on it all night.

'We've examined everywhere Linda and Giulia appear. There's

absolutely nothing out of the ordinary. No one was following them, either at the check-in or after.'

'Have the DVD sent here to me. When do they land?'

'They touch down in Los Angeles at three in the morning there, midday here, and they have a connection for San Francisco at 7 a.m. They'll be at Linda's mother's house at about 9 a.m. local time.'

'What time's that here?' Balistreri asked impatiently.

'About six in the evening. More than ten hours from now. Please don't worry. Nothing's going to happen . . .'

Balistreri ended the call. He refused to look at the information he had, at Melania and Tanja, Domnica, Beatrice. It was pointless: that case had been resolved. He knew who the killer was. He also knew where to find him. But he had to wait until Linda and Giulia had arrived safely at Linda's mother's house. He poured himself a double whisky, put a Leonard Cohen CD on the stereo at low volume and lay down on the sofa.

All I can do is wait.

At six in the evening, he was woken by the front-door bell. Staggering, he went to open the door. It was the courier with the DVD Corvu had promised him.

Balistreri had a cold shower and drank a whole pot of black coffee. He then put the DVD in the player and sat down in front of the screen.

It's a way of passing the time until they land.

He studied the footage carefully, searching for known or suspicious faces. He watched it three times, but saw nothing. Corvu was right. It seemed that no one had followed Linda and Giulia, either in the airport or on to the plane.

Then, eaten up with anxiety, he made a decision. Linda must have landed by now. He dialled Lena Nardi's landline in San Francisco. Corvu had found the number for him.

The telephone on the other side of the world rang for a long time. Then a woman's voice answered.

'Hello?' Then two coughs.

Michele Balistreri was disappointed. He'd hoped Linda would answer.

'I'm sorry, Signora Nardi, I need to speak with Linda. It's Michele Balistreri.'

He heard nothing for some time, and at one point he thought Lena Nardi had hung up.

'Signora . . .' he whispered.

'What do you want?'

The voice was now unquestionably Linda's. And her very simple question made it clear that his call wasn't welcome. And neither was he.

'Nothing, I'm sorry. I wanted to make sure.'

'That I was here?'

'That you're well.'

That you're alive.

'I'm here. And I'm well.'

'And Giulia's there with you?'

Linda passed the phone to her, without saying goodbye. Giulia Piccolo's voice had a touch of hostility about it.

'Oh, Dottor Balistreri, are you worried about us?'

'Stop joking, Piccolo. I want you to buy a gun. It's easy there. And don't let Linda out of your sight.'

Her voice became ice cold.

'I'm not on duty, Dottor Balistreri. And I'm not under your authority.'

The line went dead.

Balistreri lay down on the sofa. His knee was killing him, but that wasn't what was worrying him.

The endless running away was over. The past was becoming the present, the future the past. He had been running away from that wretched day all his life. And in exchange for a peace that had been nothing more than an endless pause, he had broken his promise to discover the truth about his mother's death. Now events had brought him back to his worst memory. Or perhaps there was even something worse. Perhaps Mohammed Al Bakri was right.

There are two sides to every truth. You only want to believe the one that suits you.

10 The Other Side of the Truth

Tripoli, Saturday, 20 June 1970

Ahmed Al Bakri

Perhaps I should just be happy. The MANK organization's going ahead full steam, and Mikey and I are closer than ever. But that's not really true. Mikey doesn't want to admit it. Or pretends not to know.

Are you in love with her?

Two seasons have passed, winter and summer. But I've never managed to ask Mikey this question. We share everything, from the money we make from the MANK to the people we've killed, but the subject of Laura Hunt is off limits. She's the only danger to our friendship, the spanner that sooner or later will be thrown into the works.

All it took was the young American *gahba* to come back from Cairo at Christmas and immediately things started up again between them.

On the plus side, the MANK organization's doing great business. This morning, Nico, Mikey and I took our last week's earnings to the strongboxes under the sea. Seven thousand sterling — one thousand a day after expenses, including the sweeteners to General Jalloun. There's nothing more useful than having an influential but cowardly man on a string. And Jalloun's both. He takes money from the MANK to close his eyes to the contraband cash and cigarettes. But now, with the arrival of Gaddafi, the monarchist old guard's in difficulty and the general's finding the ground very unsteady beneath his feet.

Jalloun arrives punctually at Mikey's place in Garden City at lunchtime, when everyone in Tripoli keeps themselves indoors to escape the heat. He's in civilian clothes, without his driver, his face hidden by his keffiyeh. He's extremely tense and this leads me to think he's bringing bad news.

'Shut the windows, please,' he tells us, as soon as he's in the house.

Mikey offers him an armchair, and Jalloun lights a Marlboro with the solid-gold Dunhill lighter we gave him. Mikey pours him out a generous dose of vintage Chivas Regal and Jalloun tells us that they're transferring him to Ghadames in the middle of the desert. I don't care about him personally, but it's a big problem for the MANK. However, the general has a plan up his sleeve.

'I want to speak to you alone, Mikey, without him,' he says, pointing at me.

Mikey shakes his head and replies politely.

'Ahmed is more than a brother to me, General. What I feel, he feels. What I do, he does. There are no secrets between us.'

Jalloun swallows a sip of whisky and regards me with his evil, watery eyes.

'Word is that your father's close to Gaddafi.'

He's an idiot; perhaps he thinks he can scare me. And yet he knows what we do to our enemies.

'I think my father looks up to him, General. But he's never spoken to me about him. It's his business, anyway.'

This is a half-truth, because I also have my suspicions that there's a link between Gaddafi and my father. I began to wonder that afternoon on the cliff top when Italia died and I found half a torn photograph in her book.

Jalloun glances nervously through the closed windows. He decides to risk it, perhaps because he doesn't have any alternative. Cowards are useful when they're worried, but they're dangerous when they're desperate.

'A few days ago I said I had an offer to make you, Mikey. I have some powerful friends, boys – friends who are not at all happy with Gaddafi.'

It's exactly what I feared. I get up immediately.

'I'm leaving.'

Mikey looks at me for a second. For the first time, there's darkness in that look. I've obeyed him since I was a child, when he gave me the part of the baddie to play in his films. I was happy to do it; what mattered was us being together.

'Sit down, Ahmed. Let's hear what General Jalloun has to say first.'

His tone is polite, like when we were kids, but – also like then – it's an order and the message is clear.

I'm your boss's son. I'm head of the MANK organization and I give the orders. Nothing's changed.

I remain standing a moment. I don't want to give the orders. What's important to me is that we stay together. But what Jalloun wants could ruin the MANK.

'What do you want from us, General?' Mikey asks.

This cowardly man studies us at length. He's running a great risk, but we're indispensable to him because we're the only ones he knows, and trusts, who are capable of eliminating our enemies.

'In a couple of months it will be a year since Gaddafi took office. And the more time that elapses, the more difficult it will be to kick him out. With my transfer, the MANK business is finished, boys. But, for this job, my friends are offering more money than you could earn in ten years. One million pounds sterling: 2,400 million Italian lira. To be divided among you. Enough to last you your entire lives, and three generations to come.'

I've never cared anything about money. I know it's important for the others: to Nico, for his prostitutes; to Karim, for his poor and needy; to Mikey so he can get away from his father. To me, money's only useful for keeping us all together.

'And what do we have to do for that amount of money, General?' Mikey asks.

Like me, he already knows the answer. But he needs Jalloun to compromise himself, and this leaves me appalled and terrified, because it means he wants to do a deal and tell him what our price will be. But this thing isn't worth all the money in the world.

The general lights another Marlboro and pours himself another whisky. His hand is trembling and his voice is down to a whisper.

'Before the end of August, you have to assassinate that bastard Gaddafi.'

I'm up like a shot. Not out of fear of dying, but at the certainty that this proposal will be the beginning of the end.

The end of the MANK, the end of Mikey and me, the end of the dream.

'I'm leaving, Mikey. I'll pretend I haven't heard a thing.'

Jalloun looks at me, his eyes full of hate and scorn.

'You'll not even get out of Garden City, Ahmed Al Bakri. Or do you somehow think we'd let you live?'

Jalloun already has his pistol in his hand, but one kick from me would be enough to send it flying and leave him with a broken wrist. Mikey knows what I'm thinking. Once again, his words are an order that reminds me of the MANK's hierarchy.

'Let's listen to everything the general has to say, Ahmed. Then we'll be able to make our own decision.'

I point to the gun Jalloun is levelling at me.

'Our own decision, Mikey?'

Mikey smiles at the general. I've never seen him so diplomatic. All of a sudden he seems like his father. I've never seen him like this at all. He must have an excellent reason, over and above any considerations of money.

'Put the pistol away, General. It's not going to help. We have a tape recorder hidden in the room. We use it all the time and give the tapes over to someone we trust who will send them to the police if anything happens to me or my friends. And I mean the Egyptian police, not the Libyan,' he says calmly.

'I don't believe you!' Jalloun bawls.

Mikey gets the previous month's tape from the desk drawer and shows it to him. Jalloun is furious and panicky, and points the gun at us again.

'Where's the tape recorder?'

Mikey shrugs.

'I don't know, General. Nico installed it and, for security, we never asked him where he put it. He sees to all that; he gives us the tapes, and we give them to Karim, who takes them to Cairo. Now that's all clear, can we get back to business?'

The general still isn't sure. He thinks for a moment, then rests the pistol on his knees. He needs people who are capable and without scruples, and we're the only ones that fit the bill. In any case, he's in no doubt about what would happen if the tape gets into other hands.

'Gaddafi is making agreements with foreign countries like East Germany. He's going to pay a huge sum for a select group of bodyguards who have seen service in communist Special Forces. They'll be here in time for the celebrations of the revolution's first anniversary on 1 September. After that, no one will be able to get to him.'

'And now?' Mikey asks.

'Now, his personal security is guaranteed by members of his tribe, the Qadhadhfa. He can trust them, but they don't really have any experience.'

'So it has to be in August,' Mikey says. 'And will there be a suitable opportunity?'

Just as I feared, for some reason or another Mikey wants to do it. And in order for us to remain united I'm going to have to go along with it. But it'll end badly – I know it will. Mikey has no idea about that half a photograph I found, and I certainly can't talk to him about it.

'Yes. Gaddafi's already limiting his public appearances, for fear of an attempt on his life. But in August several tribes, persuaded by my friends, will ask for a public audience, which the Colonel won't be able to refuse. We won't know the date until the last minute, but we do know where and how the meeting will take place.'

I really have to change Mikey's mind on this. We're heading straight for disaster and the break-up of the brotherhood. Besides, Karim would never go along with it.

'It's a suicide mission,' I say, to make him think again, but Jalloun's ready with a counter-attack.

'If they capture you alive, you'll be forced to talk, and I'd be caught in the middle.'

'So what do you propose?' I ask.

It's not difficult to predict that Jalloun's plan will have no provision for the attackers coming out alive, given they know who the instigators are.

'The audience will bring Gaddafi out into the open. We'll see to that. You'll be dressed as policemen; we'll supply the uniforms and weapons. Mikey is so tanned and dark-haired he can pass for a Libyan. Nico as well, with his bushy hair and eyebrows. You can mix in with the officers in charge of crowd control.

'And where will it be?' I ask.

Jalloun doesn't like my question – he doesn't want to reveal all his cards – but in the end he gives in.

'Piazza Castello. It's a symbolic place. Gaddafi wants to address the crowd from the top of the castle wall. He thinks that will keep him out of danger. However . . .'

He wants a sniper, the best in Tripoli. One who's motivated not only by the money but also by hatred of Gaddafi. Mikey fits the bill perfectly, we all know that. He's not going to say no.

'We'll need a precision rifle, General. Preferably a short-barrelled carbine. And a window at the same height, less than a hundred metres away.'

'We'll give you the rifle you want, Mikey, and a safe and secure apartment from which to fire, and at a lot less than a hundred metres. We can buy anything and anyone. And everyone knows about that lion in Tanzania.'

'I'll have to practise with the rifle, General. It's not that simple,' Mikey puts in.

'We'll let you have the rifle very soon, in Ghadames. Whichever one you choose. You can stay with me and practise out in the desert for as long as you need.'

'And what will Nico and I be doing?' I ask him.

Jalloun stubs out the Marlboro and picks up his pistol to let me know that, recording or no recording, there's no going back now.

'Watch his back – you'll be dressed as policemen as well – and guard the main door down on to the street and the landing outside the apartment while Mikey does the job. I'll advance you 25 per cent. You'll receive 250,000 pounds worth of sterling in American dollars before the end of July. The rest when it's done.'

'And who's to guarantee you'll pay?' I ask him.

I'm trying everything I can to make Mikey change his mind, but Jalloun's well prepared. He has an answer for everything.

'My intelligence, Ahmed. This money, which may seem a great deal to you, is spare change to these friends of mine. Once Gaddafi's dead, the country'll be in their hands, and they certainly won't want any trouble from you. And, after all, you've got the tapes, haven't you?'

What can I do? Mikey knows it's a suicide mission. I need to understand what's making him take Jalloun's proposal seriously.

I get up again, this time without asking his permission, and go into the kitchen, where he follows me. I close the door.

'This is insane, Mikey. Not only do you need a good aim, you'll need nerves of steel. Count me out.'

He doesn't get angry; he knows my objections are valid.

'Ahmed, I killed a lion which, had I missed, would have made mincemeat of me. I shot right through your brother's cheeks with a Diana 50 pellet. Before you cut his throat.'

I try another tack.

The brotherhood of blood.

'If Karim knew what we were discussing . . .'

Karim worships Gaddafi and, brotherhood or no brotherhood, he'd turn us in. Mikey knows this, but he's not even listening to me.

'Are you frightened of our fathers, Ahmed? Do you think they're on the other side as well?'

He's right. But he doesn't know about that half a photograph. I could tell him that going along with Jalloun would mean going against our fathers and against whoever's behind them, and that they'd tear us apart. But then I'd have to tell him how I know and he'd tear me apart. Frustration leads me to say the worst thing of all.

'You've gone crazy because of sleeping with that girl!'

Mikey's slap comes from nowhere. He hits me on the cheek and splits my lip. But I'm not concerned about that split right now, it's the split in something else. A split in a long-held dream.

Laura Hunt's more important to him than the MANK, more important than me. She's pure and untouchable, in another world, and one day she'll take him away with her to it.

If that's how it is, I won't be next to him when he fires at Gaddafi. And, without me, he won't be able to go any further.

'I'm sorry, Mikey, you're right. I won't say anything about Laura again. But I can't agree on the other business. It's madness, and I don't want to go behind Karim's back.'

Mikey looks me in the eyes.

'And you don't care anything about Nadia, Ahmed?'

I don't know what he's talking about.

'It's the other thing we're going to ask Jalloun for. The truth about Nadia's and Italia's death.'

So that's what you had in mind, Mikey. I should have got it straight away.

'Let's hear what Jalloun has to say, OK, Ahmed? I'm not keen on being an assassin either, but I want the information and only he can give it to us.'

We go back into the smoke-filled living room. My mind's in turmoil.

'We have a counter-proposal, General,' Mikey announces.

'What, a million sterling's not enough for you, boys? You really are quite greedy, aren't you!'

Mikey keeps his cool.

'No, the money's fine. But we want information about Nadia and my mother, which I'm certain you have. And if what you tell us doesn't ring true or prove useful, then not even 10 million could persuade us.'

Jalloun is surprised and irritated. He thought everything could be settled with money. This little extra's upsetting him because it concerns powerful and dangerous people. And he's a coward.

'We already have a truth about the deaths of Nadia and your mother. Isn't that enough? What more do you want to know?'

'Then you'd better find someone else for the job.'

'Mikey, even supposing your mother was killed – which I don't believe she was – it could have been anyone.'

'No, General, only someone who was already on the island. You said yourself that the coastguard didn't see any boats there that afternoon.'

I'm watching Jalloun. He's a weak old man who's now also drunk. He badly needs us for this job. I know he's about to give in and I hold my breath.

'The coastguard spotted a dinghy,' he blurts out at last. 'They saw it near the cliffs on the rocky side of the island, at about a quarter to four. The information's confidential, boys.'

'Did it put in anywhere?' Mikey asks.

'They're always on the move, Mikey; they don't know. Anyway, a little after four, they passed by again and the dinghy wasn't there any more.'

'Are you absolutely certain, General?'

'The only absolute certainty is death, Mikey. But the coastguard's report was clear. The dinghy drew up to La Moneta under the cliffs towards a quarter to four. Just after four, when they went past that way again, it wasn't there. Is that enough to seal the deal?'

I close my eyes. The times are more or less correct and the coast-guard has powerful binoculars.

In a few minutes I could be dead. I have to get them to change the conversation.

'No, not at all. What can you tell us about Nadia?' I ask the general.

Jalloun turns to me and pulls a derisory and disgusted face.

'What do you want to know, Ahmed? Aren't you satisfied that Jamaal the goatherd was the killer?'

Mikey cuts in.

'Ahmed wants the truth, General. Just like me. If you want to do business with us —'

Jalloun stares right in my face with all the scorn he can muster, spits on the carpet and gets up.

'Do you want to know what they did to your sister for one whole hour, Ahmed? Do you really want to know? I don't think so. It's better you forget the matter.'

I look back at him, just for a second. Jalloun is an idiot. He still doesn't know that his fate's in my hands.

Dear thieving and cowardly general, you're going to die before Gaddafi does. Jalloun's about to leave but Mikey stops him at the door.

'One last thing, General. If that dinghy wasn't important, why is the information confidential?'

Jalloun hesitates, unsure how to reply.

'I admired your grandfather, Mikey. He loved you, and you already have trouble enough.'

But Mikey throws caution to the wind and carries on.

'Why was it kept a secret, General?'

'If I tell you, will you shoot Gaddafi?'

Mikey doesn't answer. Jalloun sighs and opens the door. I'm also waiting for his answer. I can feel that it will decide a great deal. Perhaps everything. In the end, Jalloun gives in. He needs Mikey too much.

'It was a US airforce dinghy, Mikey. It came from Wheelus Field,' Jalloun says, and then leaves.

Mikey rushes off immediately to get his motorbike keys. Now I'm really worried. That dinghy will take his thoughts back to the cliff. Just where I don't ever want him to go again.

'Think about it, Mikey. Tackling William Hunt is about as dangerous as killing Gaddafi.'

But the argument of fear is a useless one with Mikey. He gets on his bike and turns the ignition.

'Go home, Ahmed. We'll talk about Gaddafi when I get back.'

I'm terrified. William means Marlene, and Marlene means Laura. And Laura means that dreadful afternoon when I found out that Italia wanted to see Laura and Mikey together, united.

★　　★　　★

There's nothing I can do but follow Mikey and see where the information about this bloody dinghy takes us. I get on my bike as well and park outside Wheelus Field. He's in there for half an hour and, when he comes out, huge dark clouds are gathering. I follow him at a distance. It starts to pour down as we're driving along the Adrian Pelt coast road and Mikey pulls up outside the Hunts' house. I hide behind a tree on the other side of the road. I've no idea what's going to happen. But I feel it's going to be a turning point, one way or another.

Mikey gets off the bike in the pouring rain and walks through the garden, his hair and clothes already soaked. He looks shocked and wide-eyed. He rings the doorbell.

Marlene opens the door, wearing only a petticoat, her shameless body exposed as usual – or, rather, more than usual.

'What do you want, Michele?'

Her tone is scornful and hostile. Mikey's voice, too, is harsh, guttural, distorted by the tension.

'I want the truth about that day. That afternoon at your house.'

I don't know what Mikey's referring to, but I'm suddenly paying more attention.

'Please leave, Michele, before I call the police.'

Her manner's so arrogant that Mikey takes a step back into the muddy garden. Then he raises his voice.

'Where was your husband when you let me tie you to the bed and fuck you?'

For a moment I'm shocked; I can't believe it. It was staring me in the face and yet I couldn't see it.

It's our Islamic education that prevents us from understanding what for Christians is normal behaviour.

Marlene starts to threaten him.

'Please leave now, Michele, while you still have time.'

The *gahba*'s voice is mocking, though, as well; it's as if she wants to provoke him.

Mikey's upset and out of control. I can almost hear his heart thumping, then I realize it's my own.

He stands his ground.

'No, I'm not leaving. First, you have to tell me what time William came home.'

She replies as if she's bored stiff by the question.

'I called him at five fifteen, as soon as you left. He was in a meeting at Wheelus.'

'I don't believe you.'

'Too bad for you. William was still at Wheelus Field. I told him to come home. And, as you know, when I call, the men come running, Michelino.'

I can see a curtain moving upstairs. My heart starts beating even faster. Now I know exactly what the great American *gahba*'s doing.

She wants to destroy Laura and Mikey's relationship. Exactly what I most want to see.

The derision in the diminutive *Michelino* is the tipping point for Mikey. He takes two strides towards her and his voice becomes a shrill cry.

'You're a whore, and he's a murderer.'

The *gahba* is ice cold and disdainful, intent on finishing the job. I can't believe my good luck.

'At five fifteen, William was at Wheelus, in a meeting with the American ambassador. You can check. Half an hour later, he arrived at Sidi El Masri with the ambassador and other guests for dinner. And he didn't leave; there are at least eight witnesses. They were all our guests at a barbecue that evening.'

Mikey grabs her by the wrist and drags her into the middle of the garden under the pelting rain. She's practically naked, and the rain makes the petticoat stick to her, rendering it transparent. Mikey screams at her with all the rage he has in him.

'He went there to La Moneta with a dinghy! It was him who killed her!'

Marlene stops and looks him in the eyes. I see the fire in those eyes, the fire that can destroy a man. There's everything in that fire: everything, and the opposite of everything: hate and suffering, happiness and regret. But the *gahba* knows very well what she wants and what she doesn't want.

'It's finished with, Michelino. And you're finished, too.'

'Liar!' screams Mikey, his voice, violent and desperate, rising above the sound of the thunder overhead.

He drags Marlene along, she falls and the petticoat rises up and exposes her pubis, her breasts as well. The *gahba*'s sprawling in the mire in which she's always lived and I see what I'd never even dared hope to see.

A gift from Allah, an undeserved gift.

Laura's on the doorstep, wrapped in a heavy dressing gown, her eyes bright with a temperature. The scene before her is unmistakable.

'Mom! Mikey!'

Her voice is drowned out by the thunder. I'm beside myself: the battle's been won without me having to do a thing. Mikey's anger and the American *gahba*'s astuteness have seen to that.

All that remains is what Laura Hunt remembers about that day, and, sooner or later, I'm going to have to deal with that.

Tripoli, Monday, 22 June 1970

Ahmed Al Bakri

Karim went with Laura to Cairo and, after the row with Marlene Hunt, Mikey's shut himself up at home for two days. *Now that the little gahba's out of the way I should feel happy. But there's another risk now: I'm worried that, having lost her, Mikey'll give up everything and go off to Italy; he might also do it because the atmosphere in the city's getting more and more hostile to Westerners.*

Today, the American base at Wheelus Field is closing and, yesterday, Brazil beat Italy in the World Cup final in Mexico.

Mikey, Nico and I take our bikes to the American base, crossing through the ghostly city streets. We ride along Shara Istikal and the Adrian Pelt coast road. Mikey slows down and reads the graffiti: 'Fuck off, America!' and 'Brazil 4–Italy 1'. At Wheelus Fields a gang of young Libyans starts shouting anti-Western abuse and so we travel back to the wooden pier at the Bagni Sulfurei. Mikey switches off his engine and looks at me.

'Ahmed, let's say yes to General Jalloun, before Gaddafi kicks the Italians out, just like they have the Americans.'

'What kind of bullshit is that, Mikey?' Nico cuts in. We haven't yet filled him in on the general's proposition.

I look at Mikey in silence. He limits himself to one short, simple sentence.

'You're either with me or against me, Ahmed.'

My mind's already made up, since the moment he flung the American *gahba* in the mud and ruined his relationship with Laura. Now that he's finally free, the MANK can last for ever. And there's only one way to get him to stay here, and that's to take up General Jalloun's proposal.

Assassinate Gaddafi and turn back time.

I look at the scar on my right wrist, and Mikey looks at it too. We'll keep Karim out of it. But the blood brotherhood will stand, we'll kill Gaddafi, and Jalloun's money will help my brother and his down-and-outs in Egypt.

I rev my Ducati, point to the pier that goes out fifty or so metres into the sparkling sea and smile at him.

'Want to play chicken, Mikey?'

For a moment he doesn't get it, then he smiles back. It's the first time I've seen him smile in days. He revs the engine of his Triumph Thunderbird.

'OK. First one to brake is chicken,' he says.

'Are you two crazy?' Nico shouts after us as we set off at full speed.

We shoot along the pier, neck and neck. It's a matter of moments: too few. Neither of us thinks of braking, and instead we accelerate at full throttle. The pier ends and we fly with our beautiful machines into the sea. It's as if we're flying together, no brakes, towards the unknown. But we're flying together.

The best moments of my life.

I surface out of the water and see Nico mounting his Guzzi, laughing. At top speed, whispering, 'Shit shit shit,' he also flies into the sea with his bike.

We're united, indivisible, invincible.

Tripoli, Wednesday, 1 July, 1970

Ahmed Al Bakri

For several days all three of us have been shut up in Mikey's house in Garden City. We've gone over every detail again and again. The general's already departed for Ghadames. Mikey's going to meet up with him there tomorrow. Jalloun's advance payment has come, and now we've stashed the latest takings in the back of the MANK van and are setting off for the port.

Once in the van, we get the waterproof bags ready before loading them on to the motorboat. The back of the van's boiling hot, plastered with nudes taken from *Playboy*, Nico's mattress for his prostitutes rolled up in a corner. But I can't stop thinking about what Mikey'll want to do once we've killed Gaddafi.

I need to know if the MANK really still exists for him.

'How are we going to divide Jalloun's money up?' I ask him.

'In three, aren't we?' Nico replies, immediately.

I ignore him. It's not his reply I'm interested in. I look at Mikey.

'What about Karim?'

'What the hell has Karim got to do with it?' Nico protests.

I keep looking at Mikey, ignoring Nico.

'My brother's in Cairo, taking care of our business there. The only business we have left, it seems.'

Nico gives me a shove and sends me banging against the van's metal partition. I don't need to wait for anything else; the knife's already in my left hand. I throw it, and the point sticks into the van wall between a Playmate's tits, a few centimetres from Nico's terrified face.

For a few seconds there's complete silence.

It's Mikey who should speak. He's the head of the MANK, if it still exists.

He goes over to the knife, pulls it out of the van wall and, holding it by the point, hands it back to me. His eyes stare into mine.

'If I see that knife out among us again, Ahmed, I'll kill you.'

When he says it, he's totally calm. I know very well he isn't joking. But that's fine. He said 'among us', and that's enough for me.

I'm satisfied: the brotherhood's holding up. The MANK still exists.

Mikey turns to talk to Nico.

'We divide it up four ways, as always.'

Nothing more needs to be done.

Just kill Gaddafi. But we're invincible. We're destiny.

Tripoli, Tuesday, 21 July 1970

Ahmed Al Bakri

Our new house in Tripoli has every modern convenience. It's too much. I slept much better in our corrugated shack near the cesspit. And Karim says these conveniences are excessive compared to the poverty he sees around Cairo.

Mohammed's called us together this morning. We're drinking tea and smoking *shisha* together. We're wondering what he wants to say to us when the radio announces one of Colonel Gaddafi's new decrees.

A monotonous voice starts up in Arabic and immediately there's silence in the living room.

'. . . Decree relating to the Italian ownership of property in Libya. Article 1 establishes the restitution of all Italian-owned property to the Libyan people and, given the damages caused by colonialism, without compensation; this to be followed by the expulsion of the Italian community. Within thirty days, Italian nationals will present themselves to the Libyan authorities with a declaration of assets, which they will renounce in writing, and then leave for Italy with no more than an exit visa. Their personal safety is guaranteed as part of these conditions.'

We look at Mohammed, shocked. He's brought us here on purpose so that we won't have any doubts about the Al Bakri family's role in the new regime. Now we know the price paid for the apartment, the furniture, the electrical goods and the carpets. Karim's happy.

'Gaddafi's right.'

My brother's changed since he's been in Cairo and Salim cut off part of his ear. But I'm not happy.

'But is robbing twenty thousand people lawful under the Koran, Father?'

'Yes, Ahmed,' Karim replies. 'The concept of *jihad* allows you to fight for repossession of what has been taken from you by force. This is our country, not theirs.'

Mohammed's observing me.

'Don't you think it's our right, Ahmed? When I was a child in the Sirte desert, the Fascists wiped out my father and my brothers and raped my sisters. Would you prefer to go back to that stinking shed near the cesspit?'

'Yes, Father. I preferred living in our shack. I knew who I was there. Here, I don't know who I am any more.'

Mohammed gets up and switches off the radio. I see a man who is completely different from the father I once knew. He is dressed well, in Western style, his cheeks are shaven, his hair is styled, his teeth are white. He closes the windows; from outside come shouts of jubilation. This means that we're not only here to listen to Gaddafi's speech. I look at him for a moment. His eyes are like ice.

'If you really do attempt this, Ahmed, your life will be saved, but not Mikey's.'

Karim looks at me, bewildered. He doesn't know what Mohammed's talking about, but I do. He says it again slowly, to make sure there's no doubt.

'Mikey will die, but you won't die with him. You'll stay alive and live with the remorse of not having saved him.'

Mikey will die, but not me. I'll become an old man, grey, elegant, sitting in a beautiful living room like this one, lonely as a stray, left to think about my late great friend.

Mohammed carries on, relentless.

'You've promised Jalloun that you'll assassinate Colonel Gaddafi. Did you think a man like Salvatore Balistreri wouldn't come to know about it?'

Karim looks shocked.

'What? Are you insane? Kill Gaddafi? You, Mikey . . . and Nico, of course.'

I look back at him, my little younger brother, so sure of his ideals.

'If it hadn't been for Mikey, Salim and Farid would have sliced off more than a part of your ear, Karim.'

Mohammed stares at me, his eyes burning. But he doesn't ask me for the truth about that night. He's not interested, not now. Now he's here to ask his sons to betray someone. He already has.

He explains to us calmly what we must do. It's clear that the plan comes from Salvatore Balistreri.

'And what will happen after the assassination attempt?' I ask when he's finished.

'It'll be up to Mikey Balistreri to choose. He can stay here and face a firing squad, or else make his escape and never come back. It's up to you to persuade him, Ahmed. You're the only one he trusts.'

Cairo, Sunday, 26 July 1970

Karim Al Bakri, the boy with the severed ear

Three years have passed since the war of 1967, but it's as if it's only been three days. Cairo is still in crisis, a chaos of beggars, refugees and ex-soldiers with no home or work. The roads are blocked with broken-down cars, motorbikes, bicycles and mule carts, and pedestrians who wander in the middle of the road, among them some who want to be hit, so they can get free lodging in a hospital.

The cafés are full of men without work. They smoke *shisha* and drink tea, which is all they can afford to do. But Mohammed assured me that, within a year, many of these poor guys will find a job in Libya, taking the place of the Italians. Gaddafi promised this to Nasser.

They've never recovered from the sense of defeat. Gaining victory over the Israelis in revenge is the first of our thoughts after every prayer in the Al-Azhar mosque. And I'll fight for this, too, first to rid Libya of those Italian Fascists and then rid our lands of the Zionists. And so I accepted Ahmed's plan to help my father, and therefore Gaddafi; not to save Mikey Balistreri's life. And it's because of this that I've come to speak to Laura.

The riverboat café is anchored in the bend of the Nile. Here, the majestic river slows down after flowing thousands of kilometres from the heart of Africa towards civilization. Civilization? I sometimes wonder what that is. Perhaps thousands of years ago, somewhere between Luxor, Aswan and Abu Simbel, a pharaoh would have resolved things in a wiser and more equitable way. Perhaps then the tribes of Israel didn't have a Zionist mentality and we could have lived in peace. But that's no longer possible today.

Laura is sitting at a table set apart in the shade. She's very beautiful, but seems to be unaware of it, unlike her mother. It's as if her physical beauty were a burden for her, perhaps because it reminds her of her mother. Her eyes are smiling when she sees me, even though they've had a veil of sadness covering them since that day she found out about Mikey and her mother.

'It always makes me happy to see you,' I tell her as I sit down.

Our meetings always start with me saying this, which is always true and aways fresh; nothing can undermine it. If Laura were Muslim, if she weren't absurdly in love with Mikey . . .

'And me, too, Karim, as always.'

But her words don't have the same meaning as mine. I'm the brother she's never had, not what I really want to be. She knows this – we've spoken about it many times – but it's fruitless, because the conclusion's always the same, a tremendous statement, with no appeal.

I'm in love with Mikey, Karim, and always will be.

Spoken by another woman, this wouldn't mean a great deal, but spoken by Laura Hunt it's definitive and holds for ever. I could tell her about the three soldiers killed in Cairo, about what happened to our brother Salim, about the contraband, the bordellos. It wouldn't change a thing, and I know why. She explained it to me in her own way one day in Tripoli when we were listening to the music of that Jewish singer-songwriter that Mikey's so fond of . . .

Laura Hunt's heart has been taken over and occupied totally by someone who'll never grow up; he encapsulates both perfect innocence and perfect evil. But, for Laura, Mikey's evil is the other side to his courage, loyalty and integrity.

And now Ahmed's plan will put him out of her life for ever. And maybe one day, without Mikey Balistreri around, Laura Hunt will see me in a different light.

'You still want to help him, don't you, Laura? And Mikey really needs help right now, doesn't he?'

I explain the situation to her: General Jalloun, the plot to assassinate Gaddafi and the fact that it's been uncovered.

'He'll be shot, Laura. Unless he gets out of Libya and never comes back.'

She doesn't say a word, just listens. I spell out our plan to her in detail, and the part she can play. There's such pain in her eyes I have to force myself not to tell her not to worry, to forget about it. Nor do I tell her that the plan is Ahmed's. Besides, it's not necessary: she knows very well that only my brother's mind could come up with something like this.

In the end she puts her hand on mine.

'Karim, can you swear on our friendship that Mikey's life will be saved? And no one will kill him later in Italy?'

I nod, but what I really want to do is squeeze the hand that's touching mine. But I manage to stop myself.

'If you do as I've said, nothing will happen to him. He'll leave the country and never come back. No Gaddafi agent will go after him. His father wants him to live, and the guarantor is my father, who's very close to the Colonel.'

She draws her hand away and looks me straight in the eyes.

'All right, Karim, you can tell Ahmed that I'll do what you've asked me to.'

There's a cold gleam in her look that reminds me for a minute of her father, William, the soldier.

'But tell your brother that, if anything goes wrong, I haven't forgotten that day on La Moneta.'

Tripoli, Friday, 14 August 1970

Ahmed Al Bakri

It looks as if the Sahara's advanced by twenty kilometres and is about to invade the city. During the day, Tripoli's a desert; no one's walking about the blazing streets. The Italians have closed up their shops, and the only ones left are those queuing up in the sun outside the Office of Alien Property to prove that they've paid off all their debts and are eligible to obtain an exit visa for a final return to Italy.

Nico is beside himself with rage. All he does is curse Gaddafi and those shits of politicians in both the Communist and Christian Democrat parties in Italy who are refusing to send in gunboats to oust the Colonel.

Mikey insists that we go over the assassination plan in obsessive detail. Now, all he's waiting for is the day when he can kill Gaddafi.

He's entrusted me with organizing the escape route, in case the attempt goes awry. I don't know how to interpret his concern here: is it yet one more act of absolute trust or is it that he has some doubts about me and wants to test my loyalty to him?

Mohammed filled me in this morning at home.

'The day has come. The Colonel's giving his speech tomorrow in Piazza Castello.'

There's one thing I'd like to do, something that would give me great joy. But, obviously, I can't leave Tripoli, or Mikey would get suspicious.

'All right, *abu*. I'll pass it on to Karim in Ghadames.'

Mohammed nods.

'Salvatore and Alberto Balistreri are coming into Tripoli today. Mikey's father's worried. He wants to change the boy's mind and persuade him to leave Italy without running the risk of an attempt on Gaddafi's life.'

'How is he going to do that?'

'Don't you worry about that. Just see to it that he does what his brother suggests.'

'Does Alberto know about all this?'

Mohammed shakes his head.

'Alberto knows nothing about the plan. He thinks he's coming to celebrate his brother's birthday. But he's the one that's going to call Mikey this evening.'

The call comes at suppertime, when Nico and I are at Mikey's house in Garden City.

Alberto tells him that the following day, Mikey's twentieth birthday, Salvatore has organized a day out in Misurata to see the annual tuna fishing – the *tonnara* – like they used to when he was a boy. Obviously, Mikey's not interested in going, it's a stupid idea, but in the end Alberto puts his father on the line and, as ever, he manages to persuade Mikey to go.

As soon as Mikey hangs up, the phone rings again. General Jalloun announces that the day of reckoning has come. Mikey tells us it will be the following day at seven in the evening in Piazza Castello. The rifle's all ready and waiting in the apartment that's been provided for us.

Neither Nico nor I make any objections, as if we think that a day out in Misurata is just a way of distracting us from the tension in the hours before the assassination.

'We need to get everything ready for the escape plan tonight,' I remind the other two.

We go out into the sultry night. Mikey and I head for the port on our bicycles and get to the Adrian Pelt coast road in ten minutes. We take the dinghy and the motorboat and go to moor them near the Waddan Hotel.

Nico goes to the Esso petrol station with the MANK van and fills the jerry cans with the petrol we'll need to get to Lampedusa. He then comes to the port and we load them into the dinghy.

We've done what we need to in less than an hour and are back in Mikey's maisonette in Garden City. No one wants to chat. They're coming to pick us up at dawn to take us to Misurata. Nico and I go to our rooms and Mikey stays in the living room.

I know General Jalloun's let him have Laura's number in Cairo and that Mikey doesn't want to leave without speaking to her. I know he's going to call her; otherwise, Karim will get her to telephone him. I know that Laura'll say it's fine for tomorrow evening at nine. Laura Hunt is a person who keeps to agreements. And wants them to be kept, as she's let me know through Karim.

Tell your brother that, if anything goes wrong, I haven't forgotten that day on La Moneta.

But I'm Ahmed Al Bakri, and I have a plan worked out for everyone and everything. And it's going to make the little *gahba*'s threat null and void, too.

Destiny is in my hands.

Ghadames, Friday, 14 August 1970

Karim Al Bakri, the boy with the severed ear

I don't care about Mikey. It would be better if he died, but not as a hero or a martyr. Laura would never get him out of her head then. I want him far away from here. Away from my country, my money and, I hope, from my woman.

Ahmed's plan is perfect, but there's one defect: Mikey has to kill him. I have my part to play and I'll do it willingly. Even Allah would agree.

It's cool here in Ghadames out in the middle of the desert after sunset. I'm hidden away in a corner of a local dive that smells of sheep and sweaty Bedouins. I kept an eye on General Jalloun, who is wrapped up in his keffiyeh, as he was speaking to Mikey on the phone here, informing him of Gaddafi's speech in Piazza Castello tomorrow evening at seven.

Now the pig'll be in a hurry to get back to his coterie of traitors. He doesn't know we shot them all while he was on his way here. I go out and wait for him, my face covered by a Bedouin *ghoutra*. I stand between him and the smelly camel waiting to take him back to the barracks. He walks quickly past me.

'General!' I call out.

The heart of the traitorous pig misses a beat. He's been recognized. Then he sees my face under the *ghoutra* and steps forwards, furious and threatening.

'Ahmed, what on earth are you doing here?'

I unwind the headscarf and he sees my severed ear. I want him to know who it is that will eviscerate him. Ahmed would slit his throat with a single blow. But he's more expert than me. He's given me the eighteen-centimetre knife and shown me how to use it effectively. One swift stab just below the sternum, down and then up.

But not as far as you can go, not if you want him to suffer.

Jalloun has no time to react. The knife goes straight into his stomach, just below the sternum, but not too far. If the blade touches his heart, he'd die straight away.

And that he mustn't do. First, you must know why.

The general's eyes open wide; a stream of blood trickles from his mouth. Slowly, I take out the knife. Blood gushes out with a piece of intestine. I speak to him in Arabic.

'This is for all the money you've stolen from the Libyan people, for my sister, Nadia, and for being a traitor to Gaddafi.'

I wait for him to die, looking into his eyes. Then I flash a torch and a truck comes along to load up the corpse.

This is the first time I've killed, and Ahmed's right: if it's an enemy, it's very easy.

And he's the first of many others I will kill.

Tripoli, Saturday, 15 August 1970

Ahmed Al Bakri

We're all silent on the trip from Tripoli to Misurata, leaving at first light. We reach the port at dawn, when the fishing boats are coming back from the night's fishing. The city, with its white houses, is still asleep. There are eight twenty-metre galleys waiting for us in the harbour, each with about twenty men on board and the lead boat of the *rais*, the head of the *tonnara*.

The silent procession of boats sets off over the tranquil sea. There are two hours of slow sailing while the sun rises, and everyone has a sleep. Everyone, that is, except me. How could I? I look at Mikey beside me. He has a three-day-old beard, bedraggled locks of hair over his forehead, dark rings under his eyes and sun-blistered skin. I look upon him as a brother about to die.

But I'm the brother who will die. Everything will be over in less than twenty-four hours. Everything.

At eight o'clock we arrive at the fishing grounds. Then, the ritual begins. We've taken part in it since we were children. The galleys form into a tight square around the nets. At his father's invitation, Mikey gets into the *rais*'s boat. All around us the water is beginning to foam with blood. The central net, known as the death chamber, is fuller than ever, as if the tuna had been there for some time, waiting for this day. There are more than a hundred fish, of between two hundred and three hundred kilos each. They spin round in a vortex, bouncing against the sides of the nets, blind with fear.

The galleys draw together on each of the four sides. Then, at a sign from the *rais*, the propitiatory songs – the *salaams* – begin, and the men start to haul up the nets. The tuna know their fate is sealed and start fighting viciously among themselves.

It's a sight that's always fascinated Mikey and me. The stronger fish ally with the fishermen in offering up the lives of the weaker victims. But in the end all of them end up dead.

The slow hauling up of the nets starts, by hand and by hoist. The fierce primordial struggle of the fish as they rise to their deaths makes the water boil, while the first tuna, the tiredest, are caught with long-poled hooks, thrown on board, hooked again by hand, grabbed by their two fins and flung into the bottom of the boat in a pool of their own blood. And there the fish die, looking their murderers in the eye. Below me, in the centre of the square, the strongest fight to keep safe.

Suddenly I glimpse a body in the bloody water, tossed about by the fish. When they manage to drag the corpse on board the boat where my father and his friends are, I already know who it is. I know it even before meeting Mikey's stare and Nico's desperate expression. Even before seeing the swollen face of General Jalloun.

Mikey looks at me, then at Nico, trying to find the answer to his tormented question in our eyes.

Have we betrayed him, or are we still on his side?

But I'm no longer either one or the other, Mikey. I'm betraying you in order to save your life. At the cost of my own.

Mohammed calls the Misurata police and speaks briefly with the young commander. Obviously, there are no problems; everything is fine. We set off back to Tripoli without being asked a single question, as if the general were nothing more than another tuna fish.

There's total silence again as the Land Rover runs along the asphalt ribbon towards Tripoli. There's no need for words. The message is clear.

Abandon the assassination.

It's possible that Jalloun said nothing about the attempt, but much more likely that he did. Any reasonable person would give up the plan and make a getaway as soon as they could. But our fathers are dreaming. Mikey's the one who goes to the final showdown with an unloaded pistol, like Kirk Douglas in *The Last Sunset*. His life means nothing to him, but it means more than anything else to those who love him. The body of this general is certainly not enough to stop him.

We arrive in Garden City at around six in the evening and pull up outside the maisonette.

'OK, boys,' says Salvatore Balistreri, 'let's not ruin Mikey's birthday. Have a good nap now and we'll see each other later at the Waddan for supper and a celebration.'

They decide to meet at ten o'clock. Perhaps his father's still dreaming. How little he knows his son. He still thinks he can change him, even save him from himself.

But I'm the only one who can really save him.

As soon as we get in the house, Nico raises a mass of objections, all rational and legitimate.

'Now that Jalloun's dead, the assassination must have been discovered, and no one's going to pay us the rest of the money.'

Mikey looks at him.

'We're not doing it for the money, Nico. We're doing it for us: for your mother, and my mother, for those twenty thousand poor folk who were robbed of everything here and then humiliated in Italy.'

Nico Gerace now nods in agreement, while I say nothing and

Mikey asks me nothing. Besides, I want him to start suspecting me. It's an essential part of the plan.

All three of us dress in the uniforms Jalloun has provided and leave Garden City at seven, heading off among the crowd for Piazza Castello, Mikey in the middle, Nico and myself at his sides. Three quarters of the MANK. Karim's gone to Laura's after coming back from Ghadames. Everything according to plan.

We walk down Shara Istikal, cross Maydan as Suhada, and get to what one year ago was called Piazza Castello but has now been baptized Piazza Verde, Gaddafi's green square. We've walked this way thousands of times since we were children, but this will be the last time and we're no longer children. That half a photograph comes to mind again, showing Gaddafi's young face, his arm outstretched to shake the hand of who knows who.

If only Italia hadn't died. If only Gaddafi hadn't come on the scene . . .

But it's too late. We're outside the main entrance to the apartment building. Each of us knows what to do. Nico stays outside on the street; I follow Mikey up the staircase. On the landing I feel him watching me, looking for signs of betrayal. He's undecided, tormented, doesn't know who he can trust any more. But he wants to kill Gaddafi.

He opens the door with the keys Jalloun gave him. From the window, you can hear the cries of celebration from the crowds in the square. Mikey looks me over one last time, then goes in and closes the door while I remain outside on the landing. From the large window on the stairs I can see the stage that's been set up for Gaddafi in the square. He's going to speak for ten minutes, starting at eight o'clock. The stage is twenty metres below the level of the window from which Mikey's going to shoot. It's an easy shot for someone like him, after twenty days' practice.

But it's not going to happen.

A cry from the crowd greets Gaddafi as he appears in military uniform, surrounded by his bodyguard. I can picture Mikey putting his eye to the telescopic sight, but of course they're not even going to give him time to focus. Our fathers aren't the kind of men to take any risks.

I can hear a whistling sound, then one of the floodlights behind Gaddafi shatters, leaving the stage in darkness. The crowd gives an *ohhh* of disappointment. It could have been a short circuit, but in fact it was a shot. I know it was; Gaddafi's bodyguard do, too, as they hustle him away as quickly as they can.

Now we have to move fast. I start banging on the apartment door. Mikey opens it, his face distraught. He still hasn't realized what's happened, but there's no time to discuss it, not here. He leaves everything behind: rifle, tripod, ammunition. He locks the door and we race down the stairs.

Nico Gerace's waiting for us outside the main entrance, looking pale, and the terrified crowd is running away. We set off amid the crush and are at home in Garden City in twenty minutes. We throw ourselves down into the armchairs. I don't say anything. Tired and panicking, Nico wants to leave immediately, but Mikey has other plans. I know what they are.

'Yes, we'll go to Italy by motorboat tonight, Nico. After supper with my father. Now, get some rest, the two of you.'

He takes off the police uniform and the holster with its pistol, then goes for a quick shower upstairs and comes back down after a quarter of an hour in a sweater and jeans. He doesn't look at us.

'There's something I need to sort out. We'll meet up with my father at the Waddan at ten.'

He makes a swift exit. He doesn't know it, but he's going just where I want him to go. The trap is sprung. But it's a trap that's set to save him for the very last time.

The MANK will end here, the blood brotherhood will end here, and my life will also end here.

Karim Al Bakri, *the boy with the severed ear*

I'm at Laura's house. Ahmed has just telephoned to say that Mikey's left the house. Since I spoke to her that day in Cairo, Laura's been hoping that none of this would be necessary, that things would work out in some other way. In short, that this day would never come.

Today, the high temperature that's plagued her for a while has disappeared. But she's very pale.

'I can't do it, Karim.'

She looks at me. She's unhappy because of Mikey, the rich spoilt fascist who plays at being the hero.

'Laura, his fingerprints are on the rifle he was going to kill Gaddafi with.'

'I know they are, Karim, but if he escapes to Italy they'll leave him in peace, thanks to his father. So I don't know why we have to do this to him, as well . . .'

'Because, otherwise, he'll try to come back here or to Cairo for you. And if he comes back they'll kill him. He's got to get both you and Libya out of his system for ever.'

There's no more time now. From the window, by the light of the street lamps, we see Mikey coming. I kiss Laura on the cheek and quickly leave.

I cross the street, get in the car and set off. Mikey's seen me, as Ahmed wanted. Everything's going to plan.

Ahmed Al Bakri

Karim arrives while Mikey's with Laura. Nico is in the living room, watching a Western, and I'm outside on the street.

'He's there now with her, Ahmed.'

'Here, take this. I've made a copy of the key,' I tell him. 'Go to the cave and take all the money out.'

Karim is more worried than ever.

'I don't like this part, brother.'

I shake my head. This is no time for discussion.

Karim mustn't have any idea of the showdown I have in mind. That's my business, and only mine.

'Don't worry, Karim. Just stay half a mile from the cave in the dark with the binoculars. And don't try to intervene, whatever happens. Just trust me.'

'When they find the money's not there, they'll kill you, Ahmed. If Mikey doesn't, then Nico will.'

'No, Karim, I have the gun and the knife. What's Nico going to do to me?'

He shakes his head.

'But what about Mikey?'

'I've already told you – he's like me. He won't fire on anyone who's a blood brother. Not for any reason.'

Karim remains fixed to the spot, looking at me. There's no way he's convinced, but I'm his elder brother. He has to obey me.

'Mikey will kill you, Ahmed.'

He's right, but destiny's in my hands, and what will be will be as I choose.

There's no longer an orchestra playing 'Magic Moments' on the Waddan terrace and no couples dancing there in black tie and evening gowns. Salvatore Balistreri has booked the usual table for eight looking out over the sea. Four older men: Don Eugenio, Emilio Busi, Mohammed and himself. And four young men: Mikey, Alberto, Nico and myself.

We just have to hope this wretched dinner goes off smoothly. For a while, everything is absolutely normal and relaxed. But those two shits Emilio Busi and Don Eugenio have to be certain what Mikey intends to do, and start talking about the terrible end of General Jalloun and the attack on Gaddafi.

'You know that someone tried to shoot Gaddafi, don't you?' Mikey's father asks him.

'No,' he says, without looking up from his plate.

'You've not heard? But there's been nothing else on the radio for at least three hours!'

Mikey's eyes circle the table.

'I know. But they didn't shoot at Gaddafi. They shot at one of the floodlights.'

Then his eyes come to rest on me. I keep my eyes lowered, staring at the piece of grouper on my plate. I'm very good at playing the part of traitor. By now, Mikey should be thinking that's what I am.

Finally, the cake with twenty candles is brought in. It's midnight and, as at any normal birthday, we have a group photograph, then Mikey blows the candles out and we sing 'Happy Birthday' to him.

Once the cake has been cut and handed round, along with the spumante, everyone raises their glass for the toast. Salvatore raises his to Mikey.

'Here's to you, Mikey.'

Mikey looks at his father and raises his glass as well, and makes a toast for his twentieth birthday.

'To Italia and Nadia. May they find justice one day.'

There's a moment's hesitation. Everyone knows that the toast is a challenge and an accusation. We drink the toast in silence. Then, while we're saying our goodbyes, Mohammed comes up to me.

'Get him away, Ahmed, or he won't live to see tomorrow.'

We get back to Garden City just after midnight. Mikey's decided to stick to the original plan and leave at about 2 a.m., when the coastguard relaxes a little. Nico and I go upstairs to rest. Nico immediately falls into a deep sleep. I haven't slept in twenty-four hours, and I still can't sleep. Not yet: there's still one important thing to do. My mind is focused on the final part of the plan, on one single thought.

I want to be sure that you never come back to Libya, Mikey.

I get up. There's a strip of light below the door to the bedroom where Mikey's finishing off his preparations. I go down to the living room, which is full of shadows. The three police uniforms are on the sofa, together with the holsters and pistols. They'll be useful in getting from the house to the beach. No one will stop us if we're dressed as police.

I check the guns and am relieved. Mikey's emptied mine and Nico's. There's very little left for me to do, then. Mikey's right. He doesn't trust me any more, and perhaps not Nico either.

Tonight I can finally prove Laura Hunt wrong, and for the rest of my life take on the role that she would never choose to assign to me.

At ten to two, Mikey comes and calls us. We don't look each other in the face, and speak only when we have to. It's as if everything has already been done. Or, more precisely, as if in his heart, each one of us wants it to be over.

Necessary actions take over from pointless words. We all know that this is the end of the MANK organization.

We quickly put on the uniforms that will prevent us being stopped, along with the belts, holsters and guns. Mikey and Nico each have a bag with a few clothes for the night crossing.

We leave, and meet no one on the streets. Tripoli is peacefully and silently asleep. In ten minutes we're at the Adrian Pelt coast road and the beach. The surface of the sea is lit only by the moon and the lights of the fishing boats leaving port. Everything is very calm, the same as any other night.

Only we three know how this scene will remain in our memories.

Tripoli seems the same, but it's not. It's totally changed. And it's men like our fathers who have changed it, not Gaddafi.

My dinghy is in the water, two metres from the shore. The motorboat is anchored further out. Now I feel a terrible need to hurry.

I'm like a patient whose heart has to be opened, lying conscious on the operating table a moment before they put him under.

I can't wait to close my eyes.

'The petrol?' Mikey asks me.

'The tank in the motorboat's full. There're extra cans in the dinghy. Nico can transfer them while we dive down for the money.'

We take the dinghy to the motorboat. Mikey and Nico stow their bags on board. As Mikey gets out of the dinghy, I want to tell him something – *I'm sorry, it's not how you think* – but I can't.

'We'll see you at the rocks, Mikey.'

I try not to think about anything as I pilot the dinghy at top speed. When we get to the rocks, I flash the torch three times and, in the dark half a mile away, Karim replies with his signal. As always, my brother has obeyed me.

At that distance he can see everything with the infrared binoculars, but there's no chance of him stepping in to reach us with the 5hp engine on his small boat. And, anyway, I've forbidden him to make any move, so that's the end of it.

I take off the uniform and put on my wetsuit and air cylinders. When Mikey and Nico arrive in the motorboat, I'm ready. They draw up alongside and I tie a rope to the motorboat's prow. It's a simple slip knot, speed being of the essence. Despite the calm sea, the current there is very strong and takes you out into the open sea.

Nico drops the anchor and switches off the engine. Apart from the moon, the only light is the one on the bows. Mikey takes his police uniform off, places the gun and holster on top of it and puts on his wetsuit and air cylinders. None of us has any desire to laugh or joke, as we always used to out here. We're about to celebrate a funeral, not a goodbye.

This is the end of the line for the MANK, the last drop in our brotherhood of blood.

Mikey's already wondering whether I've betrayed him. Soon he'll know for sure.

Nico comes aboard the dinghy to transfer the cans of petrol, while Mikey and I dive into the water. We swim easily to the bottom. I know what we won't find there. And I know what's left.

Perhaps Mikey knows as well, because he lets me go ahead as we enter the cave. Karim's done everything to perfection. The cable is free, the lock lying on the bottom. The four strongboxes have disappeared. We look each other in the eye for only a moment, then he sets off rapidly. I ascend as rapidly as possible, too, two or three metres behind him.

Kirk Douglas

When I get to the surface, Mikey's already on the motorboat and Nico's in my dinghy. He's still transferring the petrol cans and looks at me, stupefied, while I climb slowly up the ladder encumbered by the cylinders.

'So what's happened to the strongboxes?' Nico asks me.

Mikey calls out to him.

'Get in the motorboat, Nico! Right now!'

I know exactly what I have to do, having rehearsed these seconds dozens of times in my mind. Calmly, I take out my scuba knife and cut the rope that ties the two boats together. Nico stares at me. It's as if he's hypnotized by the knife.

'Where's my fucking money?' he says, still in a daze.

The dinghy starts to veer away from the motorboat, pulled more quickly by the current because it's lighter. Now I have to force Mikey into a gunfight, and I know there's only one way I can do it. I point the knife at Nico.

'Now I'm going to slit you open, you fascist swine!'

Nico looks at me incredulously. Then he explodes in anger.

'And you're a filthy Arab piece of shit, Ahmed. I'm going to kill you.'

Nico takes his gun out of the holster and shoots at me with no hesitation. I think about Karim cursing me as he watches impotently through the infrared binoculars. He warned me that Nico would shoot straight away.

But his gun isn't loaded, Karim. And it was Mikey who unloaded it.

Nico fires one shot, two, three – and, obviously, nothing happens. Now's the moment. I move towards him with the knife. The motorboat's twenty metres away from the dinghy and Mikey starts the engine to come up to us.

Rock Hudson

'Jump into the water, Nico!' I shout to him.

But Nico acts as if he can't move. He stares stupidly at his pistol, wondering who emptied it. He shoots Ahmed a look of pure hatred, and curses him. Then he whispers, '*Shit, shit.*'

I halt the motorboat five metres from the dinghy. Ahmed has the pistol in his left hand, the knife in his right.

'Leave now, Mikey! Turn that boat round and get back to your own country. Libya doesn't want you any more.'

I look at Ahmed, more incredulous than angry. Those few metres separating us are now an abyss of broken trust. Nothing in the world can bring us back together.

'Or you'll kill us, right?'

Ahmed stretches out his left arm towards me and points the gun at my chest.

'That's right, Mikey. First you, then Nico.'

I pick up my own gun. It's too late now for words. Too late for him, and too late for me.

But I can't shoot him. I've unloaded his gun.

Kirk Douglas

Mikey doesn't shoot: he can't believe that the situation has reversed. This time, he's Rock Hudson with the loaded gun, and I'm Kirk Douglas with the one he unloaded.

I can't give him any more time to think. I have to convince him that I'm a worse traitor than Judas, and that I deserve to be killed.

Ahmed, the traitor.

I meet his gaze as I start to fire at him. One, two, three shots. But again, nothing happens. In the feeble light of the moon and the motor-boat's navigation lights, Mikey sees my eyes looking first surprised, then scared, when he thinks I've discovered my gun isn't loaded.

Do you really think I'm afraid of dying, Mikey? Do you know me that little?

I've betrayed him with Gaddafi, stolen his money and fired at him, but Mikey still can't manage to shoot me. But then I already knew this would happen. I know who he is. I know because it's only been beside him that I've been happy, and because any sacrifice is worth-while to save his life.

There's only one way to make Mikey fire. I lunge at Nico.

Rock Hudson

Ahmed throws his gun away and launches himself on Nico with his knife. Everything passes through my mind in a split second.

The duels fought in the sun in front of the villas. The slit throats of Salim and the three Egyptian soldiers. His arm, which saved me on

La Moneta's cliff face. The gouged eyes of Killer, the Maltese trafficker's dog. And that slap when he said that I'd gone crazy because of my relationship with Laura.

Perhaps the end had begun with that slap. That's when the cracks started in our friendship. And, with him, there were no half measures.

Either bosom buddies or mortal enemies.

The first bullet makes him twist round on himself and fall to his knees. He grips on to the dinghy's rail, trying to pull himself up.

At last, Nico jumps in the water and starts swimming to the motorboat. As he climbs the ladder, Ahmed manages to get to his feet and, staggering, starts the outboard motor.

I fire the second shot level with his heart. Ahmed puts his hands to his breast, collapses over the railing and drops into the water.

I put the engine in top gear and steer towards the dinghy at top speed. I sail straight over it, crushing it. Then I stop twenty metres away.

Nico and I watch Ahmed's body sinking down under the weight of the air cylinders. In a moment, he disappears.

I stay there a few minutes in silence – to contemplate the smooth, dark surface that's swallowed up my best friend and the line of lights along the Adrian Pelt coast road where I forced myself on Laura Hunt.

Then I turn my back on Africa and point the bows towards Italy.

Karim Al Bakri, the boy with the severed ear

I'm going mad with anguish and rage.

Ahmed's done everything he could to get himself killed. That was the final part of his plan.

Being killed by Mikey was the only way he knew to make sure that Mikey would never set foot here again.

Now I know why he asked me to get the money in this slow boat and then ordered me to wait half a mile away without moving any closer.

It's absurd, unfair. My brother's given his life away for that fascist kid who plays the revolutionary with millions in his pocket, who captured Laura Hunt's heart having gone to bed with her mother, who wanted to assassinate Gaddafi.

My eyes are glued to the binoculars. I heard the shots and saw the motorboat passing over Ahmed, crushing the dinghy, and Ahmed's body sinking under the weight of his air cylinders. He was gone in a minute. I could make a dash for land and sound the alarm, but they would already be beyond territorial waters. And I would have to come up with hundreds of very complicated explanations.

And that's not what my father wanted. It's not what Ahmed wanted.

I look through the binoculars, while a vast rage mingles with the pain in me. I watch the motorboat set off towards Italy. The murderous fascists are escaping, but life is long.

One day, Mikey Balistreri, the score will be settled.

11 An Invitation You Cannot Refuse

Saturday, 13 August 2011

Rome

After Mohammed Al Bakri's death, and once Linda had left for San Francisco, nothing happened for a couple of days. The great public holiday of *Ferragosto* was two days away, and both Rome's historic centre and its residential suburbs were empty while, unusually – as a result of the economic crisis – the working-class districts were as packed as they were in winter.

In those three days Balistreri had left the house only to buy the newspapers. He had no interest in the investigations that were turning the corridors of power upside down on both sides of the Tiber. All he had wanted to do was keep an eye on whatever article or news there might be regarding Linda Nardi.

But now his thoughts were moving on. They were where Mohammed Al Bakri had said a coward like him would never go.

Karim is waiting for you.

Now, more than ever before, he was convinced of it.

Today's dead are the offspring of yesterday's dead. Melania and Tanja Druc wouldn't have been killed if Italia hadn't been killed.

It was difficult to stop himself thinking about it. He had had to run away from Libya, leaving the mystery of his mother's death there, and had never gone back over the events of that wretched day. But, despite this, his memory had not been corrupted.

Now he knew that Mohammed Al Bakri had been on that cliff and had seen his mother in her bathing costume before half past three, just before the coastguard sighted the inflatable with the Wheelus Field markings – that was, if he could be sure that what he'd been told was true.

But why should Mohammed have wanted to lie to me about it?

As to the civil war in Libya, it seemed to be at stalemate and all but forgotten. NATO's mission was dragging along painfully among a thousand polemics. The allies had serious problems at home, and the recession and the elections were of far greater interest to their governments than the survival of Muammar Gaddafi.

Balistreri's mood kept changing, torn between the past and the future, between action and sleep, between the desire to find his mother's killer and the need to protect Linda Nardi. But of one thing he was sure.

There are no two choices here. It's not over. And it won't be up to me to decide.

At sea near Misurata

The man from Libya had approached her politely in a bar in San Francisco two days earlier.

'I'm here on behalf of the man you are looking for, Miss Nardi.'

The Libyan spelled out his offer.

'He will guarantee your safe arrival in Tripoli. You will meet with him there and be returned safely home.'

'I don't interview killers, or the men behind them,' Linda had said, getting up.

'One final thing, Miss Nardi.'

He had given her an envelope.

An invitation you cannot refuse.

And so she had set off, arriving in Tobruk without any problems, thanks to the help of her Libyan contacts. As far as she knew, they could have been loyal to Gaddafi, or rebels, or playing any kind of duplicitous game. She had been put up for a night in the hotel she had stayed at previously in the last few months, except that it was now half empty, its façade scored by shells and bullets. From there, they had taken her to Benghazi.

She had written her article, and it had been approved by her hosts. Then, as agreed, she had switched off her satellite phone, cut all contacts and activated a Libyan mobile phone that she had been given in San Francisco.

A black Mercedes had taken her out of Benghazi to a quiet little port with thirty or so fishing boats and a few navy launches.

They had put her on to an unnamed tugboat loaded with weapons and dynamite, boxes covered in blue plastic, rocket launchers, rifles and strongboxes full of dollars. On board were seven crew and twenty militia in civilian dress, all armed and fully trained. Rebels, obviously, not loyalists.

It's difficult to tell who's on whose side.

They had sat her down in a corner, out of the baking sun. The sea was calm, but the boat was very unstable. Very soon, everyone was seasick, several of the crew throwing up, along with the militia.

Linda, however, was suffering no nausea. The turmoil was all in her head. *Where exactly are you going? Why haven't you gone back to John Kiptanu and your orphans? Why is this so important to you?*

And yet she felt no fear or regrets among these unknown men with Kalashnikovs in their hands, who were now singing a soft, mournful song on their passage to Misurata and the fighting.

If you don't really live, then you die.

Rome

Balistreri went out early, as usual, to buy the papers. Limping, he came back home and settled in his favourite place, the sofa.

He opened *Il Domani* and sat in shock, staring at the first page. An editorial by Linda Nardi. It was about Libya, not the Gruppo Italia scandal.

> *Gaddafi's regime is on its last legs. His funds are nearly finished and only his mercenaries and a close, privileged circle still support the Colonel. The resistance of the regime and its repression of the rebels is in the hands of a few fanatical and merciless killers who are loyal to it. The most feared among them is the man they call the 'Exterminator of Zawiya'. His name is not known, but he is recognizable by a severed ear.*

Balistreri felt the electricity running through him. This wasn't simply an article; it was Linda Nardi's challenge to the killer. But the worse news was the place from which the article had been written: Benghazi, Libya.

He called Corvu.

'I thought Linda was in America?' he asked aggressively.

'She is, *dottore*. I asked Giulia Piccolo to tell me if she leaves.'

'Call Piccolo, and get back to me right away.'

Corvu called back five minutes later, his voice trembling, stammering and stuttering in embarrassment.

'Linda left for Cairo. She told Giulia not to tell me . . .'

Balistreri hung up. He felt like the passenger on a train that keeps accelerating. He called *Il Domani* and got through to the head of personnel.

'Where's Linda Nardi?' he asked.

The voice of the man at the other end of the line was calm and professional.

'Linda Nardi's a freelance, Dottor Balistreri, she's not a staff writer, therefore . . .'

Balistreri knew this world, so used to hiding behind rules. He also knew how to get around them.

'You know who I am, right?'

'Of course, Head of Homicide.'

'I'm also a very good friend of Linda's.'

The man was silent for a minute, weighing up the pros and cons. Then he spoke.

'We certainly didn't ask her to go there. It's very dangerous. Nardi made the decision herself. She got into Libya via Egypt. We don't know how. She sent that copy in from Benghazi.'

'And where is she now?'

'We don't know. There's no reply from her satellite phone.'

Balistreri took down the number and ended the call. He tried ringing it, but the satellite phone wasn't switched on. He then called the consulate in Benghazi and spoke directly to the consul. Yes, he had seen Linda Nardi; she had been getting ready to go by sea to Misurata. He had tried to dissuade her, because the route was dangerous, not entirely under the control of the insurgents. But she wouldn't change her mind. No one could understand why she wanted to go.

But Balistreri knew very well why.

She's going there to find the man with the severed ear.

He called the satellite phone every half-hour. It was a waste of time. Linda had thrown herself into the hands of a pitiless murderer, one who took pleasure in massacring the innocent. It was madness. And, clearly, hopeless.

Why? Why do something so absurd? What's she hoping for? That Karim will let himself be handcuffed and taken to Italy to pay for his sins?

He tried to calm himself down and think clearly. There had to be an explanation. Linda was a courageous young woman with an extraordinary temperament, but she wasn't suicidal. And yet she'd gone to Libya to find that man.

Whose brother I killed after unloading his pistol.

He remembered what Mohammed Al Bakri had said to him.

Karim doesn't want me to avenge that wrong here, tonight. He's a poor deluded man who talks about an old brotherhood of blood and the stupid things you did as boys together. He wants you to go to Tripoli to settle matters. He doesn't understand that you're a coward like all Italians and would never go.

That had been the first invitation. The address at Via dei Pini, where Mohammed had been killed.

Michele Balistreri would never have accepted that invitation, not for fear of the future, but of the past; not out of fear of dying, but fear of the truth. And the man with the severed ear must have understood this.

So he had drawn her there. This is the last invitation. Come back here, Mikey. Come back like a man and pay off an old debt. Or Linda will die.

Outside his window, life in Rome was calm and peaceful, sleepy in the lazy summer heat.

But they're killing each other over there. There's the bloodshed of today and yesterday. Drawing Linda there, Karim's also dragging me into that hell.

He called the telegraph office and dictated a simple message: *I'm ready.*

He had it sent to PO Box 150870, Tripoli, Libya. Just as in 1983.

Sunday, 14 August 2011

Misurata

After more than thirty hours of sailing they came to the port of Misurata as the sun was setting in a deep red over the sea. Linda had already seen this city devastated by Gaddafi's artillery, but now its huge port was totally calm, with its squat white houses, the lights coming on after sunset, the stylish villas of the businessmen, the minarets, the shops open for business, and its chaotic traffic of cars, carts and bicycles.

Here, the war's over, just like Benghazi.

They let her disembark first. A bearded militiaman carried her rucksack and took her to a pick-up truck fitted with a machine gun with other militiamen on board, all in civilian clothes.

And from there began the last part of the journey.

Towards the war. Towards Tripoli. Towards the truth.

Rome

Balistreri hadn't even had his first coffee of the day when his mobile rang.

The man spoke Italian with an Arab accent. He told him to pack an overnight bag, have his passport ready and he would pick him up in half an hour. And Balistreri wasn't to say a word to anyone.

At nine, a dark Mercedes with Libyan diplomatic plates rolled up outside. The driver ushered him into the back seat, where another Libyan was waiting for him, a middle-aged man in stylish Western clothes. The car set off immediately for Leonardo Da Vinci airport, along with the stream of Romans heading for the Ostia beaches.

'Because of the no-fly zone, it's difficult getting into Libya at the moment, Signor Balistreri,' the man told him. 'We've found the only possible way for you, thanks to the few true friends we have left.'

It was clear he wasn't talking about the Americans, the French or the British. Even less so the traitorous Italians. He gave him an aeroplane ticket for the midday Rome–Moscow flight from Fiumicino to Sheremetyevo International.

'From there, one of our cars will take you to Vnukovo 2 airport, twenty-five kilometres south of Moscow. Then a Russian diplomatic flight will take you to Tripoli in time for you to spend the night in the Hotel Rixos. This kind of flight is still allowed. Even those NATO murderers wouldn't dare bring down a Russian flight.'

Balistreri had never dreamed of going back to Tripoli, nor had he ever wanted to. And never aboard a Russian air-force flight in the middle of a war in which even Italy was dropping bombs on Libya. And certainly not in answer to an invitation he couldn't refuse from Karim Al Bakri and in order to bring an end to a private war that had begun when he'd shot his brother, Ahmed. And this was a war to which no one had ever signed an armistice.

And an evil that was still remembered.

12 Return to La Moneta

Diplomatic flight, Moscow–Tripoli, Monday, 15 August 2011

Michele Balistreri

During the flight from Moscow I fell into a fitful state between waking and sleeping, like the delirium of someone with a very high temperature. Every kind of memory – thought, doubt and certainty – rose to the surface, disappeared and then returned with details I'd completely forgotten. Or had wanted to forget.

The Last Sunset *gunfight between Rock Hudson and Kirk Douglas, Laura saying to Ahmed, 'You wouldn't let yourself be killed holding an unloaded pistol'; the bodies of the young woman and child in the cesspit; Grandad's sadness beside Jet's kennel, Ahmed slitting that infected dog's throat; Nico lisping his 's' sounds while Don Eugenio touches him up, Ahmed's knife at Don Eugenio's throat; Emilio Busi telling my mother and grandfather 'the future lies under the sand, not above it'; the blood brotherhood, Cairo, the three soldiers with their throats cut, the MANK organization; the first kiss with Laura and my hands on the hem of Marlene's briefs; Nadia's corpse in the olive pressing shed; my mother's hand raised in farewell on La Moneta; Marlene's naked body and my blood; Salim with his throat cut by Ahmed after he'd severed Karim's ear; General Jalloun asking us to assassinate Gaddafi; racing motorbikes with Ahmed along the jetty; Jalloun's body among the tuna and my father's last warning look; Gaddafi in my telescopic sights and the whistling sound that sends it all sky high; Karim furtively leaving Laura's house, me ripping her clothes off and her hands on my shoulders as I force myself on her; the MANK's strongboxes lying empty under the sea, Ahmed firing at me with an unloaded pistol and me firing back at him, then running over his body in the motorboat.*

And yet while I was coming back to this city on the aeroplane, the memory of that last day in Tripoli seemed unreal, unbelievable even, as if it had been someone else whose life had been cut in two, not mine.

If I look back now on the drift of my life after forty years, everything slowly disappears from sight, but in the mists of memory what I can always make out is La Moneta. My physical body has survived its shipwreck and reached a shore somewhere, but my spirit's stayed there, facing the rocks around that island, facing the lights of the Tripoli coastline that grew more distant as I ran away from what I was: Mikey Balistreri.

Of course, young Mikey was an idealist with an inflated sense of loyalty. But he was also a criminal, a murderer and a rapist. And yet, as the plane was taking me back to where I'd grown up, something inside me was beginning to rebel against these more negative thoughts.

Yes, Michele. There are always two sides to every truth.

It came to me in waves as the plane was flying over the Mediterranean and nearing the African coast. They weren't even thoughts as such; it was more a growing feeling that, as I drew closer to that young Mikey, this physical flight towards the past wasn't a journey towards a truth or an enemy but towards *the person I really was.*

I felt like a father about to see a son who had been sent to jail forty years ago. And only in that moment does he realize that the judgement and the sentence were too harsh.

That the Mikey rejected by his father, Salvatore, and by the older Michele was better than either of them.

Someone tapped me on the shoulder to remind me to fasten my seatbelt. We were landing at Mitiga airport, once Wheelus Field. As the aeroplane slowed down, I could hear the noise of the wheels coming out from the undercarriage, the brakes, the engines whistling. And everything seemed to be happening in slow motion, as well as in an unreal, insulated silence. When I put my head out of the door and walked down the steps into the hot night, I remembered the thoughts I had as a boy seeing Neil Armstrong put his foot on the moon.

I'll stay here only a short while. Or perhaps for ever.

What I saw was a place unknown to my eyes but very familiar to my spirit. What was humble then was today false and pretentious. But what I could smell (that mixture of eucalyptus, earth and manure) and what I could hear in the quiet depths of the African night (leaves, crickets, frogs) and what I was feeling (the soft slowness of Africa) was much stronger than any external change that had taken place. This had been my home, the home I'd run away from in order to bury myself in the untroubled routine of the present.

And in order to do that I'd had to condemn a part of me to death.

The sentence we give ourselves becomes our own prison.

Suddenly, I felt relieved, light and ready. And very certain.

Michele Balistreri will die here, where Mikey was born.

A black, armoured Volvo was waiting for me at the bottom of the boarding steps. The driver was a Libyan in a uniform I didn't recognize. More likely, he was a secret agent rather than a chauffeur.

The unfamiliar and deserted Tripoli of 2011 began to roll past the window. We drove through the outskirts along an almost completely empty modern road: no cars; only a few bicycles. Petrol was evidently in short supply. These were the days of Ramadan, snipers and bombs. And also of curfew. NATO fighter-bombers could attack at any moment. But the fear of dying was the last thing on my mind.

Here I was born and here I once died. Here I was betrayed and was also a traitor. Here I've come back to meet a ghost, the ghost of Mikey Balistreri, who violated the girl who loved him and killed his greatest friend.

But these thoughts were now less certain, the judgement less safe, the condemnation less harsh. Then I pushed the doubts aside. This unexpected and unwanted return was in a noble cause.

To save the life of Linda Nardi, a life worth saving, in exchange for my own.

The driver interrupted this tumult of thoughts.

'We will shortly be at the Hotel Rixos, Signor Balistreri. There's a room ready for you. Please do not leave it. Wait there to be called.'

We arrived at half past midnight. The hotel was surrounded by an iron enclosure similar to a bamboo fence, which marked out the grounds. In front of the modern two-storey building, the activity was orderly: Western cars, some SUVs and quite a few security guards, but no more than at a grand hotel in Riad or Dubai. All in all, a normal flow of people, seeing the daylight fast of Ramadan was over. From one of the lounges came oriental-sounding music.

But ultimately this apparent normality was nothing more than a show for the few remaining journalists, the desperate tail end of propaganda from a regime that was on its knees. The show of calm that dictators put on – such as Gaddafi's game of chess with the Kalmuck president – which more often than not shortly precedes their downfall.

I entered the Ottoman-style lobby, walking past the glass cube and the two pools, and came to the reception, followed a footstep behind by my driver-minder. The conversations around me were either whispered or too loud. People shot furtive glances in my direction, wondering who on earth the poor cretin was who'd come to Tripoli when almost all the journalists had left by then. The staff evidently had nothing to do, because there were no guests in the lobby, only the secret police.

It was all to pull wool over your eyes, just like when we Italians were here. Indeed, especially when we were here. Pulling wool over your eyes like the dinner dances on terraces overlooking the sea in clubs called the Beach and the Underwater; like the card games held in Don Eugenio's parish for the people who mattered; like Sunday Mass in the cathedral, where everyone noted who was with whom and who was absent, followed by the swish of the young boys and girls walking past in their Sunday best.

What had changed now was only who was pulling the wool.

No one took my passport to register it. I was immediately given a key and accompanied by my pseudo-chauffeur to a room on the first floor.

'Just wait in here,' he told me, and said goodbye.

The window looked out on to an inner courtyard wall. No view and no possibility of escape. Inside, everything functioned normally: electricity, hot and cold water, shower, flushing toilet. The sheets were freshly laundered, pressed and perfumed. In the middle of the bed lay a presentation pack of dates. What had I expected? What had I hoped for? Burnt-out cars and rubble on the streets, beetles and spiders in the rooms? Is that what I would need to remove any last doubt from my mind that this regime – Gaddafi, my father, Mohammed, Busi, Don Eugenio – wasn't fundamentally evil?

All of a sudden, in the darkness of this alien room, I was struck by the dreadful suspicion that none of it was true.

Perhaps Gaddafi did have good reasons; perhaps my father and his associates were only shrewd businessmen, simple precursors of the Eighties; perhaps Nietzsche was a doddering old fool and my mother a haughty idealist incapable of living with the world as it was.

And perhaps neither Ahmed, Karim nor Laura had betrayed me.

Ahmed had twice saved my life: firstly, in that Cairo alley; and secondly, when I slipped down the cliff face on La Moneta. He'd come with me on the suicide mission against Gaddafi. And perhaps he'd saved my life a third time by organizing my escape from Tripoli on 15 August 1970. Karim had been close to Laura after I'd devastated her by sleeping with Marlene, and perhaps the Karim I saw leaving her house on 15 August was still only a friend. Perhaps Laura Hunt did love me and that same evening, rather than committing an act of violation, it was instead an act of love. The thoughts continued to surface, like the flashbacks I'd had on the plane. No longer shadows from the past but a foretaste of what was to come.

Nothing happened as you thought it did. There are always two sides to every truth.

I lay down on the bed, trying to focus on Linda Nardi.

She's still alive.

I was sure of only one thing. Karim Al Bakri, *the man with the severed ear*, would kill her before my very eyes. Or else he'd be content simply to take my life.

The life of his brother's killer for the life of Linda.

I remained like that, looking at the ceiling, fully dressed and ready to go.

At two there was a knock on the door. I hurriedly splashed water on my face and followed the driver to the Volvo. The temperature outside was forty degrees.

Just like that night. Fifteenth of August 1970. PO Box 150870.

We skirted past horrendous modern apartment blocks modelled on Khrushchev's *khrushchevka*, low-rise, low-cost workers' housing from the Soviet regime that Gaddafi had wanted to emulate. We travelled along what, as a child, I knew as the Adrian Pelt coast road. Who knew what the hell it was called now? It was certainly no longer the old graceful promenade lined with palms, just a horrendous motorway.

Then we came to the castle in Piazza Verde. A vast car park had been erected in the middle of the square. It was deserted except for two lorryloads of soldiers wearing the same uniform as my driver. The two monumental columns facing the sea were still there, one with its caravel, but in place of the Roman wolf on the other there was now a mounted Berber warrior.

We drove right past the apartment block where I was supposed to shoot at Gaddafi while he stood on the battlements. Only a little while ago, Gaddafi, wearing a fierce scowl, had addressed a crowd of supporters and threatened the insurgents there.

Then we took the road for the coast again, passing by hotels that were new to me: the Corinthia and the Sheraton. And, at last, out on to another modern road that led to Gargaresh and the beaches. But there was no longer any sign of the old beach clubs, the Lido, the Sulphur Baths, the Beach and the Underwater. Only an endless line of little shops. All closed.

Finally, the car turned off towards the coast. At the end of a short descent was a small private harbour with several guards. They signalled me to get into a motorboat together with two armed soldiers and the pilot.

When the boat set off, I recognized the route immediately. I'd followed it endless times as a kid. We were going precisely where I didn't want to go.

Where everything began and where everything will come to an end.

La Moneta

When I saw the jetty lit up in the distance, I realized something straight away.

This is the only place in Tripoli where nothing's changed.

The wooden jetty was just the same, the lamps beside it the same. The beach was identical to that of my youth; the sun umbrellas and deckchairs were the same make and colour. The villa was as white as ever and perfectly maintained, as were the guest house and the house for the domestic staff.

An armed guard was waiting for me on the jetty and led me to the door of what in another life had been my house or, rather, my father's house.

He opened the door and I entered a museum of memories: a dreadful torture the new owner wanted to inflict on me. Nothing inside had been touched either. Everything was the same, perfectly preserved: furniture, ornaments, lights, pictures on the wall. I passed the mirror in the hall towards the back of the house and saw a figure reflected there. But I no longer knew who it was . . .

Michele or Mikey?

The guard pointed to the last room, my father's study. The door was open and from it came the weak light of a desk lamp. I remembered that lamp; Papa always kept it lit on his desk, day and night. It was like going back towards the biggest mistake in one's life, to the moment before you make it, but without being able to make a different choice.

Nothing had happened as I thought it had. Mikey wasn't the puppetmaster but the puppet.

That shadow of a thought had now become a certainty. But instead of feeling pain, rancour, anger, I felt the world was lighter around me and stepped into that room now without fear.

The man with the severed ear was sitting in an armchair in the corner. Another armchair was facing him. They were my father's old armchairs. The one he used to sit in and the one he offered to guests. His was the one with its back facing the wall, obviously. And that was the one the man waiting for me was sitting in. He was the new owner, the new boss. There were deep furrows in the hollow cheeks under his prominent cheekbones; his hair was still thick, but now grey. Only that ruined ear hadn't grown any older.

'*Ciao*, Mikey,' he said, without getting up. 'Happy birthday. Take a seat.'

He spoke in English, as we did as boys when we didn't want people to know what we were saying. I'd forgotten about my birthday, but there was no sarcasm in my old childhood friend's greeting.

I sat down opposite him. He was in civilian clothes, a blue shirt and grey trousers. He seemed older than me. It was his eyes that aged him.

The eyes of someone who'd massacred too many innocent people.

'Make yourself comfortable, Mikey. So, at last you've come back!'

I still hadn't said a word to the man. I was observing him, *the scourge of the rebels, the exterminator of innocents, the murderer of Melania, Tanja, Domnica and all the others.* And Mikey's old friend.

Everything I'd believed for decades, all those thoughts as heavy as millstones, was no longer important. There was only one thing that mattered: the present.

'You know why I've come back? Because you called me here by cutting the tip off Tanja Druc's finger.'

He nodded.

'I did it after I shot them, while they were asleep. They didn't suffer. I wanted to be sure of attracting your attention, Mikey.'

I couldn't look at him. We'd started out by killing together, but the man with the severed ear had betrayed all our ideals.

'We never killed innocent people.'

'Beyond good and evil, Mikey. You taught us that.'

I could have reminded him that we were speaking about love then. But it was pointless.

'Is Linda here in Tripoli?' I asked him.

He nodded.

'Yes, she's here. You had many excellent reasons for never coming back. And yet you've come for a woman. In that, you haven't changed much, Mikey.'

All he wanted was to talk about the past and all I wanted to talk about was the future. I wanted him to understand that right away. Then I'd pay whatever debt I owed to settle the score.

'I came back to pay off an old debt. All I want is for Linda Nardi to go back to Italy. Then you can do with me what you want.'

He seemed upset. It was as if my statement, my immediate confession and unconditional surrender without putting up a fight, weren't at all what he wanted.

He doesn't want to kill a compliant and reasonable old man. He wants to kill Mikey.

'Is that all, Mikey? Nothing more? Is there nothing we need to explain to each other?'

'I'm here, and will stay here, but you get Linda Nardi on a plane for Rome. Then we can talk for as long as you like.'

He shook his head, amazed at my stupidity.

'You think it's that simple, Mikey? A flight to Rome through a no-fly zone? And Colonel Gaddafi doesn't trust Libyans any more, only his mercenaries.'

'But you're his right-hand man, aren't you? Doesn't he trust you?'

'For a good many years indeed I was, but since my father's friends reclaimed the Colonel's funds I'm regarded with suspicion. If I still enjoy any benefit of the doubt, it's only because I eliminated those two turncoats in Lugano.'

'Wasn't your father with the turncoats?'

'No, Mikey. He fought for the Colonel to the bitter end.'

'So you didn't kill Mohammed?'

He shook his head.

'I was helping the Colonel. I killed women and children here and in Italy. But the very last ones were those two contemptible cowards, Busi and Don Eugenio. And I did it for my father, not Gaddafi.'

'But then you did kill him. Because he wanted to kill me there and then, while you wanted me here in Tripoli.'

'You never could understand Muslims, could you, Mikey? Not even after all those years. We can disagree with our fathers, but we'd never betray them. Nor do we kill them.'

He was telling the truth. He had no reason to lie to me.

'So who did kill your father? Do you know?'

He stared at me. A thought crossed his mind.

'I'm still the head of Libya's Secret Service, Mikey. Of course I know who did it.'

'So tell me.'

He shrugged.

'What does it matter? You came here for Linda Nardi, didn't you?'

'And where is she?'

'I had her arrested and secretly brought here to La Moneta by men I could trust before I was put under surveillance. I happen to have saved her life. The guards think she's one of my mistresses.'

'Good. So let her escape and then we can deal with the past.'

He looked at me as if I hadn't understood a thing.

'I'm surrounded here, and watched over by the Colonel's body-guard. Apparently, for my own protection, but in reality so they can keep an eye on me. We're free here on the island, but under direct surveillance. It's as if I'm under arrest here, as well.'

'So where does that leave me? Am I your prisoner?'

'No, Mikey. The men out there belong to Colonel Gaddafi's personal bodyguard. I had no other way of getting you into Libya than by selling you to them. The kid who wanted to kill Gaddafi on 15 August 1970. You're their prisoner, not mine.'

I said nothing. He got up, went to the window and looked out across the sea.

'They still have a little faith in me. But not enough. At dawn they'll shoot you here on the beach. The Colonel's personal order.'

He stayed where he was in silence, still looking at the sea. Then he turned to me and an unexpected smile crossed his face. He suddenly seemed light-hearted and cheerful.

'So we don't have that much time, Mikey. We'll have to make a move during the bombardment that's coming just before dawn. While the coastguard boats take refuge in port to avoid the NATO bombs.'

I stared at him, dumbstruck.

'But, how come . . .?'

'I've been in charge of Libya's Secret Service for years, Mikey. I've got friends in NATO as well. A dinghy's moored off the other side of the island, below the cliff there. And an Italian cruiser will be there in an hour. One of my men will take Linda out to the cruiser in the dinghy.'

He opened the wardrobe, my father's old wardrobe, and took out a Kalashnikov. Then he smiled again.

'Linda Nardi's in the guest house. There are two militiamen on the jetty, two on the two doors of the villa, two over at the guesthouse. They're all armed, but it won't be a problem if someone helps me.'

I looked at him and shook my head.

'I don't shoot people any more.'

Again that intense, crazy smile.

'I know, Mikey. You've become what Laura Hunt wanted you to be. A sensible old bourgeois. But you're simply the diversion. You're under arrest, and I'll have to handcuff you. And that's how you'll help me. Like that.'

He put the cuffs on me and pocketed the key.

'I'll hand you over to the militiaman guarding the exit round the back of the house. He knows the Colonel wants you alive for the firing squad. I'm going across to the guest house to get Linda.'

'One of the men on the jetty's got a walkie-talkie,' I said.

'It doesn't matter. We should still have half an hour's advantage, and pretty soon they'll have other things to think about, when the NATO planes come in.'

I looked him in the eye for the first time since I'd entered the room, and he recited the magic formula that was supposed to take me back forty years or more.

'If you want to save Linda, there's only one way. Just like old times, Mikey. One last time.'

He dragged me to the door at the back and handed me over to the militiaman, who was drowsing in a chair in the heat of the night, a Walther PPK in his holster. He said something to the man in Arabic and then turned to me, speaking in Italian.

'I told him that you'll be here in handcuffs for a while. And that he should shoot you if you try to escape. Just get yourself *close enough*, all right?'

Close enough, Mikey. You remember how to do it?

He went off calmly, as if going for a walk along the beach. There was one militiaman on guard outside the guest house fifty metres away; the second one must have been inside watching over Linda.

I heard the guard greeting him deferentially at the door, then the man with the severed ear placed the Kalashnikov against the wall and went inside.

Linda Nardi

The militiaman guarding me got up, almost obsequiously, but still took the gun from his holster. Another man entered the room.

'Signorina Linda, Michele Balistreri's here. He's come to save you,' said the man with the severed ear, again speaking in Italian.

Throughout the whole journey I kept telling myself that I was coming here solely to kill the monster who'd shot Melania and Tanja Druc, run over Domnica Panu in a van, shattered Beatrice

Armellini's skull with a bullet and massacred rebels, as well as old men, women and children in Libya.

But it's not true, Linda. You came here to see if he'd come after you and try to save your life.

I suddenly felt a terrible regret. This could only end one way.

'He'll be shot at dawn. But you can save yourself, Signorina, if you do everything I tell you.'

'I don't take orders from a child killer.'

But he kept his cool.

'Balistreri came here only for you, to save your life. Please let him die a happy man!'

He didn't wait for a reply and addressed the other guard in English, holding out a pair of handcuffs.

'Put those on the lady.'

The militiaman hesitated a moment. Then he put the gun back in his holster, took hold of the handcuffs and bent towards my wrists. But he didn't have time to handcuff me. The saw blade of a knife slit his throat from ear to ear.

As the blood spurted in my face, over my T-shirt and jeans, I heard a sound like a sink being unblocked, a terrible gurgling noise as the life left his body. The man with the severed ear took the man's gun from its holster and gave it to me.

'Now, Signorina, either you try to help me, or we'll all die. And Michele first of all.'

The gun was in my hand, and our eyes met for a second.

'I'm sure you know what to do, Signorina. This is our only chance.'

He knocked three times on the guesthouse door, the signal that he wanted to exit. The militiaman outside opened it and the man with the severed ear shot him in the head before he was even past the door.

Michele Balistreri

I was ready even before I heard the gun shot. As soon as the guest-house door was opened, I launched a kick at the militiaman's chin at the same time as the shot was fired. The man had no time to get out of his seat.

As the spasm of pain shot from my knee to my brain, I almost passed out, but I saw the man with the severed ear come out with Linda. He grabbed the Kalashnikov left against the wall and pointed agitatedly in the direction the militiaman guarding the villa would come from. Then he ran off, going round the villa to get to the jetty.

But he hadn't foreseen another possibility. The militiaman emerged behind me from inside the house and gave me a kick in the back that sent me sprawling on the wooden decking. A moment later I felt the barrel of a gun at my neck.

Linda Nardi

Perhaps I've always been like this. Perhaps it's my true nature, the dreadful, rebellious girl who only Lena's tireless dedication had gradually been able to calm down.

I'm not going to let him die for my sake.

The man with the severed ear was right. We only had one chance. I knew what to do and how to do it. Five years ago, Angelo Dioguardi had taught me how to play poker and Michele Balistreri had taken me to a shooting range to teach me how to use a gun. So I took aim.

Use both hands, aim at the target.

The first bullet hit the militiaman exactly in the centre of his back, fracturing his spinal column. I ran to Balistreri, who was staggering to his feet. He said nothing but took the gun from my hands into his. He was still handcuffed.

The man with the severed ear was behind the corner of the house nearest the jetty, the Kalashnikov in his hand. A militiaman standing on the jetty was firing at him, while another was speaking furiously into the walkie-talkie.

Michele fired a shot randomly in their direction. The man on the jetty was taken aback for a moment, then turned towards us. It was all we needed. The burst from the Kalashnikov sent him sailing into the sea. The last of the militiamen dropped his walkie-talkie and started running for the motorboat.

'Shoot him, Mikey!' shouted the man with the severed ear. His ammunition was finished, he'd thrown the Kalashnikov down and was racing towards the jetty.

Michele Balistreri

Linda stared at me.

'Shoot him, Michele!'

I'd only shoot someone if I was forced to.

With those words I'd risked her being killed by Manfredi.

Mikey would never have allowed that.

I stretched out my arms and aimed at his legs. A Walther PPK is an accurate weapon, but the distance was huge. However, I was still a good shot.

The man went down, hit in the left calf. He started to drag himself along the jetty to the motorboat, but the man with the severed ear caught up with him. With one hand he grasped the man by the hair, lifted his head and slit his throat. He picked up the man's gun, tucked it in his belt and walked calmly towards us.

'Give me the gun,' said Linda.

'We're not here for this, Linda. You should go back to Italy now. I'll see to him.'

'Michele, that man killed Melania and her daughter and all

those others. In Libya, he's massacred old men, women and children.'

The man with the severed ear had reached us. There was a look of irony in his eyes, almost of amusement.

'Mikey isn't here for that, Signorina Linda. He's here to save you, if you want to be saved.'

He took the gun from my hands and slipped it in his belt. Then he took out a key and released me from the cuffs, pointing to the path behind the villa that led to the other side of the island.

'You remember the way, Mikey? We must get a move on. The bombs will soon be raining down.'

He turned and started running towards the path to the cliff.

'Let's go, then,' I said to Linda.

Our eyes met for a moment. She was an extraordinary woman, calm, intuitive, rational, sweet, compassionate.

But capable of killing, if need be.

If there'd still been a glimmer of Mikey in me five years earlier, we could have understood one other and continued to live happily together. Instead, we'd damaged each other more than we could have imagined.

The ice-cold anger I saw in her eyes frightened me more than our unending battle.

'That man is a cold-blooded killer, Michele.'

I tugged her violently, but she wouldn't come. Exasperated, I slapped her. She looked at me for a long moment. We both remembered another slap five years earlier. And we remembered what I'd said.

I should have fucked you like an ordinary whore.

There was something in her eyes, a look of pain or regret, which I couldn't bear or understand. I expected a slap back, or an insult. Instead, her face slowly softened and she calmed down, as if that slap had brought her to a different decision. Then she set off at a run along the path.

Neither of us spoke. While I was running along that path in the night, I was thinking about another time I ran to the cliff in the dark, on 31 August 1969.

When we came out on to the open space the man with the severed ear was already there, beside the old olive tree lit by the full moon. He pointed to the cliff edge with the Walther PPK in his hand.

'You'll have to jump from here, Signorina Linda.'

The dark sea glinted twenty metres below. I'd already leaped twice from that cliff, but for Linda it seemed madness.

'Is the water deep enough?' I asked him.

'For another fifteen minutes, Mikey, then Signorina Linda would no longer be able to jump. One of my men is below with a dinghy. He'll take her out to the Italian cruiser, which will take her back to Italy.'

The man with the severed ear looked at us. He was calm, unruffled.

'I let NATO know that Gaddafi has a stockpile of weapons on the island. In half an hour it won't exist any more. Now, please jump, Signorina Linda.'

She was staring at the rocks rising out of the sea. I thought she was terrified at the idea of jumping. But instead she whispered something.

So this is where it happened . . .

For a moment I thought I was dreaming, or simply imagining it. Linda turned towards me, tears streaming from her eyes.

She's not crying for herself, out of fear. Nor for Michele Balistreri, but for young Mikey.

Linda dried her tears on the back of her hand. She turned directly to the man with the severed ear.

'I don't care what happens to you, you'll soon be rotting in hell anyway. But Michele's going to jump with me.'

He pointed the gun at her.

'Mikey's staying here. We have some business to finish alone, he and I. Now you either jump or die. You have ten seconds. One, two . . .'

He started to count in Arabic. I knew for certain that he would shoot her.

'Linda, I have to stay here. All that matters to me is that you stay alive.'

The words were broken, uncoordinated; my look must have been desperate.

Suddenly Linda smiled at me. I'd dreamed for years that she might do this again. Her hand lightly brushed against mine. Only for a moment. Then she ran to the edge of the cliff and leaped into the air.

The man with the severed ear was holding the pistol in his left hand. The pale scar I'd glimpsed in my father's study was on his right wrist. The surgeon had done a good job with the ear.

Nothing has happened as you thought. There are always two sides to every truth.

I should have understood back then, when he sent me the photographs of his sister's killer fed to the sharks with his penis in his mouth. Karim would never have been able to kill him in that way. Nor would he have been able to handle a Kalashnikov and slaughter women and children.

Ahmed Al Bakri lit a long, slim cigarette.

'So, we have fifteen minutes, Mikey, before the water's too low and the bombs lay waste to this horrible island. There's another dinghy, and it'll be there twenty minutes. Let's sit down under this olive tree and get some things straight.'

Ahmed sat down, leaning against the tree trunk. He took a drag on the cigarette and slowly blew out the smoke, a moment that seemed to last a few minutes but which then stretched out to over forty years. I sat down facing him. The exterminator of innocent people. My greatest friend.

The other side of Mikey Balistreri. The dark side.

'On 15 August 1970 you were strung out, and it was easy to take you in. Everything was planned, and you never noticed a thing.'

I was the only puppet among all those others holding the strings. Each scene had been constructed especially for me.

The trip to Misurata, the tuna kill, Jalloun's body, the failed attempt on Gaddafi's life, taking Laura by force, the birthday party with my friends.

'When we got back to your house in Garden City, you were very upset, Mikey. You unloaded my gun and also Nico's. But then I checked.'

'And you put blanks in mine.'

He nodded, looking pleased with himself.

'I always told you, Mikey, destiny was in my hands. That night out at sea you were too tired, too upset, to notice the difference between blank shots and real ones and between a sinking corpse and a man going under from the weight of his gas cylinders. After you left I came up to the surface. Karim was nearby and he'd also thought I was dead. I lit my torch and he came to pick me up.'

She knew all this.

'Laura was in on all this with you and Karim?'

He shook his head, unhappy.

'You're always the same, Mikey. That's all you care about, isn't it? Then it was Laura, now it's your Signorina Linda.'

'Just tell me the truth, Ahmed.'

'I told Laura you'd agreed to shoot Gaddafi. All she cared about was that you didn't get shot yourself. And, for that, it wasn't enough to get you to run away. We had to make sure that you never ever came back either.'

So you had me rape my girlfriend and kill my best friend.

'Laura and I agreed on a plan to save your life, Mikey. Karim made sure you saw him as he was leaving her house. Then he went off to the reef and took the money.'

It was all so simple, so obvious. And there was only one explanation for Ahmed's severed ear.

'When did Karim die?'

'After you shot me, I went off to Cairo. No one knew I was still alive, not even my father. Only Karim. In 1973 the war with Israel started up again and Karim was blown up by a mine. His body was unrecognizable and I decided to have my ear cut and assume his identity. So I stayed in Cairo and wrote regularly to Mohammed, who thought I was Karim, but never went back to Tripoli. Only when the plot to assassinate Sadat was successful did I return, and I was treated like a hero. After all that time not even my father with his poor eyesight could tell that I wasn't Karim.'

'So it was you who sent me that letter in 1983.'

'Of course, to help you find my sister's killer, and you succeeded.'

I remembered the photograph he also sent me.

'How did you get a copy of that photograph of my father and Gaddafi?'

'Laura had the half with your father in it. She gave it to Karim, together with her letter, so that he could send it to you, but he showed it to me and I decided it was better not to send it. That was in 1971. Then in 1983, in exchange for the half of the Laura's letter I was keeping from you, I added the other half of the photograph, the part with Colonel Gaddafi. Then I dealt with Farid, and so I could send you the shot of his death.'

Up to that moment all we could hear was the calm sea, a peaceful background to our thoughts. Now, in the absolute quiet of the sultry night, we heard a faint, distant whistling, almost imperceptible but growing closer.

NATO fighter-bombers. Ready for action.

Ahmed was suddenly impatient. He was right: we only had a few minutes and he had the right to his explanation.

'But we're not here to go over those old stories, Mikey. You wanted Linda Nardi safely away, and now she is. Now I want to know why you wanted to kill me.'

Of course, this was always the real question, the reason why Ahmed had Beatrice Armellini whisper those words to me – *an old friend of yours has been waiting for you for many years* – a moment before he blew her head off. That whistling sound getting louder, coming from my world to drop bombs on his, was signalling the few remaining minutes we had to explain forty years.

'You know why, Ahmed. If you hadn't come to an agreement with our fathers, I would have killed Gaddafi and today we wouldn't be here waiting for those bombs to fall.'

Abruptly, his mood changed. I'd touched on the only point that still interested him in life, and now his face was serious, intent. He showed me his right wrist, the white scar still visible.

'Look, Mikey, I don't want any revenge. It's because of this scar that I had you brought back here. Is yours still as visible as mine?'

He was right. His could plainly be seen, whereas mine was a faint line on my left wrist.

'They already knew, Mikey. They had their sources. Your father wasn't worried about Gaddafi's death but yours. Mohammed threatened us, saying either we helped them or you'd be dead. Karim told Laura, and we decided we'd have to force you and then help you to flee the country.'

'Where's Laura now?'

The question slipped out, and Ahmed gazed out to sea beyond the cliff edge.

'On the other side of the world, Mikey. We all loved you. No one betrayed you. Laura tried to tell you, but I couldn't allow it, not in 1971 and not even in 1983.'

'So this was in the second half of the letter?'

Ahmed made no reply. He didn't want to answer the question. He got up, and I rose with him. Now the whistling sound of the war planes was much stronger. He offered me a gun.

'I killed you off back then, Mikey. I took away everything you had: your country, your money, your girlfriend. It was for a good reason, but, if you think differently, this time the gun is loaded.'

'And do you have a gun that's loaded?'

He shook his head, upset that I was so slow in understanding. Or that I didn't believe him.

'I'd never have shot you, nor will I now. We're united by a blood brotherhood and, for me, that still stands.'

I stood there staring at this man, once the boy I had grown up with.

A born killer, an exterminator of innocent people.

But one day Mikey Balistreri had created a pact of blood and sand with that boy. Whatever he'd become, whatever he'd done, it wasn't going to be Mikey Balistreri who ended the life of Ahmed Al Bakri. The insurgents, or God, or Allah, could see to that, not me.

I let the gun drop.

'I shot at you once, Ahmed. There's no point in doing it again today.'

All of a sudden the fighter-bombers appeared on the horizon in the first light of dawn. They shot high over our heads and after a few seconds the bombs began to fall on Tripoli. Huge explosions raised columns of smoke and flame. Ahmed pointed to the cliff edge.

'You have to jump, Mikey. Now the coastguard has other things to worry about, and very soon there'll be no more high tide and the planes will come over here and raze this island back into the sea.'

There was just one more thing. The promise he'd made via Beatrice Armellini before he blew her head off.

He'll tell you the truth. The one you really want to know.

I looked him in the eye.

'Did you kill my mother?'

He suddenly seemed both tired and at peace. It was as if everything else was simple now we'd established that we'd never betrayed one another, that I wouldn't shoot him now I knew who he was and that the blood brotherhood between us still existed.

He pointed to the olive tree, as if the chair and the Nietzsche book were still there.

'I got to the cliff top here about four thirty. I wanted to tell your mother that you couldn't have a relationship with Laura any more because you were a murderer, like me.'

I stared at him, taken aback.

'You came here that afternoon?'

He nodded, as if his lying to me then and telling me the truth now had no importance.

'Your mother wasn't up here reading. So I went to see if she was having a swim. But she wasn't there any more. Her book was still on the chair, and inside it I found that half photograph of Gaddafi.'

'What do you mean "she wasn't there any more"? Mohammed told me that at three o'clock that afternoon my mother's body was in a bathing costume lying twisted on the rocks below. And yet at half past four you couldn't see her, is that right?'

He looked straight at me, ever more reluctantly. Then one of the planes turned round over Tripoli's skies and came towards La Moneta. This seemed to make up his mind.

'There was the dinghy from Wheelus Field, Mikey. General Jalloun told us it was spotted at a quarter to four, and at four it had disappeared.'

'William Hunt?'

Ahmed nodded.

'He was a bastard. A spy. He had that black girl and her daughter tortured and thrown into the cesspit. She was a chambermaid at Wheelus and had stolen some secret document from him. Then he had those bastards kill my sister because she'd seen him with the girl. Your mother knew all this from Nadia and had given him forty-eight hours to disappear. I already thought it was him, Mikey, many years ago.'

I shook my head.

'William Hunt wasn't on the island that day. He was in Benghazi, and that's definite. He couldn't have pushed my mother off. Are you sure about what time it was when you went to the cliff top?'

He nodded slowly.

'Certain. It was four thirty. As I was going back to the villa, I met Laura.'

I was watching the bombers closing in on La Moneta, but I didn't care about them. The truth that Michele Balistreri hadn't tried to discover; indeed, had buried and forgotten, was now an obsession for his alter ego, Mikey. I knew that Ahmed wasn't lying to me, but I still couldn't understand.

'So who was it, Ahmed?'

He remained silent, shaking his head. He didn't want to go any further with this. The fighter-bomber passed fifty metres over our heads with a deafening roar. A few seconds later, the explosion on the far side of the villa was so powerful it sent us reeling.

'Ahmed, either you tell me the truth or I'm staying right here.'

He nodded, resigned.

'It was someone else. William Hunt had an accomplice.'

A second plane passed over our heads and another bomb exploded, even closer to us.

'Tell me the name.'

He signalled me no. And it was a final no.

'Mikey, I've already had my father tell you this. The truth has sides to it we don't want to see. If you want to live a little longer, remember why you came here and forget this island.'

I was sure he was telling me the truth and also sure he was holding back a decisive part of that truth in order to save my life yet again. For the first time I could read in his eyes an emotion that was totally foreign to him, and that was pity.

He was feeling pity for his one great friend, Mikey Balistreri, the dreamer, the idealist who'd introduced him to Nietzsche and the martial arts, whose life he'd saved many times and who, like him, had suffered a living death.

But now I'd come back. I was that Mikey. And Mikey knew what was hidden behind that pity.

William Hunt had an accomplice. Just as I'd always thought.

Ahmed's eyes resumed that expression I'd forgotten because I'd wanted to forget it. The expression he had when he cut the throat of that rabid dog, the throats of three Egyptian conscripts and that of his half-brother Salim.

'The rebels retook Zawiya today, Mikey. They're less than fifty kilometres away. The regime's lost, but Gaddafi will fight to the bitter end. I know what I have to do. You, on the other hand, have to jump off this cliff. It's now or never.'

He was right. It was now time to leave for ever this country I'd loved with my heart but never with my head.

Like a great love for the wrong woman.

For a moment I pictured those two young boys again, Mikey and Ahmed, so different and yet so similar back then. I felt no pity, no emotion, for the man in front of me, the exterminator of innocent people. But he was also the adolescent who'd saved my life and with whom I'd created a brotherhood of blood. A huge explosion shook the ground a hundred metres from us. The regime was crashing down, together with La Moneta, and it really was time for us to leave.

'Ahmed, finish what they didn't let us do forty years ago. If you can.'

Finally, Ahmed smiled, as he did in the old days.

'Now go and jump, Mikey. Go back home to your country.'

That go 'back home to your country' wasn't the angry order of 15 August 1970. And his *forget this island* was no threat but simply advice, a recommendation and a hope from Ahmed for Mikey.

I took a run-up and leaped off just as another powerful explosion shook the cliffs. It was the end of La Moneta.

A dinghy with a terrified Libyan in it took me to the cruiser in ten minutes, while La Moneta and Tripoli went up in columns of smoke and flame.

A lifeboat had already been lowered from the davits. I climbed on board and was lifted up. They told me straight away that Linda was safely on board.

On the bridge I looked around, trying to spot her, but it seemed she was already below. I didn't look for her, nor she for me. I knew I had to respect that absence and that silence.

From the ship I immediately sent an email to Floris, Colombo and Madonna, giving them a version of the facts that was almost true.

The killer of Melania and Tanja Druc, Domnica Panu, Beatrice Armellini, Senator Busi, Monsignor Eugenio Pizza *and* Mohammed Al Bakri was a Libyan secret agent in Gaddafi's pay. The murders of Melania and Tanja Druc were revenge against Emilio Busi for no longer protecting the Colonel's interests. All the rest followed as a consequence of that presumed betrayal. Linda Nardi had gone to Libya to complete her investigations and had been able to escape with me, whereas the Libyan secret agent died in the La Moneta bombing. The email concluded with my irrevocable resignation from the Italian police force.

13 Future Becomes Past

Palermo, Tuesday, 16 August 2011

Michele Balistreri

We docked at dawn, and I was among the last to disembark. I looked for Linda on the quay, but they said she'd disembarked early and had already left. However, I did find Police Chief Floris with Colombo, Corvu and Giulia Piccolo. Floris was the first to come up to me. I was thinking of what excuse to give him when he smiled and grasped me by the hand.

'Thank God you're not my son, Balistreri. I would have died of a heart attack many times over.'

Colombo also shook me by the hand.

'Thank you for saving Linda Nardi. And for having found the killer. We've compared the DNA found in Melania Druc's cabin, in the van that knocked Domnica Panu down, in Monsignor Pizza's house in Lugarno and in the house where Mohammed Al Bakri died. We don't know whose it is, but it's the same in each case. You're an excellent policeman, Michele. The best we have. And there's no question of you resigning.'

Corvu looked at me uncertainly. In all our years together, we'd never exchanged more than a handshake, together with some pats on his back from me in exceptional circumstances. Now the boy was sniffling and in the end couldn't resist and clasped me in a quick, silent embrace.

Giulia Piccolo, the soft-hearted giant with muscles of steel, stood back a couple of steps. Then she came up and we looked each other in the eye.

In the end she, too, held out her hand.

'Thanks for saving Linda's life,' she whispered.

I kept quiet about the fact that it was Linda who'd saved my life by shooting one of the militiamen.

'Come here, Giulia.'

It was the first time I'd used her first name in years. She smiled and came closer. I took hold of those hands, their nails painted green like the highlights in her hair, those hands that were so strong and so weak. She began to cry.

Giulia Piccolo's tears, Corvu's embrace, Linda's brief caress before she leaped off the cliff edge were the only things left in my life and the only things that had any meaning.

'Commissario, you're better than . . .' Giulia whispered, before she seized up and choked on the words, but they spoke more clearly than any others.

Both Floris and Colombo asked me to revoke my resignation, but I refused. It was neither obstinacy nor spite. It was simply that that part of my life had ended where it began forty years earlier. I was no longer a policeman, and I mentioned nothing about the death of Italia Bruseghin Balistreri.

A cruel death. Buried and then forgotten by men without honour. And then by me, who had sworn I'd never forget.

Tripoli, Friday, 5 September 1969

Mikey Balistreri

After Italia's funeral, General Jalloun sent us a letter of heartfelt condolences and some circumstantial details, saying that the Libyan coastguard constantly patrolled that stretch around La Moneta, where the cigarette smugglers used to slip in. He assured us that no vessel had come near the island on the afternoon of Sunday, 31 August, when Italia had died.

I know it's true that Libyan motor launches patrol the zone because the coastline facing La Moneta is full of hidden coves suitable for landing smuggled goods. I saw the launches myself that afternoon when I went in the motorboat to the Underwater Club with Salim, Farid and Marlene. And also on my return, after the furious hour with Marlene.

I know it's impossible to dock and get on to the island without being seen. But I also know that General Jalloun's too cowardly to take into consideration the adults left on the island that afternoon: Busi, Don Eugenio, Mohammed and my father.

Ultimately, Jalloun concludes in his letter, the death was accidental, a chance fall caused by an attack of vertigo or fainting. The general avoids the term 'suicide' out of consideration for his old friend Giuseppe Bruseghin. But closes the door on any other hypotheses.

But I will never forget. Never.

Rome, Tuesday, 16 August 2011

Michele Balistreri

Corvu and Piccolo took me home. They asked me nothing, not even if I wanted their company. They both knew me well enough.

I stocked up on whisky and cigarettes and stretched out on the sofa. But now Mikey was there in that flat as well. And he was looking at that ancient ruin of Michele Balistreri, who was again trying to bury himself under a haze of alcohol, cigarette smoke and Leonard Cohen.

And, against Michele's wishes, Mikey was starting to think about things again, going over what he'd known then and what he'd come to know in the last few hours; the things that had been kept from him all those years. He was examining the other side of the truth.

The side I didn't want to see. Not then, not now.

My mother left the house at half past one; she'd waved to us and set off walking to the cliff. Just afterwards, I'd gone to Tripoli with Marlene Hunt, Farid and Salim.

After that, three people had gone to La Moneta's cliff top.

Mohammed Al Bakri was there at three o'clock and saw my mother already dead on the rocks below.

Always assuming he was telling the truth.

Ahmed Al Bakri went there at four thirty, and the body was no longer there.

William Hunt went to the rocks in a dinghy between three forty-five and four.

He'd thrown her into the water to get rid of the body.

And what had Ahmed said?

'He was a bastard. A spy. He had that black girl and her daughter tortured and thrown into the cesspit. She was a chambermaid at Wheelus and had stolen some secret document from him. Then he had those bastards kill my sister because she'd seen him with the black girl. Your mother knew all this from Nadia and had given him forty-eight hours to disappear. I already thought it was him, Mikey, many years ago.'

It was an accomplice of this man that had pushed Italia on to the rocks. A cruel end. With no justification.

I'd buried the pain of that death in every possible way. Firstly, by violence in the MANK; then under Ordine Nuovo's double-headed axe; then countless faceless women; alcohol and cigarettes. And when that wasn't enough, the adult Michele had compartmentalized the pain, as if it were that of someone else: a young man called Mikey, immature, more arrogant than idealist, who wanted to change the world without making the effort to understand it.

I stubbed out my cigarette, got up off the sofa and went to open the window. In the past few years I'd become familiar with the new forms of investigation based on correlations between telephone records, databases and DNA. Methods in which younger officers like Corvu excelled and which had solved the deaths of Melania and Tanja Druc, Domnica Panu, Emilio Busi, Eugenio Pizza and Moham-med Al Bakri. But Italia Balistreri's death happened in 1969. Another world. Another era. There wasn't even anyone I could bring in for questioning. I could only remember and question the past.

With Mikey's grim determination and Michele's experience.

I went to the kitchen and poured the bottle of whisky down the sink. Then I put the cafetière on the hob and sat down at the kitchen table.

An accomplice of William Hunt pushed Italia off the cliff edge between the time that Marlene Hunt and I left the island and the time Mohammed saw the body at three.

But William Hunt already had his accomplices, and I'd known who they were since 1983, when Ahmed and I solved the case of Nadia's death.

Farid and Salim came away with Marlene and me. They couldn't have gone to the rocks before three.

But they were Mohammed's sons, and he could have lied to me about the times. They left La Moneta with Marlene and me . . .

But where did they go after that?

I started to rewind the film of the past.

Tripoli, Monday, 29 September 1969

Mikey Balistreri

Grandad takes me to the clinic in his Fiat 600. Tripoli is calm and bathed in sunshine. There are fewer policemen and more soldiers, but the shops are open, carriages on the go, and the shoeshine boys are again polishing Italian men's moccasins under the Piazza Italia arcades.

At Villa Igea they take off my cast, and now one crutch is enough.

'What do you want to do, Mikey, now you can walk?' Grandad asks me. He's pale and thin as a rake. In the last few months his shoulders have become stooped, and his calm and kindly eyes are now tired and red.

'Let's go out and take a walk in the Sidi El Masri olive groves, like we did when you took me there as a boy.'

Grandad drives the Fiat 600 towards Shara Ben Ashur and Sidi El Masri, and the scents of eucalyptus and olives gradually take over from the smell of the sea. He parks in front of the two villas that are no longer ours. Different cars, different people: the new proprietors who bought them from Papa.

We take the path that Nadia used in the mornings to come to the

Balistreri villa. We walk slowly, in silence. I'm limping on my crutch, and Grandad's tired.

We come to the old Al Bakri shack. Sheets of metal, cardboard and straw. An outside toilet built of old boards knocked together. The trickle of water that served as a sewer. The swing made out of a tyre. And that terrible stench in the heat haze.

The cesspit smells worse than ever, as it always did in the summer months, the hungry flies buzzing around it. It was here that the young woman and her baby were found. They were black, as I had confided to Nadia in great secrecy.

We walk in silence past the goatherds' corrugated huts, including the one where Nadia's presumed killer, Jamaal, had lived, and on to the olive-pressing shed. Only two months have passed since that day at the beginning of August. And everything has changed. Nadia's been murdered, my mother's dead, I've slept with Marlene Hunt and Gaddafi's taken control of Libya.

After an hour's walking Grandad's out of breath.

'Let's sit down for a moment, Michele. There, under that large olive tree.'

We rest against the wrinkled trunk, our shoulders touching, and I realize how thin Giuseppe Bruseghin has become. I can feel his shoulder bones against my muscles and count the ribs showing through his white shirt.

'You've lost a lot of weight, Grandad.'

He smiles. 'I wouldn't know. I've never weighed myself.'

Then he glances around and takes a deep breath. He brushes a bony hand through my hair. It has the same light calmness as Italia's hand did.

He lets out a long sigh.

'Last week, I signed a power of attorney for your father and sent it to him in Rome so he can sell the olive groves, all of them.'

I look at him. I can't speak.

'It had to be done, Michele. Your father's right. He's got big business plans and needs a lot of money to make them work. The sale of the groves will give him the collateral; most of the money will come as a loan from his Palermo friends and the Banco di Sicilia.'

'But, Grandad, he's already had you sell the villas. These olives are your life's work.'

'They're not much use to me now, Michele. Your father knows what he's doing. Besides, this way, we can ensure your and Alberto's future.'

I want to tell him that Alberto has a future, anyway, and that I have none at all. But that would only hurt him. It is, however, the right moment to clear up another point.

'Grandad, when I left you at the Underwater Club with Farid and Salim that terrible afternoon, were they with you the whole time after that?'

He looks at me and shakes his head.

'Yes, Mikey. We left the club in their pick-up and came to the warehouses here to store the gazebos they'd taken down. I let them go at four thirty. They had to collect Mohammed from La Moneta.'

This means that Farid and Salim are beyond suspicion. Fifteen minutes to get from the groves to the Underwater Club; thirty minutes by sea to La Moneta, where Ahmed saw them at five fifteen; another half an hour from La Moneta to the Underwater Club, where I met them with Mohammed at a quarter to six.

Grandad looks at me.

'There's something else, Michele. It's about your relationship with your father. And with yourself.'

I feel intuitively that he's asked my father to agree to something, something non-negotiable, in exchange for his signature for the sale of the olive groves. And now he's going to ask the same of me.

'I'm not going to say I'm sorry. And I'll never forgive him for –'

'There's no reason for you to say you're sorry to him. But he wasn't the cause of your mother's death. Get that out of your head, Michele.'

'Grandad, he and that woman –'

For a moment, his voice goes back to the firm one of the old soldier Giuseppe Bruseghin.

'That terrible afternoon, after Farid and Salim left at four thirty, I came back to the villa.'

I shut my eyes.

'Grandad –'

'In the forecourt were your jeep and Marlene's Ferrari, but there was no one in our house. A couple of hours later I saw you leave the Hunts' villa in a terrible state and get back into the jeep . . .'

'Grandad . . .'

He places a gnarled hand on mine.

'A father has the right to look after his son and the right to make mistakes doing it. A son has the right to protect himself and a duty to understand his father, sooner or later.'

He makes an enormous effort and completes the sentence, then his voice breaks off. His eyes stare first at me, then at the trunk of the olive tree. It's the first tree he planted here. He sits there without saying another word, his head resting on my shoulder, and there he dies.

Rome, Tuesday, 16 August 2011

Michele Balistreri

I finished drinking my coffee. The whole cafetière. Then I took a cold shower. The investigation, going backwards in time, was running along at a good pace, the memories surfacing intact and, it seemed, almost independently of me.

Good, so Farid and Salim couldn't have done it.

But William Hunt had a third accomplice. One of the perpetrators of Nadia Al Bakri's murder. My old friend in the brotherhood of blood.

Bushy eyebrows. A bit smelly.

Rome, Sunday, 23 January 1983

Michele Balistreri

'Your Esso sign, Nico. You were the one she wanted to check out.'

He makes an angry gesture.

'Sure, she came around asking a few questions . . .'

'Is that why you threw her off the cliff?'

The colour drains from Nico's face. The accusation of having killed Italia is too much even for someone like him. He shakes his head violently.

'No, Mike . . . I never laid a finger on your mother. I swear it on Santuzza's name.'

I look him right in the eyes. He'd never swear falsely on his mother's name. It hadn't been him who had caused Italia's death.

Rome, Tuesday, 16 August 2011

Michele Balistreri

The black coffee and the cold shower had totally cleared the mist from my brain. Now my backwards investigation, with memory as my only witness, was steamrollering along like a bus hurtling down a hill without any brakes.

I could believe Ahmed. His recent confession – *I went to the cliff top at four thirty . . . your mother's body wasn't there any more* – didn't invalidate anything else, everything he'd told me so far.

Tripoli, Tuesday, 16 September 1969

Mikey Balistreri

With my foot still in plaster, I can't use my bicycle, the car or my Triumph.

Forced into immobility, I stay at home inside the Garden City maisonette we moved into after my father sold the villas in Sidi El Masri.

On the wall of my new room is the photograph of Laura coming down the Spanish Steps in Piazza di Spagna in evening dress, a bewitching look on her face.

The person I'll never be.

The Al Bakris have also moved into a normal apartment, the same kind that Italians had, rented by my father near his offices in Piazza Italia, now called Maydan as Suhada. It has running water, sanitation, electric light, a room for each of the four boys and a large one for Mohammed and his two wives.

A tangible sign of change. And of what's to come.

Ahmed, Karim and Nico come to my room every afternoon to keep me company. Nico's terrified of Gaddafi and the new regime. He's afraid they'll take his money and his life, and even his Guzzi motorbike and the MANK van.

'For him, we're fascist torturers, not the ones who civilized his country. He'll have us all killed.'

Karim, on the other hand, is all for the new regime. He thinks Gaddafi and his junior officers are honest, serious men. Above all, they are anti-American and pro-Egyptian. And they'll help Nasser destroy Israel.

As usual, Ahmed's more detached. He doesn't particularly like the new apartment, preferring the old shack next to the cesspit. It's what he calls *my real home*.

The first day he comes to see me on his own I take the opportunity to question him about the only thing that really interests me.

'Tell me about that afternoon on La Moneta. Everything you saw and heard.'

He nods. The lines in his cheeks have become deeper; at nearly twenty, his beard's darker, his eyes even more serious. We've both lost the people we loved most. Nadia and Italia. His loyalty prevents him from asking me the crucial question.

And where were you, Mikey, on the afternoon your mother died?

'After you went off with Farid, Salim and Signora Hunt, we boys stayed on the beach. Laura was reading on the veranda. The grown-ups went into the living room. From the beach, we could see them through the window. Then I think they all went off to their own rooms, because at half past two there was no longer anyone in the living room.'

'And the four of you?'

'We stayed on the beach. At least another hour, perhaps more. But it was too hot and, before four o' clock, we split up.'

'And what did you do?'

'Nico went off for a nap and Alberto had to study. I think Karim joined Laura. I swam for a long time. I was nervous, and only felt happy in the water. I put on flippers and a mask and explored the rocks around the island.'

'Did you get as far as the cliff?'

'No, I stopped well before that. I was going slowly, trying to relax.'

'Did you see any boats?'

'No, Mikey, nothing.'

'And then?'

'I went back to the beach at about a quarter past five. After a few minutes, Farid and Salim arrived with the motorboat to take my father to the Underwater Club.'

'Yes, that would fit. I met them there half an hour later, about a quarter to six. They were taking him to the airport and they left me the motorboat to go back to La Moneta. And then?'

'At some point we all found ourselves back on the beach. I can't remember who came when. The grown-ups came out one at a time, and then Laura, too. We were all there before six.'

I look at him.

'And then I came back.'

'Yes.' He doesn't ask me where from or who I'd been with. Perhaps he has his own idea.

We look at each other. What should I say?

It couldn't have been Marlene, Ahmed. I know that was impossible.

Neither of us says anything. Everything is locked away inside us.

Rome, Tuesday, 16 August 2011

Michele Balistreri

I went to the window. The sun was setting over Rome. Overheated tourists were filling up the outside tables of the bars, while the locals still in the city were preparing to go out, now the blistering sun was calling it quits.

We boys stayed on the beach together. Laura was reading on the veranda, at least until half past three.

Then, when they split up, Ahmed didn't go for a swim. He went straight to the cliff top. And my mother was no longer there.

Not alive, nor her corpse.

This ruled Nico out. Between two and three thirty he was there with the others. While I was following Marlene from the Underwater Club to Wheelus Field and then to the villas.

That left the adults. Ahmed had glimpsed them through the living-room window from the beach.

But then at about two thirty there was no one left in the living room. And at three, Mohammed saw Italia's bloody corpse on the rocks below.

Was it true? Could I believe Mohammed Al Bakri? Something wasn't right . . .

A few days earlier, I'd reopened that brown envelope from 5 February 1983. I'd seen the photo of Nadia's killer with his penis stuffed in his mouth, thrown alive to feed the sharks. But I'd never wanted to read Laura Hunt's unfinished letter again.

And I didn't want to now, but I couldn't put it off any longer.

Letter from Laura Hunt, April 20, 1971

Mike,

*I wanted to write to you straight away after that night when you ran
away from Tripoli. And I did write to you in my head every night, without being able to put a word of it down on paper. You and I both know
that you can be close every day but still far apart — like our parents. Or
else far apart and yet close, like the two of us . . .*

*Today is the day that my thoughts need to be set down on paper,
because life has mysterious and wonderful ways which, in time, help us to
understand.*

*One thing always united us: the desire to be different. Me from my
mother; you from your father. We loved them as children, but they were
everything we didn't want to be. What united us was the certainty that
there was no dark side dark enough to separate us.*

*We were wrong, Mike, and you've seen that yourself. You only had
to lie to me once for me to stop believing you. If our judgements are
absolute ones, then our mistakes are unpardonable. And life is impossible
for us.*

That afternoon on La Moneta when Italia went out to the cliff, we were both wrong. You should have gone to your father and I to my mother to ask them what was going on.

Instead, we did the opposite.

As soon as you and my mother left with Farid and Salim, I made a decision. I went into the villa and sat outside the living room, where your father was alone for nearly two hours. Then I spoke to him for an hour. I won't tell you what was said. But straight after that conversation I went up to the cliff to talk to Italia.

Her book was open on the ground beside the chair. But your mother had already disappeared.

Rome, Tuesday, 16 August 2011

Michele Balistreri

I felt more and more anxious. The sequence of memories was running towards an end I hadn't wanted to see thirty years ago.

Things didn't add up back then, but I didn't want to acknowledge it or to see it.

There was a fundamental difference between what Ahmed told me then and what Laura had written. Their versions of events didn't coincide.

As soon as you and my mother left with Farid and Salim, I made a decision. I went into the villa and sat outside the living room, where your father was alone for nearly two hours. Then I spoke to him for an hour.

Laura hadn't been clear when she was writing. She hadn't gone *into* the villa but had sat outside.

On the veranda, as Ahmed had said.

And from the veranda she couldn't see into the living room very well.

Where your father was alone for nearly two hours.

While, according to Ahmed, *there was no one left in the living room by half past two.*

Now I felt the old enemy invading me, that poisonous anger circulating in my veins.

Someone had lied to me back then. And it hadn't been either Ahmed or Laura.

Tripoli, Wednesday, 24 December 1969

Mikey Balistreri

Papa and Alberto arrive in Tripoli from Rome on the afternoon of Christmas Eve. Papa still has this idea of the united family, even if Mamma and Grandad are no more. Perhaps he's dreaming of going to midnight Mass in the cathedral with his two sons by his side. But that hasn't happened since we were kids.

I only agree to dinner together so as not to offend my brother. We eat in the Waddan, on the terrace overlooking the seafront. There aren't very many Italians at the tables. The restaurant no longer has the atmosphere it used to on festive occasions, when there was an orchestra in the evening, and dancing and floor shows hosted by Pippo Baudo and Caterina Caselli. Now, it's quieter, with fewer civilians and more military.

Papa keeps us entertained throughout dinner with talk about his new deals with various Italian industrial groups: petrol, cars, foodstuffs. Every so often he comes out with terms such as 'joint venture', 'put and call options'. Perhaps he thinks this rubbish might still interest me.

Then he begins to comment on the situation in Tripoli.

'The Americans will have to give up Wheelus Field. Gaddafi doesn't want them around any more.'

'But will the Americans leave Libya just like that?' Alberto asks him. He smiles.

'Americans are businessmen. They'll find a way to make a deal.'

I remember William Hunt's words at my grandfather's funeral.

Salvo, we must talk tomorrow.

At this moment I cut in.

'What about you, Papa? Have you spoken to William Hunt? Have you made a deal with him?'

About Marlene Hunt.

Papa turns slightly pale.

'I don't know what you're talking about, Mikey.'

'You've sold all the family property, Papa. La Moneta, the Sidi El Masri villas, the olive groves, the town houses. And here we are, renting in Garden City. Why?'

My question takes him by surprise. It's not welcome. He brushes a hand through his thick hair and smooths his well-trimmed moustache. Here, too, you could see the first white hairs, like those on his temples. The lines in the corners of his eyes are deeper, the shadows under his eyes darker.

'The situation could change here, Michele. Shares in foreign companies are one thing, and property, land and commercial activity another.'

'What do you mean?' I ask him.

'That we Italians don't own Libya. One day we invaded it, and one day we'll have to leave.'

As usual, I disagree with him.

'Libya is our home, Papa. Thousands of good people like Grandad built it up without its oilfields, without "joint ventures" and "put and call options". I don't ever want to leave Tripoli. Besides, the MANK organization's doing better here than in Egypt.'

Papa looks at me in silence. He carefully wipes the beer froth from his mouth with his napkin.

'I'm happy for you, Michele. So long as your affairs don't damage our family's good name.'

There's no threat there. There's no need. He has all the weapons he requires. He pays the bill, as usual, and goes off, as usual.

Alberto and I are left alone at the table.

'Alberto, I have to ask you something.'

His eyes are on the luminous dots along the coast at the end of the seafront beyond the castle, towards the old fortifications, the beaches and La Moneta.

'Do you really have to, Mikey?'

His tone is always that of a caring elder brother. But this time there's a hint of concern I haven't picked up on before.

'That afternoon . . .'

I leave the question hanging in the air. My brother shakes his head.

'You can't let yourself have any peace, can you, Mikey?'

'No, I can't, Alberto. Tell me about that afternoon.'

'I was on the beach for two hours with the other guys. Before four, we split up, and I went to my room to study for the rest of the afternoon. I saw Farid and Salim docking at the jetty about five fifteen. They'd come to pick up Mohammed and I went out on to the beach to say hello.'

'Was anyone else on the beach?'

'Ahmed was there; perhaps Nico and Karim came along after a while. I don't remember.'

'And the adults?'

He looks at me, annoyed at my persistence, which he does not share.

'They came along later, in dribs and drabs. Mikey, you have to get used to it – Mother took her own life.'

From the mosque comes the muezzin's mournful cry. *Allah akhbar.*

Rome, Tuesday, 16 August 2011

Michele Balistreri

The sun had set over the city when I called my brother on his mobile.

'You at home?'

'Yes, Mike, we're eating. D'you want to come over and join us?'

'No, thanks. I need to talk to you. Alone.'

Alberto had no idea I'd just returned from Tripoli. Nothing had come out in the papers yet, and the police chief had promised my name would be kept out of it.

'Has something happened, Mike?'

It was a question to which there was no reply.

'I need to talk to you. Now.'

He gave in.

'All right, the boys are going out in a while and it's my wife's bridge night. See you in a bit.'

When I went to see Alberto, I usually preferred to cross Rome underground using the Metro, away from the tourists and those out for the night. But for the first time in years I decided to take a taxi that evening. I looked out of the window at all the happy people, the teeming restaurants, the illuminated Roman Forum and Coliseum. This was life. This was the world.

Do you really want to go back to it?

As I was getting out of the taxi, Alberto was at his front door, waiting for me. He greeted me with a smile, the smile he'd greeted me with, and looked after me with, since I was a child; even when he'd had to haul me out of the abyss I'd fallen into as a young man. He had aged well, much better than I had, and in that he also followed my father.

I wandered about the living room while he poured a couple of whiskies. The black-and-white photograph was still there in its wooden frame on one of the pieces of furniture.

The Adrian Pelt coast road. Two boys wearing English shorts and stockings up to their knees. Beside them, their parents. Salvatore looking down at the ground, Italia up at the sky.

We sat down in two armchairs facing each other. Alberto had the same expression as he had that evening on the Waddan terrace at Christmas 1969.

He cared about me. He eyes were saying *Leave it, Mikey, and spare yourself.*

As Ahmed Al Bakri had told me, they all loved me and, for that reason, no one wanted me to come near *that truth*. Alberto tried to talk about something else.

'The news said that the rebels are only a few kilometres from Tripoli. Perhaps it won't be long now . . .'

'I know, Alberto. But I'm not interested in now. That's not why I'm here.'

He nodded, sadly resigned to the fact.

'You want to talk about that day, don't you?'

His voice was tired, exhausted. The voice of someone who knows that a long illness is at last coming to its final conclusion.

'Yes, Alberto, about that afternoon, after Italia left the villa and I went off with Marlene Hunt. It was nearly two o'clock. What happened immediately after that?'

He rallied, and nodded.

'I've already told you, Mike. We youngsters stayed on the beach for a couple of hours. Then I went into the house to study.'

I asked him the same question I put to him back then.

'And the adults?'

And he gave me the same reply.

'I saw them all again at about five fifteen, coming out on to the beach, one at a time.'

Back then, he'd been evasive, not answering the real question. And I hadn't managed to ask it.

'But what about before, Alberto, while you boys were on the beach?'

Alberto looked at me. We'd always been like this: close and yet distant, the same and yet different.

'They were in the living room, we could see them through the window . . .'

'Ahmed mentioned this back then. But, according to him, there was no one there in the living room after two thirty . . .'

Alberto poured himself another whisky. This was already excessive for my brother.

'Can you tell me where Papa and the others were?'

Alberto got up. My whole life, my brother had only put me off when I touched on this point. But I never judged him; I just tried to understand.

He was silent for a while. Then he went over to the black-and-white photograph.

'I didn't see them come out on to the beach.'

'The villa had a back door, Alberto, which led straight out to the path. You couldn't see her from the beach. But you went into the house at about four. Was Papa there?'

Silence. Alberto placed a hand on the photo's frame, as if by holding on to it he could recreate that moment of happiness.

Our handsome, united family, just as Papa wanted.

He looked at me, and the desperate expression on his face frightened me. He was my rational, calm older brother. I'd never seen him look like this before.

'When I went back into the house at about four, I saw Laura near the back door.'

He closed his eyes, as if watching again these scenes that were his only true nightmare. And then in a whisper he said what he'd kept inside himself all these years.

For fear of Mikey.

'The back door opened from the outside, and Papa came in.'

For years I'd imagined this moment. I'd imagined the hate I'd feel, the rage, the desire for revenge. But instead of quickening, my pulse slowed down, as if my heart no longer had the strength to beat. I'd come to the point that should have been the finishing line but which, conversely, proved only to be a point of no return. I'd arrived there no longer wanting to, dragged back to La Moneta by Linda Nardi and Ahmed Al Bakri. But that journey had revived the adolescent who'd sworn to find out the truth.

'Where is he now?' I asked him.

Alberto sighed.

'I heard from him today. He's in America.'

I thought again about Mohammed Al Bakri, my father's old friend and right-hand man, lying in a pool of blood in that farmhouse. Ahmed had sworn to me that it wasn't him. And he had been speaking the truth.

It was William Hunt's accomplice.

The man at my grandfather's funeral who had said *We must talk, Salvo.*

Back then, I thought he had meant about the affair between my father and Marlene. But I was still very young then. Now I was an experienced policeman.

A shooting pain rose from my stomach to my chest.

Linda, Linda.

I took a taxi and was home in less than twenty minutes. I dashed up the stairs, my knee aching and throbbing, and rummaged about among the disordered papers on my desk.

Finally, I found the sheet of paper on which I had jotted the number Corvu had given me several days earlier.

I misdialled twice, then heard the phone ringing in San Francisco. It rang for some time.

'Hello?'

It was the one voice I hoped not to hear. Not there in America.

'Linda, it's Michele. What are you doing there?'

She was silent, then her voice came from the other side of the world.

'My mother's dying.'

Then, as always, she ended the call.

I knew that nothing would be achieved by calling back and telling her to be careful. My father's words, uttered a few days or a century ago, exploded in my brain.

I would hate anything untoward to happen to you, Signorina. You will promise me to be careful?

My hands still trembling, I managed to get on to the internet. I was lucky. Ryanair's last flight to London was at eleven and, from there, I could catch the night flight to San Francisco. I booked everything online and called Corvu on my mobile.

Ten minutes later a squad car with its siren on full blast was taking me to Ciampino airport.

14 The Truth

San Francisco, Wednesday, 17 August 2011

Michele Balistreri

The flight landed at 9 a.m., local time. I went quickly through passport control and found the driver of the limousine Corvu had hired for me from Rome. Waiting with a cardboard sign for *Mr Balistreri* was a short man with oriental features and an efficient look about him. He shook my hand and offered to carry my rucksack. Once we were in the car, I gave him Lena Nardi's address and he set off at speed.

We took the I-280 into the city, coming off at the piers before the Oakland Bay Bridge and turning north up to Fisherman's Wharf, with its bars and shops full of tourists. As we turned west towards Golden Gate Bridge, I could see the island of Alcatraz and the bay, full of sailing boats. We passed by Presidio National Park, crossed the Golden Gate and came to Sausalito. Looking back across the bay, we could see the San Francisco skyline.

We passed by the little tourist port and turned on to a quiet, empty street with white, two-storey houses fronted with gardens on either side. I had the driver pull up right there, at the top of the street.

I got out and looked for the house number. On the letterbox was a single name. *Lena Nardi.*

I went back to the limousine and told the driver we'd be waiting here. From the car window, I kept an eye on the drive up to the house.

This was the second time I'd rushed to save Linda Nardi's life. The first time, trying to tear her away from the hands of an exterminator of innocents on an island turned into a nightmare, I felt no fear. But now, in this peaceful atmosphere, I was terrified.

Why, Michele? Why should your father want to have Linda killed because of a crime committed over forty years ago, before she was even born?

There was no rational reason for my fear.

The hours passed and the sun began to set over the bay. It was almost seven in the evening when I saw two men arrive at the house in a long, black limousine, which I realized was a hearse. The men from the funeral home knocked at the door, then from the hearse took in a coffin of light-coloured wood. They stayed for an hour and, when they came out, I went up to them.

'Hi, I'm a neighbour. Has Mrs Nardi died?'

They gave a solemn nod. 'Two hours ago.'

'And the funeral?'

'Tomorrow morning at ten in the Catholic cemetery.'

My driver was being handsomely paid and raised no objections to staying where we were. While he slept, I kept an eye on the drive. I knew that Linda was there, keeping a vigil over her mother's body. And I was keeping a vigil over her.

I wasn't there out of hatred alone, to avenge Italia, but also out of love. To protect the future, which meant Linda.

It was a warm night, a soft breeze coming off the bay. That street, with its small, white houses, was the most peaceful place on earth. I got out of the car to have a smoke and walked up to the house, stopping at the letterbox.

All I could hear were the cries of seagulls and the wash of waves in the little harbour. Again I read that innocent name on the letterbox. *Lena Nardi*. I remember her voice when she'd answered my call a few days earlier when I wanted to find out if Linda had arrived safe and sound.

Hello?

It's Michele Balistreri, I'd said.

Then an unending silence. Almost as long as a lifetime.

I remembered Michelino listening to Domenico Modugno singing '*Volare*' as he sat on the sofa between those two women who meant most to him, Italia Balistreri and Laura Hunt. I also remembered Laura and I alone that evening, eating popcorn under the car-port roof as we told each other about our parents, Salvatore and Italia, William and Marlene.

I walked slowly back to the limousine. Very slowly.

Sausalito, Thursday, 18 August 2011

Michele Balistreri

The men from the funeral home rolled up at seven in the morning and quickly loaded Lena Nardi's coffin into the back of the hearse. Linda emerged at nine. Alone. She was dressed in black, wearing dark glasses. She didn't even see our car, with its tinted windows, and set off walking down the street.

I told the driver to follow her at a distance. In five minutes we were at the cemetery. I stayed in the vehicle. There was no one on the green lawn circled by white chapels, only the hearse parked by the little church. The coffin was taken inside. One at a time, a dozen or so elderly ladies arrived. They must have been Lena Nardi's friends and neighbours. Going up to Linda, they embraced her one by one.

Linda was worn out, but the atmosphere was peaceful. The calm sea, sun in a blue sky, green lawn, white chapels, old ladies chatting, the cry of seagulls.

No one dies from a bullet in surroundings like these.

Five minutes before the start of the service a black chauffeur-driven Mercedes drew up and parked outside the cemetery. My father got out and walked slowly to the little church. He was dressed to the nines, as always. A dark suit, his white hair freshly cut, the air of a wise and protective old man.

He went up to Linda and embraced her. It was brief, but unbearable; obscene, absurd and yet inevitable. Papa was a man who believed that ethics functioned by means of compensation, so that spreading a certain amount of good around meant compensation for any evil committed.

This has always been the unbridgeable gap between us.

I wasn't sure if he'd seen me or not. Perhaps he had, perhaps not. Perhaps in this case, at least, he had made the right choice: one which – all things considered – he'd already done when I was still a child and still his son, which was *to pretend not to see me at all.*

After half an hour everyone left the church and Lena Nardi's coffin was carried into a small white chapel nearby. The elderly ladies said goodbye to Linda and, one at a time, went away.

Linda and my father went into the chapel together. They stayed there several minutes, then came out and got into the Mercedes.

He wouldn't do anything to her. Not him, not here.

I went up to my driver.

'Would you follow them, please? If they go to her house, then you can wait outside. If anyone else comes or they leave, then call me on my mobile.'

The cemetery was peaceful again. I walked over to the chapel that Linda and my father had entered. The door was only pulled to. I opened it gently.

The interior was in shadow, cool and silent. Its rectangular shape was lit by three red candles placed in front of the three plaques, one set into each wall.

The sense of restfulness was all embracing. It was like finding yourself in an Eyptian tomb or a catacomb, as if the dead surrounding me had lain there for two thousand years, and me with them.

I went up to the first plaque. The photograph showed the face of a young man in civilian clothes, probably chosen by his wife, *a photograph of her husband before he became a soldier, secret agent and killer.*

William J. Hunt, Dallas, 4 February 1925 – Mogadishu, 16 April 1983.

He'd died just after we'd discovered who'd murdered Nadia. Ahmed had told me.

I took care of him many years ago, Mikey. Your mother knew about him from Nadia and gave him forty-eight hours to disappear.

I'd had further checks made on the information after having spoken with Ahmed. I went back to my old friends in the Secret Service. William Hunt was one of the most expert operatives in the CIA. He'd been killed by a hit man outside the American Embassy in Mogadishu. The guards were able to give only a general description of the man, because he had been wearing a hoodie that covered almost all of his face.

And his severed ear.

How much time do I have? That's what William Hunt had asked my mother that afternoon on La Moneta. *Two days, no more.*

That was enough for William Hunt. That night he left the party on La Moneta and went to Benghazi. And when my mother flew off that cliff edge he had the perfect alibi. He simply wasn't there.

It was his accomplice who pushed her over the edge. All William Hunt had to do was come along with a dinghy to pick up the body and deposit it out at sea. So that no one would see it and prevent the coup d'état going ahead. He was in cahoots with my father.

I turned to the most recent plaque, the one put in place a little earlier that day.

Marlene Nardi Hunt, Los Angeles, 1 March 1935 – Sausalito, 17 August 2011.

Linda Nardi had spoken a lot about Lena. An absolutely extraordinary mother who'd looked after her with love and dedication and rescued her rebellious daughter from the deep trouble she caused.

Nardi must have been Marlene's Italo-American maiden name before she married William.

Marlene Hunt had become Lena Nardi and must have turned her life around the same moment I dragged her into the mud in front of her daughter, Laura. That mud, on both her body and her soul had brought about what no reasoning, psychology, advice or threat could ever have. It transformed a capricious, dissatisfied and self-centred person into a strong, honest woman totally dedicated to her daughter.

The photograph on Marlene's plaque showed Lena as an already ill seventy-six-year-old. As with William's photograph, she must have chosen it herself, to wipe away any last trace of the extraordinary beauty that should have made her fortune but had only been her ruin. But neither old age nor illness had been able to extinguish the extraordinary light in those eyes that were now staring at me from the photograph.

She knew that one day Mikey would be here to look at her.

She'd known since the moment, several days ago, when I telephoned to find out where Linda was and had introduced myself as Michele Balistreri.

I turned slowly to the central wall that separated William and Marlene. I already knew what I would find there before I entered the chapel. Ahmed Al Bakri had already told me two days earlier on La Moneta, when I'd asked about her.

It was for that reason I'd totally avoided looking at the third plaque. But now I had to.

Tripoli, Saturday, 15 August 1970

Laura Hunt

Karim leaves the house in such a way that Mikey's bound to see him. This is what he has to remember about Laura Hunt: a traitorous *gahba*.

And Ahmed's managed it, with my help.

Mikey comes up to the house slowly, and I come downstairs. I open the door straight away, as soon as he rings the bell, so that I don't have second thoughts. How will I behave in front of him? I'm not sure I can act out the part and trick the most innocent person in the world.

If he trusted me, perhaps I could tell him the whole truth, persuade him to get out of the country and promise to join him in Italy.

'Come in, Mikey. The radio's just announced that there's been an attempt on Gaddafi's life.'

I speak in a kindly way, but he recognizes the false note in my voice and the sight of Karim has evaporated any good intentions he may have had. Exactly as Ahmed predicted.

'I want the truth, Laura.'

His voice is aggressive and yet as fragile as a child's. He's never had a father who's really loved him, he's lost his mother and now he's about to lose me. I'm full of pity for him, my eyes are brimming with it, but for Mikey this is what's most unbearable. I see the veins standing out on his neck; his eyes cloud over; his voice is full of controlled rage.

'You were there on La Moneta that afternoon. Tell me it was my father, Laura. Then I can kill him, and you and I can leave here and live happily together for the rest of our lives.'

With these words my will crumbles, along with any hope I have.

He's sure to get himself killed. All I can do is follow Ahmed's plan and try to save his life.

I feel a tear trickle down my cheek. I can't hold it back. It's a real tear. Mikey thinks it's for all the things that can't now happen between us.

And, at this point, I know that Ahmed's right. There's no other way. Ahmed suggested what I should say. Words from which there's no return.

'Your father's got nothing to do with it, Mikey, and your mother killed herself. Why don't you forgive yourself?'

I'd showed him pity, the thing Mikey detests the most. What I can see in his eyes is so awful that for a moment I forget what I have to do and just hug him. I hold on to him like a person in a shipwreck grasping on to a piece of the wreckage. But he's the shipwrecked one and I'm the wreckage. I can't hold on to him.

When I let go, we stand there, motionless, silent, by the door. We're both thinking the same thing.

We'll never, ever see each other again for the whole of our lives.

It's a dreadful thought.

My poor, dear love, I know what you're thinking.

Mikey's thinking about Karim, who he's seen leaving furtively. And about his mother, and my words about her. *Why don't you forgive yourself? Your mother killed herself.*

He's thinking that if I've cheated on him with Karim, I'd lie about that afternoon.

About that, you're right.

His voice is now full of anger and scorn.

'I don't believe you. You're a liar. I know you're sleeping with Karim.'

Just like a child, a beautiful, innocent child. Just like that evening back in 1958, Michelino sitting on the sofa between Italia and me as we all watched the Sanremo Song Festival and listened to Domenico Modugno's great hit '*Volare*'. A dream that never could return. He took Italia's hand, and I took his.

But neither Italia nor I would be in his dreams any longer. Or only as ghosts.

I force myself to go through with the last act and make my eyes look cold, distant, so as to say a goodbye that'll separate our bodies for ever but also unite us for ever. Mikey can read my expressions. He throws himself on top of me and we land on the carpet. He lifts my skirt and rips off my briefs. I'm lying underneath him on the floor, neither helping nor hindering him, my head buried in his shoulder and my eyes closed. I don't feel his weight, his heavy breathing. All I can feel is his pain.

I place my hands lightly on his shoulders, so as not to leave him alone in this terrible moment that will destroy his life. I don't want him to feel completely alone as he enters me. I want him at least to hope, each time he remembers this moment, that I was there with him.

My body's already distant, but my soul's here with you, Mikey. And always will be.

Sausalito, Thursday, 18 August 2011

Michele Balistreri

The oldest plaque there was for the youngest person to die.

Laura Nardi Hunt, San Francisco, 25 April 1952 – San Francisco, 29 April 1971.

Ahmed hadn't wanted to lie to me, or to cause me pain.

On the other side of the world, Mikey. We all loved you, no one betrayed you. Laura tried to tell you, but I couldn't allow it, not in 1971 and not even in 1983.

But, in my deepest thoughts, I'd always known she was dead. I'd thought about her countless times those years. And I'd never managed to visualize her concretely with a husband and children, at home or at work, whether it was in Tripoli, California or anywhere else. All I could do was remember her with me, and then nothing else, as if both our futures had ended together on that day, 15 August 1970.

She'd died on 15 April the following year, shortly after writing me that letter, of which Ahmed had first refused me and then allowed me to see only a part.

I'd never received the second half, because he'd wanted to protect his friend Mikey from a truth that would have brought about his downfall. I could imagine what Laura Hunt had said to me in the rest of that letter.

Your father was coming back from that path.

Ahmed had saved my life that time as well. The Mikey of 1971 and the young Commissario Michele Balistreri of 1983 were both too impulsive and violent. They would have discovered an unacceptable truth and got themselves killed because of it.

Then I saw that there were two photographs on Laura Hunt's plaque. They were there for me and for me alone.

The other side of the truth.

My anger had led me to this place of peace. It was the anger of a child, Michelino, who'd fought a titanic battle in every way against a father who *didn't like him as he was*, going so far as to make that father an icon of evil, of all the evils in the world, and making him a killer for ever.

But, together with his accomplices, Papa had only murdered Italia, not Italy. The other side of that truth, the real truth, was a far worse nightmare. Ahmed had mentioned it to me for the last time before I leaped off the cliff top.

Mikey, I've already had my father tell you this. The truth has sides to it we don't want to see. If you want to live a little longer, remember why you came here and forget this island.

Part of that truth had been staring me in the face without me recognizing it — except perhaps in the most unconscious recesses of my soul: that evening five years ago when I couldn't bring myself to kiss Linda Nardi, and that dreadful night when I stopped myself just in time before raping her. And with Laura on 31 August 1969 on the beach at La Moneta, watching that gesture *that wasn't a goodbye*.

Now I was looking at the truth in the two photographs on Laura Hunt's plaque.

One for Mikey; the other for Michele.

The first was the one a fearful adolescent who felt betrayed and full of anger had left on his bedroom wall in Tripoli. Laura, looking ravishingly beautiful in an evening gown, walking down the Spanish Steps in Piazza di Spagna, imitating her mother, Marlene.

The shot of how I'll never be.

The second was an extraordinary photograph in black and white, taken in a hospital room a little before she died. Laura was propped up on pillows, her pale complexion contrasting with the dark shadows under her eyes, but those extraordinary eyes were lit by the sunlight coming in from the window.

That beautiful young woman was dying, yet she was happy, smiling at the very tiny newborn girl in her arms who was looking up at her mother with one half of her face in the sun, the other in the shade.

The second side of the truth.

I didn't need that image to tell me who the baby was. Nor the dates. Although I'd celebrated Linda's birthday with her years ago. She'd been conceived on 15 August 1970 and born on 28 April 1971, a little prematurely. Probably because Laura was dying.

Now I knew where I'd seen Linda Nardi's eyes before: they'd taken their shape from her grandmother Marlene, their colour from her mother, Laura, and their expression from her grandmother Italia.

And from her father, Mikey, she had that shadow that cut her face in half.

And the courage to walk across hell.

I looked at Marlene Hunt's eyes again. I knew she was pleading with me.

Forgive me, Mikey. The fault was mine, and mine alone. Forgive yourself, and her, too.

The chapel door opened and then closed behind me. He said nothing but came and stood by my side. Now that I could really see him, Papa was nothing but an old man of eighty-six. His stance was a little more bowed, his steps less sure, his arms trembled slightly. His eyes were more sunken and appeared tired under his tinted lenses.

The two of us stood in silence, each of us with his own thoughts. I knew he was waiting for me to say something, anything at all, but nothing came from my heart to my lips.

I know a long time's passed, Papa. But nothing's distant between a father and son; everything is close, as if it happened yesterday.

Close, and yet very distant. What both united and separated us was blood, his and my mother's. My mother, Italia, would have said so, had she been able to.

But I can't, Papa. You can forgive a moment of madness; you can forget the past, but not the present.

Without saying a word, I turned my back on him and went out, pulling the door to behind me. Outside, there was splendid sunshine, the cemetery's green lawn, the little church, the white chapels, the glittering bay with its sailing boats below the Golden Gate Bridge. I went back to my hired limousine and told the driver to take me back to San Francisco airport.

15 The Evil that Remains

Ostia, Thursday, 20 October 2011

Michele Balistreri

Tripoli had fallen to the rebels two months ago and the media was now speculating whether Gaddafi had left the country or not.

I thought how much Ahmed and Mikey would have laughed at the idea. The West had exploited the dictator for forty years or more but continued not to see the difference between a desert Bedouin brought up in a tent and an employee brought up in the West. The Colonel was neither a Saddam Hussein nor a Slobodan Milošević: he would never surrender. It wasn't a question of good or evil. Gaddafi was certainly evil, but he'd never run away.

Each day of those two months had seemed never-ending. I'd been waiting for that meeting, wondering how it might come about, and I hadn't even managed to think of the first words I would say to her. Everything seemed either insincere, or too serious, or ridiculous. And so for two whole months I'd resisted getting in touch. And, for that matter, so had she. But then I had no illusions about that.

I'm the father who abandoned her.

Except once, coming back from Palermo, where he'd gone to see my father, who was having problems with his heart, Alberto had mentioned that Linda was there with him, a few miles west in the small town of Isola delle Femmine. Picturing her there, near Palermo, keeping a man she now perhaps called 'Grandad' company, and who I could no longer call 'Father', was unbearable. I was sad for all that had been lost and happy for what remained, but the things I couldn't forget made the two feelings as inseparable as poison from water.

As I was every day, I was in Ostia sitting at a table in a bar, looking out at the sea. The weather was glorious, the tail end of a summer that seemed it would go on for ever. Only people like me without work or family could enjoy being there, taking a walk, reading the papers, taking the sun if it was out and, at sunset, going off to the pier to fish.

Why this routine? Because the eternal repetition of nothing was all that was now left to me. I went there every day and waited for another day to end.

Then one day I was caught by surprise as I was eating, my fork in mid-air while the bar's television announced that Colonel Gaddafi had been killed in Sirte. Watching the bloody scenes of what had evidently been a massacre, I wondered what I really felt.

Are you happy now someone's done what they stopped you from doing all those years ago?

I realized with some surprise that the images gave me no real satisfaction, only the mixed feelings of justice and repulsion that any civilized adult would feel about the death of a dictator, in itself nothing more than a massacre.

My mobile kept ringing, but I didn't answer the calls, nor the messages of congratulation, as if I'd won something. Then came a message from a number I didn't recognize, with a photograph attached. The text was very simple.

As promised.

I opened the photo. The television in the bar was broadcasting scenes of Gaddafi's last minutes, but this shot – slightly out of focus and shaky – had been taken at a different angle, obviously with a phone. A group of young men was dragging along the obviously wounded Colonel.

It took me some time to pick out the small revolver in the middle of the crowd. Then the hand holding it, followed by the arm, the shoulder and the neck, then a face in profile you could just make out. Below the baseball cap, an ear could be seen. The picture wasn't clear, but I knew that I was looking at a severed ear.

Alberto called me that evening.

'Papa saw the pictures of Gaddafi's death, then he put himself to bed and went to sleep.'

He said nothing more for a minute. It seemed a long time. Never in his life had my father slept in the afternoon; he thought it was a stupid waste of time.

In the end, I rallied.

'All right, Alberto. I'm coming,' I said.

Isola delle Femmine, Friday, 21 October 2011

Michele Balistreri

On the edge of the town, a track led to a gate that was identical to that of the villa in which we lived at Sidi El Masri outside Tripoli, with the linked 'S' and 'I' of my parents' initials. The two villas beyond the gate were identical to the ones I grew up in.

Nothing remained of the tight security in place in 1983 when I showed my father the photograph of him with the young Gaddafi; gone, too, were the security guards, the CCTV and high boundary wall. All that was left were the two villas, surrounded by eucalyptus, and behind them the beach, the jetty, the sea and the exact copy of the white villa on La Moneta.

Papa had asked Alberto not to bother with a large funeral, simply to cremate him and scatter the ashes on the bay there. When Alberto and I arrived with the urn, Linda was waiting for us on the wind-blown beach that was glowing gold in the sun.

No one said anything. Alberto opened the urn, and my father's ashes were scattered by the wind, mingling with the water and the sands. Then Alberto went indoors and left us alone together.

Me and my daughter.

Around us there was only wind, water, sky and sand. She was staring at me with those eyes inherited from three extraordinary and very different women: her grandmothers Italia and Marlene and her mother, Laura. The wonderful creature I had in front of me was Laura Hunt's present to Mikey Balistreri.

There were two deckchairs by the water's edge. We sat down. The sun was beginning to set and a kitesurfer was shooting past a hundred metres away.

'Michele, there's something I have to tell you.'

I wanted to tell her that it wasn't necessary. I knew everything about my daughter because I'd loved her in a different kind of love before I knew she was my daughter and had twice stopped myself acting on it; once on the verge of paradise, the second on the verge of hell. And now I knew that what had stopped me wasn't an act of will, but Laura Hunt, wherever she was.

But there was no way of stopping the daughter of Mikey and Laura, of telling her *Let's not talk about it, there's no point in going back over old truths.*

Once back in Rome, having seen Marlene Hunt's eyes staring at me from the funerary plaque after her funeral, I'd watched the DVD of Linda and Giulia leaving together for San Francisco under police surveillance many times. It was the evening I went to the farmhouse where Mohammed Al Bakri was later killed.

I'd done this before, looking for faces that stood out as possible killers who were after Linda and Giulia. And I'd found none, because there were none.

But in that DVD were Mohammed Al Bakri's killer and my mother's murderer.

The kitesurfer performed an elegant twist and turned towards the open sea and the disc of the sun as it was setting over the horizon.

'Go on, then, Linda, let's hear it.'

Tuesday, 9 August 2011

Ciampino

At twenty to eight, Linda Nardi came out of the toilets in Fiumicino airport. She met Giulia Piccolo's friend Francesca, who was waiting for her outside the terminal with the Ducati Monster 900.

She knew she had limited time, thanked Francesca and got on the bike. She drove at top speed down the motorway towards Rome and then took the intersection on to the Appia Nuova and Ciampino.

After the airport exit, she turned down on to Via dei Pini, towards the address that Emilio Busi and Eugenio Pizza had given her before they were killed. In the darkness, lit only by the moon, she rode the few kilometres through the countryside. The narrow road became an unmetalled track and ended in a large green gate with the number 1952.

Just in front of the gate was a Fiat Ritmo, parked by the verge. She knew that car from the trips to Ostia with Michele Balistreri five years ago. When she heard the sound of a motorbike in the farmyard, she quickly hid Giulia's Ducati behind Balistreri's Ritmo. The Kawasaki rider shot past without seeing her.

If Balistreri's here, then the man with the severed ear must be here as well.

She climbed over the gate and crept silently into the farmhouse.

Then straight away she heard the voice. It was that of an old man speaking on the phone in Arabic and he sounded upset. But Linda could make out nothing of what he was saying, except the word 'Balistreri'.

She peeped along the dimly lit hall. An old man was talking into a satellite phone. He was wearing thick, dark glasses, had a few sparse white hairs on his head and lots of dark blotches on his skin.

And he doesn't have a severed ear.

His back was to her. On a small table lay a Smith and Wesson, which Linda slipped into the pocket of her grey sweatshirt. Then she made out a word. Five years ago, Michele had taught her two words of Arabic, only two: one was the word for 'love', and the other was the word for 'death'.

I don't remember which was which, but it's not difficult to guess.

The old man ended the call, turned round and saw her with the Smith and Wesson in her hand.

'Signorina Nardi, from that night on the cruise I knew that in the end we would have to kill you as well.'

'Like Melania Druc and her baby girl?'

He raised his shoulders and coughed.

'Yes, like them all. My son saw to it. I thought I'd only see an end to Michele Balistreri this evening, even though my son's against it. But I see I'll have the pleasure of doing away with you as well.'

Mohammed Al Bakri had been born and brought up in a culture in which women were, at best, obedient mistresses. He felt sure of himself and took a step forwards. Linda Nardi shot him without a moment's hesitation.

She put the gun and satellite phone in her pocket and rushed back to Giulia Piccolo's bike, stopping only to throw the gun and the phone into a well. She reached Ciampino airport in a few minutes, just in time to catch the last flight to London and from there the night flight to San Francisco.

Friday, 21 October 2011

Isola delle Femmine

Balistreri listened in silence to what Linda had to say, all the while watching the kitesurfer.

'Mohammed wouldn't have killed me, even if you hadn't come. His son had forbidden it.'

'How did you know it was me?'

'When I saw the photographs on Laura's plaque, and Marlene's eyes in her eyes. When I came back from Sausalito I checked the DVD of the Fiumicino airport CCTV footage and the other reports from Ciampino airport that I'd asked Corvu to get. It was all there.'

Right in front of my eyes, only I didn't want to see it.

9 August 2011 – Fiumicino Airport, Rome

    Time 19:17

    Linda Nardi and Giulia Piccolo enter the International Departures hall. Linda has a single trolley and a bag, almost looks at the CCTV camera. They queue up at the check-in, then go through baggage check and passport control. Linda goes to the toilets and comes out at 19.38. Giulia waits for her outside.

Time 19:40

A young woman in a baseball cap with no logo, sunglasses, grey tracksuit and trainers comes out of the toilets after Linda Nardi. The young woman quickly leaves the International Departures hall.

Time 20:35

Linda and Giulia are sitting down and reading in a corner of the waiting room, then they get up, walk to the jet bridge, hand in their embarkation cards and show their passports, and are aboard at 20:45.

9 August 2011 — Ciampino Airport, Rome

Time 22:21

The same young woman who left Leonardo da Vinci airport at 19:40 wearing a baseball cap with no logo, sunglasses, grey tracksuit and white trainers, enters the International Departures hall and goes straight to baggage and at 22:50 gets on the 23:00 Ryanair flight for London.

The kitesurfer was twisting and turning, shooting along and going ever further out to sea. Balistreri kept his eyes trained on him.

'Corvu even had you tailed, poor lad. Passengers L. Nardi and G. Piccolo appeared on the manifest and disembarked in Los Angeles. But there's only the initial on the embarkation card. And at Ciampino you also used your initial, L. You took the same flights I did to get to Marlene's funeral, the last flight of the day from Rome to London, then the non-stop to San Francisco.'

Linda nodded.

'Lena and Giulia left from Leonardo da Vinci at nine, while I left Ciampino at eleven. They got to San Francisco an hour before me.'

'And you got there in time for my phone call, when Marlene answered and passed me on to you and Giulia.'

Linda sighed.

'Lena had come to Rome to help me, because I told her about the man with the severed ear that I saw with Melania Druc in Tripoli, and she was worried about me.'

'Naturally. She knew who he was.'

Except she thought it was Karim.

'She told me everything: who my real mother was, my grandfathers, and that the man with the severed ear was a childhood friend of my father's. But she didn't tell me who my father was. I learned that in San Francisco, from the man Ahmed Al Bakri sent to persuade me to go to Tripoli.'

'Persuade you?'

Linda was also keeping her eyes on the sea.

'He wrote to me. Told me who you were, who I was. And that I should trust my father, that you would come and get me.'

To trust her father, Mikey.

'Are you going to arrest me now?' Linda asked.

I should have spoken to her like a father. Told her that Michele wouldn't have acted as she had done but that he understood her. And told her that Mikey would have acted as she had but wouldn't have understood her, as he'd never understood her exceptional mother.

The kitesurfer did a splendid turn westwards, where the rays of the setting sun were shining over the sea and the sky was beginning to turn red.

'There's no proof,' I said. 'I've destroyed the DVDs and I'm not a policeman any more. And you couldn't have acted any differently, like that day with Manfredi.'

'Lena acted my part out brilliantly.'

She was smiling as she stared at the curvature of the earth where sea and sky met. The sun's red-gold semicircle was starting to sink and colour the sea the same red as the surfer's kite.

Something started there that I'd never had time to feel for Laura, her wonderful mother, and that was a sense of responsibility. It's that feeling – sometimes unfair, but irrepressible – that leads you to want to spare your children from too much suffering. But it was difficult. Very difficult.

I turned towards her and looked her in the eye.

'Yes, your grandmother Marlene could have become a great actress.'

She already had, Linda. Many years ago, in another time and another world. She was still Marlene, but playing another person.

I closed my eyes against the sun, as on that day.

She looked at us fleetingly from behind those large dark glasses, her hair tied up in the usual scarf, and wearing the long linen kaftan that left only her pale white arms bare. A book was protruding from a pocket, most probably Nietzsche. She raised an arm halfway up without smiling, a sort of interrupted wave. Then she stopped, as if she'd already done everything possible, turned and went off at a brisk pace.

Now I knew that those arms were only so white thanks to the cream which Marlene would wash off only minutes later in the shower, and that the wave wasn't a farewell gesture from a mother about to commit suicide. It was a small act of consolation given by Marlene Hunt to Mikey, the young man she would shortly take to bed to give herself an alibi and whose mother she had just killed. She'd pushed her off the cliff that morning and put on her clothes, scarf and dark glasses. She'd even fooled Alberto, who'd seen her from a distance, thanks also to her accomplices, Farid and Salim, who she could always blackmail into doing what she wanted. Then, right under my eyes, she'd given the bag with my mother's clothes to William Hunt, who'd just come back from Benghazi. He'd shot over to La Moneta in the dinghy, dressed the body again, because the disappearance of her clothes would have given rise to suspicions, and then dumped her in the sea so that no one would find her until the next day, when the *coup d'état* would already have taken place. Marlene Hunt had been William Hunt's accomplice. Her and no one else.

And I'd given her the alibi that saved her life. The worst side of the truth.

I'd seen Marlene Hunt's eyes in the funerary photograph on the plaque.

Forgive me for killing your mother. Forgive yourself for that afternoon with me. Forgive your daughter for killing Mohammed. And please cause her no more pain. Ever.

Linda held a brown envelope out to me. I knew what was in it straight away.

'That man gave it to me on La Moneta. He told me to give it to you one day.'

I took the envelope. It contained a sheet of white paper, the second page of Laura's letter to me, written a few hours before she died. A single line, that was all. And, obviously, it spoke of love, not death. Of the love that endures beyond death:

Goodbye, my love. Take care of our daughter.

That line contained in it as much as a novel. Everything was there. A whole lifetime.

Linda looked at me, questioningly. I had to reply.

'A note from your mother. A line of advice I intend to follow. But it's private, if you don't mind.'

Laura Hunt, as ever, was right.

Love's stronger than any evil. Always.

Marlene killed my mother because she envied her for having a life she couldn't have herself. And to save her husband from a Libyan firing squad. But that Marlene Hunt existed only in Mikey Balistreri's time, a time when everything was smothered in the *ghibli*'s sand and coloured red with blood.

A time in which anger against my father justified everything, including going to bed with the mother of the girl I loved, slitting the throats of three soldiers in Cairo and Salim Al Bakri, and shooting at Gaddafi. Marlene Hunt was no worse than Mikey Balistreri. And, in contrast to Ahmed, she'd been able to transform her life from one of hate to one of love.

The kitesurfer performed another risky manoeuvre and ended up in the water. Instinctively, I made to get up, but Linda put a hand on my arm.

'He can get along without you.'

She smiled, and her hand brushed mine. I felt empty, but not tired; melancholic, but not sad. I was happy.

There I was, next to my daughter, just like Michelino that day in 1958 when I was sitting between Laura and Italia, Linda's mother and grandmother, with Domenico Modugno singing about flying up into those bluest of blue skies.

What remained of the evil, of all that evil, was now there beside me. Her hand was holding mine. Was it only in this moment or had it been there for forty years?

These years haven't been lost. It hasn't been a question of departures, destinations, arrivals. Only journeys, should we choose to travel.

A few seconds later the kitesurfer was again gliding across the water towards the shore, while the sun's last sliver glimmered in the autumn twilight and somewhere around us the first lights came on.

ACKNOWLEDGEMENTS

My thanks, firstly, to my editors Marco Di Marco and Jacopo De Michelis, who have shown even more patience than usual.

For help in reconstructing places and settings, I should like to thank the following: ex-Consul Guido De Sanctis for Tripoli in 2011, where he was stationed during the bombs and the shooting; the journalist Pietro Suber for the adventurous sea trip between Benghazi and Misurata; Salah Omar for Cairo in 1967, a city of the living and the dead; and Moses Juma for present-day Nairobi. Thanks also to Professor Maurizio Bellacosa for assistance with legal aspects and to Carabinieri Colonel Luigi Ripani, Head of Forensic Investigations (RIS) in Rome for assistance with investigative procedure.

And, lastly, two friends who know they made an enormous contribution. They wish to remain anonymous and, certainly, neither of them needs the publicity.

ALSO AVAILABLE

THE DELIVERANCE OF EVIL

COMMISSARIO BALISTRERI: BOOK 1

Roberto Costantini

On 11 July 1982,
Elisa Sordi was beautiful.
Commissario Michele Balistreri was fearless.
Italy was victorious.
A killer was waiting . . .

On 9 July 2006,
With Sordi's case twenty-four years cold
And Balistreri haunted by guilt and regret
Italian victory returned.
And so did Sordi's killer . . .

AVAILABLE IN PAPERBACK AND EBOOK

Quercus
www.quercusbooks.co.uk

ALSO AVAILABLE

THE ROOT OF ALL EVIL

COMMISSARIO BALISTRERI: BOOK 2

Roberto Costantini

One man alone killed them all.
And it all began in Tripoli.

I had to go back to the real starting point:
Nadia Al Bakri, 3 August 1969.

If I could find out Nadia's killer, then I find out who
killed all the others. I had to go back to the very
point that I tried in every way to forget.

To the roots of evil.

AVAILABLE IN PAPERBACK AND EBOOK

Quercus

www.quercusbooks.co.uk

THRILLINGLY GOOD BOOKS FROM CRIMINALLY GOOD WRITERS

CRIME FILES BRINGS YOU THE LATEST RELEASES FROM TOP CRIME AND THRILLER AUTHORS.

SIGN UP ONLINE FOR OUR MONTHLY NEWSLETTER AND BE THE FIRST TO KNOW ABOUT OUR COMPETITIONS, NEW BOOKS AND MORE.